TRAPPER'S BLOOD

"This is terrible, most terrible!" Pepin said in his animated way. "The Indians in this country are too brazen, too vicious. They deserve to be hunted down and made to pay."

"By now the war party might be many miles away," Shakespeare said.

"So?" Pepin touched the tomahawk at his belt. "In Canada we would never let such a foul act go unpunished! It boils the blood to think about it!"

Nate, busy starting a fire, looked at the fiery trapper. "If it's the same bunch I saw, there are nine of them and only four of us. We'd be committing suicide if we went after them."

"Are we yellow?" Pepin said gruffly. "I say we teach these savages a lesson and get back all of the hides and horses that were stolen. I say we kill each and every one of the braves responsible."

Nate, with a sinking sensation in the pit of his stomach, saw that his real troubles were just beginning.

MOUNTAIN CAT

Nate idly glanced to his right and felt the short hairs at the nape of his neck prickle. A pair of fiery eyes had left the ring of wolves and was moving toward the tethered mounts and pack animals.

In a flash Nate was on his feet and racing to a point between the advancing wolf and the horses. "Go away!" he shouted, motioning with his knife hand.

The wolf slowed briefly, then crept nearer. In the forest beyond, others, made bold by the first, were slinking closer.

"I don't like this," Nate muttered, drawing his pistol. The metallic click of the hammer sounded eerily loud in the dreadful stillness.

"Don't shoot unless you have no other choice," Shakespeare advised. "If you hurt one, the rest will be on us like crazed banshees."

Other *Wilderness* Double Editions:
KING OF THE MOUNTAIN/LURE OF THE WILD
SAVAGE RENDEZVOUS/BLOOD FURY
TOMAHAWK REVENGE/
  BLACK POWDER JUSTICE
VENGEANCE TRAIL/DEATII HUNT
MOUNTAIN DEVIL/BLACKFOOT MASSACRE
NORTHWEST PASSAGE/APACHE BLOOD
MOUNTAIN MANHUNT/TENDERFOOT
WINTERKILL/BLOOD TRUCE

WILDERNESS

TRAPPER'S BLOOD/ MOUNTAIN CAT

DAVID THOMPSON

LEISURE BOOKS NEW YORK CITY

A LEISURE BOOK®

October 1999

Published by

Dorchester Publishing Co., Inc.
276 Fifth Avenue
New York, NY 10001

TRAPPER'S BLOOD Copyright © 1994 by David L. Robbins
MOUNTAIN CAT Copyright © 1994 by David L. Robbins

ISBN 0-8439-4621-0

Printed in the United States of America.

TRAPPER'S BLOOD

To Judy, Joshua, and Shane.

Chapter One

Life was good.

Or so rugged Nathaniel King decided as he rode along the bank of a gurgling stream high in the pristine Rocky Mountains. A free trapper by trade, young Nate had just completed the spring trapping season, and as proof of his skill there were 175 prime beaver pelts bundled on the three pack animals trailing his big black stallion.

Nate was already imagining how he would use some of the money he would get at the upcoming Rendezvous when he sold his plews. At the going rate, he stood to earn upwards of 900 dollars, and that was for just the hides he had collected on this trip. During the preceding fall trapping season he had acquired 210 prime hides which were safely stored in his remote cabin. Added to his current haul, he'd leave the Rendezvous with 1900 dollars, minus however much he spent for fixings such as powder, ammunition, new traps, grub, and the like, and what his wife spent on whatever struck her womanly fancy.

In a day and age when the average mason or carpenter made less than 500 dollars a year, Nate reflected that he was doing right fine. He was justly proud of his ability to provide for his family, and looked forward to the look on Winona's lovely face when she learned he would finally go along with her plan to buy a fancy rug for their home. She had been pestering him about it for quite some time, ever since he made the mistake of taking her to St. Louis and letting her see how white women lived. Since then he'd been persuaded to install an expensive glass pane in their window, to board over the dirt floor, and make a few other changes that Winona felt improved their homestead.

Women! Nate thought, and snorted. Men were unable to live without them, yet living with them was sometimes as trying as living with a cantankerous grizzly. Still, as he fixed his wife's shapely form in his mind's eye and dwelled on the many grand times they had shared, he realized he wouldn't trade being married for all the plews in the world.

The black stallion suddenly nickered, shattering Nate's daydream. He promptly reined up, hefted the heavy Hawken in his left hand, and gazed in all directions, seeking whatever had caught the stallion's notice. No mountain man survived very long being careless, and Nate had every intention of living to a ripe old age.

The streams Nate had trapped were situated on the west slope of the Rockies, well to the north of his usual haunts. No one Indian tribe claimed the territory, yet many hunting and war parties passed through the area regularly. Some of them were Blackfoot, Piegan, and Blood war parties, all of whom would slay and scalp a white man on sight. Nate had to constantly exercise the stealth and caution of a panther if he hoped to see his family again.

Nate was at the edge of a dense pine forest. Before him unfolded a spacious valley lush with green grass. Beyond the valley reared a solitary mountain crowned by a jagged peak tipped with snow. On the slope of that mountain figures were moving, riders moving from north to south. He counted nine, and although the distance was too great to note details, he felt certain they were Indians.

For one thing, there were no packhorses, which whites invariably had. For another, the riders were strung out in single file, a customary practice of war parties whether mounted or afoot. And finally, sunlight glinted off what could be the tips of several lances.

Nate stayed right where he was to avoid being detected. The trapping had gone so well he hated to risk spoiling it by tangling with hostiles. He thought of his four friends, free trappers like himself who had entered the region with him and then scattered to various points to lay their trap lines, and he hoped none of them had encountered the band.

It took five minutes for the Indians to cross the mountain slope and disappear in fir trees. Nate waited another five before jabbing his heels into the stallion's flanks and moving down the valley. Warm sunshine on his bearded face and the cries of sparrows, jays, and ravens served to relax him and reassure him that the danger had passed.

During the eventful years Nate had spent in the wilderness, he had learned to read Nature as some men read books. When the wildlife fell silent, he knew to expect trouble. When the animals frolicked and chattered, all was well. The habits of the birds and beasts, the moods of the fickle weather, and the rhythms of the wild in general were as familiar to him as his own countenance in a mirror.

Often Nate's knowledge had meant the difference between life and death. The Rockies were no place for the squeamish, the weak, or the ignorant. Those who didn't learn fast paid for their laziness with their lives. Of the hundreds of hopeful greenhorns who entered the mountains each year, the majority never got to return to the States.

Not that Nate ever would anyway. He had grown to love the untamed frontier, to revel in a life of freedom unmatched by anything back East. Here he could do as he saw fit, accountable to no one but himself. There was no boss standing over his shoulder, telling him how to go about his work. There were no deceitful politicians trying to rule his life with their petty laws and rules. He was truly as free as the eagle, ruled by nothing but his heart's desire. Could any man ask for more?

Nate shook his head and grinned. He was becoming too wrapped up in his own musings for his own good. Staying alert was the key to staying alive, so he kept his eyes on those fir trees on the mountain until he reached a point abreast of a gap in the hills to his left. Toward this he made his way, knowing that in the next valley over he would find one of his four friends.

The blazing morning sun climbed to the midday position, and still Nate forged on. Weeks had elapsed since last he had talked to another human being, and he was eager for company again. Loneliness was part of a trapper's life, a part he had become accustomed to, but unlike some trappers who preferred to be alone the whole year through, Nate couldn't wait for companionship when the trapping season was over.

A red hawk soaring high on uplifting currents caught Nate's attention. He watched it glide over the hills, and spotted a magnificent black-tailed buck in a clearing on one of them. Had the range been shorter, he would have been tempted to drop the deer.

Nate's nostrils tingled to the rich, dank scent of bare earth as he entered the gap. Here little sunlight penetrated. He saw many tracks of elk, bear, and deer, but only four sets of horse prints, and they were so old they were barely visible. He knew who had made them, and he grinned in anticipation.

The next valley was narrower but contained more vegetation. At a ribbon of a stream dotted with large beaver ponds, Nate turned to the left to follow the waterway to his friend's camp. He covered two miles, then caught the faint acrid scent of smoke. A little further on he saw a clearing ahead, and to one side, under the spreading branches of a towering tree, a small fire crackled. Four horses were tethered nearby, but there was no sign of their owner.

Halting, Nate cupped a hand to his mouth and hailed the camp, a practice that prevented those with itchy trigger fingers from making a fatal mistake. "Shakespeare! Where the devil are you?"

"Right behind you, Horatio."

Startled, Nate shifted in the saddle and glared at the speaker. "You ornery varmint," he declared, feigning anger. "Don't you know any better than to go sneaking up on someone?"

Shakespeare McNair threw back his white-maned head and laughed lustily. Then he made a grand show of bowing at the waist, declaring, "So please your majesty, I would I could quit all offenses with as clear excuse as well as I am doubtless I can purge myself of many I am charged withal."

"Let me guess," Nate said, and deliberately guessed wrong. "*Romeo and Juliet?*"

"Pitiful. Downright pitiful," the older man grumbled. "What are the young'uns coming to nowadays? Didn't you have a proper education?" He came alongside the stallion. "That was from *King Henry the Fourth*. Part One, if I'm not mistaken."

"I'll take your word for it," Nate said. He had long ago discovered the folly of arguing with his mentor over the works of William Shakespeare. No one, absolutely no one, knew the writings of the Bard better than the grizzled mountain man whose nickname was a token of his peculiar literary passion. Shakespeare could quote his namesake by the hour, and to Nate's knowledge no one had ever proven a single quote to be wrong. "But what's this nonsense about you having an excuse for scaring the daylights out of me?"

"'Tis true, young sir," Shakespeare said good-naturedly. "I was only helping to keep you on your toes."

"You needn't worry in that regard," Nate said, moving toward the tree. "The war party I saw earlier did the trick."

"What war party?" Shakespeare asked. He was somber now, since he well realized the implications, and he listened attentively while Nate described the band. "Blackfeet would be my guess. This is one of their main routes south to Ute country."

"My thinking too," Nate agreed. Dismounting, he tied his horses, then walked to the fire, and was handed a tin cup brimming with steaming coffee. "They're long gone by now, though. We can be well on our way before they return."

"I suppose," Shakespeare said. Squatting, he poured himself a cup, and quoted thoughtfully, "Nimble mischance, that art so light of foot, doth not thy embassage belong to me, and am I last that knows it?"

"In other words, we shouldn't let down our guard for a minute," Nate translated.

"Exactly." Shakespeare sipped loudly and stared at the bundles on Nate's pack animals. "Appears to me you did right fine."

"How about you?"

"One hundred and ninety-four plews."

"You beat me again."

"Did I?" Shakespeare grinned. "Well, I had to work my britches off to do it. Must of scoured the valleys and parks westward for better than forty miles."

"The same here." Nate sat back against a log and took a swallow. "The beaver are becoming harder and harder to find. Each season it gets a bit worse."

"And it will continue to get worse," Shakespeare predicted. "There are just too blamed many trappers. Why, not ten years ago, before the fancy ladies and fashionable gentlemen back in the States took to craving beaver hats and collars and such, there were so many beaver in these mountains that a man couldn't kneel down to take a drink without bumping heads with one. The critters chopped down so many trees to make their dams, there was hardly any timber left to use for making firewood."

"Oh, please," Nate said, chuckling. "I'm no longer a child."

"Don't believe me if you want," Shakespeare responded. "I only exaggerated a little." Sighing, he encompassed the neighboring mountains with a sweep of an arm. "There's been a lot of change since the trappers moved in, and not all of it has been for the better. If things keep going the way they are, before you know it we'll have settlers spreading out over the countryside like a swarm of locusts, driving off the Indians and killing off all the game. Out here will be just like the East." He shuddered. "God help us."

Nate shook his head. They had been over the same subject countless times, and nothing he had said had been able to convince McNair that the prairie and the mountains would last forever as glorious bastions of freedom and adventure. Most Easterners wouldn't think of crossing the Mississippi; they regarded everything west of that mighty river as wasteland, part of the Great American Desert, as explorer Stephen H. Long had called the plains during his brief expedition some years before.

"I hope I don't live to see that," Shakespeare was saying. "I want to remember the wilderness as it should be, wild and uninhabited."

"It must be all your white hairs," Nate joked. "You've turned into a first-rate worrier."

Shakespeare fixed his narrowed eyes on the younger man. "Your mind is all as youthful as your blood," he quoted, adding, "You'll learn, though, One day you'll see that I knew what I was talking about."

Their banter was suddenly interrupted by a crackling in the woods to the northwest. Nate leaped to his feet, his right hand dropping to one of the twin flintlocks adorning his waist. In addition to the pistols, he had a butcher knife in a beaded sheath and a tomahawk tucked under his wide brown leather belt. Slanted across his broad chest were the powder horn and ammo pouch for his guns.

McNair had also risen. "It's him again," he muttered.

"Who?"

"The same contrary cuss who has visited my camp every few days for the past month. If I had any sense, I would have shot the nuisance weeks ago."

"Who are you talking about?" Nate asked, tensing as the crackling grew louder. Vaguely, he spied a bulky form moving toward them through the heavy undergrowth.

"Not who," Shakespeare corrected him. "What."

The brush parted, revealing a young black bear, a male no more than a year old, if that. It squalled on seeing the camp and came forward at a lumbering shuffle. McNair's horses showed no reaction; evidently they were accustomed to the bear's visits. But Nate's animals whinnied and fidgeted.

"Stand still until he gets to know you," Shakespeare advised. "I don't want you spooking poor Brutus."

"*Brutus?*"

"Well, I couldn't very well call the thing 'It' all the time, now could I?" Shakespeare responded testily. Setting down his coffee, he moved around the fire and stood with his hands on his hips. The bear displayed no fear whatsoever as it came right up to the mountain man and rubbed its head against his buckskin-clad leg. "See? As friendly as a Flathead." Shakespeare stroked the creature's neck and scratched behind its ears.

"You're getting awful softhearted," Nate said. "Wait until I tell our wives."

"We can't go around killing every animal we see," Shakespeare countered. Reaching into his possibles bag, he pulled out a thin strip of jerked deer meat, tore the piece in half, and gave it to their visitor. The bear knew just what to expect, and delicately took the dried meat between its tapered teeth, then chomped hungrily.

"Are you fixing to take Brutus back with you?" Nate asked.

"Not hardly." Shakespeare gave the bear the rest of the jerky. "This coon might be softhearted, but I'm not as addlepated as you'd like to think."

Nate studied the bear a moment. "That's a nice hide you're passing up. And all that meat and fat. It makes my mouth water just to think about it."

"Oh?" Shakespeare glanced up, triumph lighting his face. "Would you kill that pet wolf your son is so attached to?"

"Blaze? Never."

"Then don't be poking fun at Brutus." Shakespeare patted the bear's front shoulders and the animal flinched and whined. "What's this? What have we here?" Shakespeare leaned down, examining the fur. "Looks like something got its claws into you."

Nate bent over the bear for a look. There were three slash marks, so fresh blood still seeped from them, each at least an inch deep. "Panther, you figure?" he asked.

"Could have been," Shakespeare said, although his tone implied he was not quite convinced. Straightening, he surveyed the primeval forest, particularly the various shadows under some of the giant pines. "There aren't many creatures that will tangle with a bear, even a small one like Brutus."

"Another bear would," Nate mentioned casually.

"True," Shakespeare said, his lips puckering.

The object of their concern was now rummaging in the stack of supplies at the base of the tree, sniffing loudly as it poked its black nose under the flaps of closed parfleches and into whatever other nooks and crannies it could find.

"Your friend just makes himself to home, doesn't he?" Nate asked.

Shakespeare had been deep in reflection and had not noticed. Uttering a squawk, he bounded at Brutus and gave the bear a swat on the rump. "You pesky bottomless pit! You'll wait until I fix some biscuits for supper."

"You still have flour left?" Nate marveled. "I ran out weeks ago."

"There's an art to conserving grub," Shakespeare boasted. "When you have as many gray hairs as I do, no doubt you'll be almost as good at it as I am."

"White hairs. Your hair is white. How many times must I remind you?" Nate said. "And now that you mention it, yes, I would like to be as old as these mountains."

"Most shallow man! Thou worms-meat, in respect of a good piece of flesh indeed! Learn of the wise, and perpend: civit is of a baser birth than tar, the very uncleanly flux of a cat. Mend the instance, shepherd," Shakespeare stated.

Chuckling, Nate walked to the black stallion and began stripping off his saddle. "If it's all right with you, we'll start after the others at first light."

"Fine."

"I wonder how they've fared?"

"Pointer and Jenks will be lucky if they have a hundred pelts between them. They're as tender as the soles of a baby's feet and as ignorant as granite."

Nate glanced over his shoulder. "I had no idea you held such a high opinion of them."

"Don't misconstrue my remarks, Horatio. I like them despite their shortcomings or I wouldn't have agreed to having them join our party." Shakespeare was keeping his eyes on the black bear, which had wandered to the other side of the clearing and was sniffing at the remains of a rabbit Shakespeare had skinned and eaten the day before. "They're young, but they're sincere. They truly want to be good trappers. And if they live long enough, they will be."

"What about Pepin?"

"That feisty *voyageur* might beat us both." Shakespeare stroked his beard. "He's about as skilled a woodsman as you're ever likely to run across."

"To hear him talk, he's the best."

"That's a *voyageur* for you. I haven't met one yet who didn't love to flap his gums just to hear himself talk."

Nate laughed. Canadian trappers were a colorful, hardy breed who lived each and every day as if there would be no tomorrow. He'd known others in his time besides Pepin, some as friends, others as enemies, and there was no denying they could hold their own against any free American trapper alive.

"I'm mighty curious about what brought him here," Shakespeare commented. "If I've heard him say he loves the North Country once, I've heard him say it a thousand times. It's odd he'd leave it for the southern Rockies."

"You figure he got into a fight and killed someone and had to make himself scarce?"

"That would be my guess, but this child isn't about to pry into another man's personal affairs."

Nor would Nate, although he was as curious as his mentor. The only fact Pepin had revealed was that he had been a *coureur de bois* up north, which roughly translated to a ranger of the woods, or the Canadian counterpart of an American free trapper. The rest of the man's past was a complete mystery.

"Enough about him," Shakespeare said. "What say we go hunt ourselves a deer and make dog of the critter? I have coffee left too. If I throw in some biscuits and berries, we'll have a feed fit for royalty."

"Count me in," Nate said, his stomach grumbling at the mention of food. "Just give me a moment to set my pelts aside." He swiftly unloaded his pack animals and placed the plews beside McNair's. His possibles bag, which had been hanging from his saddle, was draped over his shoulder and angled across his chest below his powder horn. He then checked his rifle and the pistols.

The Hawken was fairly typical of those widely used by company men and free trappers alike. Made by the renowned Hawken brothers of St. Louis, it boasted a 34-inch octagonal barrel, a set trigger, accurate sights, a ramrod housed under a metal rib, a heavy butt stock, and a butt plate in the shape of a crescent. Powerful enough to drop a bull buffalo, it was .53-caliber. A half-ounce lead ball and 214 grains of black powder were the standard load. Nate's flintlocks were both .55-caliber, smoothbore single-shots. At close range they were as effective as the Hawken.

"There's a small lake west of here," Shakespeare said as he retrieved his rifle. "Deer like to hole up near it during the day. It shouldn't take us no time at all to track one down."

"All we need is some wild onions and I'll . . ." Nate immediately stopped talking when he saw the young black bear suddenly rear up on its hind legs and sniff noisily, swiveling its head as it tested the air. "What's gotten into Brutus?" he asked.

Shakespeare looked and frowned. "He must have the scent of something."

The bear took a few awkward steps, then dropped onto all fours, spun, and sped off into the underbrush, plowing through the vegetation as if in fear for its very life.

"Maybe it's time you took your annual bath," Nate joked. He turned, laughing, and happened to gaze in the direction from which Brutus had approached the camp earlier. Every nerve in his body tingled and a shiver rippled down his spine when he saw another bear standing 20 yards off Only this one wasn't a black bear.

It was a full-grown grizzly.

Chapter Two

There wasn't a trapper alive who had more experience with grizzlies than Nate King. By a curious quirk of fate it had been his lot to run up against the fierce beasts time after time, which had resulted in his earning the Indian name of Grizzly Killer. Among the Shoshones, his adopted people, his prowess as a slayer of grizzlies was almost legendary. Yet ironically, as Nate was often the first to admit, usually he had prevailed more by accident than design.

Nate regarded the great brutes with deep respect, if not outright dread. Whenever he saw one, if possible he made it a point to head the other way just as fast as his legs or his mount could carry him. The times he had been forced to fight were those where no other recourse was open to him.

Such as now.

The sight of the grizzly lumbering forward was enough to cause the bravest soul to flee, but Nate stood his ground. He knew how destructive grizzlies could be, how they would wantonly tear apart everything they found in a trapper's camp, and he could ill afford to let that happen. There were his horses and supplies to think of, not to mention the pelts he had worked so hard to gather. So, firming his grip on the Hawken, he took a few strides, putting himself between the grizzly and his plews. "Shakespeare," he said urgently. "We have more company."

The older man whirled. "Damn! Now we know what took a swipe at Brutus!" He moved up beside his young friend, admiring the determined set of Nate's jaw. At times such as this, Shakespeare was proud to have been the man who taught Nate all there was to know about wilderness survival. Shakespeare had known many frontiersmen over the years, but none had taken so naturally to the arduous life than the one he fondly regarded as the son he had never had. "If he charges, go for the head," he cautioned.

"A heart shot is better," Nate said. Having carved up a lot of grizzlies for their hides, he'd seen firsthand that their brains were protected by enormous skulls as well as layers upon layers of thick muscles.

"We can't get a good heart shot from head-on," Shakespeare noted.

"Try for the eyes, then."

The grizzly slowly advanced as they talked. It had its ponderous head low to the ground, its nostrils quivering, as if it was still on Brutus's scent. Steely sinews rippled under a lustrous coat. Long claws glinted in the sunlight. Here was the most massive killer known on the North American continent, its height at the shoulders being five feet, its length over seven feet, and its weight in the vicinity of 1500 pounds. A huge hump, characteristic of the species, bulged above the front shoulders.

The horses had seen the bear and were working themselves into a frenzy, snorting and stomping and tugging at their tethers.

"On my cue," Shakespeare said, tucking his rifle to his right shoulder.

"Wait," Nate said. "I want to try something." He would rather run naked through a briar patch than have to fight another grizzly. In desperation he resorted to a tactic that worked on lesser beasts, but which he had never yet witnessed do any good against the terrors of the Rockies; he took a long stride, lifted his arms, and screeched like an enraged banshee while jumping madly up and down.

The effect on the grizzly was interesting. It halted, a paw half raised, and stared at the screaming human. Never had it beheld the like, and in the depths of its dull mind it didn't know what to do. It wasn't afraid, since fear had no meaning to a creature capable of shredding an elk's neck with a single blow. Instead it was puzzled, as it would be if it came on the spoor of an animal it had never seen before. Humans were familiar to this bear as timid things that fled at its approach. The antics of this one, though, were so different as to give it pause.

Nate jumped higher, yelled louder. He flapped his arms, hoping against hope he could drive the grizzly off and avoid a bloody clash.

The bear lowered its foot and glanced from the humans to the horses and back again. It had never tasted the flesh of either and so was not impelled by its stomach to go after them. And since 90 percent of its actions were motivated by its belly, the grizzly began to depart, to go find quieter morsels, but as it did, the wind shifted and abruptly the grizzly registered the tantalizing scent of rabbit blood. Blood of any kind always had the same effect. Instantly the bear's mouth watered and there were rumblings in its paunch, the age-old signal for the grizzly to do one thing and one thing alone—attack.

Shakespeare's keen eyes saw the bear's front claws digging into the soil. "Look out!" he shouted. "Here it comes!"

As if shot from a cannon the grizzly hurtled straight at them, moving with astonishing speed for such a heavy animal. When aroused, grizzlies were capable of moving as fast as a horse, and this one was a credit to its kind.

Nate was sweeping the Hawken level when Shakespeare's rifle boomed. The bear's head jerked, blood spurted from its brow, but it never slowed a whit. Nate sighted on the monster's right eye, then realized the grizzly would be on them before he could fire. "Move!" he cried, and did exactly that, leaping to the left just as the bear raced between them. Perhaps dazed by the lead ball, it made no attempt to claw them, but barreled into their supplies and pelts, scattering belongings every which way.

Pivoting on a heel, Nate aimed as the grizzly slid to a halt and turned. The beast was broadside to him for a few seconds, all the time he needed to fire into its chest, going for its heart.

At the retort the grizzly arched its spine and roared, its mouth agape, its lips curled up over its fearsome teeth. Seared by acute agony the likes of which it had never felt before, the bear focused on the cause of its pain and charged again.

Nate had his back to the tree. In pure reflex he tossed the Hawken aside and drew both pistols, cocking the flintlocks as he did. The bear was coming for him like a bolt of furry lightning. He had no time to think. He had no time to plan. All he could do was what he did, fire both pistols at point-blank range and vault to the right. His shoulder was struck a resounding blow that tumbled his head over heels. His head hit a stone or other hard object, and for several seconds the world was spinning like a child's top. When the spinning ceased he was lying on his back, the empty flintlocks clutched tight, while directly above him was the hind end of one of the horses.

"Son, are you all right?"

Strong hands gripped Nate's shoulders and assisted him in sitting up. Blankly he stared at the grizzly, lying slumped on its stomach next to the tree, blood oozing from the holes where its eyes had been. The impact had partially cracked its skull, and a bubbly froth was trickling from the fracture.

"I reckon the damn thing killed itself," Shakespeare declared. "Busted its own head wide open." He cackled and gave Nate a smack on the arm. "I never saw the like."

"Me neither," Nate mumbled. Grunting, he slowly stood.

"How many does this make now?" Shakespeare asked.

"I've lost count."

"Wait until the Shoshones hear. You keep this up and they're liable to start thinking there must be something supernatural about you."

"Don't be ridiculous."

"You know as well as I do that Indians are not only deeply religious in their own way, they're awful superstitious too. They're forever calling on the Great Mystery or the Great Spirit for help, and they believe in things like guardian spirits, animal spirits, and such." Shakespeare paused. "Course, we do pretty much the same thing, only we call on God and believe we're looked after by guardian angels. When you think about it, the white and the red cultures are more alike than most realize."

Nate walked to the dead giant and shook his head in amazement at his deliverance. By all rights he should have been slain. Once again Providence had seen fit to spare him, although he had no idea why. Sinking onto the log, he worked at reloading the pistols and his rifle. After a while he realized his friend was staring at him and he looked up. "Yes?"

"What's bothering you, son? You're a mite flushed."

"Wouldn't you be after what just happened?" Nate extracted the ramrod from his rifle. "These close scrapes always leave me flustered. My blood is pumping so hard I can practically hear it."

"Which is perfectly normal." Shakespeare sat down and began reloading his gun. "Why, I recollect the time I was up in the geyser country, hunting elk. I shot a big old bull and tracked his blood trail deep into the woods. Hadn't no more than set down my rifle and drawn my butcher knife than there was this terrific roar and a grizzly twice the size of this one came rushing toward me out of the brush."

"Twice the size of this one?" Nate asked skeptically.

"This took place when I was about your age," Shakespeare said, unruffled. "Bears were bigger back then."

"The tall tales must have been bigger too."

Shakespeare arched an eyebrow. "Do you want to hear this yarn or not?"

"I'm all ears."

"All right then. Anyway, there I was, standing next to this dead elk with just my knife in hand, and here came this snarling grizzly. It was too close for me to try and run away, and there wasn't time for me to scoop up my rifle, take aim, and shoot."

"So what did you do?" Nate asked when McNair stopped.

"That's the strange part. To this day I don't know what made me do what I did." Shakespeare made a show of fiddling with his ammo pouch.

"Which was?"

"Well, before I tell you, you have to keep in mind that this here bear was coming straight toward the front of the elk. And what I did was, I grabbed hold of the top antler and lifted with all my might, raising the head and the whole rack clear off the ground." Shakespeare gazed off into the distance. "That elk had the biggest rack I ever did see."

"And? And?" Nate prompted.

"Why, the darn fool bear couldn't stop and ran smack into the antlers. Must of knocked me a good twenty-five feet. When I sat up, there wasn't a scratch on me. And there was that grizzly, stuck fast with those antlers ripped deep into its neck and face. The noise that thing made! It spooked every creature for fifty miles."

"Did the bear die?"

"Not then. It tore loose and went off into the trees without another look at me. The thing was bleeding like a stuck pig. Likely bled to death later on, but I didn't go see."

"Your point?"

"My point is that I was so rattled I sat there shaking for the better part of an hour. Just shook and shook like an aspen leaf, and nothing I did helped." Shakespeare smiled. "Being scared is nothing to be ashamed of. Every man is at one time or another. It's how you handle the fear that counts. In that regard, you have no cause to be ashamed."

"Thanks," Nate said sincerely.

Shakespeare studied the kill. "It would be a shame to let a fine specimen like this go to waste. I suppose we'll have to spend the rest of the day skinning it." He smacked his lips. "Which isn't all that bad a proposition. Painter meat can't shine with this, but meat is meat to a hungry man and I've always been rather fond of bear steaks myself. How about it?"

"Bear meat will do fine."

So the remainder of the afternoon and evening was devoted to dressing the grizzly. Its hide was removed intact, and Shakespeare insisted on having Nate take possession since

Nate, as Shakespeare put it, "was the one the bear seemed to like the most." Since they had no caskets in which to put the oil, they left that task unattended. Shakespeare made a point of carving out the heart, which was as big as the heart of a large ox, and added it to the thick slabs of meat they had selected for their supper.

"Ever eaten bear heart, son?"

"Can't say as I have."

"I'll share with you. Heart meat is a delicacy too delicious to pass up. Got hooked on it once up in Flathead country when I shot a deer that was in poor order. Sickly thing it was, and the meat was terrible. But I was starving and needed to eat something, so I roasted the heart and some of the other organs." Shakespeare scrunched up his face. "The liver about made me gag, but the heart was so tasty I wished I'd had five or six more. Ever since I've been a heart man."

"I'll bet you're partial to tongues as well."

"As a matter of fact, I am," Shakespeare responded. "Buffalo tongue in particular. The first time . . ." He broke off, his eyes narrowing. "You danged upstart."

"I beg your pardon?" Nate said innocently.

"Don't play dumb. You landed a broadside fair and square, and I'll take my licks without complaint." Shakespeare laughed lightly, then quoted, "I am a very foolish fond old man, fourscore and upward, not an hour more nor less. And to deal plainly, I fear I am not in my perfect mind."

"I could have told you that."

"Twice! Twice!" Shakespeare clutched at his chest. "You wound me to the quick, young sir! And to think that you were weaned at the nipple of my wisdom!"

"William Shakespeare wrote *that*?"

"No. I just made it up. Wasn't it grand?"

Both men roared.

That night, seated by the crackling fire, warm and with a full belly, Nate listened to his mentor read from the thick book McNair never went anywhere without, a rare collected edition of the famous playwright's works. This night Shakespeare read from *Hamlet*. Later, after they had turned in and Nate was on his back, his head propped in his hands and staring thoughtfully at the myriad of sparkling stars, he asked, "Do you think Hamlet did the right thing?"

"In what respect? Treating Ophelia as he did? Acting mad? Which?"

"Neither. In taking so long to decide what to do. If he'd killed the king outright, he would have spared himself a heap of grief."

"Think so?" Shakespeare shifted, his eyes almost luminous in the glow of the fire.

"Don't you? All that agonizing was a waste. When a man sees that something has to be done, he should go out and do it and not worry himself to death over it."

"If only life were that easy," Shakespeare said wistfully.

Nate was to have bitter occasion to remember his words later on, but for now he closed his eyes and drifted into an undisturbed slumber that lasted until the chirping of sparrows awakened him well before dawn. Throwing off his buffalo robe, he rose and went into the bushes. He yawned loudly, scratched his thick beard, and was hitching at his leggings when he saw something which instantly brought him fully awake.

A gray wolf sat on a knoll ten yards away staring curiously at the two-legged oddity that wore the hides of deer on its body and the fur of beaver on its head. The faint scent of roasted meat had brought the wolf close to the camp, but its natural wariness had prevented it from drawing any nearer.

Nate's first reaction was to reach for a flintlock. Then he hesitated, sensing the wolf was no threat. Feeling exposed with his leggings down around his knees, he quickly finished adjusting them and tightened his wide leather belt. When next he looked at the knoll, the wolf was gone.

Forest creatures were that way. Ordinarily they lived quiet lives, going about their daily routines as stealthily as they knew how, the predators because without stealth they would rarely catch the prey they needed to sustain themselves, and the prey because if they made too much noise they might attract the unwanted attention of a predator. There were exceptions, as there were to every rule. Grizzlies often plodded along heedless of the noise they made; they had no natural enemies, and they ate anything and everything that caught their eye, from roots to wild fruits to living things.

Nate reflected on this as he strolled back to his bedding. There were those who would view him as peculiar for having forsaken the security of life in New York City for the savage uncertainties of the mountains, but he would not give up his life in the wild for all the gold in the world. The element of constant danger added a certain zest to a man's life, and made him appreciate each and every moment of his life that much more.

"Morning, Horatio," Shakespeare greeted him.

"About time you got up. You're turning into a lazy lay-about," Nate said, nodding to the east where the first pale rays of the rising sun were visible. "Half the day is wasted."

"When a man has lived as many years as I have, he's entitled to sleep in late once in a while."

Within half an hour they had broken camp and were riding northeastward at a slow pace so as not to tire their fully laden pack animals. Nate had the lead, the Hawken across his thighs. "Refresh my memory," he said at one point. "Is it Jenks or Pointer we collect next?"

"Pointer, I do believe," Shakespeare said.

"Let's hope he remembered that we agreed to head on home about this time and he has all his traps in."

"If he doesn't, no harm done. We'll lend a hand." Shakespeare skirted a pine. "It's easy to lose track of time out here. One day is so much like the rest that they all become a blur after a while."

"Until the first snow."

"True enough."

Their course took them toward a row of stately mountains whose majestic peaks reared to the very clouds. High up a steep, rocky slope they climbed, to a pass which would take them to a lush valley. They were well into the sunlit pass when Nate spotted impressions in the ground and abruptly reined up. "I don't like the looks of this."

"What is it?" Shakespeare called.

Swinging down, Nate knelt and examined a series of unshod hoofprints made within the past week or so. "Indians," he announced. "Seven or more, heading into the valley."

"Maybe it was the same bunch you saw," Shakespeare guessed.

"Maybe," Nate said, although he doubted that was the case. The band he'd seen had been heading due south. This party had been going due north, days ago. If it was the same band, then for some reason they had turned around at some point and swung a little to the east, then made to the south. Such aimless meandering made no sense. Rising, he stared at the end of the pass. "What concerns me most is whether they spotted Pointer."

"We'd better hurry. And keep your eyes peeled."

The mouth of the pass widened out onto a curved shelf overlooking the valley proper. Here Nate halted to scour the countryside. A bald eagle was soaring over the high grass flanking the blue stream, and to the east several cow elk were browsing. No smoke marred the scenic picture, nor was there any sign of Pointer's camp.

"He must be at the west end of the valley," Shakespeare said.

A serpentine game trail brought them to the valley floor. Nate was riding on the south bank of the stream when he saw hoofprints in the soft earth at the water's edge. Halting, he checked, then declared, "It's the same bunch. They went this way."

"Damn."

At a trot they proceeded into dense timber, now and again coming on more of the week-old tracks. At length they came to a beaver pond. The dam showed evidence of recent repair. Close by the opposite shore was a large lodge, and as the two trappers watched, a young beaver swam from the shore to the lodge and disappeared under the water with a slap of its flat tail.

"This would be the first place I'd lay some traps if I was trapping this neck of the woods," Shakespeare said somberly.

Nate poked his heels into the stallion. He was growing more concerned by the minute, and he prayed his fears were unjustified. He thought of Harold Pointer, an amiable 18-year-old from Illinois, and of Pointer's parents, who were patiently waiting for their son to return with the money they needed to save their farm from the auction block, and he wanted to curse but didn't.

Shakespeare was equally anxious about the young trapper. He'd known literally hundreds of hopeful greenhorns who had come to the Rockies bound and determined to make their fortunes in the fur trade, the majority of whom had wound up dead, victims of their ignorance and their brashness. He always tried to warn them. He always stressed the hazards a trapper faced. But whatever he said invariably went in one ear and out the other. They were young; they were full of vim and vinegar; they were invincible, in their estimation; and they knew better than some old geezer who sported more wrinkles than a dried prune. The only way they would learn was the hard way.

A clearing materialized ahead, so Nate slowed and placed a thumb on the hammer of his Hawken. He glimpsed a black circle that had to be an old campfire, but no other sign that anyone had ever been there. Stopping at the tree line, he slid off the stallion and tied his horses to low limbs. Then, rifle leveled, he walked into the open. There were horse tracks everywhere. And footprints. Nate bent down to inspect a set, turning as he did, and involuntarily stiffened when he heard his mentor bellow.

"Behind you!"

Straightening, Nate spun as the brush erupted in a flurry of crackling and snapping.

Chapter Three

Ordinarily Shakespeare McNair was not the jittery sort. With his age had come wisdom, and in his wisdom he had learned that every now and then life offered up unpleasant surprises and there was nothing any man could do to avoid them. They had to be taken in stride, met calmly and overcome patiently. Every living person had to swallow the bitter with the balm and pray everything worked out in the end.

Staying composed when under pressure was a trait Shakespeare prided himself on. So he was more than a little embarrassed when, because of his abiding affection for his companion, he blurted out a warning on seeing the undergrowth across the clearing move without first verifying there was a threat. For out of the brush, flapping mightily, popped a large raven.

Nate held his fire when he saw the black bird take wing. It uttered an irritated squawk as it banked above his head and soared off up over the pines. On passing above him the raven dropped something from its big beak, and the object fell almost at Nate's feet. He glanced down, not knowing what to expect, but certainly not expecting to see a grisly, stringy eyeball dotted with peck marks. A human eyeball, no less. "Dear Lord!" he breathed, and hurried to the spot where the raven had first appeared. Extending the Hawken barrel, he parted the weeds.

First to hit Nate was the awful stench. Gasping, he turned his head aside long enough to gulp fresh air, then leaned forward to stare at the partially decomposed body of Harold Pointer lying sprawled on its back. Pointer had been stripped naked and mutilated. His stomach had been torn open and his innards ripped out and left draped over the ground. His throat had been slit wide. And there were other things that had been done, unspeakable things only the most diabolical of minds could have conceived, horrible things no human being should have to see.

"The poor kid," Shakespeare said over Nate's shoulder. He had seen worse in his time, but not much worse.

"About five days or so ago, you figure?" Nate asked, holding his breath so he could edge a bit closer and search the surrounding area. Not a single one of Pointer's clothes was anywhere around. Every last article the man possessed had been stolen.

"About that," Shakespeare said, backing away to scan the clearing. "I'll find which way they went."

Nate also backed away until he could breathe freely again. He tried to remember the exact town in which Pointer's folks lived so he could send them word of their son's death, but for the life of him he couldn't recall what it was. "We should bury him," he remarked forlornly.

"Whatever for? Let Nature take its course," Shakespeare said from over near the stream.

"He deserves a burial. He was our friend."

"If he hadn't started to rot away, I'd agree," Shakespeare said, looking up. "There isn't much I'm squeamish about, but touching rotten flesh is one of them."

"Then I'll plant him myself."

Shakespeare sighed. "Hell. You and your principles. All right. I'll help. But don't blame me if I'm a mite whiffy for a spell."

The burial was a nightmare. Since they lacked proper digging implements, they resorted to thick limbs sharpened at one end to pry apart clods of earth. The ground was hard, the chore grueling, raising blisters on their palms and fingers. But the digging was a picnic compared to the job of getting the corpse from the weeds to the hole. Nate tried grabbing an ankle and pulling, but the soft flesh was like mush in his grip and he wound up with gory bits clinging to his hand. Shakespeare came up with a better idea; they used the limbs to flip the corpse over and over until they rolled it into the grave. Then they took turns covering the body so that neither of them would become too queasy from the smell.

"There," Nate said when the last bit of loose dirt was on the pile. "Now he can rest in peace."

"You do know, don't you, that some animal is likely to come along, dig him up, and make dog of him?" Shakespeare said.

"No matter. We'll have done what we can. That's all that counts."

"Not quite," Shakespeare said. "There's still the matter of the bastards who did this." He returned to the stream and squatted, scrutinizing the tracks. "They're a canny bunch, I'll give them that. After doing their dirty work, they rode smack into the water. The current has long since washed away their prints so there's no telling if they went back out the valley the same way they came in or whether they continued on to the west."

"That's odd."

"What is?"

"I've never heard tell of a war party going to so much trouble to hide their trail before. Indians are proud of the coup they count. Sometimes they leave sign just so others will know who did it."

"Maybe these were shy," Shakespeare said.

"Or maybe," Nate declared, "they knew there were more trappers in this region." His eyes met his mentor's, and without another word they hurried to their horses, mounted, and headed back down the valley until they came to a creek that fed into the stream. This they followed northward for over five miles, into a verdant paradise in the midst of a ring of towering peaks.

"Jenks should be here somewhere," Shakespeare said.

"If the war party didn't find him too."

Anxiously they searched, going up one stream and down another, always on the lookout for hostiles. They were nearing a fork when Nate spied a stretch of churned-up earth, and as he trotted forward his stomach muscles tightened. The hoofprints were so plain there was no mistake. "Seven riders. Three or four days ago."

The tracks took them to the northwest, to a meadow. They were still a ways off when Shakespeare spotted a telltale black circle in the grass near the water. "Did they make that fire, or did Jenks?"

Nate galloped to the site, and was off the stallion before the horse stopped moving. Touching the charred pieces of wood confirmed the campfire was days old. He discovered a number of moccasin prints of different sizes, and deduced that considerable activity had taken place.

Shakespeare had gone to a nearby cottonwood. "Here's

where Jenks had his horses tied," he said, indicating a line of hoofprints and patches of flattened grass where the animals had bedded down at night.

"But where is he?" Nate wondered, fearing the worst. Hawken in hand, he walked in a loop, probing the high grass for the body he was certain must be there. When he found nothing on his first sweep, he conducted others, widening the loop each time. He canvassed an area 50 yards in diameter, and was both relieved and puzzled when the hunt proved fruitless. "Maybe they took Jenks with him," he speculated as he walked up to Shakespeare.

"Could be. The Blackfeet, those scoundrels, like to take captives to their villages to impress the women and the sprouts. They hold grand feasts, and the high point of their festivities is when they torture their captives to death."

Nate was already painfully aware of the Blackfoot custom. Once he'd fallen into their hands and been forced to run a gauntlet, to dash between two rows of armed warriors, an ordeal which he had barely survived.

"The tracks go into the stream again so we can't follow them," Shakespeare said.

"We have to see about Pepin," Nate said urgently. "If they haven't gotten him yet, he has to be warned." They both mounted and rode in a northeasterly direction. Dense timber proved a frustrating barrier, slowing them down, and it was late afternoon by the time a new mountain range hove into sight. Nate, again in the lead, was emerging from cover into the open when the glint of sunlight off metal in the high grass 60 yards away gave him a fraction of a second in which to throw himself from the saddle. He heard a rifle crack, even as he yelled, "Take cover!"

Shakespeare had not been caught napping. He'd seen the gleam of light almost at the same time and sprung from his white horse. Keeping bent at the waist, he glided through the grass to where Nate was crouched. "You hit?"

"No. Whoever it is rushed his shot." Nate stared at their horses, which had scattered but not fled far.

"It could be one of the warriors in the war party," Shakespeare said. "We'd best kill him quick and make ourselves scarce before the rest show up."

"You go left, I'll go right," Nate proposed, then did so, hugging the ground and parting the grass with exquisite care. He hadn't gone more than 20 yards when movement to his left alerted him to someone creeping in the opposite direction, directly between McNair and him. It had to be the one who had shot at them, he realized. The man was making enough noise to rouse the dead, cracking dry stems underfoot and brushing loudly against every blade of grass he passed.

Nate flattened and crawled to intercept the creeping figure. Either the ambusher was incredibly careless, he reasoned, or the man was in an almighty big hurry. He couldn't believe an Indian would act so stupidly, not when from earliest childhood warriors were taught how to use supreme stealth when necessary. A buckskin-clad form materialized. Nate froze, let go of the Hawken, and slowly drew his tomahawk.

The figure was pumping his limbs furiously, apparently trying to reach the horses.

Digging in his knees and toes, Nate waited until the man was directly abreast of his hiding place. Then, venting a Shoshone war whoop, he leaped up and pounced, aiming a terrific blow at the figure's head. In the nick of time he recognized the startled, upturned face below him and managed to swerve the tomahawk just enough to one side to miss the man's skull.

"King!" the man blurted out.

"Jenks!" Nate responded, appalled at how close he had

come to splitting the greenhorn's head in half. "What the hell are you doing taking a shot at us?"

"I didn't know," the younger man declared, sitting up. Perspiration beaded his smooth brow. He was a lean youth, only 17 years of age, with square, bony shoulders and knobby knees. His brown eyes brimming with moisture, he pushed upright and exclaimed, "Thank God! Thank God it's you!"

From out of the grass a few feet behind the greenhorn rose Shakespeare, wearing a wry grin. "I can't say I think much of the way you greet your friends."

"Forgive me," Jenks said, smiling idiotically at both of them. "I didn't stop to take a good look. I just saw riders coming and figured it was them."

"Who?" Nate asked, although he already knew.

"I never saw them clearly," Jenks said, and unexpectedly commenced shaking, trembling from head to toe.

"Are you all right?" Shakespeare inquired. He put a hand on the young man's arm and could feel the arm quiver.

"Just glad is all." Jenks exhaled loudly while holding out his quaking hands. "I reckon I'd better sit down." He sank onto his buttocks and stared at his rifle. "To think I almost killed one of you!"

"Shucks. You never came close," Shakespeare said to relieve the greenhorn's anxiety. "You were aiming at Nate, but I think you hit a squirrel over in the next valley."

Laughter burst from Jenks, nervous laughter, the kind typical of a person so overwrought he desperately needed to release his pent-up emotions.

Nate squatted and waited for their trapping partner to fall silent. "Why don't you tell us what happened?" he prodded. "Talking might help calm you down."

"There's not much to tell," Jenks said. "Three days ago, about sunset, some men showed up at my camp. I'd been off gathering the last of my traps, and was late getting back. It was almost dark, and when I first saw them through the trees I figured it was you coming to fetch me as we'd agreed. Then I heard voices, but I couldn't quite make out what was being said or even what language it was. I stopped and tried to get closer, but I must have made some noise because the next I knew one of them let out a yell and took a shot at me and five or six of them came running toward me." Jenks licked his lips. "I don't know how the hell I got out of there in one piece. All I remember is dropping my traps and running until I couldn't run any further."

"Did they come after you?"

"I should say they did! I'd collapsed on a log when I heard them moving through the pines behind me." Jenks shook again. "So I snuck off and spent the next hour working my way up the valley until I was sure they had given up." He paused. "The next morning I went back and they were gone. So were all my pelts, all my gear, all my horses, everything."

"At least you're alive," Shakespeare said. "Which makes you a far sight luckier than Pointer."

"Harry?" Jenks said in alarm, gazing all around. "I just noticed. Where is he? What happened to him?"

"The same band that tried to kill you got to him first," Nate explained. He didn't deem it appropriate to go into much more detail. "We buried him earlier."

"Oh, God," Jenks said, blanching.

"Don't fall to pieces on us, Lester," Shakespeare advised. "We all need to keep our wits about us because the band might still be in this area."

"What do we do?" Jenks asked stridently.

"Shakespeare and I will rearrange our packs and free up one of the pack animals for you to ride," Nate said. "Then

we have to check on Pepin." He noted the position of the
sun. "It's too late to reach him today. We'll have to make
camp in an hour or so and go on in the morning."

"Is that smart? I mean, shouldn't we push on through the
night?"

Nate shook his head. "Riding at night is dangerous enough
without having a string of packhorses to keep an eye on. And
the trail Pepin took is one that would give a bighorn sheep
second thoughts."

"I just hope we reach him in time," Jenks said.

"You're not the only one."

Nate tossed and turned all night long. Occasionally he
would lie and listen to Shakespeare's snoring and marvel
at the mountain man's iron constitution. In the morning he
was up first, and had all the horses ready to go before the
other two woke up.

The cocky Canadian had insisted on trapping an extremely remote area, so secluded there was only one trail in and
out and so high up the temperature dipped to near freezing
at night even in the spring. The game trail was easy enough
to locate, but the ascent, winding up a series of switchbacks
with sheer cliffs on one hand and steep rock walls on the
other, was nerve-racking. At times barely enough space
existed for the horses to walk, and Nate would peer down
at the boulder-strewn ground hundreds of feet below and try
not to imagine what it would be like to fall and be dashed
to pieces.

Eventually the trail brought them to a plateau abundant
with wildlife. Elk, deer, and bighorn sheep sign were everywhere, and lesser animals were constantly sighted.

Nate had no sooner cleared the crest than he saw a
spiral of gray smoke a half mile off. Was it from Pepin's
fire? he asked himself. Or had the war party beaten them
there? He waited for his companions to join him, then held

out his lead rope to Lester Jenks. "I'm riding on ahead
with Shakespeare. You come on after and bring all the
packhorses."

Jenks blinked. "I don't much like the notion of being left
behind."

"If the war party is already here, we can't very well outrun them hauling our pack animals along," Nate explained.
"This way, if Shakespeare and I see it isn't safe, we'll
gallop back and let you know not to come on in."

"What if there's a fight? I'll miss out."

Nate almost grinned. This from a man who had never
once fought Indians? "If there are hostiles, and if they
spot us, you'll have more than your share of fighting.
Trust me." Handing over the rope, he rode forward at a
walk until Shakespeare came alongside him. Together they
brought their mounts to a gallop.

"I don't see any tracks yet," Shakespeare mentioned,
surveying the ground.

A grassy field brought them to a thick forest, through
which a crystal-clear stream flowed. They veered into the
brush, using the thickets and undergrowth to screen their
movements, but stayed within sight of the stream.

The *voyageur* had picked a wondrously picturesque spot
for his camp. Nestled in an oval clearing at the base of an
aspen-covered slope down which the stream wound like
a glassy ribbon, it afforded protection from the wind and
plenty of forage for horses. A lean-to had been constructed
on the bank of a pool formed by a glittering waterfall. At
this high altitude the air was crisp, invigorating. A striking
azure sky completed the picture.

Nate spotted the five horses belonging to the Canadian
right away, each staked out in the clearing and nipping at
the sweet grass. He also saw pelts ready to be transported
and supplies piled near the lean-to. All appeared serene, but

as Nate had long ago learned, appearances could be deceiving. Reining up behind a spruce, he glanced at McNair. "I'll go on in alone, just in case."

"Why you?"

"I'm younger."

"So?"

"I run faster when someone is after my scalp."

"This is a hell of a note. A whippersnapper like you throwing my age back at me." Shakespeare frowned. "My pulse, as yours, doth temperately keep time, and makes as healthful music."

"Maybe so. But now isn't the proper time to put it to the test," Nate said. Bracing the stock of the Hawken on his leg and holding the barrel so the rifle slanted upward, he went around the spruce and made a beeline for the lean-to. The five horses all looked up, but displayed no alarm. He was within yards of the pool when he heard loud whistling in a stand of pines beyond, a lively tune he knew to be *Mon canot d'ecorce*, or "My Birch-bark Canoe," a popular *voyageur* song Pepin was inordinately fond of singing. Sure enough, a few seconds went by and out of the trees strolled the man himself, bearing an armful of firewood.

Pepin was characteristic of his hardy breed: short, stocky, and as powerfully built as a bull. A red woolen cap crowned his shock of curly hair. He wore a fringed buckskin shirt, which was likewise common among American free trappers, but the deerksin leggings which ran from his ankles to a bit above his knees, leaving his thighs exposed, and the short skirt, or breechcloth, he wore were both distinctly Canadian. So was the red sash about his waist, complete with a large beaded bag that resembled somewhat the possibles bags of the mountain men.

Pepin had no sooner emerged than he looked up, spied

Nate, and broke into a broad grin. "*Mon ami!* Allo! Allo! *Depuis quand êtes-vous ici?*" He ran around the end of the pool, the flat soles of his moccasins slapping on the earth.

"Hello, Pepin," Nate greeted him. "It's good to see you again."

"And you, my friend!" Pepin declared, reverting to English as he dumped the wood by the lean-to and hurried over to the black stallion. "Give us your paw!"

Nate bent over to shake and nearly lost his perch, so vigorously did the *voyageur* pump his arm. It was impossible to know Pepin and not like him, and Nate liked the man a lot. Pepin was so full of energy, so full of life itself, that his robust attitude was often contagious. "How has the trapping been?"

"*C'est formidable!*" Pepin answered. "Just great. I have over two hundred prime pelts."

"Shakespeare was right. I should have known."

"What?"

Sliding down, Nate gazed out over the vast plateau. "Have you had any trouble?"

"Difficulty? *Non!* No." Pepin's weathered brow creased. "Why do you ask, my friend? What is it you are holding back?"

"Just a moment," Nate said. Turning, he waved an arm so Shakespeare would know all was well. Then he draped the same arm over the Canadian's wide shoulders and said, "I bear bad news."

Pepin listened attentively to the story of Pointer's horrid fate and Jenks's misfortune, flushing a deep scarlet the whole while. When Nate finished, Pepin slammed a fist into his open palm and gave expression to a long string of oaths in French. He was still cursing vehemently when Shakespeare and Jenks arrived.

"Thank goodness the murdering devils didn't get to you,"

the youth told the *voyageur*. "We feared we wouldn't get here in time."

"This is terrible, most terrible!" Pepin said in his animated way. "The Indians in this country are too brazen, too vicious. They deserve to be hunted down and made to pay."

"By now the war party might be many miles away," Shakespeare said.

"So?" Pepin touched the tomahawk at his belt. "In Canada we would never let such a foul act go unpunished! It boils the blood to think of it!"

Nate, busy starting a fire, looked at the fiery trapper. "If it's the same bunch I saw, there are nine of them and only four of us. We'd be committing suicide if we went after them."

"Are we yellow?" Pepin said gruffly. "I say we teach these savages a lesson and get back all of the hides and horses that were stolen. I say we kill each and every one of the braves responsible."

"I'm with you!" Jenks cried.

Nate, with a sinking sensation in the pit of his stomach, saw that his real troubles were just beginning.

Chapter Four

Shakespeare McNair also saw the danger in the direction the talk was taking. A full lifetime had permitted him to see rash folly for what it truly was, and since he had no hankering to lose his hair at such a ripe age, he sided with Nate by saying, "It could take us weeks, and there's no guarantee we'd ever find them."

"The effort will be worth it if we avenge the memory of our fallen fellow!" Pepin replied.

Jenks nodded. "I have nothing to lose. They've already got my goods."

"But not ours, nor our plews," Shakespeare said bluntly, "and I don't figure to give them the chance to get their hands on any of my fixings."

Pepin nodded at his own hides. "But that is easily solved, *mon ami!* We can cache all the pelts here with most of the supplies. The extra horses can be let loose to roam as they please since it is doubtful they will try to go down the cliffs by themselves. Simple, *non?*"

"Some of us have families to think of," Nate mentioned.

"Is this the famous Grizzly Killer talking?" Pepin rejoined. "Is this the man I heard so much about I couldn't wait to be his partner? The man the Blackfeet, Piegans, and Bloods consider their greatest white enemy? The man who has beaten the Sioux? The man who saved his wife from a life of captivity among the Apaches?"

"I had no choice in those instances," Nate lamely said.

"And you do now? After Pointer has been slain? After Jenks was nearly killed?" Pepin made a clucking sound. "How can you say such a thing? What about the next trappers who lay their lines in this region? Are they to be butchered and scalped because we did not have the courage to deal with this?"

Such unexpected eloquence caught Nate off guard. He didn't know quite what to say, so he said nothing.

"I'll go with you, Pepin, if no one else will," Jenks said scornfully. "I'm not afraid of any damn hostiles, and I mean to have my things back come hell or high water."

"That is the spirit, my young friend!" Pepin faced McNair. "And you, *Carcajou*? Will you see justice done? Will you join us in our noble cause?"

"Noble causes have a habit of getting folks killed."

"Does that mean no?"

"It means I'll ponder some and let you know when I make up my mind," Shakespeare promised.

"As you wish, *mon ami*."

Pepin produced a short spade from his supplies, and the remainder of the day was spent digging the hole where the hides and other possession would be cached.

There was a certain technique the trappers always employed. First a straight, round hole was dug, usually to the depth of five or six feet. Next a chamber was made adjacent to the hole, a chamber big enough to accommodate all the items to be cached. Afterward, the hole was filled in with dirt. Any excess earth was scooped up and scattered, in this case into the pool. Finally branches were used to rake over the top of the hole and bits of grass and leaves were added to completely cover it. When all was done, only an experienced eye could tell that the ground had even been disturbed.

Nate helped dig, but his heart wasn't in it. He had liked Pointer as much as any of them, and he was as outraged as they were by Pointer's death and the theft of Jenks's peltries. By the same token, he had learned the hard way that vengeance was a two-edged sword; those who sought it often reaped it. He did not care to die without seeing his family again. But—and that word seemed to stick in his throat—he did have an obligation to his trapping partners, a responsibility to do what was best for all of them. It would be selfish of him to think only of his own interests.

By evening most of the stores had been cached. Pepin took Jenks off to hunt supper. Nate strolled to the pool and sat glumly down at the water's edge. He swirled the surface with a finger and saw the reflection of his mentor appear. "Have you made up your mind yet?"

"I was waiting for you to make up yours first."

"I made my feelings clear earlier."

"Did you?" Shakespeare asked, sinking down. "I heard your common sense speaking but not your heart."

"Women think with their hearts. Men don't."

Shakespeare chuckled. "Men like to pretend they don't, but they do. Just as much as women. We just lie about it because we don't like to admit we let our emotions get the better of us." He tossed a pebble into the water. "No man likes to 'fess up to losing his self-control. It makes him seem weak."

"If we go after that war party, we're as dumb as turnips."

"You'll get no argument from me."

"It'd be plain stupid."

"As stupid as anything."

"Who knows when we'd get home?"

"Time would tell."

"It would be a dunderhead thing to do."

"True enough."

"Feebleminded is a better description."

"Then feebleminded it is. Throw in featherbrained, empty-skulled, and doltish too."

Shifting, Nate stared into Shakespeare's kindly eyes. "But we have it to do, don't we?"

"As surely as the sun rises and sets every day."

"Damn."

"That's what we get for being men and not boys. A boy can always make up excuses to get out of doing what has to be done, but a man, *if* he's a man, has to face facts and do what has to be done without complaint."

"Sometimes I wish I'd never grown up."

"Don't we all, son. Don't we all."

Pepin and Jenks returned an hour later with a bighorn sheep. "You should have seen the shot I made," the Canadian boasted. "There was this gorgeous sheep, so high up on the rocks his horns were touching the bottoms of the clouds, and I put a ball through his head with my first shot!"

"Amazing," Nate said dryly, and coughed. "There's something you should know," he continued. "Shakespeare and I have decided to go along." Before he could elaborate, the *voyageur* sprang at him, embraced him in a bear hug, and spun him in circles while whooping like a demented Comanche.

"*Tres bien! Tres bien!* I knew you would! Does a panther run from chipmunks? Does an eagle flee from jays? Does a bear hide from ants? *Non!* Never!"

Nate was spun a few more times for good measure. He couldn't help but laugh when Pepin stepped back. "You're plumb crazy. You know that, don't you?"

"*Oui*. But without a touch of craziness, life can be so dull, *non*?"

"Dull, maybe. Longer, definitely," Shakespeare muttered.

That night Pepin regaled them with exaggerated tales of his escapades in Canada. He told of Lake Winnipeg, "so deep a *coureur de bois* once found a Chinaman floating on the top." And of rivers where the current was so swift, "a man can fire his rifle, paddle a few strokes, and be in position to catch the ball as it comes down." He claimed "the grizzlies in Canada are so big, the full-grown ones you have here are no bigger than their cubs." And after dark had settled, he mentioned the time he found mammoth tracks.

"What the dickens are mammoths?" Jenks asked. "No one ever told me about them."

"That's because no white man has ever laid eyes on one," Pepin said. "And the Indians who have seen the things don't like to talk about the creature because they're mighty bad medicine. The Indians believe that anyone who sees a mammoth will die soon after doing so if the mammoth doesn't kill the person first."

"Sounds like another one of their nature spirit yarns to me," Jenks said.

"Not the mammoth, *mon ami*. The Lillooet, the Bella Coola, the Yuroks, they all say that mammoths are flesh and blood." Pepin pulled out his pipe and tobacco pouch. "And after what I saw, young one, I think they are right." He pondered a bit. "It was eight years ago. I was crossing the Canadian Rockies through Yellowhead Pass when I saw these peculiar tracks. The Indians with me went into a panic and begged me to leave the area before the thing found us."

"Certainly," Jenks said. "We're not murdering savages."

"Neither are they," Shakespeare responded.

The greenhorn was incredulous. "How can you say such a thing, McNair? They butchered Pointer, stole everything I own."

"We don't know yet whether the Blackfeet or the Bloods or some other tribe is to blame, but it doesn't matter. Every one of them has made no secret of the fact that white men are their enemies. In their eyes, we're trespassers, invaders who are killing off all the beaver and a lot of other game and spreading our diseases among them wherever we go. In their eyes, they're doing what they think they have to do to protect their people, what they believe is right."

"That doesn't make it so!"

"As you go through life I think you'll learn that being right or wrong, good or bad, often depends on which side of the fence you're on."

"Are you saying that you excuse what they did to Pointer?"

"I wouldn't go that far," Shakespeare said, wishing he could make the younger man understand. Many trappers despised Indians on general principles, and many Indians returned the favor for the same reason, or lack of it. He'd long speculated that if both sides could see the world through the eyes of those they hated, the constant bloodshed might stop, or at least taper off. The Shoshones and Flatheads were living proof that the red man and the white man could live together in harmony if they wanted. The pity was that so few cared to make the effort. "I'm only saying I understand it."

Nate saw Jenks open his mouth to argue and spoke up himself. "Let's keep going. I don't aim to sit here on this mountain all afternoon listening to the two of you squabble." Applying his heels, he moved out, following the prints. No rain had fallen in the interval since he'd sighted the war party, so the tracks were quite plain.

The younger man's attitude bothered Nate. There had been a time, back before Nate had ventured from New York City to the frontier, when Nate might have sympathized with Jenks's point of view. Since then he had learned that Indians and whites were more alike than either was willing to admit. And having lived with Shoshones for so long, he had learned to highly admire the Indian way of life. When someone branded them as evil, he took issue.

The Shoshones were friendly to all whites and always had been. Whenever a trapper visited a Shoshone village, he was made welcome with food and drink and a lodge to sleep in if he so desired. And the man need not fear for his belongings either. Unlike the Crows, who were addicted to petty thievery, the Shoshones were scrupulously honest in all their dealings.

Nate thought of them later that evening, after camp had been made and chunks of rabbit meat were roasting on the fire. "Did you happen to notice which direction the war party is heading?" he remarked.

"I did," Shakespeare said. "Toward Shoshone country."

"You'd think they'd be satisfied with Pointer's hair and my peltries," Jenks said bitterly.

"If these devils are Blackfeet," Pepin said, "they won't be content with anything less than a scalp for every one of them, and a new horse besides." He adjusted the stick suspended over the fire, turning the meat so the uncooked portions were nearest to the flames. "Maybe they're fixing to steal a few Shoshone women as well."

"Not the Blackfeet," Nate said. "They aren't much for taking wives from other tribes." He remembered a battle in which he had taken part some years back. "Men, women, children, it's all the same to them. The Blackfeet kill everyone."

"Like I said," Jenks mentioned smugly. "Savages, pure and simple."

The next day was a repeat of the first. About mid-morning Nate came to a creek where the war party had stopped to water their mounts. Not far beyond was a gravel bar the Indians had crossed. Mixed liberally with mud, the bar gave Nate a chance to study each and every set of hoofprints in detail. As he was doing so, he spotted a set of tracks much deeper than the rest. "This one was packing a heavy load. Maybe pelts."

"Could be," Shakespeare said, "although Jenks claims he had enough for two horses." He scratched his beard. "But where are all the other pack animals? What happened to all the supplies they stole? And Pointer's peltries?"

"Maybe we have the wrong band."

"Keep looking. We might find a clue."

Nate continued searching, and on a long muddy strip where the warriors had ridden strung out instead of in single file he found something odd. "I count eleven horses now."

"Me too," Shakespeare confirmed. "I thought I did back yonder and this proves it."

"Two more than I saw," Nate said thoughtfully. "This answers our question. I didn't see the whole band. There must have been more in the trees, and some of them are taking most of the plunder back to their village even as we speak."

"It's possible," Shakespeare conceded. "They wouldn't want to traipse all over the country with a lot of pack animals and provisions slowing them down."

"Especially if they're mainly after scalps," Nate said, pleased by the cleverness of their deduction.

That night they camped in a ravine sheltered from the blustery winds and enjoyed venison thanks to Pepin, who downed a small doe at 70 yards. Their horses were pushed to the limit the next day, and the next. Jenks's mount, normally used as a pack animal, was hard pressed to keep up the pace.

Nate was beginning to think it would be three or four days more before they caught their quarry when they had a stroke of luck. They discovered a spot where the war party had camped for two days, and the remains of an elk explained why.

"Soon now!" Pepin cried. "Soon we avenge our friend!"

It was the following day, early in the evening when the sun was slowly sinking behind a stark range of glistening peaks, that Nate came off a bluff and spotted in a basin below a pale pinpoint of light. Instantly he reined up and pointed. "There they are," he announced.

"At last," Jenks said. "I can't wait to get my hands on my furs."

"You'll have to wait a while longer," Shakespeare said. "We can't go barging on in there. First we scout out their camp, then we decide how best to kill them."

"I'll do the scouting," Nate said to forestall the others. He was concerned either the hotheaded Pepin or the brash Jenks might make a blunder that would prove costly to them all. Slanting into a stand of slender aspens, he climbed from the saddle, looped the reins to a limb, and started down the slope.

"Mind some company, son?" Shakespeare asked, falling into step.

"Not at all," Nate said gratefully.

A stretch of shrub and pines brought them to the basin floor, which was covered with high grass shaded greenish-gray by the gathering twilight. Halfway across the basin, at the base of a hillock dotted with trees, was the campfire.

"Cocky bunch," Shakespeare said. "Most war parties wouldn't bother with a fire this close to enemy territory."

"I've got three plews that says they're Blackfeet."

"You're on. I think they're Bloods."

Dropping low, Nate entered the grass and snaked forward. He loosened both flintlocks in case he needed them quickly, and slid his butcher knife partway out of its sheath once. The wind was on his back, a bad place for it to be since the war party's horses would pick up his scent if he wasn't extremely careful.

Three hundred yards were covered in virtual silence. Nate had learned the art of being stealthy from the Shoshones, some of whom were so adept they could sneak up on a bear and swat the beast on the rump before it knew they were there. He knew just how to lower his feet—toes first, with the weight born on the balls—to muffle the sound of his footsteps.

Low voices and laughter brought Nate up short. He guessed he was 20 to 30 yards from the fire, too close to dare rising for a look since his pale face would be a dead giveaway against the dark background. Easing onto his hands and knees, he crawled forward, glancing to the right where Shakespeare had been a few moments before. His friend was gone.

Nate wasn't worried. No other white man alive could handle himself like McNair, who would probably sneak so close to the camp he'd hear the warriors break wind. Nate, on the other hand, had no desire to push his luck; he crawled until he glimpsed the flames, then halted and contented himself for the time being with merely listening.

The tongue being used wasn't Blackfoot. Nate couldn't claim proficiency in the language, but the time he'd spent as a captive had given him an ear for recognizing it when he heard it spoken. Which narrowed the choices down to Piegans or Bloods, both allies of the Blackfeet in a fierce confederacy that controlled the northern Rockies and plains.

Presently, satisfied the band had no idea there was any-one else within 50 miles, Nate worked his way to the right, toward the hillock. He needed to know what sort of arms the warriors had, how many guns and bows and lances. At least one gun had been fired at Jenks, and they had to have at least one additional rifle and two pistols because that was how many guns Pointer had owned. Nate also wanted to learn where the horses were tied since he hadn't heard so much as a nicker out of them yet.

A faint rustling caused Nate to stop and look to his left. The rustling grew closer and closer. His gaze dropped, and so did his mouth when he distinguished the outline of a long, thin shape crawling directly towards him. *A snake!* he realized, instinctively tensing to draw back. Only he couldn't. He was closer to the camp, too close. The warriors might notice any sudden swaying of the grass.

The next moment the head of the reptile appeared, and Nate had to bite down on his lower lip to keep from crying out. Of all the types of snakes it could have been, this one turned out to be one of the deadliest of all: a rattlesnake.

Chapter Five

Even in the gloom of gathering night the distinct triangular shape of the rattler's head was plain to see. The markings on the scaly skin were harder to discern, not that they mattered. Nate knew that rattlesnakes did their hunting at night, knew that the one creeping slowly toward him was seeking prey, any warm-blooded prey it could find. He held himself rigid, hoping against hope the venomous reptile would simply pass him by. But such was not to happen.

When only a foot away from Nate's right hand, the rattler suddenly whipped its head high and coiled, its tiny forked tongue darting out to test the air. Its rattles shook, but not loudly.

Nate stared into the creature's unblinking eyes, into its bizarre vertical pupils, and felt his skin crawl with gooseflesh. The snake swayed, the tongue repeatedly flicking in and out. At such short range it could hardly miss if it chose to strike. Nate fought to resist an impulse to snatch his arm away since any movement would provoke the reptile into doing just that.

Nerve-racking seconds passed. Nate had no idea what the rattlesnake would do. Of all God's creatures, only grizzlies were as unpredictable. The Hawken was clutched in his left hand, of no use in swatting the snake aside even if he dared do so, since by the time he lifted the rifle the reptile would bite. All he could do was lie there and pray.

A full minute went by. Then, so lightning-quick its body was a virtual blur, the rattler whirled and sped off through the grass.

Nate exhaled in relief. His hands trembled slightly in reaction to his narrow escape. Waiting until he was composed, he resumed crawling around the base of the hillock, and once on the side opposite the camp he rose into a crouch. The wind had temporarily died, enabling him to hear the chirp of a cricket and the distant hoot of an owl. Even further off a lone coyote yipped its melancholy cry.

Holding the rifle in both hands, Nate advanced up the slope, wending around boulders, scrub thickets, and occasional pines. Three-fourths of the way to the top a log barred his path and he started to step over it. As his leg lowered, strong fingers abruptly clamped on his ankle. Thinking that an Indian had grabbed him, Nate elevated the Hawken to bash in the warrior's head. A barely audible chuckle stopped him.

"Getting a mite careless in your young age, Horatio. I heard you coming clear down at the bottom. Are you trying to get yourself killed?"

"You pick the darnedest times to play games," Nate whispered irately. His ankle was released, and he slipped over the log to squat beside his mentor. "Have you already spied on them?"

"Yep."

"Who won our wager?"

"See for yourself," Shakespeare said softly. Rising, he padded upward to the crest and lay down in a patch of cool grass.

Doing the same, Nate held his head low to the ground so the dancing firelight wouldn't reflect off him. Ten robust warriors were seated around the fire, all listening to one of their number who was going on at length about something. Nate noted the style of their hair and their buckskins and identified them as Piegans, which meant Shakespeare and he had both been wrong and neither of them had won their friendly bet.

Nate glanced to the right. At the base of the hill, shrouded in inky shadows, were the horses. He scanned the camp, spotting a number of bows and lances and a single fusee, but he saw no sign of the peltries and fixings stolen from Jenks and Pointer. He reasoned the goods were piled near the horses and couldn't be seen from his vantage point.

The Piegan doing the talking stopped, and another squared his shoulders and began speaking.

Nate had learned enough to know how best to spring the ambush. Easing backwards, he went a few feet before he pushed off the ground and hastened down the hillock. Shakespeare trailed him.

"Did you hear what they were saying?"

"You know I don't speak a lick of Piegan," Nate whispered.

"I've picked up a smattering of words," the mountain man said. "And if I'm right, they're fixing to attack a Shoshone village the day after tomorrow. They plan to steal a lot of horses and maybe count a few coup."

"Not if I can help it," Nate said. Now he had another reason for attacking the war party. The Shoshones were his adopted people, and he could not stand idly by while their enemies raided them.

Once on level ground the two trappers bore to the south and worked their way in a roundabout fashion to the aspens. They were at the edge of the trees when a clear metallic click stopped them in their tracks.

"*Non! Non!* It is our friends, young one."

"Yes, it's us," Nate confirmed, going on to find Pepin with a firm hand on the barrel of the greenhorn's rifle, which had been deflected downward. "Didn't it occur to you that it might be Shakespeare and me?" he asked Jenks.

"I wasn't thinking. I heard a sound and I assumed it might be Indians."

"That makes twice," Nate said, recalling the incident when Jenks had shot at them. "Keep it up and one of these times you'll make a mistake you'll live to regret."

"*Enfant!*" Pepin declared, and laughed.

Although Nate did not find the close call so amusing, he let the matter drop and turned to the issue at hand. "Here is what we found," he began. The Canadian and the youth were rapt listeners, and when Nate was done the Canadian smiled and slapped a thigh.

"Ten scalps to share! This is better than I dreamed."

"Our main purpose is to reclaim the stolen hides and such," Shakespeare mentioned.

"All I want is revenge," Jenks said eagerly.

"A dagger of the mind, a false creation, proceeding from the heat-oppressed brain," Shakespeare quoted.

"What?"

"Never mind," Shakespeare said, unwilling to waste words. There was nothing he could say or do that would change the young man's attitude, and rather than waste energy trying, he leaned against a sapling and crossed his arms. Some lessons could only be taught by life itself. Jenks would learn of his own accord, if he survived to learn at all.

Nate detailed the arrangement of the Piegan camp, concluding with: "They have no idea we're here, so if all goes well we can take them completely by surprise. I think we should sneak up on them from four directions and at a signal from me, open fire."

"I will take up position near their horses to keep any of the savages from getting away," Pepin said.

Nate suspected the *voyageur* had an ulterior motive. At the first blast of gunfire the Piegans would naturally dash for their horses to flee, enabling Pepin to drop more than he might otherwise, thereby giving him the chance to collect more scalps.

"What about me?" Jenks inquired. "I've never fought Indians before. What do I do?"

"You go to the top of the small hill," Nate suggested. The hillock, he figured, would be the safest place to be since it was highly unlikely any of the warriors would try to scale the slope while under attack. "If any of them go for the high ground, cut them off."

"I'll drop them like flies," Jenks pledged. "But where will you be?"

"Shakespeare and I will go through the grass, right up to their camp."

Jenks grinned. "Better you than me, King. If the Piegans spot you before you're ready, you'll be turned into pincushions."

"Thanks for the warning." Nate craned his neck to see up through the foliage. Every trapper learned early on how to tell the passage of time by the relative positions of the stars and the constellations, and by his reckoning it was then close to eight o'clock. "We'll wait until midnight to move out. By then most of them should be sound asleep."

"What do we do until then?" Jenks wondered.

"I don't know about you, but I aim to get some rest," Nate answered. Going over to a clear space amidst the saplings, he sat down with his back to a trunk, rested the Hawken across his legs, and tried to nap. The long day in the saddle had left him fatigued, but the impending clash had him too on edge to permit sleep. Shifting and squirming, he tried his best, until he heard a soft snicker.

"Ants in your britches, son?"

Nate looked around as McNair walked over and took a seat. "It's times like this I wish I had your knack for falling asleep anywhere, anytime."

"Blame Winona."

"You've lost me. What does she have to do with anything?"

"If your wife nagged you, you'd know how to drop off at the drop of a pin. No man likes to listen to a woman squawk at him from dawn to dusk, day in and day out. So men who find themselves in that situation learn to shut their wives out by falling asleep at will."

"And where did you pick up this tidbit of information? Your wife doesn't nag you either."

"No, she doesn't. But years ago I lived with another woman, a plucky Nez Percé, who just about wore my ears to a frazzle. I loved her too much to leave her, yet I couldn't take all that carping. Then one day she up and got herself taken by the Bloods during a raid, so I imagine some lucky Blood warrior has had to put up with her all these years." Shakespeare grinned. "There is justice in this old world, no matter what anyone says to the contrary."

"You're always full of surprises," Nate commented. His gaze drifted to the Piegan campfire. "Let's hope we're not in for any nasty ones when we make our move."

"You did right by having Jenks on the hill," Shakespeare said. "It'll keep him out of danger." His voice lowered.

"Course, he's not the one who worries me."

"Pepin? He can handle himself."

"You'll get no argument there. But the man is too sure of himself. And he's got a powerful hankering for scalps. Worse case I ever saw. He would have been happier if he'd been born a Blackfoot."

"There you go again. Exaggerating as always."

"Think I do?" Shakespeare shrugged. "Well, let's hope so, for both our sakes."

For the next several hours Nate made small talk. He was too on edge to do anything else. Despite the many times he had engaged in mortal combat with enemies white and red alike, he could never get used to the idea. He wasn't one of those who liked to fight for the mere sake of fighting. If he had his druthers, he'd rather live in peace with everyone, but that was an impractical ideal, especially for one living in the untamed wilderness. Running into enemies, both human and bestial, was a common part of life in the mountains, and any man who wanted to last long had to accept that fact and live accordingly.

The crunch of a twig heralded Pepin. "It's about that time, my friends," he declared, pointing heavenward. "Are you ready?"

The location of the Big Dipper showed the Canadian was right. Nate stood, worked his legs to restore circulation, and checked the Hawken. None of them uttered a sound as he walked out of the trees and paused to regard the basin. "Spread out and stay low," he cautioned. "If you get into trouble, the rest of us will come to your aid."

"That's good to hear," Jenks said. His tone, his posture indicated his nerves were taut.

"Good luck," Nate offered. He touched Shakespeare's arm, then stalked forward as before. The light from the Piegan fire had dwindled to a few fingers of flame that would soon go out, which forced him to hurry in order to be in place before that happened.

Dread of encountering another rattler prompted Nate to stop every time he heard rustling. In each case it was the wind, which had intensified and was rippling the grass much as a gale rippled waves on the sea. Nate was halfway to the hillock when he thought to glance over his shoulder at the horizon and saw a mass of dark clouds blotting out many of the stars. A storm was coming. And if it got there before they were ready, it would spoil everything. In a driving downpour they wouldn't be able to see more than a few feet.

Disregarding caution, Nate hurried faster, parting the grass with his head and shoulders. He wondered if his companions had noticed the approaching storm and if they were doing as he was. Once his right hand came down on something wriggling and slippery, but there was no answering rattle and he plowed on ahead without bothering to find out what the thing had been.

The wind had an unforeseen effect. Nate was still 50 feet from the camp when the flames were smothered, plunging the immediate area into total darkness. Now Nate couldn't see where the Piegans were sleeping. Indeed, he had no idea whether a guard had been posted and where the warrior might be.

Frowning at the unwanted development, Nate moved steadily nearer. He didn't fear detection because the waving grass smothered any faint noises he made. About 20 feet out he sank onto his belly. Another ten feet brought him close enough to make out a few dark lumps on the ground by the fire. Sleeping Piegans, but he only counted five. Where were the rest?

Nate lifted his head to see better, then turned to ice on hearing a yawn off to the left. A slender figure was moving toward the fire, the lone man on watch, evidently. The Piegan knelt at the fire. Nate saw sparks blossom and promptly sank down. The guard was trying to get the fire going again.

Persistence paid off. After a dozen tries the brave rekindled the flames and held his hands out to shield them from the wind.

In the pale glow Nate saw the warrior's hawkish features. He now counted seven sleeping forms, which left two unaccounted for. The possibility of there being more than one guard was terribly worrisome. He scanned the hillock and the black shadows where the horses were tethered, but saw no one.

The Piegan, meanwhile, was feeding branches to the fire, raising the flames to new heights. He added too many, or maybe the wind flared the fire, but whichever was the case, the flames suddenly shot so high the Piegan had to leap back to keep from having his eyebrows singed.

At that moment a horse whinnied.

Instantly the Piegan was on his feet, and he wasn't the only one. Three others leaped up, bows in hand. They spoke in muted voices while gazing all around. Two of them then headed for the horses.

Nate was in a quandary. He wasn't sure if Shakespeare and Jenks were in position yet, and if he jumped the gun before they were ready, the whole element of surprise would be wasted. He watched with bated breath as the two warriors vanished in the murky shadows. The same or another horse nickered. There was a commotion but no outcries, no gunshots. He began to breathe a smidgen easier.

On the top of the hillock another commotion erupted. Someone cursed—in English. A tremendous crashing in the underbrush brought more of the sleeping Piegans to their feet in time to see a pair of men rolling down the slope, men who were locked together as each sought the other's throat. Rolling over and over and over, the combatants finally came to rest at the bottom.

Nate let out a gasp. Lester Jenks was grappling with a muscular brave, a brave who must have been on top of the hillock. A second sentry. The Piegans had not been as cocky as Shakespeare thought; they had taken prudent precautions against an attack.

Fierce yells broke out among the Piegans, and several moved to help their fellow. One drew a knife and coiled to plunge the blade into Jenks's back.

Something had to be done. Nate could wait no longer. Raising the Hawken, he took a hasty bead on the Piegan with the knife. But his thumb was in the act of curling back the hammer when another rifle cracked in the grass off to his left. Shakespeare's rifle it was, and the slug caught the knife-wielder squarely in the center of the back, ripping through the man's spine and bursting out his chest.

As the first Piegan fell, the rest whirled to confront the new threat. Nate shifted, sighted on a burly warrior, and gently squeezed the trigger. At the retort, the burly one was lifted from his feet and slammed lifeless to the ground.

The war party was in turmoil. They didn't know how many enemies they faced, and the deaths of two of their number in as many seconds had disconcerted the majority. Some broke, running for the horses. A few lifted bows, seeking targets to shoot. And a lone warrior turned back to assist the man grappling with Jenks. This warrior had a tomahawk, which he started to swing in an overhand arc.

Reloading the Hawken was out of the question. Nate drew his right flintlock, rising to one knee as he did. He snapped off a shot without aiming, and was gratified to see the ball strike the tomahawk-wielder in the armpit. The man jerked to one side, twisted, and fell.

Another pistol banged. Shakespeare had dropped a fourth
warrior.

Barbed arrows sought the trappers.

Nate flattened again as a whizzing shaft streaked over his
head, almost clipping his beaver hat. Yet another warrior
dashed for the horses, leaving only two by the fire, one
armed with a bow, the last holding a war club. Jenks was
getting the worst of his fight; the Piegan was slowly choking
the life from him.

Wedging the spent flintlock under his belt, Nate girded
his legs, drew his other pistol, and surged forward, shooting
as he straightened. The bowman, hit high in the chest, staggered and dropped his bow but did not fall. Nate unlimbered
his tomahawk, uttered a Shoshone war whoop, and rushed
to close quarters.

The Piegan bearing the war club charged to meet Nate.
They clashed in front of the fire, the Piegan swinging first,
a brutal blow that would have smashed Nate's skull to
fragments had it landed. A swift parry with the tomahawk
deflected it. Nate pivoted, slashing at the warrior's stomach.
His foe, as nimbly as a chipmunk, danced aside.

Meanwhile, the wounded bowman had drawn a knife and
was seeking an opening.

Nate was caught between the pair. He had to keep one
eye on the man with the club, the other on the brave with
the knife. Working in concert they might have downed Nate
swiftly, but the wounded man was unable to do much more
than stab ineffectively.

Suddenly Shakespeare McNair entered the fray, swinging
his rifle as if it was a club, the stock crunching the wounded
Piegan's nose and felling the warrior on the spot.

The warrior with the war club shrieked and made a frantic
bid to cave in Nate's forehead. Nate countered, blocking
the blow. In the process he hooked his right leg behind

the Piegan's legs and shoved with his elbow, tripping his adversary. The Piegan landed on his back, got an elbow under him, and started to rise. Nate stopped him. Or rather, the keen edge of the tomahawk did by splitting the warrior's face right down the middle.

Nate wrenched the tomahawk loose and whirled to help Jenks. Aghast, he saw that he was too late. Lester Jenks lay limp in the grass, the hilt of a knife jutting from the youth's chest. There was no sign of the warrior who had killed him. "Where—?" he blurted out, glancing around.

Shakespeare was looking around also. "I think he ran for the horses," he said, and headed in that direction.

Nate immediately followed. There were still four Piegans unaccounted for. He'd expected to hear Pepin cut loose as warriors made for the string, yet there hadn't been a sound out of the Canadian, leading Nate to fear Pepin was dead too.

A body materialized in the night.

Both Shakespeare and Nate slowed. The corpse was that of a Piegan, his throat slit ear to ear. They went further and found another. A few yards more and there was a third, and bent over it, slicing off the scalp, was the grinning *voyageur*.

"*Magnifique!* Three scalps, all mine!" Pepin unbent and waved his grisly trophy in the air. "*Formidable*, eh, my friends? They never knew what hit them!"

Nate halted, breathing deeply as the swirl of violence caught up with him. His blood raged through his veins and he felt almost out of breath. He understood now why Pepin had not fired. The Canadian had not wanted to alert the fleeing Piegans to his presence, so he had dispatched them silently.

"Where's the last man?" Shakespeare asked, peering into the night.

"We missed one?" Pepin said. "That will not do. We cannot waste a scalp."

Coming as it did so soon on the heels of losing Jenks, Nate found the *voyageur*'s bloodthirstiness appalling. Turning, he walked toward their fallen friend. Behind him Pepin addressed McNair.

"Where is our young companion, *mon ami*?"

Nate did not hear Shakespeare's low response, but the Canadian's bellow of anger was like the bellow of a bull moose. Nate halted beside the dead greenhorn, sank to one knee, and took hold of the knife hilt to yank the weapon out. Jenks's eyes were wide open, staring blankly at the heavens. Nate let go of the knife to reach down and close the hapless trapper's eyelids, and as he did, rushing footsteps came at him from the right. He looked up just as the last of the Piegans, tomahawk in hand, screeched and sprang.

Chapter Six

Moments ago Nate King had tucked his own tomahawk under his belt. His hands were empty, his pistols also. But his left hand was near his knife. With the speed of thought he went to grab for it, then realized he could not possibly bring the knife into play before the Piegan slammed into him. So he brought both arms up, barely in time to cushion the impact as the heavy warrior bowled him clean over.

Nate landed flat, the Piegan astride his midsection. He tried to hurl the warrior from him, and the movement of his head as he lifted it saved his life because he moved it a hair to the left just as the brave's tomahawk cleaved the air, fanning his right ear. A punch to the Piegan's flat stomach elicited a grunt. The warrior, snarling, swept the tomahawk on high.

Getting his feet firmly on the ground, Nate bucked as a wild horse might, which threw the brave forward onto his shoulders. Nate was ready. Seizing the man's thighs as the Piegan slid upward, he heaved, throwing the warrior from him. In an instant Nate was in a crouch and clawing for his tomahawk.

The Piegan divined Nate's intent and aimed a blow at Nate's wrist, forcing Nate to pull his arm up or lose his hand. Nate scrambled backwards, trying to gain distance so he could employ a weapon, but the Piegan came after him, swinging constantly, a series of vicious swipes that would have ripped Nate to shreds if they had connected.

In the heat of personal combat a man's reflexes take over. If he tries to think, to reason out strategy, more often than not he loses his life during the precious seconds he is distracted by his own thoughts. Quite frequently inspiration saves the day, inspiration so elemental it stems from the most basic of instincts, the instinct for self-preservation.

Nate King had a strong sense of self-preservation. That instinct had carried him through dozens of conflicts with men and beasts alike. And it served him in good stead now. For as the Piegan delivered a particularly powerful blow that left the warrior momentarily off balance, Nate took a step toward the man instead of away from him and gouged his fingers into the Piegan's eyes.

Howling, the Piegan retreated a few feet, blinking furiously as his eyes filled with tears. He brushed his free hand over them, attempting to clear his vision.

In that crucial interval, Nate took the offensive. He leaped, grasped the warrior's wrist to keep the tomahawk at bay, and drove his other hand, fist clenched, into the Piegan's jaw. The warrior rocked on his heels. Nate punched again, and a third time, and suddenly the dazed Piegan crumpled, the tomahawk falling loose.

Nate pulled his knife and lifted it for the fatal stab. Helpless at his feet lay the Piegan, ripe for killing. Blade glinting in the firelight, the knife reached its apex, then froze there as Nate paused, his brow knitting. He wanted to bury the blade in the brave, but something stopped him, something stayed his hand at the very moment of making the kill. Whether it was the fact the Piegan was totally helpless or another factor, Nate didn't know. He just couldn't bring himself to finish the warrior off.

"Are you all right, son?"

Nate glanced up at Shakespeare and slowly nodded. "Fine," he said breathlessly. "Just a mite winded."

"Are you going to kill this rascal, or not?"

"No."

"Oh?" Shakespeare was perplexed, but they were such close friends that he offered no criticism or objections. Sliding his butcher knife out, he cut several strips from the Piegan's buckskin shirt and used them to securely bind the warrior's wrists.

A small boulder offered Nate a place to sit. He mechanically began reloading his pistols and commented, "Well, I guess that's that."

"We were lucky."

"Not lucky enough," Nate responded, looking at Jenks.

"What do you have in mind for this one?" Shakespeare asked, giving the Piegan a smack on the shoulder.

"I don't rightly know yet."

"I know what Pepin will want to do."

As if on cue, the fiery *voyageur* strolled up to them. Hanging from his belt were three fresh scalps, all dripping blood. He frowned down at Jenks, then glanced at the bound Piegan and looked startled. "What's this? You've spared one of the murdering bastards?"

"Yes," Nate said.

"How can you, after what they have done?" Pepin laid a hand on his knife. "Leave it to me, my friend. I will take care of this one for you, and to show you my generous nature, you can still have his hair."

"Don't touch him," Nate said.

Pepin paid no attention. "You're being foolish, and that's not like you." Grinning in anticipation, he leaned over the unconscious warrior and inched his knife from its sheath. "This will be all over in no time. A quick cut, and *voila*! It is done."

"No!" Nate practically roared, rising. "This one is mine, to do with as I see fit. Touch a hair on his head and so help me I'll put a ball into you."

"Into me?" Pepin said in amazement. "But we are friends, are we not? Surely you would not kill me to save one such as this?"

"I don't want him harmed," Nate reiterated.

"Most strange," Pepin said, stepping back and replacing his knife. "I do not understand but I will respect your wishes. Just remember this warning. You are making a mistake if you do not finish this man off here and now. A big mistake."

"I've made them before."

The Canadian glanced at McNair, who shrugged. "*Je ne comprends pas,*" he muttered. "I will find the peltries and be right back." Shaking his head, he walked toward the horses.

Nate finished reloading one pistol and concentrated on the other. Without having to raise his head he knew that his mentor was staring at him, so he said, "Is something the matter?"

"Not with me."

"With me, you figure?"

"Alas, how is it with you?"

"Meaning?"

"Use every man after his desert and who shall escape whipping? Use them after your own honour and dignity: the less they deserve, the more merit is in your boun-ty," Shakespeare quoted, casting a meaningful look at the

Piegan. "In this instance, though, I have to agree with our impulsive friend from the North Country. You're making a mistake that could prove costly to you and yours. If you let this warrior go, he'll never rest until he's buried each and every one of us."

"He'd have to find us."

"Never put anything past fickle Fate."

Annoyed, Nate rose. "I have to fetch my Hawken." He entered the grass, following the trail of bent stems he had made to the spot where the rifle lay. Picking it up, he blew bits of grass and dirt off the barrel and the stock. Inwardly he was more upset with himself than the others because he knew in his soul they were right. To not slay the Piegan would be plain stupid, yet he balked at the notion and could not explain why. Was it because he was growing too softhearted for his own good? Was it because there had already been enough bloodshed, more than enough to make up for what the band had done to Pointer? Or was there some other reason altogether?

Shakespeare was examining the Piegan when Nate returned. "Uncanny, isn't it?" he remarked.

"What is?"

"How much this man resembles Drags the Rope. Why, they look enough alike to be twins."

Nate looked, and it was as if he saw the Piegan for the first time. He wondered why he had not noticed himself, and chalked it up to the heat of combat. Drags the Rope, after all, was one of his oldest friends, a Shoshone brave who had always treated him with the utmost respect and kindness. The two of them were like brothers, and there was nothing the one would not do for the other.

"Two peas in a pod," Shakespeare went on. He gave the warrior's left cheek a light slap, then did the same to the right. The Piegan's eyelids quivered but did not open, so

Shakespeare grabbed the man's chin and shook vigorously until they did.

Instantly the warrior tried to sit up. Shakespeare shoved him back down, and he snarled like a cornered beast and tugged in vain at the strips securing his wrists. When he discovered he was helpless he unleashed a string of furious words at his two captors.

"There's no need for me to translate," Shakespeare said. "Suffice it to say he has his dander up."

"Ask his name," Nate prompted.

Shakespeare spoke haltingly in the Piegan tongue, then relayed, "Black Badger. And he claims to have taken the scalps of seven whites."

"He's at our mercy and he tells you that?"

"No, he boasted of it."

The warrior went on at length with many angry glares at Nate and nods at his dead companions. On finishing he held his head high, proudly defiant.

"What was that all about?" Nate inquired.

"Black Badger wants you to know that one day he is going to cut open your stomach and rip out your entrails with his bare hands," Shakespeare reported. "He aims to make all of us suffer for our unprovoked attack, but you he hates the most. No one has ever bested him before. He thinks you must have a special charm given to you by your guardian spirit or else you are an evil spirit yourself."

"Tell him I'm just a man," Nate said, "and point out that we were justified in repaying them for what they did to Pointer and for stealing the hides they took."

Shakespeare passed on the information and listened intently to the Piegan's answer, his features troubled. "He claims he doesn't know what we're talking about. His war party hadn't set eyes on a single white man since leaving their village until we came along, and they didn't steal any pelts."

"Tell him we know better. Tell him that honest men don't speak with a forked tongue."

The warrior made a hissing sound on hearing the insult. His next words were barked out, clipped and precise.

"Black Badger says that your father was a Pawnee and your mother was a coyote. If he wasn't tied, he'd challenge you and let the Great Spirit show which one of you two has a straight tongue." Shakespeare paused and looked up. "I know an honest man when I meet one and this here is no liar."

"But what about the packhorse?" Nate mentioned. "War parties travel light and live off the land. Why did they bring an extra horse? What was on that one animal that made its hoofs sink so deep into the ground?"

The question was posed to the Piegan, who answered with bitter resentment.

"One of the warriors brought along a spare because his favorite war horse had just healed up after being wounded in a battle with the Sioux and the man wasn't sure if it would last the whole journey," Shakespeare disclosed.

"And the deep tracks?" Nate said.

"They shot an elk their fifth day out, and rather than let the meat go to waste, they packed as much as they could onto the extra horse and brought it along to eat along the way."

Nate was thoroughly confounded. The warrior's explanation made perfect sense, but he refused to believe it. If true, it meant that blaming the Piegans had been unjustified. It meant that tracking the war party down had been wasted effort. And it meant something far worse.

Pepin ambled toward them, a thumb hooked in his bright sash. "You will not believe this, my friends," he said. "I could not find the peltries anywhere. The savages must have cached their plunder along the trail and we will have to backtrack them to find it."

"Did you happen to see any elk meat lying around?" Shakespeare inquired softly.

"Was that what it was?" Pepin scrunched up his nose. "There's a lot of overripe meat wrapped in an elk hide over by the horses. Smells so awful a wolverine would pass it up!" He shook his head. "How they ate it is beyond me."

"Oh, Lord," Nate breathed, and had to sit down. His gaze fell on Jenks, on the youth's upturned, slowly stiffening face. The poor greenhorn had given his life needlessly. Nate felt a twinge of remorse, until he remembered that he had objected to going after the war party, that it had been Pepin and Jenks who'd insisted on the mission of vengeance. Had they listened to him, the youth would still be alive.

"What's wrong?" Pepin asked.

Nate told him.

"Can it really be?" the *voyageur* declared. "Well, *c'est la vie*! Mistakes happen sometimes, and there is nothing we can do about them except pick up the pieces and go on with our lives. *Oui?*"

"How can you—?" Nate began, and checked his anger before he made a statement they would both regret.

Shakespeare, touched by the turmoil he read in his friend's expression, commented, "Before any of us go around blaming anyone else, we all have to remember this worked out for the best."

"How do you figure?" Nate demanded.

"These Piegans were set to attack a Shoshone village. Think of all the lives we saved by stopping them before they could carry out the raid."

There was a point Nate had overlooked. They had indeed spared the Shoshones much death and misery, and he should be thankful he had been able to help his adopted people. His guilt started to evaporate. To take his mind off the affair completely, he worked at reloading the Hawken, but someone else wasn't content to let the matter drop.

"We must also remember, my friends, that Indians such as the Piegans live for war. Counting coup is everything to them, the measure of their manhood, their status in the tribe," Pepin stated. "When they ride off to attack their enemies they know full well they may never see their village again. We did no worse to them than any other tribe would have done."

Shakespeare nodded. "Honest plain words best pierce the ear of grief."

"What?" Pepin said.

"Old William S."

"When will you stop reading those silly plays and buy the works of a real man?" Pepin joked.

"Do you know of one?" Shakespeare asked drolly.

"What? You think Canadians can't read?" Pepin puffed up his chest. "Try the works of Rousseau. Or if you need your books in English, try Sir Walter Scott. Or Byron's masterpieces. Either knew more of life than your English bard."

Nate listened with half an ear to their exchange. It would have surprised many back in the States to learn that reading was a popular pastime for the trappers during the long, cold winter months when trapping was impossible. Books were freely traded back and forth, and in the course of four or five months a man might go through twice as many volumes. Not all the trappers indulged; some were content to lie abed with their Indian wives and not come out from under the blankets for days at a time.

Suddenly, while Pepin and Shakespeare were distracted by their conversation and Nate was busy with his rifle, the surviving Piegan leaped to his feet and bounded toward the end of the hillock with an agility and speed a black-tailed deer would have envied.

"Stop him!" Pepin bellowed. Suiting action to words, he lifted his rifle and took aim on the fleeing warrior's back.

"No!" Nate said, leaping up and pushing the barrel aside. "We take him alive."

"Not if we don't hurry," Shakespeare urged.

Whirling, Nate sped after the brave. He was upset with himself for not thinking to bind the Piegan's ankles as well as the wrists, and he wondered if perhaps, deep down, he secretly wanted the warrior to escape. A lone brave was no danger to the Shoshones. Once in the clear, the Piegan would no doubt head for home.

Black Badger glanced back, his face a study in determination. He came to the end of the hill and bore to the left, into the trees flanking it.

Nate was hard pressed to keep the warrior in sight. The thick brush, the quilt work of light and dark shadows, the low-hanging limbs, they all conspired to camouflage Black Badger, to render the man virtually invisible. Fortunately, the pumping motions of the brave's legs gave him away.

Nate also relied on his ears. The Piegan was making a lot of noise plowing through the undergrowth, cracking twigs underfoot and snapping off small branches. So whenever Nate temporarily lost sight of the brave, he only had to listen to know he was going in the right direction. For several minutes he tried hard to overtake the Piegan without success.

Then the noise stopped.

Nate ran another ten feet before he realized it. He halted, every nerve aquiver. About 40 or 50 feet to his rear Pepin was calling his name, but Nate wisely stayed quiet. Black Badger might be close by and Nate didn't want to give away his position. He crouched, breathed through his nose, and waited for the Piegan to resume the chase. But nothing happened.

Puzzled, Nate scoured every square inch of the fore-boding forest. Other than the wind rustling the leaves, there was no sound. He figured Black Badger was lying low, waiting for him to give up and go back. The war-rior was in for a surprise. Nate intended to stick on the trail.

Pepin fell silent. There was crashing in the undergrowth to the northeast which moved farther away with each pass-ing second.

Still Nate didn't budge. He sensed that he was close to his quarry. A little patience, and he could march Black Badger back to the camp. And what then? Would he release the Piegan unharmed? If so, why bother going to all the trouble of hunting the man down?

Nate decided he was being outright foolish. He had no real wish to hurt the Piegan and no real desire to keep him a prisoner, so he might as well let the warrior go. Having made up his mind, he straightened and reversed direction, walking as he normally would, making no attempt to conceal the fact he was leaving so the Piegan would know it too. Ten yards he went, and then a slight noise behind him made him look over his shoulder.

A vague shape disappeared into a cluster of small pines.

Nate knew it was Black Badger. But what was the warrior doing following him? The brave should be in full flight else-where, making good his escape. Chuckling at the Piegan's stupidity, Nate went on. He hadn't gone more than five yards when his intuition blared and he spun around and saw a figure dive from sight in the undergrowth.

What a fool! Nate reflected, hiking northward. Had the situation been reversed, he would have been half a mile off already, not shadowing the very man he was trying to get away from.

The thought jarred Nate like a physical blow. There was only one reason the Piegan would be doing such a thing. *The hunter had become the hunted!* Again he stopped and spun, only this time there was no shadow to see. Of course not. The Piegan wouldn't make the same mistake a third time.

Raising the Hawken, Nate walked backward. He was the one who qualified as a fool for expecting the warrior to flee when Black Badger had clearly stated his intention to get revenge. Somehow, the warrior had slipped his wrists loose from the leather strips. Now the warrior was stalking him, biding time until a chance presented itself to close in.

Shouting for help would have been easy. Nate knew Shakespeare and the Canadian would swiftly come to his aid, but he couldn't bring himself to call their names. This was strictly between Black Badger and himself. He was the one who had fought the Piegan; he was the one who had spared the brave's life. If he had done as he should have done and slain Black Badger outright, he wouldn't be in the tight spot he was in.

The woodland took on a whole new aspect. Every shadow seemed sinister; every rustling leaf might be made by the man intending to take Nate's life. Nate looked right and left, trying to see everywhere at once. He cocked the Hawken, not caring if Black Badger heard the metallic click or not. Moving backwards as he was, he had to walk slowly, feeling his way so as not to trip over a root or a log. A single mistake would be all the Piegan needed.

Nate's right heel bumped something. Risking a look, he found a downed branch still bearing leaves. He lifted his leg high to step over, did likewise with the other leg, and kept retreating. Suddenly the vegetation on his left crackled.

Finger on the trigger, Nate pivoted, set to fire, and caught a glimpse of a rabbit leaping madly off. Any other time, he would have laughed at his jumpiness. Now, he grimly scanned the closest trees, his heart beating so loud he swore he could hear it.

Nate's heel scraped another object. This time it was a log as high as his knees. He had to twist in order to take a full stride, and as he did, during the instant when he took his eyes from the forest and was looking at the log, the night was rent by a bloodcurdling scream, a mixed whoop of feral hatred and rage. Nate tried to swing around, but he was standing sideways when a heavy body slammed into his right shoulder with all the force of a charging buffalo.

Chapter Seven

Nate King was borne backwards as iron arms banded around his own, preventing him from using the Hawken in any way or from grabbing for a pistol. His lower legs smashed into the log, which sent him tumbling hard onto his shoulders on the other side. The contorted features of Black Badger were inches from his own, the gleam of intense hatred in the Piegan's glittering eyes giving him the aspect of an enraged demon.

At the instant of slamming onto the ground, Nate's finger involuntarily tightened on the trigger and the rifle went off, booming loud in his ears. The ball thudded into the ground. Nate tried to ram the barrel against the warrior's head, but was unable to raise his arms high enough. A knee gouged into his groin, flooding him with agony. In order to defend himself he let go of the rifle, and the two of them commenced rolling back and forth as each sought to get a grip on the other's throat.

Black Badger succeeded. Nate winced as fingernails bit into his skin, digging deep into his flesh. He gripped the brave's wrists and pulled, but he might as well have been pulling on the wrists of a bronze statue. Black Badger seemed endowed with inhuman strength. Stark hatred, it was said, could do that.

Nate tried flipping the Piegan off, but it was like trying to flip a slippery eel. Black Badger knew just how to twist and shift to frustrate every attempt Nate made. And all the while his bony fingers dug ever deeper into Nate's neck, cutting off Nate's wind.

In the distance there were yells. Shakespeare and Pepin were on their way, but Nate knew they would arrive too late to be of any help. Only he could preserve his life. To do that, he abruptly stopped pulling on Black Badger's arms and swooped a hand to his butcher knife.

Black Badger must have felt the movement, for he released his hold and clutched at Nate's wrist just as the knife leaped free of its beaded sheath. Nate angled his arm to stab and was thwarted by his foe. Straining with all their might, they struggled for an advantage: Nate to break loose so he could use the knife, Black Badger to wrench Nate's arm hard enough to compel Nate to drop the weapon.

A boulder settled the issue for them. They rolled against it, and Nate nearly cried out when his forearm smashed into the obstacle and the knife was knocked from his grasp. Thinking fast, he drew his tomahawk. Equally fast, Black Badger seized his left wrist.

Again they tussled. Nate wound up on top. He managed to tear his arm free and whipped the tomahawk overhead for a killing stroke. Black Badger lashed out with both legs, his heels lancing into Nate's midsection. Nate was hurled backward, tripped, and fell. By the time he scrambled to a knee, the Piegan was on him again.

Both of Nate's wrists were snatched and held as he was propelled rearward into a tree trunk. Nate put every ounce of energy he had into pushing the warrior from him, yet it wasn't enough. It appeared he had finally met his match; more than his match.

Those were awful moments. Nate was nose to nose with a crazed fiend who thirsted for his blood, and he was powerless to keep the man at bay. He tried hooking a leg behind the Piegan and shoving, but Black Badger was too crafty for him. He tried ramming a knee into the warrior's groin, but Black Badger avoided the blow. Nothing Nate did worked.

Then, unbidden, a memory flashed through Nate's mind, a memory of a talk he'd had with Shakespeare some years ago, shortly after the pair met. They had been discussing hostiles, and Shakespeare had said, "As sure as you're breathing, there will be times when you find yourself going at it tooth and nail with some brave who fancies your scalp. When those times come, remember this: Anything goes in a fight. There are no rules. There's no right or wrong way to save your hide. Do whatever the hell you have to in order to survive. Biting, scratching, kicking, you name it. Whatever it takes."

Those words were like soothing ointment on a burning wound. Nate remembered them as if they had been spoken the day before, and with the memory came action. Closing his eyes, he drew his head back, then brought his forehead crashing down onto the Piegan's nose. Cartilage crunched. Blood gushed. The warrior's grip weakened and Nate immediately shoved, throwing the brave from him. Black Badger stumbled but didn't fall.

Nate stepped to the left, gaining room to move, drawing both pistols and cocking them as he did. Black Badger wiped a forearm across his eyes, snarled, and sprang. "Not

this time," Nate said, firing the right flintlock. The ball
cored the warrior's chest, spinning Black Badger completely around. The Piegan looked down at himself, blinked
once, then unexpectedly pounced, his arm upraised, his
lips curled in fury. Nate shot again, the left flintlock this
time, and a hole appeared in the center of Black Badger's
brow. Carried along by its own momentum, the body toppled toward Nate, who nimbly darted out of the way. The
thud of the warrior hitting the earth signified the end of
the clash.

Nate was suddenly very tired. He walked to the log and
sat down, his arms hanging. Through the brush came a pair
of buckskin-clad figures who drew up short on spying him
and the corpse. No one spoke for a bit.

Shakespeare lowered his Hawken and came forward.
"You okay, son?"

"Never better."

"Hurt anywhere?"

"Not a scratch."

"You don't sound so good."

Sighing, Nate wagged a pistol at the Piegan. "I tried to
do the right thing and look at what happened. I nearly got
myself killed."

"No one ever claimed doing right would be easy. Sometimes our head tells us it's one way while our heart tells
us it's another. Choosing is where wisdom comes in."

Pepin chuckled and swaggered to the dead Piegan. "Lord,
McNair! Sometimes you're worse than a Bible-thumper.
King has no cause to be upset. He did what he had to do."
Pepin nudged Black Badger with his toe. "He just should
have done it sooner and spared himself a lot of trouble."

"Is it really that simple?" Nate asked.

"It is to me, *mon ami*," Pepin said. "It's useless to fret
yourself sick over killing an enemy. *Certainment*, no one

in their right mind ever wants to take another life, but if it has to be done, if you have no choice, then do the killing and forget about it and you'll be better off. That is my outlook."

Nate slowly stood, and went about collecting his scattered weapons. He had to search long and hard for the butcher knife, which lay hidden in thick grass. Then he reloaded his guns. His friends waited patiently, both well aware that it was unwise for a trapper to go anywhere unarmed. As they made their way toward the hillock, Nate asked, "What now?"

"What else? We go dig up our cache and head back," Pepin said. "I don't know about you, but I can hardly wait to see my woman again. She'll have missed me so much, I don't think we'll come out of the lodge for a week."

"The Nez Percé have their villages along the Snake at this time of year, don't they?" Shakespeare commented.

Pepin nodded. "That's where I'll find my sweet *femme*."

"What about Jenks?" Nate brought up.

"What about him?" the *voyageur* responded.

"What are we going to do with his belongings?"

"We divide them up between us."

"That wouldn't be right."

"*Mon Dieu!* Here you go again."

"Jenks has kin back in the States," Nate reminded the Canadian. "I say we sell his stuff for whatever it will bring at the upcoming Rendezvous and send the money back with the supply train to St. Louis. Someone can relay the funds to his family from there."

"What a waste," Pepin lamented. "We won't get more than fifty dollars for his rifle and possibles."

Fifty or ten makes no difference."

"You are a hard man, Grizzly Killer," Pepin said, and cracked a grin. "But yes, we will do what is right by our former partner. Our consciences will be clean." He clapped

Nate on the shoulder. "Being around you is having a bad influence on me. At this rate, you'll have me giving up drinking and women before I know it." He glanced around. "But what about the Piegan mounts? Surely we're not selling them too? Can't we split them up among us?"

There was no reason not to, and Nate remarked as much.

"Good. There is hope for you yet."

The storm struck shortly after they buried Lester Jenks. Nate had already gone after their own animals, so they moved all the horses into the shelter of the forest. A lean-to was erected to protect them from the elements, and while lightning blazed and thunder rumbled, they sat snug and dry in front of a tiny fire, each man lost in his own thoughts.

Dawn broke crisp and clear. They were in the saddle before the sun had completely risen, wending their way northward. With so many horses to manage, they were spaced out over 40 yards or better. Pepin had the lead, Shakespeare was halfway back, and Nate brought up the rear with the four horses under his care.

The next day the same arrangement prevailed. As usual, wildlife was everywhere, and Nate lost himself in the wonders of the mountain paradise he'd chosen to call home. He never tired of studying wild creatures; they were a constant source of entertainment and instruction. Tiny scampering chipmunks or huge grazing elk, they all fascinated him equally.

On the third day, as they were crossing a luxuriant valley, Nate glanced to his right at hills bordering the grassy flatland and spotted a splash of red among the pines. Curious, he reined up. The shape of the red object was circular and didn't appear to be moving. Since Nature never painted her handiwork such a bright crimson hue, it had to be something man-made.

"What's the matter?" Shakespeare called.

"Come have a look-see," Nate answered.

Pepin rode back also. "A flower, you think?" he said when he saw the red dot.

"Too big," Nate replied.

"A marker of some kind, then?"

"There's only one way to find out." Nate gave his lead rope to Shakespeare. "Watch my horses don't run off."

"You be careful," McNair cautioned. "It might be a Blackfoot trick. Once I saw a band fly an American flag so unsuspecting trappers would walk right into their camp, thinking they were friendly. A few dunderheads did too. They lost their hair so fast, they didn't have time to blink."

Resting the stock of the Hawken on his thigh, Nate galloped to the bottom of the hill. From there the red object was difficult to see, screened as it was by a thicket and pines. Dismounting, he ground-hitched the black stallion so he could ride off swiftly if he had to.

On panther's feet Nate padded upward, always staying low to the ground to minimize the target he presented. He caught glimpses of the red object now and then, but not enough of a glimpse to tell him what it was. At length he squeezed through a thicket, and lying in an open patch of ground was what had drawn his interest: a red woolen cap, similar to Pepin's.

Perplexed, Nate picked up the cap to inspect it and found dark stains made by dried blood. A lot of blood. Looking down, he saw red splotches dotting the earth, leading off into a bunch of spruce trees. Leveling the Hawken, he followed the dots.

In the valley below, the *voyageur* turned to McNair and asked, "What the hell is he doing? If he goes into those trees we will not be able to see him at all."

The same thought had occurred to Shakespeare, and he did not like it one bit. "I taught him better than that," he grumbled. Lashing his reins, he made for the hill. "Come on. We might as well stay close in case he gets into a fix again."

"*Oui*. He does have a flair, does he not?"

"In faith, he is a worthy gentleman, exceedingly well read, and profited in strange concealments, valiant as a lion, and wondrous affable, and as bountiful as mines of India."

"Are we talking about the same man?"

"Lord, Pepin. You're a regular barbarian."

"And loving every minute of my barbaric life."

Shakespeare observed Nate disappear in the spruce stand and cursed under his breath. The younger man took too many needless risks. He rode faster, leaped from the saddle before his white horse fully stopped, and was off up the hill like a spry mountain goat. Since haste was called for, he didn't try to move silently. Behind him came Pepin.

A faintly bluish tinge set the spruce trees apart from other nearby pines. They formed nearly even rows, an impenetrable phalanx to the unaided eye. Shakespeare saw Nate's footprints next to a trail of blood, divined why Nate had gone into the stand, and advanced with his senses primed.

In the center the pines widened. There, prone in a patch of grass, lay the mutilated body of a trapper. Beside it squatted Nate, who looked up and frowned. "Another one," he said grimly. "Just like Pointer."

The similarities were obvious. Like Harold Pointer, this man had been stripped, his abdomen sliced wide, and his intestines strewn about. His neck had been severed. Additional atrocities had rendered the body as ghastly in every respect as Pointer's.

"The Piegans, you figure?" Pepin speculated.

"You know better," Nate said. "This was done within the past twenty-four hours. Look." He pointed. "The ravens haven't even gotten to the eyes yet."

"Then who?" Pepin said, stepping forward. He saw the cap in Nate's hand, stiffened, and grabbed it. "Can it be? This is the cap of a *voyageur*! But who?" Leaning down, he took hold of the dead man's shoulder and slowly flipped the body over. On seeing the man's face clearly, he exhaled loudly and clapped a hand to his brow. "*Qu'est-ce que c'est?* Labeau! What a terrible end, my old friend!"

"You know him?" Shakespeare said.

"Yes. Some years ago in Canada. We worked for the same company for a while, then went our separate ways. I'd heard that he ventured south, but I had no idea he was in this territory."

Nate lowered a finger close to bruise marks on the trapper's wrist. "It looks like some of them held him down while someone else did the carving."

"The bastards!" Pepin declared. "Wherever these murderers are, they must pay for their crimes! This vile act must not go unpunished."

"Here we go again," Shakespeare muttered.

The grass had been torn up by the struggle. Nate studied the various tracks, and discovered where a half-dozen men had headed east out of the spruce stand. He stuck to their path, which brought him, minutes later, to a clearing where horses had waited, 18 or 19 in all. Most of the hoofprints dug deeply into the soil, as they would if the animals were heavily burdened. He was scrutinizing them when a low voice to his rear made him jump.

"We owe it to the Piegans, if not ourselves."

Nate locked his eyes on Shakespeare's. "Oh, we owe it to ourselves, all right. They're not more than a day ahead of us, and with all the pack animals they have, they won't make very good time."

"There are seven of them."

"There were nine Piegans and that didn't stop us."

"But these aren't Indians, and you know it."

"Yes," Nate admitted. The idea had been growing ever since Jenks described eluding the men who stole his hides. Jenks had been a greenhorn, as inexperienced as a new-born baby; he'd known next to nothing about wilderness lore, hadn't the vaguest idea how to hide his tracks. Any self-respecting Indian would have hunted Jenks down with ease. And no war party would have given up the search for Jenks so readily, not when one of their number stood to gain a fresh scalp, which warriors prized above all else. No, now that he thought about it in depth, he fully realized that the band responsible for slaying Pointer and taking Jenks's belongings had to have been a band of white man. "But who would do such a thing?" he wondered aloud.

"Cutthroats of one sort or another," Shakespeare said. "Men who value the price they can get for a stolen pelt more than they do the value of a human life." He scoured the clearing. "Who knows how many innocent trappers they've killed?"

Nate stiffened as a recollection came to him. "Do you remember the last Rendezvous?"

"How could I forget it? My wife bought so much it about left me broke."

"This is serious," Nate said. "Do you remember that talk we had with Bridger and Meek one night?"

The light of understanding brightened Shakespeare's eyes. "Sure do. Bridger told us that it seemed the Blackfeet were a lot more active of late than they used to be. Meek said that by his calculations there were close to twenty trappers who didn't show up for the Rendezvous who were supposed to."

"Twenty," Nate repeated, the full implications appalling him. "And everyone just naturally figured the Blackfeet were to blame."

"There might be a lot more we don't know about," Shakespeare said, "since we have no way of telling how many seasons this bunch has been going about their vile business."

"Whoever cooked this scheme up is no idiot," Nate said.

Shakespeare nodded. "They must concentrate on a small region at a time and murder every trapper they can find, making it look as if Indians are to blame. Then they clear on out and no one is the wiser."

"We fell for their trick," Nate said bitterly. "We were all too eager to pin the blame on the Piegans."

"Now we know better."

"Whoever these vermin are, we have to hunt them down and put an end to them before any more trappers lose their lives," Nate declared.

Shakespeare, in the act of moving around the clearing, paused, his brow knitting. "There's something else about that last Rendezvous. Everyone was talking about a certain trapper who'd supposedly caught more beaver in one year than anyone else ever had. He even beat out Jed Smith."

"I heard the same story," Nate confirmed. "But I can't recall his name." He pondered a bit. "All I remember is that he brought in over eight hundred peltries." Something else came to mind. "And there were a few others who had good years too. Real good years. I'll bet they're the ones we want."

"Don't jump to conclusions," Shakespeare cautioned. "Some of them might have been legitimate. We won't know who to hold accountable until we catch this outfit."

"And catch them we will, *mon ami*!"

Both Nate and Shakespeare turned at the angry bellow and saw Pepin striding toward them, Labeau's cap still clutched in his brawny hand.

"I heard some of what you just said," Pepin informed them, "and I have never been so mad in my life!" He gave the cap a furious shake, as if throttling a throat. "The ones who butchered poor Labeau will not live long enough to butcher anyone else. This I vow!"

"We're in this together," Shakespeare said, "and we can't go rushing off half-cocked. We have to be mighty careful. The men we're after are utterly ruthless."

"So?" Pepin touched his knife. "I can be just as ruthless when the need arises." He spat, then wiped a sleeve across his mouth. "Just thinking of these sons of bitches puts a rotten taste in my mouth. We must go after them and stay on their trail until we catch up, no matter how long it takes us."

"What about all the extra horses we have?" Nate mentioned. "They'll slow us down."

"We'll have to let them loose in a meadow and hope they're still there when we get back," Pepin proposed.

Shakespeare walked over. "I have a better idea. We can do like the Comanches do when they hunt wild horses."

"The Comanches?" Pepin said. "They are the Indians who live far down in the Red River country, are they not? I do not know much about them."

"All you need to know is how they hunt mustangs." Shakespeare grinned as he went into detail. "Several warriors will go out together, each with a string of two or three mounts. When they spot a wild herd, they give chase, and as each one of their mounts tire, they change to another horse without their feet so much as touching the ground."

"I get it," Nate said, excited by the possibilities. "They run the wild herd into the ground and then catch whichever ones they want."

"Exactly," Shakespeare said. "There's no reason we can't do the same thing. With all the horses we have, we should overtake these butchers in a third of the time it would ordinarily take us."

"*Très intelligent!*" Pepin exclaimed. "Why did I never think of that?" He held out his hand, palm downward, and said, "Now we make the pledge."

Nate looked at him. "Pledge?"

"*Oui.* Put your hand on mine and I will commit us to our noble cause."

Feeling somewhat sheepish, Nate obeyed the *voyageur*. Shakespeare added his hand, his expression grave.

Pepin gazed skyward and cleared his throat. "We solemnly pledge to track these fiends to the ends of the earth, so help us God! And if we fail, may maggots eat our innards and worms crawl in our ears!" Pleased, he smiled at each of them and nodded. "Now we are committed."

Together they headed down the hill. Nate, bringing up the rear, couldn't shake the mental picture of maggots squirming in his entrails, which he sincerely hoped wasn't a harbinger of things to come.

Chapter Eight

For the rest of that day the three trappers put the Comanche system to the test, and found it worked extremely well. Where possible, they held their horses to a steady trot, and when an animal flagged they simply switched to another and added the tired horse to their individual strings. In this way they covered twice as much ground as they ordinarily would have, and by sunset they were many miles from the hill where Labeau lay in a shallow grave, and at a much lower elevation.

Camp was made in a gully where they could build a small fire without fear of it being seen from afar. Supper consisted of jerky and water. Afterward, they turned in so as to be able to get an early start the next day.

Sunrise found them already on the trail. The killers had tried to hide their tracks, but with so many pack animals in tow, they had wasted their energy. Even on the rockiest ground there were plenty of chips and scratch marks to guide the three trappers.

Toward the middle of the day, as they came to a narrow valley, Shakespeare, who was in the lead, suddenly drew rein and gestured. "Smoke," he announced.

Two miles distant a tendril of gray was rising to meet a puffy white cloud.

"It's them!" Pepin cried. "Now we make good on our pledge! Soon the ground will run red with their blood!" Working his legs, he began to swing his horse past McNair's string so he would be the one in front.

"Hold on," Nate said. "Charging on in there would only get us all killed. We'll take it nice and easy, just as if we were up against hostiles."

"Bah!" Pepin waved his rifle at the smoke. "I say we ride in with our guns blasting and cut them down before they can so much as lift a finger against us."

Shakespeare leaned on his saddle horn and grinned. "There isn't much that amazes a man my age. When you've seen and done practically everything, surprises are few and far between. But Pepin, you fit the bill."

"How so?"

"I don't know how in the world you've lived as long as you have," Shakespeare said. "As impetuous as you are, you should have gone under by the time you were ten." He lifted his reins and his horse moved out. "Since Nate and I aren't partial to the notion of pushing up buffalo grass, you'll do as we say and go about this slow and careful."

A few mumbled words were Pepin's only comment.

Another mile fell behind them. Shakespeare slanted north-ward, sticking to thick cover but never losing sight of the smoke. When within half a mile of the camp, he drew rein, dismounted, and secured his horses to a cottonwood. "One of us has to go on ahead for a look-see."

"Me," Nate said.

"Not this time," Shakespeare replied, hurrying into the

woods before anyone could stop him. He heard Nate curse, and chuckled. The younger man's concern was touching, but Shakespeare didn't need anyone mothering him and felt that it was high time Nate realized the fact.

Holding his Hawken in his left hand, Shakespeare stealthily crept closer and closer to the few wisps of smoke still hovering in the air. The fire, evidently, was going out. He was puzzled as to why the band had stopped so early, but was glad they had. The sooner the whole gory business was done with, the happier Shakespeare would be.

The acrid scent of burning wood brought Shakespeare to a stop behind a pine. Peering out, he spied several tiny flickering flames at the edge of the forest, where the grassy valley floor began. Oddly enough, he saw no one, nor any horses.

Bending low, Shakespeare advanced cautiously. The area around the fire was completely deserted, causing him to conclude the band had already gone on. Prudently, he didn't show himself until he was at the very last tree and had verified it was indeed safe to step into the open.

Tracks were everywhere, both the footprints of the cutthroats and the hoofprints of their many horses. Shakespeare walked to the fire, then gazed out across the valley. The band had no more than an hour start, he deduced. "We'll get you soon," he said softly, and was about to leave when his eyes fell on moist drops of blood.

Shakespeare touched a fingertip to the largest drop. Having skinned so many beaver and other animals over the years, he knew exactly how fast blood dried. The sticky consistency of the drops indicated they had been made within the past two hours. A trail of them led into the high grass.

"Not again," Shakespeare said to himself. Cocking the

rifle, he followed the trail, noticing how the drops grew bigger and bigger the farther he went. About 30 feet out he saw the body, lying face down. Unlike the other victims, this one was fully clothed. "Damn!"

Shakespeare knelt, set the Hawken down, and gripped the man's shoulders to roll him over. Suddenly a hand darted out, a bloody hand grasping a gleaming dagger, the blade spearing at Shakespeare's throat. Shakespeare jerked his head to the right and felt the man's sleeve brush his neck. He grabbed the arm, then held fast. "Hold on there! I'm a friend."

"McNair?" A bearded, lined face, seamed with pain, gaped up at him. "Is it really you?"

"Nelson?" Shakespeare released the arm and quickly rolled the man onto his back. "Tim Nelson?"

"Help me, please."

Shakespeare was already lifting the trapper to carry him to the fire. He'd met Nelson at a Rendezvous four years ago, and on several occasions since they had played cards and shared drinks. "Hold on. We'll do what we can to patch you up."

"Help—" Nelson said, his voice fading as his eyelids fluttered and trembled as if having a fit. Gasping loudly, he passed out.

A rare rage seized Shakespeare McNair as he hastened out of the high grass and gently deposited Nelson close to the fire. He drew a pistol, pointed it at the ground, and banged off a shot as a signal to his friends. Then he bent down.

The cutthroats had done a thorough job. Blood seeped from bullet holes in both ankles and both knees. The left shoulder, broken by a ball, was bent at an unnatural angle. And as if those wounds weren't enough, someone had stabbed Nelson three times low in the back.

Shakespeare marveled that the man was still alive. Depending on how severe the stab wounds were, Nelson might survive provided he had a lot of doctoring. That in mind, Shakespeare rekindled the fire and had the flames crackling when his companions showed. "We need hot water," he announced.

Nate was first off his horse. He stared, then commented, "I know him from somewhere."

"That you do," Shakespeare established, and quickly explained, finishing with, "If we can stop the bleeding, maybe he'll pull through."

Pepin was standing a few yards away, his arms folded across his chest. "Why go to all the bother?" he asked. "It might be a waste of our time, and those we are after will get farther and farther away."

"I can't believe you can be so cold-blooded," Shakespeare snapped. "So what if they gain a little lead on us? This is a fellow trapper we're talking about."

"Is it?" Pepin said. "I wonder."

"What the devil do you mean?"

"How do we know he isn't one of *them*? How do we know he didn't have a falling out with the others and they left him for the vultures, no?"

The idea had not even occurred to Shakespeare. He studied Nelson's face while reflecting that he actually knew very little about the man. And now that he thought about it, he hadn't seen Nelson for a year or better. What had the man been up to in all that time?

While the grizzled mountain man pondered, Nate was searching for water. It stood to reason that no one would make camp where water was unavailable, so he was certain there must be some within short walking distance of the fire. Since there was no stream anywhere in sight along the valley floor, he concentrated on the forest behind the camp and located a small spring. There, as he knelt to fill the coffeepot, he noticed a small footprint in the soft mud at the water's edge. The size was such that it had either been made by an extremely small man or a woman. Assuming a man had to have been responsible, he thought no more about the track as he hastened the filled pot back to heat it over the rekindled fire.

Nate told Pepin about the spring, and the *voyageur* took the horses to drink. Then Nate turned to his mentor. "What do you think? Could Pepin be right?"

"Nelson always struck me as the honest sort, but honest men go bad on occasion. I don't know," Shakespeare admitted. "It would explain why he's the only one we've found who wasn't stripped and hacked apart."

Shakespeare drew his knife and leaned over Nelson's left leg. Nate did likewise with the right. Together they carefully cut the buckskin leggings open to fully expose Nelson's severely swollen ankles and knees. They did the same with the shoulder wound.

"We'll have to set this broken bone soon," Shakespeare mentioned. "It'll hurt like hell. I hope he doesn't come around until after."

But Nelson revived as they were dabbing hot water on his ankles. Groaning, he sluggishly tried to lift his head but couldn't.

"You lie still, Tim," Shakespeare said. "Save your energy for later."

"Can't," Nelson said weakly.

"Mister, you do as we tell you," Nate advised. "We'll do our best to pull you through, but you have to help."

"Forget about me," Nelson said. "This coon is a goner."

"Nonsense," Shakespeare responded.

"You saw where I was stabbed," Nelson said, and winced. "I'm bleeding inside. I can feel it." He coughed once. "The knife Belker uses is over a foot long."

"Belker?" Nate said.

"One of those riding with Galt." Nelson coughed some more, and when the fit subsided there was a drop of blood at the corner of his mouth.

Nate and Shakespeare exchanged knowing looks.

"Forget about me," Nelson reiterated. "Save her."

"Who?" Shakespeare asked.

"Clay Basket, my woman. They took her, the scum!" Nelson flushed with outrage and the drop of blood became a trickle. "She fought them as best she could, kicking and clawing like a wildcat, but they tied her to a horse as if she was some animal and rode off with her. They all laughed at me too as they went by, laughed and bragged of how they're fixing to treat her." He tried to raise a hand to seize Shakespeare's wrist, but couldn't. "She won't last two days in their clutches. Promise me you'll go after her, McNair! Promise me you'll get her safely to her people, the Crows!"

"Calm down," Shakespeare said. "We'll do what we can for her just as soon as we tend to you."

"No!" Nelson cried. "Haven't you been listening to a word I've said? I'm not important. She's the one you have to help." His skin turning ashen, he tried to push up on his elbows.

"You're making yourself worse," Nate said, putting his hands on the man's chest and pressing. "Just lie quietly."

"I don't care about me! Save her, damn it!" Nelson glanced from one of them to the other. "Haven't either of you ever had a wife? Haven't either of you ever been in love? Clay Basket is everything to me! Don't let those bastards have their way with her."

"We'll head out in a bit," Nate said, touching the wet strip of buckskin he held to the blood on Nelson's chin.

"Fill us in, Tim," Shakespeare coaxed. "We need to know who we're up against."

Nelson gave a curt nod, then closed his eyes. "They showed up about sunset yesterday, just as we were sitting down to supper. Acted real friendly at first. They hailed us, then rode on in with their hands empty to show they meant us no harm. When I found they were white, the first white men I'd laid eyes on in over a year, I was glad for the chance to chaw and catch up on the latest news."

"You've been living with Clay Basket's people?" Nate guessed.

"Yep. They took me in when I was about froze to death, and half starved to boot. Clay Basket herself doctored me." Nelson's voice acquired a wistful quality. "I've never known a woman like her. So kind, so caring. She brought me back from the dead, and ever since I've been with her village, helping hunt and fight off the Blackfeet and such." He stopped, took a lingering breath, then continued. "About a month ago I got the fool notion of taking up trapping again. I'd lost all my fixings, but I figured I could find someone to stake me at the next Rendezvous."

Nate saw that the man was weakening fast. "About the men who did this to you? About Galt and Belker?"

"There are seven of them. Galt is the brains of the bunch," Nelson said. "When they first rode in, I couldn't believe how many peltries they had. Eleven horses piled high as could be! They claimed they'd had a run of luck and like a jackass I believed them."

"When did they turn on you?"

"This morning. We had just finished up breakfast when Galt grinned at me, said he'd taken a liking to my woman, and wanted to know if I'd be partial to selling her.

When I told him she was my wife and I wouldn't give her up for all the furs they had, Galt laughed and said he'd just have to take her." A low moan escaped Nelson's lips. "I wouldn't let any man talk that way to me, so I jumped up and was set to bash his face in when all the rest of them pounced on me and pinned me down. Clay Basket tried to help but one of them wouldn't let her."

"You don't have to go on," Nate said.

"I want to." Nelson opened his eyes. "They taunted me, called me an Indian-lover. Galt bragged of how he and his friends are growing rich by robbing every trapper they can find. They were going to let me live when they learned I didn't have any pelts, but then Galt took a fancy to Clay Basket." His voice broke and he sobbed. "They beat me, and they made her watch. They shot me in the knees so I couldn't walk, then they made me crawl. But that wasn't enough for them. They put balls through my ankles and shoulder. And Belker finished the job by stabbing me."

"What about that dagger you had?" Shakespeare inquired.

"I always keep one hid under my shirt for emergencies," Nelson said. "I knew they'd kill me right off if I tried to draw it, so I waited, hoping Galt would come close enough for me to kill him. But he never did." His mouth twitched. "I remember how it felt when Belker's knife plunged into my back, then everything went black. The next I knew, you were turning me over." He stared at McNair. "You be careful of that Belker. He's a natural-born killer and he has a wicked streak a yard wide."

Nate had encountered the type before. "I'll take care of him personally," he said.

"Thanks," Nelson said, turning his head until his left cheek rested on the ground. Almost immediately his body went completely limp as he succumbed to the deep sleep of utter exhaustion.

"Like I told you, an honest man," Shakespeare commented rather sadly.

"Do either of those names he mentioned ring familiar to you?" Nate asked. "I seem to recall having heard of Belker somewhere before."

"You probably have," Shakespeare said. "Two years ago at the Rendezvous there was a wrestling match that got ugly. Both men grabbed their knives and went at it tooth and nail. Belker was one of them."

"The one who won," Nate said, remembering. "There was talk for a while of kicking him out of camp and not letting him attend again, but nothing ever came of it."

"Galt I've heard of also," Shakespeare disclosed. "He was trapping partner with a man named Wilson. About four years back they headed north into Blackfoot country and only Galt returned. He spread the word that the Blackfeet had lifted Wilson's hair."

"Everyone believed him?"

"No one had cause to do otherwise. Of course, now that I look back, I remember that Galt had a lot of furs to sell."

"Maybe that's where he got his start," Nate speculated. "For some reason or another he killed Wilson and took Wilson's peltries. When he learned how easy it was to get away with it, he must have figured he'd found the perfect way to get rich quick."

"He's about to learn differently."

Nate touched Nelson's hot brow. "He has a high fever. Do you really think he can pull through?"

"Can't say for sure. I have to dress those stab wounds next. If I can find the right herbs, I'll be able to make a poultice that should help some." Shakespeare gingerly examined the broken shoulder. "I do know he doesn't have any chance at all if we leave him."

"If we stay here too long, what will happen to Clay Basket?"

"You know the answer to that as well as I do," Shakespeare said. "Here." He shifted so he was straddling Nelson's upper arm. "Lend me a hand setting this bone."

Horrifying images of the fate facing Clay Basket bothered Nate as he worked. He kept thinking of his own wife, and how he would feel if the same thing had happened to Winona. Once the wounds were crudely bandaged and Pepin had a minty broth simmering on the fire, Nate stood and declared, "I'm going after them. The two of you catch up when you can."

"You're being hasty," Shakespeare said.

Pepin, who had been filled in after bringing the horses from the spring, nodded. "I agree with *Carcajou*. We are all in this together."

"I won't do anything stupid and get myself killed," Nate said. "I'll just keep an eye on them until you show up. And who knows? Maybe I'll have a chance to save the Crow woman."

"I'll go with you," Pepin offered.

"No," Nate said, dreading the Canadian's fiery temper would land them all in trouble. "If Nelson gets his strength back, it'll take both of you to bring him along. I'll do this alone."

"I don't like it," Shakespeare said.

"Neither do I, but we don't have much choice."

Pepin grumbled, and Shakespeare offered a few more objections, but in five minutes Nate was on the trail. He didn't admit as much to them, but his main reason for hurrying on ahead was specifically to rescue Clay Basket. Once the cutthroat gang stopped for the day, she'd be in for a terrifying ordeal. Nate was going to catch up to them before dark and spare her from a fate worse than death.

The tracks were plain to see. Apparently Galt and company were growing cockier the longer their bloody spree continued, because they hadn't even bothered to make any effort to throw off possible pursuit. Nate was grateful for their oversight since he could fairly fly in their wake.

Once again Nate resorted to the Comanche tactic of constantly changing horses, which he did once every hour no matter how tired a particular animal might be. In this way he kept his mounts fresh, able to cover ground swiftly. Small wonder, then, that by the middle of the afternoon he spotted a long line of riders in the distance. Instantly he angled into pines, and from then on until nearly sunset he shadowed the band, never narrowing the gap for fear of being spotted.

Galt's route was taking the killers steadily lower, and from the direction of travel Nate had a hunch they were making for the Green River region so as to be there early for the upcoming Rendezvous.

Twilight's gray veil shrouded the landscape when Nate saw an orange glow three-quarters of a mile off. Galt had finally made camp. Nate reined up, stepped from the stirrups, and hid the horses in heavy brush before venturing to a hill that overlooked the campfire.

The camp had been made in a shallow basin filled with grass watered by a crystal-clear pool. From a vantage point under a tree on a slope above, Nate enjoyed an unobstructed view of the activities taking place. One man was breaking and feeding small limbs to the fire. Another had the task of watering their many horses. Three men were sitting around doing nothing, while a fourth was hovering near a pretty Indian woman in a buckskin dress whose black hair flowed to her ankles: Clay Basket. She was making their supper.

Nate could not see their faces very well. Beyond noting that all the men were bearded and dressed much like trappers everywhere, he saw little of interest. Clay Basket, however, was a genuine beauty, not over 20 years of age to judge by her youthful appearance, with a noble bearing that spoke eloquently of her contempt for her abductors.

Deciding to sneak closer for a better look, Nate rose and picked his way down the slope. The wind was blowing to the southeast, so he wasn't worried about the horses picking up his scent. All he had to be concerned about was blundering into the open and being seen, or so he thought until he rounded a boulder the size of a carriage just as another man came around the boulder from the other side. Too late, Nate realized there had only been six men in camp, not seven. Too late, he saw this seventh cutthroat point a rifle at him and cock the hammer.

Chapter Nine

Nate King began to jerk his own rifle up, but realized instantly he would be shot if he tried anything, so he held himself still as the cutthroat walked toward him wearing a quizzical expression. His mind racing, Nate plastered a welcoming smile on his face and blurted out, "You're white! Then I'm safe at last! Am I glad to see you!" He knew his fate would be sealed if the band of bloodthirsty killers suspected he was after them; his life depended on convincing them he was totally harmless.

"Are you now?" the man responded suspiciously. Halting a few yards off, he scrutinized Nate from head to toe. "Who the hell are you and what are you doing spying on our camp?"

"Spying?" Nate laughed long and loud. "I just saw the smoke from a fire and was working my way close enough to see if I'd found whites or Indians. After what I've been through, I had to be sure before I showed myself."

"You haven't told me your name."

"Jess Smith," Nate lied. Hiding his identity seemed like a good idea. He was fairly well known among the trapping fraternity, and he had a widespread reputation for being an honest, forthright man in all his dealings. Should the killers learn the truth, they'd fear the worst and slay him on the spot. "What's yours?"

"Roarke," the man said. He scanned the forest. "Are you all alone?"

"That I am," Nate said. "My two partners were captured by the Blackfeet two days ago and I've been running from the devils ever since."

"Blackfeet? In this area?" Roarke didn't like the news.

"Yep. They can't be more than a day behind me if they're still on my trail," Nate said. He nodded at the other man's gun. "There's no need to cover me, friend. We're on the same side. It's us against them, isn't it?"

Roarke lowered his rifle, but only slightly, and motioned for Nate to precede him. "You go first, mister. My friends will want to hear this."

A crawling sensation broke out all over Nate's skin as he headed for the camp. All eyes were on him the moment he appeared, and the renegades gathered in a group to await him. None were men he knew, but he was able to pick the deadly Belker out of the bunch by the exceptionally long knife Belker wore. Stout, hairy, and grimy, Belker had the aspect of an undersized but ferocious black bear.

Nate noticed Clay Basket at the fire, watching him. He studiously paid no attention to her, since any interest he showed might arouse suspicion. Bestowing his phony smile on the group, he called out, "Howdy, gents! What a sight for sore eyes you are!" None of them answered him. A few whispered back and forth, and each one had a hand close to a weapon when Nate stopped and regarded them with what he hoped was a convincing imitation of heartfelt relief. "I never thought I'd set eyes on another trapping party again!"

Roarke halted behind Nate, and to one side. "This here is Jess Smith. He says he's on the run from Blackfeet."

"Oh?" said a skinny man sporting a wicked scar on his left cheek and three pistols jammed under his belt.

"That's right," Nate declared good-naturedly. "Like I told your friend here, a war party jumped Bill, Adam, and me two days ago. I saw old Bill go down with a lance in his shoulder, and Adam was set upon by three whooping warriors and taken alive. I've been on the run ever since."

"How is it that you escaped?" the skinny man asked.

"Sheer luck," Nate said. "I was answering Nature's call, and I'd just gone into the brush when I spotted one of the Blackfeet peeking at me from over a log. I gave a yell, but it was too late. They were already swarming into our camp, so I bolted." Nate shook his head as if in amazement at his own good fortune. "I tell you, the Good Lord must have been watching over me! Arrows and lances were raining down thicker than hail, yet I didn't get so much as a scratch."

"Remarkable," the skinny one said. "But I've heard of it happening before. Hell, once the Bloods came after me, shooting and firing until they ran out of bullets and arrows, and I still got away." Grinning, he offered his hand. "The name is Ira Galt. I'm the booshway of this here outfit."

"Pleased to meet you," Nate said, hiding his revulsion. "Any chance of another Mountanee Man getting himself a bite to eat and some coffee? I don't mind telling you I'm starved to death."

"It'll be a while before the grub is ready, but you're welcome to join us," Galt said. "Never let it be said we don't show hospitality to a brother trapper." Draping an arm over Nate's shoulder, he steered him toward the fire.

The others had relaxed. One of them chuckled. Another winked at a companion.

"Are you partial to kinnikinnick?" Galt asked Nate. "We've got plenty to share."

"Thank you, no. I never did pick up the tobacco habit."

"No? Most do sooner or later. How long have you been trapping?"

"A year, or thereabouts," Nate said.

Galt's dark eyes raked Nate from head to toe. "Really? I would have expected you to be an old hand."

Nate saw Clay Basket staring at him. Since they were making straight for her, he couldn't very well continue to act as if she didn't exist. Consistent with his acting the friendly fool, he commented, "My goodness! A woman! I haven't seen one of those in a coon's age."

"She's mine," Galt said, his harsh tone belying his grin. "So don't be getting any notions."

"I have a wife in the States," Nate said. "She'd shoot me if she caught me so much as looking at another woman."

"Just so you know how things are," Galt said. "Clay Basket is her name, and she's the best damn cook this side of the Divide."

"Do tell," Nate said, trying to sound suitably impressed even though he knew there hadn't been time for the Crow woman to prepare a single meal for the band since being abducted. "I can hardly wait to fill my belly."

Galt indicated a spot close to the flames. "Have a seat and we'll chaw a spell."

Easing down, Nate set eyes on dozens of bundles of prime peltries lying over near the horses. He let his eyes go wide and exclaimed, "Land sakes alive! You gents must be the best trappers around! You've enough hides there to set all of you up as kings!"

"Not quite," Galt said, laughing. "But there's no denying the past two seasons have been the best ever for us. We were raising so many beaver a day, at one point I thought my elbows would give out."

"So you're on your way to the Rendezvous?" Nate casually asked.

"That we are. We'll get there early and wait for the caravan to show."

"I envy you," Nate said. "I've lost everything but the clothes on my back. This trapping business isn't at all what it's cracked up to be. Between the weather, the Indians, and the animals, it's a wonder a body lives out his first year."

"Thinking of quitting?"

"Yes," Nate said. "I'm going back to New York and take up accounting like my pa wanted."

"Accounting is a nice, safe profession," Galt said, smirking. "The worst you'll have to worry about is smearing ink on a page."

Nate leaned the Hawken against a leg and held his hands out to the flames. Out of the corner of one eye he observed Clay Basket cutting up a doe. Out of the other eye he saw Roarke hovering in the background. The rest were taking seats around the fire. He was, in effect, hemmed in, as effectively as if they had built a fence around him.

"Ain't I seen you somewhere before?" Belker suddenly inquired. He was directly across from Nate, his right hand idly resting on the hilt of his big knife.

"It's possible," Nate said. "I was at the Rendezvous last year. Were you?"

"Yep," Belker said, "but I don't think it was then. Another time, maybe?"

"I've only been to one Rendezvous," Nate responded. "If you've seen me, that's where it was."

Belker's forehead creased and he tapped a finger on his knife. "I suppose."

It was like being the lone coyote among a pack of ravenous wolves. Nate was acutely aware of the cold, probing eyes fixed on him, but he didn't let on that he was in the least bit bothered. A plan was taking shape, a daring scheme that would result in the freeing of Clay Basket and reunite him with his friends, provided all went well. If not, he'd wind up like Nelson or Pointer, a most unappealing prospect.

In order to carry out his idea, Nate needed to convince the cutthroats he was no threat to them whatsoever. So he smiled and babbled about his limited trapping experience, about the problems he had faced and how few beaver he had caught.

The latter perked Galt's interest. "What about your friends? Did they have many furs?"

"About two hundred and ten, as I recall," Nate said, adding, "They were more experienced than I was." He glanced at the ring of faces, at the greed reflected by the firelight. "But now the Blackfeet have laid claim to them."

"What a waste," Galt said.

"True enough," Nate agreed. "Over a thousand dollars worth of hides gone, just like that." He snapped his fingers for emphasis.

"A thousand dollars," one of the men repeated longingly.

Galt thoughtfully scratched his scrawny beard. "How many Blackfeet did you say there were?"

"I didn't," Nate answered. He disliked the direction the talk was taking. The renegades were so eager to add to their spoils, they just might seriously consider going after the Blackfeet to get the extra pelts. In which case Nate had to discourage them. "There were over a dozen shrieking braves I saw with my own eyes and more off in the brush. Too many for one man to handle, which is why I lit out of there like my hind end was ablaze." He lowered his hands so he could readily grab his pistols if need be. "Too many for even an outfit this large to tackle."

"Sounds that way," Galt said, and cursed. "Too bad, Smith. We'd have liked to do the neighborly thing and help you reclaim your hides."

"That's awful decent of you," Nate said, continuing the charade. "But I wouldn't want complete strangers to lose their lives on my account. It's better this way anyway. I'm not cut out for the mountain life."

"Some are, some aren't," Galt said, and the issue was dropped.

Clay Basket stepped to the fire, a large pot and tripod in her hands. She pointedly looked at Nate, and because he had glanced up on hearing her footsteps, their eyes locked. For a fleeting second Nate thought he read an eloquent appeal for help in hers, yet all he could do was smile dumbly and act as if nothing was wrong. A flicker of disappointment etched her face as she bent to set up the tripod, and Nate deliberately gazed at the brightening stars.

Nate had to admire her courage. Here she was, in the clutches of the men who had attacked the man she loved, at their complete mercy, her life forfeit if she gave them any grief, yet she had the poise of a princess. Small wonder Nelson had been smitten by her.

"Hurry it up with the food, woman," Galt growled. "We're hungry, damn it."

Clay Basket wasn't intimidated. She finished arranging the tripod, hung the pot, and moved off.

"Squaws!" Galt chuckled and jabbed his elbow into Nate's ribs. "They can't hold a candle to white women. Lazy, uppity biddy hens is all they are."

"I wouldn't know," Nate said, though in truth he considered his Shoshone wife a competent, hardworking woman, and every inch a lady. Arching his back, he slowly stretched, turning his head to the right and left as he did, which gave him the opportunity to study the camp. The horses were to the south, strung in a long row. Saddles and parfleches were nearby, to the right of the mountain of peltries. To the east reared dense forest. The same to the north. To the west was the hill Nate had descended before being caught by Roarke. Which reminded him. What had Roarke been doing up there?

Nate half turned and discovered Roarke was gone. He nodded at Galt and asked, "Where did our friend get to?"

"To make a circuit of our camp. As you learned the hard way, it doesn't pay to let your guard down in this country. We always survey the countryside before we turn in."

"A smart practice," Nate said. "I wish we'd done the same."

Again Clay Basket returned, this time holding a wooden spoon with which she stirred the contents of the pot. Again Nate had to ignore her, although it pained him to do so. He figured she took him for the biggest fool in all Creation, as did her captors, and for the time being the illusion served his purpose admirably.

The renegades loosened up and talked about matters of no special consequence. Nate contributed little. When the stew was done, he ate heartily, two heaping helpings and part of a third. Nate often caught Galt lecherously ogling Clay Basket, and wondered if the cutthroat would try to force her to submit with him present.

And Nate had another concern. Would the renegades let him live or see fit to slay him when the whim struck? Countless corpses were testimony to their callous lust for money, yet he had nothing of great value. Nor did he have a pretty woman to catch the eye of Galt, as Tim Nelson had. No, he reflected, the killers might be inclined to let him be, if for no other reason than to show up anyone who might later point the finger of blame at any of them in connection with the murders. They might say something along the lines of: "See? Jess Smith spent time with us and we didn't kill him? So how dare you accuse us of going around killing every trapper we met?"

Regardless, Nate never let his vigilance down for a minute. When he was eating, one hand or the other was always next to a pistol. When drinking coffee, it was the same. He kept the different renegades in sight at all times, and when one or another went off into the brush, he never turned his back to that part of the forest.

Eventually Roarke showed up.

"Anything?" Galt asked.

"No campfires, no smoke, nothing. If the Blackfeet are after Smith, we'll be long gone before they show."

Galt and two of his men walked over to the peltries, and Galt selected a grassy spot on which the pair began constructing a conical structure of limbs and brush similar to the makeshift forts used by the Blackfeet on occasion. This one was smaller, suitable for two people at the most. Nate didn't need to ask who the structure was for, and he couldn't help but see Clay Basket's apprehension.

It ruined everything. Nate had hoped to wait until the cutthroats were asleep, then spirit the Crow woman to safety. Now he had to change his plan and embark on a riskier venture: to spirit her away right from under their noses before she was forced to go into the fort with Galt.

Doing his best not to be obvious about it, Nate kept watch over Clay Basket, always noting her position in relation to the forest and the horses in case a chance presented itself.

None did. The renegades bossed her around freely, keeping her busy doing minor chores such as fetching them coffee or jerky and gathering fuel for the fire. A killer always went with her when she went after branches, and hovered over her in camp like a hawk over its prey.

Nate was so preoccupied with watching Clay Basket that he didn't realize someone had addressed him until a hand clamped onto his shoulder and he twisted to see Galt eyeing him critically. "What?" he blurted out.

"I said," Galt repeated slowly, "what are we going to do about you?"

"How do you mean?"

"We don't have any extra horses to spare. All the pack animals are carrying as many peltries as they can, so we can't double up the loads." Galt stared at the animals. "You could ride double with one of us until we get to the Rendezvous site. Would that do you?"

"I'd be very grateful."

"We don't mind the company," Galt went on as if he hadn't heard, "but never forget that I'm the boss here and what I say goes. If I want you to lend a hand with the work, I expect you to chip in."

"That's only fair," Nate said, adopting his fake smile. "Hunting, cooking, chopping wood, you name it, I'll do what I can."

"There should be more folks like you," Galt said, the corners of his eyes crinkling. "Most don't know the first thing about gratitude nowadays."

Strange words, Nate reflected, coming from a confirmed murderer. He nodded and responded with: "How true. You've hit the old nail on the head. One of the reasons I left the States was because I'd grown so fed up with the cold way people in New York City treated others. I wanted something different."

"So did I," Galt said softly. "But the first few years I was out here, nothing went right for me. I was like you. Barely caught enough beaver to stake me for the next year. Had brushes with the Bloods and the Piegans. Nearly lost my hair more times than I care to remember."

"Yet you stuck with it." Nate bobbed a chin at the furs. "And now look! What's the secret of your success?"

"Hard work." Galt's smirk returned. "My pa always used to say that no matter what line of work a man picks, he should always do it the best he possibly can. I never thought much of his preaching when I was a kid, but now I see he had a point. I'm doing better than I ever dreamed I could by doing what I found I do best."

"Trapping," Nate said.

"What?" Galt glanced at him.

"Trapping beaver. Collecting pelts."

"Oh, yes. Collecting peltries is all I live for, you might say."

One of the men, Belker, had a coughing fit.

Nate played the innocent and leaned back, letting them think he didn't have any idea of the true meaning behind Galt's words. He glanced around, seeking Clay Basket, and was surprised to find she was gone. So was Roarke. They were probably off getting additional wood, he figured, and didn't think more of it until a sharp cry pierced the night and there was a loud crashing in the underbrush to the north.

Every last cutthroat leaped erect and had a gun ready when Clay Basket burst from the trees and halted to catch her breath. Her left cheek was bleeding from a small cut and there were red marks on her throat.

"What the hell!" Galt roared, racing over with his gang close on his heels.

Nate followed, but at a slower pace. He held back as Galt grabbed Clay Basket's wrist and gave her a vigorous shake.

"What happened to you, woman? Where's Roarke?"

"He tried to take me," Clay Basket said.

This was the first Nate had heard her speak, and he was struck by the musical lilt to her pleasant voice. Her English, while heavily accented, was almost as good as his wife's. Placing a finger on the hammer of his Hawken, he edged closer.

"Tried to take you?" Galt was saying. "In what way?"

"You know in what way."

"The son of a bitch!"

"I slapped him and he fell," Clay Basket said.

"I'll turn the bastard into a gelding!" Galt snarled. Drawing a knife, he plunged into the forest. His men stayed right with him.

In the excitement and anger of the moment, Nate and Clay Basket were left alone. He took a bound, snatched her hand, and declared, "There's no time to explain. I'm here to help you, to take you back to Nelson. You must come with me." Whirling, Nate headed northward, glancing once at the horses. He would much rather have cut them loose and stampeded them, but there were so many it would take a minute or two to drive every last animal off, and by then the renegades might return. He couldn't risk that. The only alternative, he felt, was to reach his own horses and ride like a bat out of hell back to where he had left his friends.

Clay Basket offered no protests. As fleet as a deer, she sprinted beside Nate, casting anxious eyes on the pines.

They crossed the open space, and were almost to the tree line when a strident shout erupted to their rear. Glancing around, Nate saw one of the killers.

"Galt! Galt! He's stealin' your woman, damn it! They're headin' west!"

Furious yells broke out. Nate raised his rifle to swat a limb aside as he sped into the woods. He could have shot the man who gave the warning, but he preferred to save the ball for when he would need it the most. Darting around a tree trunk, he ran flat out, Clay Basket matching his pace if not his stride. He was angling up the hill when the night thundered to the blast of a rifle and a searing pain lanced his left thigh.

Chapter Ten

Nate was knocked forward by the impact. He automatically let go of Clay Basket's hand as his left leg twisted and he fell, smacking onto his knee. Grimacing, he looked down at his thigh. In the dark, the spreading stain on his leggings seemed almost black. He gingerly touched the wound, tracing a furrow several inches long and less than a quarter of an inch deep. Nasty, but not life-threatening.

"Can you stand, Jess?" Clay Basket asked, sliding her hands under his arms. "I will help you."

"I can manage," Nate assured her. He pushed upright, took her hand again, and resumed running.

"You're bleeding!"

"I'd rather be bleeding than dead."

And dead Nate would be if Galt had his way. Nate could hear the enraged renegade bellowing orders, instructing the cutthroats to fan out, to spare the woman no matter what. As for his fate, that was sealed if the killers got him in their clutches. They'd either slay him outright, or more likely, drag him to their camp so they could give him the same treatment they had given their lengthy list of victims.

Nate tried to remember exactly how far they had to go to reach the black stallion and his other mounts. For the life of him, he couldn't. Was it 300 yards? Or 400? He knew exactly where the animals were tethered, but he had been concentrating on the camp as he went down the hill and hadn't kept track of the distance.

The renegade trappers were coming on fast, as evidenced by the crackling of brush and the pad of rushing feet. Nate shot a glance over his shoulder, and counted four figures strung out in a ragged line from north to south. They were at the bottom of the hill, starting up.

Surely, Nate reflected, Galt would have every last man taking part in the chase. Where, then, were the missing three? Had Galt stayed behind? Was Roarke dead?

Nate spied a log in his path. "Jump!" he whispered, and did just that. Clay Basket matched his feat, and side by side they alighted and dashed onward. To Nate's dismay, he then heard what he feared the most, the drumming of heavy hoofs. A look showed a pair of horsemen galloping in determined pursuit. Already the riders had passed the four men on foot.

Being caught was inevitable. There wasn't a man alive who could outrun a horse, especially on a hill. Nate saw a thicket to his left. Slowing, he pulled Clay Basket down next to him as he stooped to enter the prickly maze. The hoofbeats were drawing rapidly closer and closer. Nate squeezed through a gap and squatted in a small enclosed space. Clay Basket joined him. Between them there wasn't enough room left for either to lift an arm.

Seconds later the monstrous shapes of the riders, looming in the night like ancient creatures called centaurs Nate had once read about, appeared. They reined up ten feet from the thicket and one of them vented his spleen.

"Damn it all! Where the hell are they? I thought I saw them at this very spot a few seconds ago!"

Nate was surprised to recognize Roarke's voice.

"Keep it down!" the second man hissed. "Do you want them to hear you?"

"What difference does it make? They know we're here," Roarke replied testily. "And we're going to find them, even if we have to stay up all night."

"You're just mad because that squaw walloped you good and made you look like an idiot."

"You'd be mad too, Sterret, if she'd caught you off guard like she did me. Stinking treacherous females!"

"Were I you, I'd be more worried about whether Galt believes your story. If he asks her, and she sticks by her tale of you trying to get up her dress, Galt will skin you alive."

"I'm not scared of him," Roarke said with less than sterling confidence. "Now come on! We have to find the bitch!"

Nate watched the pair gallop westward. When they were gone, he leaned over and smiled. "Too bad you didn't bust his skull wide open."

"He lies," Clay Basket said. "He attacked me first and I slapped him, just as I said. He fell and pulled his knife, so I ran back. I would rather have gone deeper into the woods, but I was afraid he would shoot me if I tried."

"You've done right fine so far," Nate complimented her. "Nelson would be proud of you."

"He is alive, then?" Clay Basket asked anxiously. "You were speaking with a straight tongue?"

"I left him with friends who are trying to patch him up."

Clay Basket's eyes shimmered in the dim light. "You do not know how happy you have made me. I believed he was dead."

"We have to get you—" Nate began, and froze on discerning more voices. Some of the renegades on foot were approaching. He tensed, lowering a hand to a pistol since the flintlocks would be easier to use in the confined space and at short range were just as accurate as the Hawken.

"—ain't seen hide nor hair of them. I say we go get horses and torches."

"And I say we keep lookin' until Galt tells us otherwise. He's riled up, and you know how he gets when he's riled. Anyone who complains is liable to wish they hadn't."

Nate could see one of the cutthroats moving at the edge of the thicket. Would they think to check inside it? he wondered. Fingers touched his arm and squeezed. Clay Basket was terrified, as her low gasp proved when the cutthroat stopped. The man faced the thicket and bent down.

"What is it?" another asked.

"Thought I heard something," the man said, swinging from side to side.

"Probably a damn rabbit," said the other. "They wouldn't go in there with us on their trail."

The cutthroat examining the thicket grunted. "I guess not." He slowly straightened, motioned at his companion, and both were soon lost in the murky vegetation.

"Stay close to me," Nate cautioned, easing onto his elbows so he could crawl to the opening and peek out. A cool breeze stirred the trees and the grass. He scanned the shadows, saw no one, then eased out and helped Clay Basket to stand.

"Which way?" she wanted to know.

That was the crucial question. To go west would be flirting with death, yet to the west was where the horses waited. Going east would take them to the basin and Galt. Nate stared southward and northward, debating, and he had not quite made up his mind when the metallic rasp of a gun hammer being cocked sent a tingle down his spine.

"Don't move, either of you!"

Two of the renegades strode from cover, the same pair who had stopped next to the thicket. The taller of the duo snickered and remarked, "I knew I saw something in there!"

"That you did, Johnny," said the other.

Nate had his right arm at his side, holding the Hawken. His left arm was slightly behind him, out of sight of the approaching killers. Relying on the dark to blanket his movements, he inched his finger to his butcher knife and clasped the hilt.

"Drop that long gun, you ornery greenhorn," the one named Johnny commanded. "Then step back and put your arms in the air where we can see them."

"And don't try nothin' clever unless you want to eat lead," his companion said. "I've got a ball in this here barrel with your name on it."

Nate had no choice but to obey, but he didn't do exactly as they wanted. He slowly lowered the Hawken's stock to the ground, exaggerating his motion. Both renegades kept their eyes on the rifle in case he should suddenly reverse his grip and try to bring it to bear. With their attention on the gun, neither noticed the sleight of hand Nate resorted to, for while they were momentarily distracted by the movement of his right arm, he slowly raised his left arm, drawing his knife as he did and holding it flush against his forearm so they couldn't see it. He then elevated his right arm and stood awaiting further directions. "Satisfied?"

"Sure am," Johnny said, coming closer. "I thought for certain you'd do something stupid and get yourself killed."

"Which would spoil the surprises Galt has in store for you," said his companion.

Johnny wagged his rifle. "George, take his pistols before he gets any contrary notions. And his tomahawk and knife too."

Nodding, George warily stepped forward and stopped to the right of Nate. He touched the barrel of his rifle to Nate's stomach and said, "You heard the man. Hand 'em over. And remember, no tricks."

"Don't worry," Nate said meekly to make them think he would do as they wanted. "I'm not looking to get myself killed."

"Then you shouldn't of run off with the squaw," George said, and laughed.

Nate glanced down at George's rifle as he slowly reached for his right flintlock. The rifle wasn't cocked. He glanced at Johnny and saw that Johnny's rifle was leveled at his midsection but not at any specific spot. As risky as it was, there might not be a better time. So, when his finger curled around his pistol, he tensed his body and ever so slowly began to ease the pistol clear.

George looked at Johnny and snorted. "Well-behaved greenhorn, ain't he?"

And in that instant when Johnny was focused on George, Nate sprang into action, whipping the pistol from under his belt and cocking the hammer in a single smooth draw while simultaneously he firmed his hold on the butcher knife and arced his left arm across his chest, spearing it around and in. Both killers were swift to react: Johnny to raise his rifle a bit higher, George to begin to turn back toward Nate.

Nate fired before Johnny did, the heavy-caliber flintlock belching smoke and bucking in his hand. At almost the same moment he twisted and sliced his big blade into George's chest, just below the sternum. George clutched at the knife, then tried to cock his rifle. Nate, pivoting, slammed his pistol into the renegade's temple, and George dropped the rifle and staggered, his knees buckling. The butcher knife jerked loose, dripping crimson drops. A second blow brought George down. Nate, fearing the other cutthroat might not be mortally wounded, spun, but he need not have worried.

The man called Johnny was flat on his back, his lifeless eyes fixed on the heavens, a hole in his chest bubbling blood.

Nate turned back to George to finish him off. Shouts in the forest to the west changed his mind, since it meant the rest were on their way and might get there before he could escape with the woman. He slid the butcher knife into its sheath without bothering to wipe the blade, wedged the pistol under his belt, and stooped to grab the Hawken. "They'll be on us quick. We have to hurry," he said, offering his hand to the Crow.

Clay Basket paused, looked down at George's rifle, and hastily retrieved it. "I will keep up," she pledged.

A horse and rider were barreling through the undergrowth less than 30 yards away. Nate whirled and fled once again, southward this time, skirting the thicket and crossing a moonlit glade. Clay Basket might have been part of him, so smoothly did she run at his side. When he swerved, she did. When he vaulted over a log, she did the same without breaking stride or causing him to either. Whatever he did, she duplicated it flawlessly. They ran in virtual silence thanks to the thick carpet of pine needles underfoot.

"Quince! Roarke! The rest of you! Over here!"

Nate knew that Johnny and George had been found. Soon the others would be in pursuit, provided they could track at night. Some Indians could. The average trapper became a fair hand at it out of necessity, but few became adept enough to rival the Indians. Then Nate thought of Belker, and something told him that there was a man who could track an ant over solid rock.

At least, Nate reflected, he had reduced the odds by one, possibly two, since if George lived he would be in no shape to pose a threat. Which left Galt, Belker, Roarke, Sterret, and Quince. Nate needed to remember those names. If he survived, if the renegades got away, he would let all the other trappers at the upcoming Rendezvous know who had been part of the bloodthirsty band. The word would spread like wildfire to all friendly Indian tribes, and be taken back to St. Louis with the caravan traders. Galt and company would find themselves the objects of the biggest manhunt in the history of the frontier. Their lives wouldn't be worth a pile of buffalo chips.

Galt was smart. He had to realize that. So Nate couldn't count on the renegades giving up easily. They'd scour the countryside for miles around, take days if need be. Evading them was going to be a chore.

Just how much of a chore became apparent when Nate heard the pounding of hoofs. Darting behind a pine, he crouched down in the nick of time. A pair of renegades galloped past, not 50 feet to the east. They neither slowed nor spoke and were presently out of sight.

"That was close," Nate whispered in Clay Basket's ear. "We'd best sit tight for a minute. They just might swing on around."

"You are very brave, Jess Smith. I can never thank you for what you have done."

"King. Nate King," Nate corrected her. "I gave them a different name because they might have heard of me."

"I do not understand."

"If they'd known who I really was, they'd have killed me as soon as I stepped into their camp."

"Are you a friend of the Blanket Chief?"

That was the Indian name for Jim Bridger, without a doubt the most widely respected trapper alive. His word carried more weight with the Indians than the word of practically all other white men combined. Only Shakespeare

McNair had an equal reputation. "I am," Nate admitted. "And I'm an even closer friend of the man your people know as Wolverine Killer."

Clay Basket was trying to study his features in the darkness. "How else are you known?" she inquired.

"The Shoshones and Flatheads call me Grizzly Killer."

"I have heard of you. Once, many moons ago, Wolverine Killer and you visited the village of our high chief, Long Hair. It was said you brought him horses and eagle feathers to restore the honor of a warrior who died in disgrace."

Nate had nearly forgotten about that day. "He was a good man. I owed it to him," he answered, and let it go at that.

To the southeast the two riders could be heard sweeping the area. Nate elected to stay put for the time being since they were safe from detection.

"Is it true you are an adopted Shoshone?" Clay Basket whispered.

"It is."

"My Nelson wants my people to adopt him," she said proudly. "I hope they will agree."

"He loves you very much," Nate mentioned. "When we found him, he told us to forget about him and go after you. Your safety came first. He didn't care about himself."

Clay Basket's head bowed, her hair falling across her face. "My heart is his forever. I could not live without him."

Just then Nate stared northward and caught a hint of someone moving. He put a hand to her mouth and pulled her lower. The stout figure glided nearer, a lone renegade bent at the waist, examining the ground. Nate didn't need to see the man clearly to know who it was: Belker, he of the huge knife and sinister eyes.

Nate put a hand on his left pistol. He'd let Belker get closer, right up to the pine in fact, and fire at almost point-blank range so he couldn't miss. Then there would be two down and only five to deal with. But the cutthroat thwarted him.

Belker halted 20 feet away and bent down to touch the ground. His head snapped up, but he looked to the southeast, not at the pine. For several seconds he was like a statue. Unexpectedly, he turned and headed due west, dashing into the trees.

The move perplexed Nate. Why, if Belker had been tracking them, had the killer gone in an entirely different direction? And why had Belker stared to the southeast? Nate did the same, and saw the two riders returning. Spaced a dozen yards apart, they were searching around every bush, under every tree.

"Damn," Nate whispered. He gestured at Clay Basket, turned, and bore to the southwest. There was plenty of cover, so he had no difficulty in eluding the horsemen. Once he felt they had covered enough ground, he rose and resumed running.

Nate often thought of being abroad in the forest at night as a dream-like experience. The delicate play of shadows and pale moonlight lent the terrain an eerie aspect heightened by the often total silence and complete lack of wildlife. It was so different from the same forest during the day when the sun blazed and the wild creatures were singing or scampering about, when the forest was so vibrant with life.

Ten minutes elapsed. Nate stopped at the edge of a meadow to reload the spent pistol and to allow Clay Basket to catch her breath. Somewhere close at hand an owl hooted.

"They will keep looking for a long time, will they not?" she asked.

"Yes."

"Do you have horses?"

Nate nodded as he opened the flap on his ammo pouch. "But the only way to get to them without attracting attention is to swing wide to the west. If we push ourselves, and if we don't run into any problems, we can reach the spot by dawn."

"Then let us keep going. I want to see my Nelson."

"Whatever you want."

Nate had a course worked out in his head. Since the renegades were concentrating on a narrow area, all he had to do was outflank them. He did so by bearing to the southwest for an hour and then turning westward. Besides a few crickets and coyotes, they had the night to themselves.

"Do you have a woman, Grizzly Killer?" Clay Basket asked at one point.

"Yep. The prettiest Shoshone ever born," Nate boasted, grinning. "And we have two sprouts too. A boy and a girl."

"Do you ever regret taking her for your wife?"

The unanticipated question prompted Nate to glance at her. "Never. Why would you ask such a thing?"

"I sometimes think Nelson will one day believe he made a mistake and he will go back to his own people."

"If you'd heard him urging us to save you, you'd know how silly you sound," Nate told her. "I've never met a man anywhere more in love than he is. He'll stick by you through thick and thin."

"I hope so," Clay Basket declared.

The conversation made Nate think of his own wife, and he longed to be holding her in his arms again and inhaling the fragrant scent of her hair. As much as he enjoyed the life of a free trapper, there were certain drawbacks every trapper had to accept, one of them being long periods away from loved ones. He was about to remark as much to the Crow woman when there arose a loud crackling in the trees directly ahead.

Nate halted and motioned for her to do the same. He trained his Hawken on a dark blotch of trees, then crouched. Clay Basket imitated him, ready to back him up with the rifle she had taken from George.

The trees moved, some of the limbs swaying violently.

Nate saw, and blinked. Those limbs were seven or eight feet off the ground. Whatever was in there had to be enormous. Mentally, he ticked off a short list of likely creatures: an elk, a grizzly, or something smaller in the tree itself. Whatever it was suddenly grunted, a deep, guttural grunt such as a bear would make, only much deeper than any bear Nate had ever heard.

"What is it?" Clay Basket asked softly.

"I don't know," Nate admitted. Unbidden, he remembered the tale Pepin had told of the mysterious Canadian mammoth. He peered intently into the inky gloom, and swore he saw the vague outline of a gigantic beast standing on two legs. Yet when he closed his eyes a second and opened them again, the outline was gone.

"I thought I saw something," Clay Basket said.

Nate listened to the crackling as the strange animal moved about. The thing didn't seem to be in any great hurry to move on, so to avoid a confrontation, Nate took Clay Basket's wrist and slanted to the right to go around.

There was a crack, as of a tree limb being broken, followed by a disturbing silence.

Nate didn't stop. He wanted no part of the unknown creature. As he hurried along, he experienced the sensation of unseen eyes watching him, and the short hairs at the nape of his neck prickled. A glance at Clay Basket confirmed she was equally anxious. Frayed nerves, he figured. The two of them had been under a constant strain for so long that their minds were playing tricks on them.

After several minutes Nate allowed himself to relax. The

animal hadn't given chase, so they were safe. He surveyed the landscape, trying to guess their position in relation to where the horses were tied, and calculated they were a mile or more to the southwest. On all sides reared heavy timber, with a lot of downed trees and thick brush that would slow them down. They would be lucky if they reached the horses by first light, as he wanted to do.

Half an hour went by. Nate had the Hawken resting on his shoulder and was strolling along the bottom of a gulch they had stumbled on. Here there were fewer obstacles and the going was easier. He checked on Clay Basket, and saw her fiddling with a moccasin. And then, as he was partially turned toward her, there was the rattle of dirt on the gully slope, a swishing noise, and something heavy pounced on his back.

Chapter Eleven

Nate King's first thought, on hearing the rattle of the dirt, was that the creature they had encountered earlier had stalked them and was attacking him. He tried to spin, but was way too slow. The impact smashed him to the ground so hard the breath whooshed from his lungs. He felt the Hawken being torn from his grasp, and through a haze of pain he saw Clay Basket bringing her rifle to bear even as a sharp object gouged him in the side of the neck and a gruff voice spoke.

"Try it, squaw, and this son of a bitch dies!"

It was Belker! Nate realized, and tried to move, but the renegade was on his back, kneeling on him, pinning him in place. Clay Basket glanced at him, then at the killer. Reluctantly, she lowered her rifle and took a step back.

"How touching!" Belker quipped. "I knew there was more to this bastard than he let on. What, is he your lover?"

"He is a friend," Clay Basket answered indignantly.

135

"And I'm the king of England," Belker said. "The two of you didn't fool me for a minute. I saw the way he was watchin' you when he thought no one else would notice. Idiots!"

Nate was trying to get his right arm out from under him so he could reach for his tomahawk. He had almost succeeded when the knife point gouged deeper into his neck and a hand seized hold of his hair and yanked on his head.

"Try that, fool, and I'll slit you from ear to ear!" Belker hissed. He slid off Nate and stood, hauling Nate erect by the hair. "Give me any excuse and you're a dead man, no matter what Galt wants."

Nate was given a rough shove that sent him stumbling toward Clay Basket. He kept his balance, drew up short, and was poised to draw a pistol when he saw the renegade had already done so.

"Drop all your weapons, Smith. Nice and slow."

Only a fool resisted while staring down the barrel of a .55-caliber flintlock. Simmering with anger at being caught so handily, Nate removed all four of his belt weapons. The smirk on Belker's grimy face only aggravated him more.

"That's a good boy," the cutthroat taunted. "I knew you'd be reasonable about it." Chuckling, he wagged his pistol. "Now back up."

Nate's blood boiled as he helplessly watched Belker taking possession of their arms, and he wanted to kick himself for being so careless. He had to rein in a suicidal urge to make a mad dash at the renegade. Presently he was looking down the barrel of his own Hawken instead of a pistol.

"Next we march out and around to the top of this gully so I can fetch my rifle," Belker said. "Keep your hands where I can see them, because I assure you I have no qualms about shootin' either of you in the back if you give me the slightest cause."

Nate believed him. Turning, he allowed Clay Basket to go first. That way, he could block Belker's view of her if he had to. He tried to catch her eye and signal her with a bob of his head to let her know she should make a bid to escape if the opportunity presented itself, but she was staring at the ground, dejected. They retraced their steps to the mouth of the gully, and began climbing a gradual incline to the top.

"I've got to hand it to you, Smith," Belker commented. "You gave the others a merry chase. But then, they're not the tracker I am. I found your trail right away and almost blundered onto you when you were hiding behind that pine. Remember?"

Nate wasn't going to respond, but a sharp poke between the shoulder blades changed his mind. "I remember," he said sullenly.

"I knew the two of you were hidin' there, so I went off into the brush and waited for you to show yourselves. Then I followed you until I saw my chance. Pretty clever, huh?"

"Was that you in the trees?" Nate asked.

"What trees?"

"In that stand a while back, breaking limbs and making those sounds?"

"I don't know what you're talkin' about. I never got too close because I didn't want you spottin' me before I was ready to make my move."

Nate came to the rim of the gully. Grass and bushes grew to the very edge, and he was obliged to step around some of the latter as he followed Clay Basket toward the spot where Belker had jumped them from the rim. A germ of an idea formed, and he scanned the slope in front of them. He glanced back, measuring the distance between the renegade and him, and suppressed a grin.

"Have you ever seen someone have their belly slit and their innards ripped out?" Belker was saying. "I have. It ain't a sight for the squeamish." He snickered. "I expect I'll get to see it again when Galt starts in on you. Trust me, pilgrim. He's not the kind of man you want to rile. Something inside of him snaps and he goes all crazy. Why, once I saw him carve a man up so bad the man didn't hardly look human no more when Galt was done."

"I bet you've done your share," Nate remarked.

"Meaning?"

"I've heard about you, Belker. You're no saint."

The renegade chortled. "No, I ain't. I've planted a few jackasses in my time. But I always do the job neat and clean, not like Galt. He likes to see people suffer, likes to see them squirm and hear them beg for their lives. One time he reached inside a guy he'd cut open and pulled the fella's heart out with his bare hand. Lordy, was that a sight!"

Nate had slowed a bit so Clay Basket could gain a couple of yards on them. He didn't want her to be too close when he made his move.

"I swear that Galt was born wrong," Belker had gone on. "He should have been born a Blackfoot or an Apache instead of a white man. He'd have been right at home with them."

"And you don't mind riding with someone like him?"

"Mind, hell! He's making us rich, ain't he? I don't care how crazy he gets just so we keep on filling our pokes with fur money."

Another bush appeared in front of Nate, the largest yet, over three feet high. This time, instead of going around the plant on the left side, where the ground was level, he went around on the right side, where the slope dropped away to the bottom of the gully. Almost immediately the loose earth gave way under his foot and he started to slip.

"Not that way, damn you!" Belker bellowed.

Nate deliberately fell onto his stomach and clawed at the slope, pretending he was caught in gravity's grip, while at the same time he dug in his toes to arrest his descent. He also pretended to pay no attention at all to the renegade, who stepped close to the edge and glared down at him.

"Get back up here!"

"I'm trying," Nate lied, scrambling faster, his left hand moving closer and closer to Belker's legs each time he dug his fingers into the earth.

"Try harder, idiot." Belker motioned impatiently, and when he did the barrel of the Hawken swung to one side.

This was the moment Nate had been waiting for. Braced on his toes, he lunged upward, still pretending to be clawing at the slope when in reality he was diving at Belker's legs. His left arm looped around both of the cutthroat's ankles and with a tremendous heave he upended Belker and pulled.

Venting a string of oaths, the renegade plummeted over the edge, tumbling downward, one rifle flying but not the Hawken. Together they rolled to the very bottom, where Nate released his hold and seized the Hawken by the barrel. With a terrific wrench he gained control of the gun, but as he did it went off almost in his face.

"Damn you!" Belker roared, rising. His hand swooped to his belt and flashed out holding the long knife he favored. "To hell with Galt! I'm putting you under right here and now!"

Nate barely backed away quickly enough to avoid a wicked slash that would have gutted him. He swung the Hawken at Belker's head, but the wily killer ducked under the swing and stabbed at Nate's legs. Nate had to leap backward. As he did, Belker grasped the rifle barrel.

There they stood, not more than a yard apart, each with a hand on the Hawken, Belker waving his long knife in small circles in the air. "Think you're clever, don't you, smart boy?" he said mockingly. "Well, we'll see how clever you think you are after I cut out your tongue."

Nate didn't waste breath replying. He gave a tug on the Hawken, pulling Belker toward him, and leaped straight at the shorter man. His hand closed on the renegade's right wrist to keep the knife at bay while his knee drove into Belker's groin. They both toppled, Belker clamping his other hand on Nate's throat.

Back and forth they rolled, each struggling mightily to gain an advantage. Nate was amazed at the renegade's strength. Strive as he might, the knife edged ever nearer to his face.

Belker growled as he fought, much like the black bear he so resembled, his lips curled to reveal his clenched teeth. "You're mine! Hear me? Mine!" he cried.

Nate strained his utmost and pushed the renegade's arm back a few inches. Their rolling brought them up against the slope, with Nate on the bottom. Belker angled the razor-edged blade inward, seeking Nate's neck. Nate, in desperation, snapped his head forward, butting his brow into the cutthroat's nose. Something cracked, and Belker shrieked and tried to rise.

Coiling his legs, Nate rammed both feet into the renegade's midriff. Belker went flying rearward to crash onto his back in the middle of the gully. Nate pushed into a crouch and charged just as Belker was rising. His shoulder caught the killer in the side, bowling Belker over, but as Belker went down he cut upward with the knife, ripping Nate's buckskin shirt and slicing the skin.

They parted. Nate could feel blood trickling from his wound. He balled his fists and waited for his foe to make the next move.

Belker was in no hurry. Ready to strike, he held the knife at his waist. He was getting his breath back while letting the pain in his ribs subside. And too, he was studying Jess Smith more closely. For a greenhorn, Smith was a hellion. Or was Smith a greenhorn? Belker stared, and suddenly remembered the Rendezvous several years ago. "Damn! I knew I'd laid eyes on you before. You're Nate King, aren't you?"

Long ago Nate had learned not to talk when in a fight. Talking served as a distraction and might cost a man his life. So he simply nodded and circled to the right.

"I thought so!" Belker said. "That explains a lot! Wait until Galt hears."

Nate continued to slowly circle, planting each foot carefully.

"The great Grizzly Killer!" Belker said, and snorted. "Who would have thought it?" His brow puckered. "Wait a minute. You're married to some Shoshone bitch. What's this Crow squaw mean to you?"

Seldom had Nate fought anyone who talked so much. He saw a rock between them, and on an impulse he flicked out his foot, kicking the rock at the renegade, who stepped to the side. Nate kicked again, only this time a spray of dirt that made Belker raise an arm to protect his eyes. Instantly Nate leaped and gripped Belker's right wrist in both hands. Pivoting, Nate whirled, throwing every last ounce into a swing that propelled the cutthroat into the gully wall.

Belker landed on his back and endeavored to rise. Nate, taking swift strides, got there first and lashed out with his left foot. The long knife went sailing into the dark. Belker, incensed, reached for the tomahawk he had taken from Nate, but Nate closed and down they went again, punching one another furiously.

Nate landed a right to the jaw and received a left in the stomach. He blocked a flurry, then drove his left fist into Belker's cheek, splitting the flesh. Belker's forearm clubbed Nate on the ear. Nate connected, his knuckles flattening the renegade's lips. In unison they rose to their knees, slugging away all the while.

The blows were brutal, bone-wrenching. Nate shut out the agony and tried to knock the cutthroat out with a solid right to the jaw. It was like striking metal. Belker merely flinched. Nate took a punch to the temple that made him see stars. He pushed backward, shaking his head to recover, and was tackled about the chest. Once more he wound up flat on his back.

Belker seemed determined to end the fight at all costs. His fists were blurs as he pounded without letup.

Nate was losing and knew it. He brought his left arm high so his face would be spared, and shoved against the cutthroat with his right hand. Belker was immovable. Bucking his hips, Nate simultaneously twisted and threw the renegade off. His head swimming, he straightened, then froze upon hearing a click.

One of Nate's pistols was now aimed at his head. Belker grinned, wiped blood from the corner of his mouth, and said, "Enough of this. I should have shot you the minute I first saw you. Meet your Maker, King."

A single shot sounded, resembling a blast of thunder, echoing along the gully in both directions.

Belker's grin faded. He tried to lift an arm to touch the ragged cavity in his forehead, but couldn't. The pistol drooped, his arm sagged. His whole body went limp and he pitched forward.

Nate darted out of the way and stared down at the killer in bewilderment. A sigh drew his gaze to the rim, where Clay Basket was lowering the smoking rifle she had just used. Belker's own gun had been turned against him. "Thanks," Nate said softly. Absently, he brushed at the gore that had spattered the front of his shirt.

Clay Basket came down the slope, sliding half the way, the rifle employed as a crutch to keep her erect. In a swirl of dust she stopped and gazed at the man she had slain. "If ever a man deserved to die, he was one."

"You'll get no complaints from me," Nate assured her. He held up his hands and saw the skin peeled from his knuckles. Bruises and welts covered him from his face to his groin.

"Now we are safe, Grizzly Killer," Clay Basket said. "Now we can hurry to my Nelson."

"If none of his friends heard the shot," Nate observed. He would have liked to sit down and rest, but he had already grown careless once and wasn't about to make the same mistake again. Swiftly he scaled the east side of the gully and stood listening. No shouts sounded anywhere. The night was as quiet as a tomb.

"We were lucky," Nate said as he rejoined her. "We're too far away for them to have heard." Taking Belker's rifle from her, he loaded it and gave it back. He also gave her Belker's pistol and knife. His own weapons soon adorned his waist. Carrying the Hawken in one hand and George's rifle in the other, he resumed their interrupted trek at a faster clip.

Neither of them spoke for the longest while. The cut Nate had sustained stung terribly but wasn't life-threatening, so he ignored it. Which was typical, not just for him but for most trappers. Whiners and weaklings had no business being in the mountains. Those who fainted at the sight of blood were better off in the States where civilized society spared them from the grimmer realities of life.

Gradually the sky to the east lightened. Not much, but enough to signal the advent of dawn within the hour. Nate was extremely tired, and imagined Clay Basket felt the same. He had to admire her fortitude in holding up as well as she had, and he rated Tim Nelson a very fortunate man in having earned the love of such a remarkable woman. Back in the States there were many who looked down on Indians, who regarded Indians as somehow inferior to whites, as little better than animals. He'd often wondered if those people would change their minds if they could live with Indians for a while and get to know the so-called "savages" as they really were. Doing so had certainly changed his outlook. Ignorance, it seemed to him, was a prime breeding ground for hatred and bloodshed, and he thought it a shame that so many were afflicted with a lack of human understanding.

Out of consideration for Clay Basket, Nate halted on a rise and remarked, "Let's rest a few minutes. It won't do us any good to wear ourselves to a frazzle."

"If you will," she replied, not sounding very pleased by the delay.

Nate looked at her and debated whether to say something, whether to prepare her for the grim possibility that the man she loved might be dead. Tim Nelson, after all, had been in grave condition when Nate rode off. But when he saw her gazing westward, an eager gleam animating her eyes, he couldn't bring himself to shatter her hopes. Instead, he commented, "By tonight you should be back with Tim."

Clay Basket's throat bobbed. "He is all I think about." She grinned self-consciously. "I always thought I would one day marry a man from my own tribe. I never thought I would love a trapper."

"Love is strange that way," Nate agreed. "There's no telling when it will strike. If someone had told me when I was younger that I'd wind up taking a Shoshone woman as my wife, I'd have laughed right in their face."

"When this is over, maybe you and your wife would see fit to visit us."

"I'm sure she'd like that."

"I wish—" Clay Basket said, and abruptly stopped.

Nate turned and gazed in the same direction. An enormous mountain lion was descending the nearest mountain. The great cat was just below the snow line, barely visible crossing an open space. It moved with a fluid grace that was apparent even at that distance, and with the first pale glow of dawn dappling its tawny coat, the predator presented a stirring sight. "Lord, I love these mountains," Nate said to himself.

"So do I," Clay Basket said.

They watched until the mountain lion disappeared in high timber. Then Nate hefted the two rifles he held and resumed their hike. How different life had been back in New York City, he reflected, when the only wild creatures he had seen were stray dogs and cats and flocks of pigeons. Perhaps his city upbringing explained why he never tired of the wildlife in the wilderness. To see a grizzly or a buffalo or an eagle was always a thrill; each experience added a certain spice to his life that far surpassed anything he had ever known in civilization.

Presently Nate had a more pressing matter to consider. He had guided them by instinct, relying on his sense of direction to bring them right to where he had left his horses. He had roughly calculated the time it would take them, and had believed they would get there before the sun rose, but now, with the eastern sky growing steadily brighter, there was no sign of the hill he sought. Granted, he was

approaching the spot from a different direction, but he had
learned enough about noting and memorizing landmarks to
be certain he would know the area when he saw it.

Halting, Nate studied the lay of the land. There was a
mountain to the west, a hill to the north, and another to the
northeast. One of those hills must be the one overlooking
the basin in which the renegades had camped, but which
one? Neither was familiar.

"Is something wrong?" Clay Basket inquired.

"Just getting my bearings," Nate said, striding to the
northeast. Logic told him that must be the right hill, but
when they came on a narrow creek he hadn't seen before,
he began to doubt his judgment. Since the two of them
hadn't had a drop to drink in many hours, they stopped
and quenched their thirst. The water was cold, refreshing.
Nate wiped a sleeve across his mouth when he was done.
Then he splashed water on the wound in his thigh, which
was smarting terribly and had swollen up, and on the cut
he had sustained fighting Belker.

"That leg should be bandaged," Clay Basket remarked.

"When we have the time."

Across the creek Nate found fresh elk tracks, which
was reassuring. If any of the cutthroats were in the area,
the elk wouldn't have strayed from cover to drink. Still,
he stayed alert as he wound through the forest toward
the hill.

"How long will it take us to reach my Nelson?" Clay
Basket asked.

"About four hours at the most."

"Is that all?" Clay Basket said, and smiled.

Nate studied the west slope of the hill. There was a certain pine he looked for, a towering fir, a patriarch among
the trees that had been struck by lightning in years past.
The bolt had split the crown of the fir down the middle

and charred the wood. Nate remembered passing it shortly
before he spotted the renegades.

With the golden crown of the sun creasing the eastern
horizon, the wild creatures were stirring to life. Sparrows
and finches chirped, chipmunks climbed onto logs and boulders to chatter and flick their tails, noisy squirrels were
again abroad in the trees, and larger animals were coming
out to forage.

To Nate, the many sounds were akin to listening to
an orchestra tune its musical instruments before launching
into a masterful composition. The creatures were likewise
preparing for another active day of living out their lives
in accordance with the melody of existence Nature had
decreed for them. He breathed deep and smiled.

Nate's smile widened when he spied the split fir tree.
"We're close," he announced, and made for a patch of
underbrush 40 yards off. A low nicker sounded as he
approached, and pushing past a bush he saw the black
stallion and the other horses. "We did it," he told Clay
Basket. "We're safe now."

"Is that a fact?" someone else responded, and from out of
concealment stepped Roarke and two other renegades with
their rifles cocked and leveled.

Chapter Twelve

Ira Galt put his hands on his hips and sneered at the defiant bound pair in front of him. "Did you really think you'd get away from us? Hell, we've been outfoxing fools like you for a couple of years now." So saying, he suddenly lashed out and slapped Nate King across the face.

The blow was so powerful that Nate staggered and would have fallen had he not bumped into Clay Basket, who stood firm. His cheek stung and he tasted blood on the tip of his tongue.

"That's for giving us such a hard time, you bastard," Galt said. Without warning, he swung again. "And that's for killing Johnny and stabbing poor George."

Nate's lower lip was split, the side of his head throbbing. Holding his head high, he refused to show any pain. Over by the bales of peltries he saw the renegade named George lying on blankets, glaring hatefully. There was no doubt what the killer would like to do to him.

Galt rested a hand on one of his pistols. "I should blow

your brains out, but that's too easy. You deserve to suffer for the aggravation you've caused us, to suffer like no one has ever suffered before."

"Cut off his oysters and cram them down his throat," suggested one of the men.

"There's a fine notion," Galt said, smirking.

"Stake him out and skin him alive," proposed another.

"Another good idea, Quince," Galt responded.

Roarke cleared his throat. "Give him to me. I know how to make him suffer." He chuckled. "I saw a prospector done in by the Comanches once. He'd had stakes driven into his arms and legs and slivers driven under his nails. Besides that, the red vermin gouged out his eyes and chopped off his ears and his nose. This polecat deserves the same treatment."

"Those Comanches can be so inventive," Galt said. Reaching out, he gripped Nate by the chin. "What do you think? Would you rather have us do it Quince's way or Roarke's?"

Nate remained silent.

"I asked you a question," Galt said, his grin transforming into a throaty growl as he brutally lashed out with his right fist.

Nate was helpless to dodge the blow. His stomach exploded in agony and he doubled over, wheezing noisily. Fingers twisted his hair and his head was yanked up.

"I want you to take days dying, Smith," Galt declared. "Days and days of torment, until you plead with me to end your rotten life. And when I'm done, maybe I'll make me a tobacco pouch from your hide and carry it with me wherever I go."

"Make me one too," Quince said.

"Say, ain't we forgettin' something?" said the last member of the gang, the one named Sterret. "What about those Blackfeet he mentioned? He claimed they were only a day or so behind him. They could show up at any time."

"I bet he was lying," Roarke said.

"Do we want to gamble all our pelts on whether he is or isn't?" Quince threw in.

All eyes were fixed on Nate. He had forgotten all about the yarn he had told, but now he saw a way of using it to delay his torture for a while, perhaps to even buy himself the whole day in which to devise a means of escaping. "I wasn't lying," he declared with fake conviction. "A war party will be here before you know it."

"Like hell!" Roarke snapped.

"Don't believe me. I don't care," Nate said. "I'd rather you stay here and get your hair lifted anyway. If I'm going to die, I want to take the whole bunch of you with me."

Bluff or fact? That was the crucial question Galt had to answer, and his puzzled expression showed he didn't know how he should take the assertion. "I'm inclined to go along with Roarke. You've already shown yourself to be a liar," he said. "You told us that you were afoot when you had horses hid nearby. You acted and talked like a damn greenhorn, but it's plain you're not. And you tried to take the Crow from us, which proves you know her."

"I never set eyes on her before I came into your camp," Nate stated.

"Then why'd you run off like you did?"

It was Clay Basket who answered. "That was my doing, Galt. I told him you were bad men out to hurt me, and I begged him to get me to safety."

"And he took your word just like that?" Galt said skeptically, snapping his fingers. "We hadn't done anything to him. Why should he believe you without proof?"

"What would you have done if you were in his place, alone among strangers?" Clay Basket shot back. "Walked up to them and demanded the truth?"

Galt's cloud of indecision darkened. He gazed westward, then at Nate, then at the peltries. "I still think you have a forked tongue, Smith, but I can't take the chance you're telling the truth. We've worked hard for our hides and we're not letting the Blackfeet or anyone else take them from us."

"We're pulling out?" Sterret asked.

"Yep. And we're taking these two with us."

"What about George? He's in no shape to ride."

The cutthroat in question overhead and called out, "You can't leave me here, Galt! It wouldn't be right. I'm entitled to my share and I aim to collect."

Roarke, Quince, and Galt walked over to their wounded companion and stood looking down at him. Nate glanced at Sterret, who was covering Clay Basket and him with a rifle, and decided not to try making a bid for freedom just yet.

"I mean it," George insisted. Coughing, he attempted to rise on an elbow but was too weak to do so. "We agreed we were all in this together, and we'd stick together through thick and thin."

Galt nodded. "That we did. But none of us counted on a situation like this cropping up. We can't let one man slow us down."

"I can keep up. Just get me on my horse."

"Who are you kidding? You couldn't sit a saddle in your condition."

"Damn it all, you can't up and desert me!" George said, a pitiable whine in his tone. "You owe it to me to take me along!"

"We owe you nothing," said Roarke.

"Not a thing," Quince added.

Sighing, Galt squatted and placed a hand on George's shoulder. "You can see the fix I'm in, can't you? If we stay to nursemaid you back to health, the Blackfeet might show up. We risk losing everything on account of you."

"But—" George began, and stopped when Galt raised a hand.

"I'm sorry, my friend. I truly am. If we could, I'd rig a travois and haul you to the Rendezvous. But doing so would delay us, let the Blackfeet overtake us. I owe it to the others not to let that happen."

"What are you saying?" George asked fearfully.

"We're going to have to leave you here with enough food and water to last you a while," Galt said. "If the Blackfeet don't show up in a day or two, we'll send someone back to stay with you."

"You lying scum!" George cried. "You will not! You'll leave me here to rot! And I'll be damned if I'll let you get away with it!" Infuriated, he tugged at a flintlock tucked under his belt, but in his feeble state he was unable to move very fast, and had yet to clear the barrel when there was a tremendous boom and his right temple burst outward in a spray of blood and flesh.

"You didn't give me any choice," Galt said, rising. He blew on the smoke curling from the end of his pistol, slid the flintlock under his belt, and grinned at his fellows. "I guess this means we divide up his share among us."

"More money for our pokes," Quince said.

Nate had seen too many men and women killed under much gorier circumstances to be very affected by the death of a murderous renegade trapper. He watched as George's companions stripped everything of value from the body and rolled it into high weeds. Then the cutthroats hastily loaded the stolen peltries onto the packhorses, threw their epishimores and saddles onto their mounts, and put out the fire. The preparations completed, the band gathered around the embers.

"I'm mighty surprised Belker ain't shown up yet," Sterret commented.

"What about it, Galt?" Roarke asked. "Are we going to wait for him or not?"

"You know how he is," Quince said before Galt could answer. "He told us he wasn't coming back until he tracked these two down, so he must still be out there beating the brush."

A suspicious glint lit Galt's gaze as he turned to Nate and the Crow woman. "The two of you wouldn't happen to have seen him, would you?"

"If I did, I'd have killed him," Nate said.

Several of the men laughed. "Kill Belker?" Sterret said. "Mister, the man ain't been born who can best him. He's tougher than a whole pack of Blackfeet and Bloods combined."

"He can take care of himself better than any man alive," Galt said. "So I say we ride on, but leave his horse here for him so he can catch up later."

"Yeah," Roarke said. "If he came back and didn't find his horse, he'd think we deserted him and likely hunt down each and every one of us, no matter how long it took." He paused. "I know that I sure as hell don't want him mad at me."

Even though there were now mounts to spare, Nate and Clay Basket had to ride double, Nate behind Quince, Clay Basket behind Galt. In single file the band moved out, each man leading pack animals. Quince was the last renegade in line, with three packhorses and the black stallion behind him.

Nate had to clamp his legs tight to keep from being thrown as the killers goaded their mounts into a trot and headed eastward through dense woodland. Immediately Nate began working his wrists back and forth, striving to loosen the rope binding them. His arms had been bent so sharply behind his back that his shoulders ached constantly, but he gritted his teeth against the discomfort and persevered.

The rope was terribly tight, chafing Nate's skin with every little movement. He hadn't been at it for five minutes when a trickle of blood ran down his wrist. Regardless, he continued straining and pulling and tugging. Whenever Quince glanced back, Nate froze. In this manner he went on for the better part of the morning, until his wrists and palms were slick with blood and the loops of rope had loosened a fraction.

Galt was canny about the route he took. Avoiding ridges and hills and high slopes, he stuck to the lowlands and the best cover. Plenty of practice had made him a master at avoiding detection, and he did all he could to throw the Blackfeet off the scent, including riding down the middle of a wide stream for over an hour.

Nate kept an eye on the sun. He expected the renegades to call a halt about midday to rest the horses, and he worried they would see the blood on his arms and realize what he had been up to. He had to free himself before they stopped.

In due course a spacious, verdant valley opened out before them. Buffalo grass waved in the wind, and at the far end of the valley was a small herd of mountain buffalo, shaggier counterparts of their brethren on the plains, grazing peacefully.

"Look yonder!" Sterret cried.

"Meat on the hoof," Roarke said. "What do you think, Galt? We haven't had fresh buffler meat in a coon's age. This child is plumb starved for some."

"Have you forgotten about the Blackfeet?" Galt responded.

"Blackfeet, hell," Roarke said. "We can camp over in the

trees and keep our fire low. If we keep our eyes peeled, they won't catch us napping."

Nate was secretly pleased when Galt agreed and the whole party rode to the right into the woods. A suitable clearing was soon found, and leaving Quince to serve as guard, the other three renegades galloped off after the buffalo. Nate contrived to always face the cutthroats so none got a look at his wrists, and as soon as the trio left, he set to work with a vengeance. He was on his knees, close to the pack animals. Beside him, on a stump, sat Clay Basket.

Quince paced back and forth a score of feet away. Now and then he would mutter to himself, often loud enough to be heard. "I don't like this, I don't like this one bit," he was saying. "Now isn't the time to be thinking of our stomachs, not with a war party in the area. No, we should be hightailing it for the Green River. To hell with a bunch of mangy buffalo!"

Nate saw the renegade shift to stare at him, and he stopped moving his arms. When Quince resumed pacing, he resumed the rubbing action that was steadily loosening the rope. By now he had almost a quarter of an inch leeway.

Clay Basket had noticed his efforts. She sat tense with anticipation, and when he looked at her, she smiled encouragement.

Suddenly Quince stopped pacing and came toward them.

Relaxing, Nate sank onto his buttocks and partially twisted his body so that he faced the grubby renegade. He feared Quince was going to check his wrists, but Quince walked on by. Nate twisted further, and almost laughed when the cutthroat rummaged in a parfleche on one of the pack animals and drew out a handful of jerked deer meat. "How about a bite for us?" Nate asked.

"Starve, bastard," Quince responded, taking a hearty bite

as he moved back across the clearing.

Rising on his knees once more, Nate worked harder than ever. He peered through the trees, but saw no sign of the rest of the renegades, who were probably circling around to get up close to the buffalo before firing. More blood dampened his wrists, making the ropes extremely slippery. He yanked hard, trying to wriggle a hand free.

Quince was standing still, staring off across the valley at the herd. "Hurry it up," he grumbled. "It doesn't take all damn day to drop a buffalo."

Inch by gradual inch Nate was freeing his right hand. The rope slowly slid down over the fleshy part hand above his thumb, gouging in deep as it did. Then it caught and wouldn't budge. His arms muscles became cords as he exerted all of his strength. There was excruciating pain and more blood flowed, but seconds later, his hand slipped completely out.

"Damn them," Quince still complained. "I have half a mind to ride off by myself and let them get themselves killed."

Freeing the left hand was easy. Nate flexed his fingers, restoring the circulation. Slowly, he rose into a crouch and padded forward, on the lookout for twigs and dry grass. He had to strike swiftly to prevent the renegade from giving a cry or getting off a shot that would bring the others back on the run.

"Galt is just too cocky," Quince groused. "That's always been his problem. He doesn't know when to stop pushing his luck."

Nate wiped his palms on his leggings as he closed the gap. His weapons had been divided up among the cut-throats, and if he remembered correctly Quince had one of his pistols. In addition, Quince had another pistol, a butcher knife, and a fine Kentucky rifle.

Only six feet separated Nate from the unsuspecting renegade when the unforeseen reared its unwanted head in the form of a chattering squirrel in the trees beyond the horses. One of the pack animals whinnied and shied, which caused Quince to glance over his shoulder. He saw Nate.

"What the hell!"

Nate King took a swift bound and leaped, his arms outstretched. He tackled Quince about the waist just as the cutthroat was bringing the Kentucky rifle to bear, and they both went down. Nate delivered a right to the jaw, or tried to, but his blow was deflected by the rifle barrel. He swung again, managed to connect with a glancing left, and then was rammed in the forehead by the Kentucky's stock. Pinwheels of light flickered before his eyes. Befuddled, he punched wildly. Something smashed him in the stomach, doubling him over, and the following instant he was bucked off and landed on his side.

"You're dead, you son of a bitch!" Quince rasped as he rose on one knee and began to take aim.

Since to lie there was to invite death, Nate did the only thing he could do; he went on the attack, surging up and springing even though he couldn't see the renegade clearly. His shoulder knocked the Kentucky to one side, and his fingers found purchase around Quince's skinny throat. Again they toppled. This time Nate was determined to finish his foe off.

Quince had other ideas. He pounded the Kentucky against Nate's chin, rocking Nate backward, but the fingers gouging into Quince's throat didn't let up. Frantic now, Quince released the rifle and groped at his waist for his knife. A single stroke was all it would take and the fight would be over.

Nate's vision was rapidly clearing. He felt rather than saw Quince's hand groping about under him, and he divined

Quince's intent. Letting go of the cutthroat's neck, he seized Quince's arm and rolled, pulling Quince's hand away from the knife hilt. Fiercely they struggled, Quince to get the knife, Nate to stop him, until changing tactics, Nate made a grab for the knife himself. His fingers closed on the smooth hilt and he began to draw the blade when Quince locked a hand on his wrist, pinning his arm in place.

For such a skinny man, Quince was endowed with exceptional strength. Or perhaps the excitement of the moment lent him more than his normal share. Whichever, he wrested Nate's hand from the knife and shoved, temporarily separating them and giving Quince time to reach for one of the pistols.

Nate lashed out with a knee, catching Quince in the groin. Gurgling, Quince scrambled backward, a hand over his privates. He pulled on the pistol, and almost had the flintlock out when Nate drove his knuckles into Quince's jaw, dazing him. Nate followed through with another fist, and saw the cutthroat go limp.

Thinking Quince was unconscious, Nate caught his breath while slowly rising. The Kentucky rifle lay a few feet away and he stepped over to it and bent down.

"Behind you!"

Clay Basket's yell brought Nate around barely in time. Quince had the knife out and was slashing the blade at his chest. Nate twisted sharply, feeling the keen edge slice into his shirt and nick his skin. His right hand closed on Quince's wrist and they grappled, dancing in a tight circle.

Nate saw his own flintlock on Quince's right hip. Breaking Quince's grasp on his arm, he snatched the pistol, cocking the piece as he did. Quince was elevating the knife for a death stroke.

"Die!"

The shriek ended in a gasp of surprise when Nate jammed

the pistol barrel into the renegade's stomach and squeezed the trigger. The muffled retort was no louder than a hand clap. Quince stiffened, whined, and clutched at himself.

Nate pushed to his feet and claimed the rifle. Another shot, however, wasn't in order as Quince was in the midst of his death throes, convulsing and blubbering as spittle frothed his lips. His wild gaze roved the clearing and settled on Nate.

"You . . . You . . ."

Whatever the cutthroat intended to say would remain a mystery. Exhaling all the air in his lungs, Quince wordlessly moved his lips, his fingers formed into claws, and he died.

Nate checked for a pulse to be certain. Once he was, he scooped up the knife, hurried to Clay Basket, and cut her loose. "Thanks for the warning."

"Did the others hear the shot?"

If they had, Nate had no way of knowing, for a survey of the lower end of the valley revealed only the buffalo. The renegades were still hidden in the trees. "You have to leave now," he advised. "Take Quince's horse and head west."

"What about you?"

"I have a score to settle."

"Not alone."

"There's a time and a place for being stubborn and this isn't it," Nate said, taking her elbow and propelling her toward the mounts. "I can't fight them and worry about you at the same time."

"You have done much for me, Grizzly Killer. I will not leave you when you need my help."

"What about Nelson?" Nate tried a new tack. "He needs you too, more than I do. He needs doctoring real bad. Head on back to where you saw him last and lend my friends a hand."

"No," Clay Basket said, digging in her heels.

"Damn it all," Nate huffed. "I don't want you hurt."

"I am staying."

Arguing was a luxury Nate could ill afford since he had no idea of how soon the other renegades would show up. "All right," he said in compromise, "you can stay provided you keep low while I do what needs doing."

"Give me a gun and I will fight alongside you."

"You'll do no such thing." Nate walked to Quince and retrieved the butcher knife and Quince's powder horn and ammo pouch. He reloaded the spent pistol, then verified the second flintlock and the Kentucky were loaded. Armed to the teeth, he stepped to the horses and cut the black stallion loose. The whole time Clay Basket anxiously watched him.

"I am Crow, not Osage," she mentioned, referring to a tribe whose members were notoriously inept at fighting. "I have fought the Blackfeet and the Sioux when they raided our village. I am no coward."

"Never claimed you were," Nate responded. "But these are whites. I'm white. We'll let it go at that." He swung up and wheeled the stallion, but could go no further because she blocked his path.

"For the last time," Clay Basket pleaded.

A jab of Nate's heels, a flick of the reins, and he was past her and crossing the clearing. He drew up halfway across to look around. She hadn't moved. "Get on Quince's horse and go off into the brush. If I go down, you know what to do."

"You lied, Grizzly Killer."

"What?"

"Your skin is white but inside you are one of us."

Those words rang in Nate's ears as he rode to the edge of the trees. At last he spied one of the renegades, the man named Sterret, creeping through the grass at the far end of the valley toward the two dozen or so buffalo. Evidently the cutthroats had circled completely around the herd to get between the hulking brutes and the nearest forest. That way, if the buffalo spooked, they'd be able to drop one or two before the herd reached cover.

Nate brought the stallion to a gallop, hugging the tree line. He hoped Galt and Roarke were also in the high grass. In one fell swoop he could wipe out all three if they didn't spot him first.

A tall bull on the west flank of the herd lifted its huge head to stare at the still-distant stallion. The bull showed no alarm and stood munching on the sweet grass.

Bending low so his outline would blend into that of the horse, Nate whipped the stallion to go faster. Buffalo were unpredictable creatures, like grizzlies. Sometimes they'd flee at the drop of a feather, while at other times they'd belligerently stand their ground against all comers. They were less likely to flee from men on horseback if they couldn't see the men, no doubt because they had no ingrained fear of horses. This was why many Indians had learned to swing onto the sides of their mounts as they approached herds and then rear up at the last instant to loose their arrows, thus taking their quarry unawares.

Nate intended to do the same. He rode another hundred yards along the edge of the trees, shifted onto the off-side of the stallion, and broke into the open, making straight for the herd. Peeking past the animal's neck, he could see more and more of the buffalo staring at the onrushing horse. None displayed any alarm, yet.

A buffalo was a massive engine of destruction. Standing six feet high at the shoulders, weighing well over a thousand pounds in many instances, and endowed with wicked, curved horns boasting a spread of three feet, it was capable of bowling over and goring a horse or a man with equal ease. Multiply that by dozens, or hundreds, or many thousands, and it was understandable why anything or anyone that got in the path of a fleeing herd was reduced to so much pulp and broken bone.

Nate was counting on this particular herd to do the job he had to do for him. He galloped ever nearer, until he was within 30 yards of the foremost bull. Then, straightening, he vented a series of piercing war whoops that would have done justice to a full-blooded Shoshone. Simultaneously he waved his rifle and flapped his arms.

The effect on the herd was instantaneous. As one the mighty beasts spun and fled, their heavy hoofs pounding the ground in a thunderous staccato beat. Bulls, cows, and calves alike sped eastward as if the valley was on fire and flames nipped at their tails.

Beyond the herd, Sterret leaped erect. Panic lined his features as he whirled and raced toward the sanctuary of the forest, but he was closer to the buffalo than the trees and the buffalo were much faster than he was. He glanced back repeatedly, his eyes wide, his mouth agape, and when it became apparent the herd would be upon him in the next few seconds, he turned and fired at the nearest animal, a large bull. The single shot had no effect.

Nate saw Sterret throw up his arms, heard the man's wavering scream. The renegade tried to dodge the bull but failed, and he screamed louder as a slashing horn ripped into his stomach and he was hurled high into the air. Sterret came down on his back directly in front of a compact mass of buffalo. A final scream was torn from his throat just as he disappeared under their flailing hooves.

Eagerly Nate scanned the grass, hoping both Galt and Roarke would be caught in the stampede. He spotted a figure in the trees, fleeing toward a waiting horse, but couldn't tell which one of them it was. The horse panicked and ran, stranding the figure, who quickly darted to a nearby tree and began climbing with the alacrity of a squirrel. Moments later the herd swept by, snapping saplings and flattening brush. The thin tree swayed as the man clung for dear life.

Nate was 50 yards out when the tree broke and went down. There was no sound from the man as he fell. The clouds of dust being raised by the buffalo prevented Nate from seeing whether the renegade had been trampled. He rode to the tree line and leaped off while the stallion was still in motion, diving behind the trunk of a pine.

By now the herd was lost in the maze of trees, but the diminishing din of their passage told of their continued flight. Nate covered his mouth to keep from coughing as the dust settled around him. He focused on the spot where the renegade had gone down, but could see no body.

Cautiously, Nate worked his way forward, going from trunk to trunk. The odds were still against him and he had to have eyes in the back of his head if he wanted to stay alive. Galt and Roarke would slay him on sight.

Suddenly a rifle cracked, the lead ball smacking into the trunk inches from Nate's head. He went prone, saw puffs of gunsmoke off to the right, and twisted to aim. A buckskin-clad figure appeared for just a heartbeat, then was gone.

Nate changed position too, dashing to another tree, one with a wider trunk. His eyes raked the undergrowth to no avail. A glance back confirmed he was safe from that direction, for the moment at least.

A hint of motion near a boulder heralded another sharp retort. This time slivers stung Nate's cheek and he ducked down, the Kentucky pressed to his shoulder. But whoever had fired had vanished.

Easing onto his stomach, Nate crawled to his right, closer to the boulder rather than away from it. He slanted behind a waist-high bush and paused to scour the general vicinity. About 25 yards off a man materialized next to a tree. It was Roarke, and he was staring at the spot Nate had just vacated. Nate slowly brought the Kentucky rifle up. The .40-caliber rifle was less powerful than his Hawken, but a bit more accurate at longer ranges thanks to its longer barrel. At this close distance, aligning the front and rear sights was child's play. Nate took a bead on the center of Roarke's chest, and when the cutthroat leaned a bit further out to look for him, he gently stroked the trigger.

Roarke toppled backward, the rifle he held flying. He crashed onto his back, tried to stand, and collapsed.

Drawing his pistol, Nate sprinted across the intervening space, then halted as Roarke attempted again to rise. Roarke spotted him and made as if to draw a flintlock. "Don't!" Nate warned.

But Roarke paid no heed. His hand was closing on his pistol when Nate's pistol blasted and a second ball cored his chest, knocking him flat. Coughing uncontrollably, he spat blood and feebly tried to sit up.

Several rapid strides brought Nate to the cutthroat. He slammed down a foot on Roarke's pistol, pinning the gun to the ground. There were two holes in the renegade's chest, side by side, from which crimson stream poured. Roarke tried to speak but produced only a strangled whisper. "Where's Galt?" Nate demanded.

"Go . . . to . . . hell," Roarke croaked, and died, vindictive to the last.

Nate lowered into a crouch and picked up the rifle Roarke had dropped, which was his own Hawken. He checked it, set down the Kentucky, and commenced reloading his pistol, all the while gazing around about him. There was still Galt to deal with, and he had to be ready.

Total silence shrouded the forest. The buffalo were long gone, and the birds and lesser creatures had either fled or sought shelter in their burrows or elsewhere.

For the time being Nate left the Kentucky and Roarke's other weapons where they were and moved into the brush. Taking a seat on a log, he waited and listened, confident that if Galt was sneaking up on him, he would detect the renegade first. But there were no sounds to be heard; there was no movement anywhere. Close to ten minutes went by, and the only thing Nate saw was a solitary butterfly fluttering among some flowers.

Standing, Nate warily advanced to the edge of the high grass. He entertained the notion that Galt must have been trampled along with Sterret, and with that in mind he moved into the open seeking Galt's body. Hoofprints and droppings were everywhere. Wide tracts of grass had been crushed flat by the stampede, making his search a bit easier.

Presently Nate came on Sterret, or what was left of the renegade. As he stood staring down at an eyeball that was being swarmed over by ants, he caught a faint glint of sunlight on metal out of his right eye. Nate spun, bending at the knees as he did. There was the bang of a rifle and a hornet buzzed his ear. He promptly replied in kind.

To the south, 60 yards away, Ira Galt was perched in the low fork of a mountain alder. At the crack of the Hawken a scarlet spray gushed from the back of his skull and he threw out his arms in involuntary reflex. Slowly he did an ungainly pirouette. Then his foot slipped and he plummeted to the earth. He made no effort to rise, not even when a small leaf, dislodged by his fall, fluttered from above and landed in his open mouth.

Nate King saw the leaf when he reached the body. "You're

the one who got off too easy," he said gruffly as he took Galt's weapons and turned to go. Then he paused. "This is for all those you butchered." Drawing back his right leg, he kicked Galt full in the face. "May you rot in hell."

Epilogue

Nate King and Clay Basket spent the rest of the day riding westward. They were only a few miles past the basin when they met Pepin, sent ahead by a very worried Shakespeare McNair to see how Nate was faring. Nate asked Pepin to bring the pack animals and pushed on, relying once again on the Comanche trick of often changing horses to cover the miles swiftly. It was well after midnight when a small fire in the narrow valley came into view.

Clay Basket was first on the ground. Her face aglow, she ran to the man lying by the fire and threw her arms around him, tears flowing down her smooth cheeks as she smothered him with kisses.

Tim Nelson had been sleeping. He awoke with a start, saw who was holding him, and added his tears of joy to hers.

"You're alive, my love!" Clay Basket declared.

"And he'll stay that way, if you don't squeeze him to death," Shakespeare McNair said, grinning. "That man of yours has an iron constitution. That and the herbs I've given him have pulled him through. He'll be laid up for quite a spell, but he'll be good as new in time."

"Thank you," Clay Basket said, gazing warmly at the grizzled mountain man, then at Nate, on whom her eyes lingered. "For everything."

MOUNTAIN CAT

To Judy, Joshua, and Shane.

Chapter One

They came silently out of the night, gliding through the dense pine trees to encircle the small clearing where the two men had made their camp. In the glow cast by the crackling fire, only their eyes were visible, fierce crimson slits that lent them the aspect of disembodied demons.

"We have company," announced the older of the two trappers, a grizzled mountain man by the name of Shakespeare McNair. Picking up one of the broken branches collected earlier, he placed it in the flames.

The second man, who was busily honing his long butcher knife, glanced up and scanned the ring of red eyes. "So I see," he said, not at all concerned by the feral arrivals. This man was much younger than the first, much broader of shoulder and with more rippling muscles packed on his hardened frame. Nathaniel King wagged his knife at the newcomers and added, "Should we throw them what's left of our supper?"

"Not unless you want to go hungry tomorrow,"

Shakespeare responded while jabbing a thumb at the pot containing the remainder of their rabbit stew. "That there is breakfast. Let the mangy varmints hunt for their food, like we had to do." Twisting, he cupped a hand to his mouth and bellowed, "Go find someone else to bother!"

None of the eyes so much as blinked.

"Let them watch us if they want," Nate chided. "More often than not, wolves are harmless."

"But not always, as you well know," Shakespeare said. He touched his left shin. "I still have a nasty scar from the time a wolf attacked me when I was toting a dead doe to my cabin."

"I've tangled with them too, on occasion," Nate admitted. "But if this pack doesn't bother me, I won't bother them."

"Getting right peaceable in your young age, are you?" Shakespeare asked, grinning.

"I just see no need to cause trouble where there is none," Nate said. "All I care about is getting this trapping season over with so I can see my family again."

"Spoken like the good husband that you are."

"Are you poking fun at me?"

"Would I do that?" Shakespeare rejoined innocently, and chuckled. "It's just that this old coon isn't hog-tied by apron strings, as are some men I could mention. It doesn't do me any harm to get away by my lonesome every now and then."

"You're trying to get my goat," Nate said, "and it won't work. You, of all people, should know that being in love isn't the same as being hog-tied."

"That depends on the woman," Shakespeare said. "Some wives dig their claws into their men and don't let their husbands so much as breathe without their permission. Others, the smart ones, put their men on a longer leash."

Nate lowered his whetstone and said, "This from the man who is always quoting from *Romeo and Juliet*?"

"You should pay more attention when I do," Shakespeare said, giving a beaded parfleche at his elbow an affectionate pat. In it was the thick volume that had earned McNair his nickname, a book containing the collected works of the Bard of Avon. Shakespeare could recite his namesake by the hour and was often called on by fellow trappers starved for entertainment to do just that. "Here's a quote you must have missed," he commented and coughed to clear his throat. " 'Alas, that love, so gentle in his view, should be so tyrannous and rough in proof!' "

"Shakespeare said that?"

"Old William S. was a heap wiser than most folks give him credit for being."

"Maybe so," Nate said, "but I have a hard time understanding him. It's a shame he couldn't have written in plain English."

"Plain English?" Shakespeare repeated, his eyes sparkling with building mirth. "Where do you think he was from? Spain?"

Nate sighed and touched the edge of his knife to the whetstone. He had been all through this discussion with his mentor before, and he wasn't about to let himself be drawn into another lengthy debate over McNair's literary passion. As he resumed sharpening the blade, he idly glanced to his right and felt the short hairs at the nape of his neck prickle.

A pair of fiery eyes had left the ring of wolves and was moving toward the tethered mounts and pack animals.

In a flash Nate was on his feet and racing to a point

between the advancing wolf and the horses. He slid the whetstone into his possibles bag, draped a hand on one of the flintlocks wedged under his wide brown leather belt, and faced the oncoming predator. "Go away!" he shouted, motioning with his knife hand.

The wolf slowed briefly, then crept nearer. In the forest beyond, others, made bold by the first, were slinking closer.

"I don't like this," Nate muttered.

Shakespeare had risen. "They must be awful hungry."

"Maybe they have a taste for horseflesh," Nate remarked, drawing his pistol. The metallic click of the hammer sounded eerily loud in the dreadful stillness.

"Don't shoot unless you have no other choice," Shakespeare advised. "If you hurt one, the rest will be on us like crazed banshees." Stooping, he grabbed his rifle in one hand and the end of a burning branch in the other. "I'll try to scare them off."

"Be careful."

"Don't fret yourself. I don't intend to end my days in a wolf's belly." Shakespeare waved the firebrand in circles and strode purposefully toward the oncoming wolf. In the flaring radius of light, the beast became clearly visible. It was the apparent leader of the pack, an enormous male sporting a black mask and unusual white markings on its forelegs. The wolf crouched and retreated a few yards, glaring balefully at the firebrand over its shoulder.

"You've got it on the run," Nate said, but, as it developed the very next moment, he had spoken prematurely.

Venting a guttural growl, the leader of the pack suddenly whirled and charged straight at the horse string, streaking across the ground so fast its hairy body was a virtual blur.

Nate instantly fired. In his haste, he missed. The wolf was almost abreast of him, so he took a quick step to the left and slashed with his gleaming knife, causing the pack leader to veer wide. As it did, a rifle boomed and the wolf tumbled. Nate moved in, prepared to dispatch the creature before it could stand. A chorus of snarls stopped him in his tracks.

The majority of the wolves were converging on the camp, their lips drawn back to expose their tapered teeth, their features alight with ferocity.

Dropping the spent pistol, Nate drew his other flint-lock, took a hurried bead on a large specimen, and fired almost at the very same moment that Shakespeare fired a pistol. Two wolves crashed down, one to lie motionless, the other to rise again and limp off.

At the twin blasts, most of the wolves broke off their attack and bolted into the woods. The rest began to circle, seeking an opening.

Nate wanted to reload but feared being set upon while doing so. His Hawken was over by the fire, too far off, for if he ran to retrieve it the poor horses would be unprotected. Instead, he shoved the second pistol under his belt and whipped out his Shoshone tomahawk.

Three wolves were still circling. One darted in close and then darted out into the darkness again, as if daring them to do something or testing their reactions.

Backpedaling to the agitated horses, Nate tried to keep all three wolves in sight at once. A set of eyes disappeared off to his right. Expecting the beast to sneak through an adjacent thicket, Nate dashed to its edge and crouched to peer into the dense vegetation.

McNair, meanwhile, had his hands full with the other two, both of which were padding warily toward the horses but each from a different direction. He had his second pistol out and cocked, and covered first one wolf and then the other, waiting to shoot whichever charged first. If they both charged simultaneously, one was bound to reach the string. Given that wolves regularly hunted large game such as elk and deer and knew how to bring their quarry down by severing leg muscles and tendons, one of the horses might wind up hamstrung, or worse. And every horse was essential. He stepped lightly toward the string, his every nerve tingling.

Over in the thicket, something stirred. Nate tensed, bracing for the rush certain to come. When it did, the wolf sprang with such lightning speed that all Nate could do was bring his tomahawk up to keep the wolf's slavering jaws from closing on his face. Together, they fell backward, the wolf in a frenzy of thwarted blood lust, snapping again and again at Nate's throat. By a sheer fluke, Nate had jammed his forearm under the wolf's chin. He held the beast at bay long enough to bury his knife in the creature's side, the blade spearing in between the wolf's ribs. The wolf yelped and leaped back, almost tearing Nate's arm from its socket. Dripping blood, the knife slipped free. Before Nate could stab a second time, the wolf whirled and fled.

Shakespeare had heard the commotion and glanced around in alarm. To him, Nate King was more like the son he'd never had than just another free trapper, and while he would never admit as much to anyone, he'd gladly sacrifice his own life for the younger man's should the need ever arise. He saw Nate go down and took a few steps towards him. Then he glimpsed one of the wolves racing toward the horses. Pivoting, he snapped off a shot that appeared to strike the wolf in the leg. The wolf went down in a whirl of limbs and tail but bounded up and off without missing a beat. The last wolf followed.

"Nate?" Shakespeare said, running over as the younger man stood. "Are you hurt?"

"No, but it was close," Nate said. "Too close for comfort." His blood pumped madly in his veins and his temples were pounding. He had to clench his fists to keep his fingers from shaking.

"They're gone," Shakespeare announced, surveying the benighted forest. "They were hungry, but not that hungry."

"Hungry enough," Nate grumbled, turning to the horses. His black stallion was the calmest of the bunch, standing with ears pricked and nostrils flaring. The others, including McNair's white mare, whinnied and fidgeted, some pulling at their ropes. Nate moved among them, speaking soft, soothing words and stroking a neck where needed.

Shakespeare was busy reloading his pistols. "We were darned lucky, son. I told you we should have scared those devils off the moment they showed. You'd think that you'd know enough to heed me after all this time."

"Between you and my wife, I should never have to make another decision again," Nate said sarcastically.

" 'Oh, let it not be so! Herein you war against your reputation, and draw within the compass of suspect the unviolated honor of your wife. Once this—your long experience of her wisdom, her sober virtue, years, and modesty, plead on her part some cause to you unknown.' "

"They call it love."

Shakespeare beamed. "I knew you understood old William S. better than you've been letting on."

Their banter was cut short by a piercing howl to the north of their camp, more a wavering wail of despair than the mournful cry so typical of wolves.

"It's one of those we wounded," the mountain man declared.

"We should put it out of its misery."

"It would be downright foolish to go traipsing off through the brush in the dead of night just to finish off a critter that's going to die soon anyway."

Another fluttering wail pierced the night and echoed off the mountains bordering the valley in which they were camped. Many of the peaks were pale, ghostly crags sheathed in white sheets of snow.

"I'll go," Nate proposed.

"We should both stay here," Shakespeare insisted.

"I won't let anyone or anything suffer because of me. It won't take but a few minutes to find the animal and put a ball in its brain."

"What if it still has some fight left? Or there are others still in the vicinity?" Shakespeare shook his head. "You'd be taking too great a risk for no good reason. Let's just sit back down and finish our coffee."

As if to contradict him, the wolf cried a third time, louder and longer than before, a great, sad, pitiable sound that caused Nate's skin to erupt in goose bumps. He went to where his Hawken was propped on his saddle, scooped up the rifle, and headed for the gloomy woods.

"You're being a dunderhead," Shakespeare commented.

"Force of habit," Nate responded, trying to sound carefree and cheery when in fact there were butterflies flitting about in his stomach. A fourth howl drew him into the murk beyond. He proceeded cautiously, bent at the waist with the Hawken tucked to his shoulder, ready for anything.

"If you need help, holler!" Shakespeare called out.

Nate didn't answer. The wolf would hear and know he

was coming. His thumb rested lightly on the Hawken's hammer as he skirted a spruce, passed a boulder, and ducked under a low limb. Away from the fire, the darkness was nearly total. Once his eyes adjusted, his sight would improve a little, but that would take a minute or two.

The undergrowth crackled off to Nate's left and his first thought was that Shakespeare had been right and some of the pack had lingered and were stalking him. Crouching, he waited for whatever was making the noise to appear. To his relief, the animal went the other way and the sounds soon tapered to silence.

Hoping for another howl to guide him, Nate continued deeper into the forest. He set each foot down delicately, as if walking on eggshells, the smooth soles of his moccasins pressing soundlessly onto the thick mat of fallen pine needles that carpeted the earth. His buckskins and his beaver hat blended well into the shadows, making him hard to detect. Unless he blundered, he figured he should be able spot the wounded wolf before it spotted him.

Not ten seconds later, Nate did. He had paused beside an evergreen and leaned against the trunk while scouring the rugged terrain ahead. At the limits of his vision something moved, something low to the ground. Focusing on it, he distinguished a lone wolf crawling on its stomach. From the size of the silhouette, he judged it to be none other than the huge leader of the pack.

Bracing the Hawken against the bole, Nate sighted carefully. Just as he did, the wolf reached high grass and vanished. Thwarted, Nate angled to intercept the beast. At the edge of the grass he stopped, expecting the wolf to soon show itself. Yet time went by, and other than the wind rustling the grass and the leaves of nearby aspens, there was no hint of movement anywhere.

Eager to get back to camp, Nate impatiently crawled into the grass. He held the Hawken in front of him, his palms clammy where they contacted wood or metal. Perhaps, he told himself, Shakespeare had also been right about something else—the stupidity of trying to end the misery of an enraged wild beast that would rip him to shreds without hesitation if it could.

Nate advanced slowly, parting the long stems with his rifle barrel. Even though the crisp mountain air was cool, his brow became dotted with perspiration. His mouth, by contrast, was exceptionally dry. He covered six feet without incident. Eight feet. Ten.

Suddenly a black shape hurtled out of the grass on Nate's left. Twisting, he tried to bring the Hawken to bear but the wolf was on him before he could shoot, its heavy body knocking the rifle aside. Razor-sharp teeth sought his throat. Nate just managed to clamp both hands on the creature's neck as he was bowled onto his back. His shoulders straining mightily, he held the wolf at bay, barely able to retain his grip as the beast snarled and snapped and thrashed.

Drops of saliva fell onto Nate's face. He could feel blood on his fingers and he worried they would become slick and he'd lose his grip. Claws raked his right leg, lancing his body with pain. Nate rammed his knees into the animal's belly, then kicked upward while at the same time he heaved with all his strength. He succeeded in flipping the wolf from him.

Scrambling upright, Nate drew both his knife and his tomahawk a split-second before the wolf closed on him again. It came at his legs but swerved when he tried to cleave its skull with the tomahawk. Rumbling deep in its chest, the wolf then circled him. There was a dark stain on its side but the wound seemed to be having no effect.

Nate had his knife extended and held the tomahawk close to his right shoulder. He turned as the animal circled, always keeping his eyes on it. Somewhere in the nearby grass was his rifle, but he dared not look for it, dared not lower his guard for a moment.

The wolf abruptly sagged, then shook its head and straightened. Apparently the loss of blood was having an effect, but not swiftly enough to suit Nate. He took a gamble and lunged, the tip of his knife catching the wolf on the shoulder as it leaped aside. Incensed, the beast sprang at Nate's legs, and Nate arced the tomahawk at its skull. Exhibiting uncanny reflexes, the wolf evaded the blow and resumed circling.

Nate wanted to kick himself for not taking the time to reload his pistols. How many times had he told his son to never, ever venture into the wild with unloaded weapons? How many times had he pointed out that such forgetfulness could prove fatal? Yet here he'd gone and done the same thing. Sometimes he wondered if he had rocks for brains.

The wolf abruptly charged, and Nate, preoccupied with his thoughts instead of paying attention, jumped to one side too late. He heard the crunch of the wolf's teeth as its jaws closed on his leggings, heard the buckskin tear as the wolf tore into him. Twisting, he speared his butcher knife into its side. The predator jerked back and vented a yelp. Tripping over its own feet, it went down. Nate promptly took a stride, raised the tomahawk on high, and drove it deep into the wolf's skull, connecting as the wolf was in the act of rising. Its head split wide, like a furry cantaloupe. Blood and gore sprayed out.

Nate let go of the tomahawk and sank to one knee.

His pulse was racing again, and he took a minute to calm himself down while observing the wolf's death throes. When the animal finally lay still, he pulled out both the knife and the tomahawk, then wiped them clean on the beast's hide. "You were a tough one," he said softly, standing.

The northwesterly breeze picked up, cooling Nate's brow. Replacing his weapons, he searched until he found the Hawken. Next he stooped, lifted the wolf, and draped its body over his left shoulder. Then he turned his footsteps toward the flickering glow of the fire.

Shakespeare was seated on his blankets, his rifle resting across his legs. He smiled when he saw Nate approaching and lifted his tin cup in a salute. "Well done, son. I was getting a mite worried." His gaze fixed on the wolf. "What do you intend to do with the carcass?"

"Skin it and give the pelt to Winona," Nate said. "Zach has been pestering her for a new hat."

"Had me one made from wolf hide once," the older man mentioned. "It didn't shed water good enough to suit me." Reaching up, he ran a hand over the beaver hat crowning his white hair. It was a perfect match for Nate's own headpiece, except that Shakespeare's wasn't adorned with an eagle feather. "There's nothing like beaver for keeping a man warm and dry."

"True enough," Nate agreed, setting the wolf down next to their supplies. He squatted to examine the tear in his pants and a small cut on his leg. "Any sign of the others?"

"Nope. They high-tailed it elsewhere, and good riddance." Shakespeare nodded at the horses. "If we'd lost them, we'd be up the creek without a paddle."

"I just hope this new territory is all you claim it is," Nate said.

"Would I lie to you?" Shakespeare said indignantly. "I'm telling you the country is crawling with beaver. No white men have been there yet, so we don't have to worry about the streams being trapped out."

"There's a good reason no white men have been there," Nate noted. "It's too close to Blood hunting grounds for anyone to take the risk."

"If we keep our eyes skinned, we should be all right."

Nate hoped so. Dealing with hostile Indians was part and parcel of a trapper's life, but it was a part he could do without. In addition to the Bloods, there were a dozen other tribes that hated all whites; they regarded trappers as invaders deserving torture and death. If the Bloods took him by surprise, he'd suffer a lingering, terrible death.

"Besides," McNair had gone on, "the Bloods should be out on the prairie hunting buffalo at this time of year. It's been a long, hard winter so they're probably low on jerky and pemmican and such. They need a lot of fresh meat and new hides for their lodges. It'll be late Spring or Summer before they move back into the mountains."

"You hope."

Shakespeare arched an eyebrow. "If I'd known you were turning into such a worrier, I would have come alone." He paused. "It's not like you. Why are you so bothered? We've trapped in dangerous territory plenty of times."

"I know," Nate said, shifting to stare northward at a range. "I have a feeling, is all. A bad feeling."

"Bah! You're imagining things! Being a homebody has turned you into a milksop."

"I hope that's all it is," Nate said sincerely, although deep down he wasn't so sure. Was it the chill wind, or was it something else that caused an anxious ripple to course down his spine?

Only time would tell.

Chapter Two

Nate King had an abiding passion for the Rocky Mountains. Ever since he'd initially set foot in them, he'd been entranced by their pristine beauty. The towering, regal peaks, the stark, barren crags, the magnificent forested slopes, verdant valleys, and crystal streams had stirred his soul as no other landscape ever had. And he found that as time went on, to his surprise, he didn't tire of the stirring scenery. Rather, he became even more enamored of the wilderness. He considered it his home, and he would never leave it.

The Rockies always reflected the changing seasons more drastically than Nate's home state of New York ever had. In the fall the aspens glimmered with brilliant hues of red, orange, and yellow, and the grass turned a deep brown. In the winter a white mantle invariably covered everything, lending the terrain a pure, virgin aspect. In the spring, when Nature rekindled the spark of life in the dormant plants and animals, the mountains came alive with all manner of wild creatures and the vegetation flourished. Trees budded and turned green, flowers sprouted and displayed their various beautiful shades, birds chirped gaily, squirrels and chipmunks chattered, and insects buzzed about their daily business.

Paradise on earth, Nate reflected as he wound down a steep slope into the valley where Shakespeare was going to set traps. He could see a wide blue stream half a mile or so off, and grazing near it were a number of elk. Overhead, among pillowy clouds, an eagle soared. To the west, a hawk crested a rocky spire. Sparrows flitted in a fir tree mere yards away. Nate inhaled the pine scented air and smiled in delight.

"No Indian sign anywhere," Shakespeare commented. "We'll have the region all to ourselves."

Nate simply nodded. A boulder the size of a wagon barred his path so he swung to the right, hauling on the lead rope when the foremost pack horse balked. They each had three pack animals, only one of which was burdened with their provisions and traps. The other two would be used later to transport bales of peltries to their cabins.

"It was Broken Paw who told me about this area," Shakespeare said, referring to a Flathead Indian they both knew. "He'd been up here last year hunting and noticed all the beaver dams."

"If there are as many beaver as he claims, when we get back I should give him a gift to show my thanks."

"Don't bother. That crafty coyote already got a knife and some ammo from me for his fusee, as well as a lot of foofaraw and a new blanket for his wife." Shakespeare snickered. "The man drives a hard bargain."

Presently, they came to the valley floor supplies where

Mountain Cat

Nate spied a game trail and rode along it toward the stream. In the dank earth were imprinted a variety of deep tracks; deer, elk, mountain buffalo, and a fresh set of gigantic prints that caused him to draw rein in consternation. "Grizzly!" he exclaimed.

"Damn. The last thing I want is to get in a racket with one of those monsters."

"That makes two of us," Nate said grimly. By a curious quirk of Fate, it had been his misfortune to tangle with the savage bears frequently. So often, in fact, his bad luck had become a running joke among the trapping fraternity. Nor was his reputation in that regard any better among friendly Indians. Long ago he had been given the name of Grizzly Killer by a Cheyenne who had witnessed his clash with one of the vicious bruins, and now the Shoshones, Flatheads, Crows and other tribes all knew him by that name.

Nate goaded the stallion forward while alertly scanning the valley. He guessed the bear had passed that way sometime since dawn, sometime in the past three hours. It might be long gone. Or it might be hidden in a thicket, dozing. Since grizzlies were prone to attack without warning, he studied the nearest coppices with extra vigilance.

The tracks ended at the stream. Here the bear had either waded to the east or west and the swiftly flowing water had erased all prints.

"Too bad," Shakespeare said. "I was hoping to find out which way the damn thing went."

"We could follow the stream until we find where it came out."

"Why go looking to have our innards ripped out?" Shakespeare said, dismounting. "Leave a grizzly alone and nine times out of ten it'll leave you alone." He glanced up at Nate and grinned. "For most people that's how it works. In your case, grizzlies go out of their way to show you just how nasty they can be. Must be your scent."

"My what?"

"Your scent." Shakespeare stepped to the water's edge, cupped his palm, swallowed a mouthful, and smacked his lips. "Animals have a keen sense of smell. You know that. Some can scent prey a long ways off. Most, when they smell man, head for the hills. But maybe you're special. Maybe there's something about your odor that draws grizzlies like flowers draw bees."

Nate threw back his head and roared. "That has to be the craziest notion you've ever had!"

"Stranger things have happened," Shakespeare said, unruffled. "There are more things in heaven and earth, Horatio, than are dreamt of in your philosophy."

"I don't smell any different from anyone else."

"Care to make a wager?" Shakespeare countered. "The next time you're in a crowded lodge on a hot day, take a few sniffs. See if everyone has the exact same scent or whether they all smell differently."

"I'm not about to go around sticking my nose in armpits to prove you wrong."

"Suit yourself."

Nate slid from the saddle and let his stallion and the pack horses drink. He saw a large fish swimming further out and was tempted to rummage in his pack for his line and hook. But the day was still young and he had a long ride ahead of him if he wanted to reach the next valley before nightfall. "Any idea where you'll make up camp?" he casually inquired.

McNair jabbed a thumb to the west. "I'll set up a lean-to in the trees where hostile eyes won't be likely to spot it." He regarded the gurgling water a moment. "Shouldn't take more than five or six weeks to work a stream this size."

"How about if we meet right at this spot in six weeks then?" Nate suggested.

The mountain man scratched his bushy beard. "Sounds fine, but I still think you should let me take the next valley and you should take this one."

"I lost the toss."

"There's a certain knack to flipping a coin," Shakespeare joked, doing a poor job of concealing his misgivings. "I wouldn't mind switching."

Nate suspected why his mentor was making an issue of a matter already decided. The farther north they went, the closer they would be to Blood territory. "You won fair and square," he reiterated, "so you get to trap this stream and all its branches." To forestall an argument, he stepped into the stirrups and gripped the reins. "Shoot sharps the word."

"Same to you," Shakespeare said rather begrudgingly. "And hold onto that hair of yours."

Bobbing his chin, Nate departed. He jabbed his heels into the stallion and rapidly crossed to the opposite bank. The last pack horse slipped and almost fell but was able to dig in its hoofs and lurch onto firm footing. With a wave, Nate turned his back on his friend and was soon surrounded by woods.

Parting brought a degree of melancholy. Nate liked being with his mentor, liked the company of others. As fond as he was of the mountains, of the remote recesses where few men had ever trod, he wasn't one of those trappers who could go a year or two without seeing another living soul. He wasn't the kind who would rather frolic with wild creatures than with other human beings.

David Thompson

Give Nate his loving family all snug in their sturdy cabin and he was as happy as the proverbial lark. Venturing into parts unknown was exciting, but it was just another aspect to the line of work he had chosen, to the everyday life of a free trapper. Had he been able to collect all the peltries he needed just by walking out his door to the nearest body of water, he would have been perfectly content. But he couldn't. He had to do as other trappers did and seek out the haunts of the beaver.

Once, many years ago, before beaver fur became all the rage in Europe and the States, beaver had existed in great abundance, their lodges decorating every stream of any fair size the length and breadth of the vast Rocky Mountains. Then came the fashion craze and the influx of fur men eager to make their fortunes in the fledgling market. Before long, to the dismay of many Indian tribes, the beaver in wide areas were trapped to extinction.

Now, much to Nate's displeasure, it became harder and harder every season for him to find enough beaver to suit his needs. Every time he went out, he had to travel farther and farther afield, into areas others hadn't thought to penetrate yet, into areas where the risks were higher than he liked.

This particular venture was a case in point. Ordinarily, Nate would have shunned the region he was entering as if the land itself was infested with the plague. He had no inclination to tangle with the Bloods or their allies in the dreaded confederacy that controlled the northern Rockies and plains, the Blackfoot confederacy as it was known since that tribe was its leading member. United with the Piegans, the Bloods and Blackfeet held sway over an area larger than most States, fiercely resisting the influx of whites by exterminating every trapper they encountered.

Mountain Cat

There were no exceptions to the rule. There were no white men who had been caught and let go again as an act of mercy on the part of the confederacy. If you were white and you fell into the hands of either tribe, you were as good as dead. Every trapper knew it, and every trapper stayed clear of the territory the confederacy claimed as its own.

Even other tribes did the same. The Blackfeet, Bloods, and Piegans were three of the most warlike tribes in all creation. They made ceaseless war on the Crows, the Shoshones, the Flatheads, the Sioux, the Utes. In short, on anyone and everyone who wasn't Blackfoot, Blood, or Piegan. A man might fault their bloodthirsty natures, but there was no denying they slaughtered their enemies fairly, without regard to race or disposition.

Nate had fought warriors from all three tribes on occasion, and the thought of doing so again was enough to cause him to gnaw nervously on his lower lip. A lesser man would have refused to trap in the region they were working. But Nate, despite his reservations, hadn't batted an eye when Shakespeare proposed doing so. Nate had his family to think of. And himself, too. It was his belief that a man did whatever was needed to improve the welfare of those for whom he cared, and if that meant traveling into an area where he was just as likely to lose his life to a wandering grizzly or his scalp to a war party of roving hostiles, so be it.

A man couldn't shirk his responsibility and still wear the label of a man. Not west of the Mississippi, anyway. In the East, in the larger cities in the States, he'd known men who didn't care at all about those who depended on them for a livelihood. Those men would rather spend their evenings at a tavern than with their children, rather spend the night with a soiled dove than with their wives.

Such men didn't know the true meaning of manhood, and Nate had never enjoyed their company.

A meadow appeared ahead, putting an end to Nate's musing. He paused before riding into the open, checking the meadow from end to end and the slopes on either side to be sure no unpleasant surprises awaited him. A trapper could never be *too* cautious.

Nate saw a few black-tailed deer, all does, grazing at a low elevation on the mountain to the east. Across the meadow a solitary magpie pranced about on the ground. There were no bears, no Indians. Reassured, he trotted on, grinning when the magpie rose into the air voicing its distinctive *Mag! Mag! Mag! Mag!*

"A little high up, aren't you?" Nate joked as the magpie flapped into a fir tree. It perched lightly and gave him a cold stare.

"What are you so upset about, you stupid bird?" Nate asked.

And then he saw it. Lying in the grass at the edge of the meadow was a body, not an animal carcass either, but the body of a man dead at least five or six months. Nate immediately reined up and out of pure habit glanced in all directions. Satisfied there was no threat, he climbed down, ground-hitched the stallion, and advanced on tiptoe as if afraid his footsteps would disturb the slumber of the dead.

Nate saw where the magpie had been pecking at tattered ribbons of dried flesh clinging to the skull and felt an impulse to shoot it. He couldn't blame the bird, though. Magpies were greedy feeders, eating anything and everything that caught their fancy. It was magpie nature to peck at corpses.

There was little smell after so much time had elapsed. Still, Nate covered his mouth and nose with a calloused hand and walked around the pale bones, taking note of the few details that might offer a clue to the dead man's identity. Right away he deduced it had been an Indian. The tattered vestiges of a breechcloth clung to the hip bones, as did what was left of a pair of moccasins to the man's feet.

A jagged cavity in the sternum and the fact several ribs had been broken were evidence the warrior had met his end in combat, most likely at the hands of another warrior wielding a tomahawk. Only a tomahawk could cause so much damage to thick human bones. Arrows and knives left nicks and scrape marks. Lead balls left neat furrows or shattered bones into splinters.

Nate couldn't tell which tribe the man had belonged to. His best guess was that a Flathead or Shoshone or some other hunter from one of the friendlier tribes had been caught by a party of Bloods. There were no markings to confirm it, but Nate figured the warrior had been scalped since no self-respecting Blood would pass up such a trophy. There was no trace of torture, although such traces would be hard to discern after all this time unless they were glaringly obvious.

"Poor soul," Nate said, returning to the stallion. Once in the saddle, he by-passed the bones and entered the forest.

The implications of the find were disturbing. Nate had entertained the hope that the valley he would be trapping was far enough south of typical Blood haunts to be spared a visit while he was there. The dead warrior, however, might be proof parties of Bloods did visit the region regularly, perhaps to hunt, perhaps to acquire specific types of wood for their bows, perhaps to gather quartz or rocks used in making arrowheads.

Whatever the reason, the discovery had shattered

Nate's hope and impressed upon him as nothing else could the reality of the dangers he faced. Thinking about them was one thing, finding their potent legacy quite another. His lips compressed into a thin line and he firmed his grip on the Hawken.

For the next several hours Nate wound steadily northward along the base of several mountains and through several emerald hills. Above him reared ivory heights resembling alabaster temples beckoning to lofty deities. Dense growth of spruce and other pines covered the slopes like green cloaks. Everywhere there was wildlife, a teeming variety of animals going about their daily routines in characteristic style. Some, such as the big gray squirrels and ravens, were noisy to the point of being pests. Others, such as rabbits and raccoons, were so quiet a man didn't know they were there until he spooked them. Then there were the larger animals usually seen only from a discreet distance, such as the elk and the noble bighorn sheep.

Nate never tired of admiring the spectacle. During his early years, he'd been fascinated to the depths of his being by accounts in books written by explorers and missionaries of the countless kinds of exotic animals found in distant places such as Africa and Asia. Never in a million years would it have occurred to him that he could find the very same thing on the North American continent.

Wasn't that the human way, though? Nate asked himself. As the old saying went, the grass always looked greener on the other side of the fence. Natural wonders might be right in front of a person's face, but they'd never see them if they were too busy craning their necks for a glimpse of the far horizon. How odd that so few recognized the truth.

Mountain Cat

Once past the mountains and among the hills, Nate was troubled to note the animals all fell silent. Silence wasn't Nature's normal state. A profound quiet served as a sure sign of looming peril. The cause might be something as simple as the advent of a severe thunderstorm, or it might have a more sinister genesis: prowling predators, whether four-legged or two-legged.

Nate rode uneasily, shifting often to survey the impenetrable woods. Pines, when clustered close, formed a seemingly solid wall capable of hiding a full-grown grizzly or an entire war party. Many a trapper had lost his life when set on without warning by an enemy that appeared almost at his very elbow, too late for the trapper to do more than blink. Nate had no intention of being one of them.

The hills gave way to a low ridge that formed a barrier between them and the valley. Here a whole slope had been devastated by a lightning strike resulting in a widespread fire that reduced thousands of patriarchs of the forest to mere charred fragments and stumps. The ground had been darkened by the inferno but was now sprinkled with islands of hardy grass.

Nate threaded among gnarled black steeples and around ebony logs once home to thriving insects and birds and animals but now reduced to pitted, lifeless hulks. There wasn't so much as a solitary chipmunk abroad on the blistered slope.

At the top, Nate stopped and breathed in relief, glad to be up where the air lacked an acrid taint and the trees rustled with vitality. His breath caught short when he gazed out over the valley he would call home for the next six months. There were valleys, and there were *valleys*.

Ages past, a giant cyclops must have taken a crooked

scythe to the land, creating a deep, ugly scar that had healed in the course of time and resulted in a valley with so many twists and bends that from high in the air it must have the appearance of a knotted snake. The faces of the ringing mountains to the north, east, and west were strangely barren and so inclined that they shielded the valley floor from much of the sunlight that would otherwise penetrate.

A cool breeze wafted up and out over the ridge, making Nate shiver. He shook himself, turned the stallion, and moved along the ridge eastward, giving his new home a thorough inspection. A wide stream was visible, which confirmed there would be beaver. Or should be, at any rate. No other animals were in sight, which in itself wasn't remarkable. Early afternoon was a time for deer and elk to lay low in thickets and the meat eaters to rest up for their nightly hunting.

That reminded him. Nate squinted up at the sun, judging he had five or six hours of daylight remaining. Less in the valley, where the peaks to the west would cause an artificial sunset an hour or so earlier. He had to hurry.

Ten minutes of looking failed to reveal a game trail, so Nate made his own, picking his downward course with care, keenly aware he couldn't afford to lose a single horse. The incline was steep, in spots almost severe. It required an hour to gain the valley floor.

Birds were singing again when Nate trotted on a beeline for the stream. The temperature was cooler, but that would be an advantage when he began working hard. He heard the bubbling of rapid current before he broke from the pines onto a grassy strip bordering the source of his livelihood. As with the majority of high mountain streams, the water in this one seemed in an almighty hurry to get to a lower elevation. A stick went flashing past, bobbing with the ebb and flow.

Nate turned westward. Beaver didn't make their lodges in the middle of rapids. They needed still water. Which was no doubt why they spent most of their adult lives building and rebuilding the dams so critical to their existence. In a sense, beaver had a set of responsibilities similar to his own. The fate of their families rested on their ability as providers and protectors. It was a bit sad, Nate reflected, that the latest fashion craze hadn't been chicken feathers instead.

Around a bend was a sight so glorious that Nate quivered with excitement: a tremendous dam, the work of generations of beaver, built at a critical point, an ideal spot to stem the rapid flow without causing so much pressure to build up during times of flood that the dam would be swept away. Over the top cascaded the overflow, re-forming at the bottom into the current contributing to the rapids.

Nate rode past the immense jumbled bowl of trunks, limbs, and odds and ends. A tranquil pond unfolded before him. All along the shore were recently felled trees or the upthrust spikes of those downed long ago. A dozen feet out from the bank rose the hump forming the roof of the lodge. There was no sign of activity, and there probably wouldn't be until later. In the early evening beaver came out to treat themselves to fresh bark and inspect their dams, while most of the actual construction work was done at night.

Going on, Nate presently discovered another dam. And another. There was so much beaver sign, in his mind's eye he was already seeing the thick bales of prime pelts he would be taking to the next rendezvous. At a muddy stretch flanking a straight section of rushing water, he saw something else, something that made him jerk on the reins so hard the stallion titled its head quizzically.

The mud bore dozens of tracks, some old, some new, testimony to the drinking habits of a variety of creatures. Most prominent were the telltale pad marks of the one animal able to hold its own against a riled grizzly, the pad marks of what had to be the biggest panther in all existence.

Chapter Three

That first night in the new valley Nate slept in a small clearing at the base of a cliff located almost a full mile north of the stream. With the rock wall at his back, he only had to worry about something coming at him from the front. He gathered several loads of dry wood, bedded down the horses close to the cliff, and spread out his blankets between them and the fire. The long day on the trail had left him too tired to bother hunting his supper. He settled for some of the pemmican his wife had thoughtfully packed.

As Nate munched, he pondered. The gigantic panther tracks weren't much cause for alarm since the big cats were known to roam over a wide range and the one responsible for the prints might not show up in the valley again for many days, if not weeks. And when it did, the odds were that the panther, or mountain lion as a few of the trappers had taken to calling the breed, would just go about its business without bothering him.

Like wolves, panthers normally wanted nothing to do with humans.

Seated there close to the crackling flames, warm and content and drowsy, Nate felt a bit ashamed of his earlier misgivings. The valley was really no different from any other. Oh, its shape was extraordinary, but it still had a stream and grass and trees, just as others did. And while the surrounding peaks tended to shade the valley floor more hours of the day than was typical, shade in and of itself was hardly sinister. He laughed at his former feelings and took a swig of piping hot coffee.

Nate knew how a mind could play tricks on a person, especially in the rugged Rockies where the awe-inspiring landscape was a heady spectacle that stirred the emotions to undreamt of heights. The imagination was free to soar with the eagles, and if left unchecked, might soar into stormy clouds of worry and despair. Many a trapper had fallen prey to the ravings of his own mental fancies, and Nate had no intention of joining their ranks.

There had been one man in particular whose story Nate recalled vividly. The trapper, a greenhorn from North Carolina or some such Southern state, had outfitted himself in Missouri and traveled west with a rendezvous caravan. At the annual gathering he'd announced to all and sundry that he was going to bring back more furs the next year than any trapper had ever done before. And off he went to trap on his own. A few of the men offered to be his partner, but he'd refused each and every one.

The next rendezvous came along and the Southerner failed to show. Some wondered about the loud green-horn, speculating on his possible fate. Indians, a wild beast, a natural disaster like an avalanche, or an innocent accident might have cost the brash youngster his life.

Hundreds of trappers perished every year from those common hazards, and others.

Afterward, the North Carolinian was forgotten about until later that fall when a group of trappers riding into unknown land to the west found a crude cabin near a high pass. Bleached bones of horses long dead dotted the weeds choking the front of the structure. Inside they found human bones, a single skeleton in a heap beside a chair. They also uncovered a journal.

Evidently, the greenhorn had come on an area rich with beaver and decided to winter there. He'd built the cabin from downed trees, stored his bales inside, stocked up on jerky, and prepared to wait until Spring to head east. About halfway through the winter, however, the isolation got to the man.

His journal related the entire story. At first, the trapper complained of being spied on by unseen eyes. He thought he was being watched as he went about his daily chores, and he was certain hostiles were sizing him up to take his hair. Then he began hearing peculiar noises, mostly at night, scratching and rustling and low whispering. Yet when he dashed outside to confront the intruders, no one was there.

Several weeks of this ordeal had a terrible effect on the trapper's fraying mental state. He wrote in his journal of seeing large, strange bugs crawling about in the forest behind his cabin and of hearing them on his roof after dark. He'd shoot at them, to no avail. He'd rail at them, and throw sticks and stones, but they refused to leave.

Finally came the day when the trapper barricaded himself inside. In his journal he told of a fierce seige by the bugs, and how he was valiantly fighting them off. Some, though, were getting in through cracks in the walls or chinks in the floor and crawling up under his buckskins to bite and tear at his flesh. He was doing the best he could to resist the dark tide, but he labored at a disadvantage since many of the bugs were invisible.

The trapper's last entry spoke eloquently of his abject state. He'd stripped off his clothes so the bugs couldn't hide on his person. He'd stabbed himself a few times in the belief he was stabbing attacking bugs. Desperate, in terrible agony, he'd decided to put an end to himself before the bugs crawled into his mouth and nose and ears and ate his innards, burrowing from the inside out. The man had sat in a makeshift chair, cocked a pistol, stuck the tip of the barrel in his mouth, and squeezed the trigger. Simple as that.

Nate had seen the journal and touched the drops of blood scattered over its last two pages. He remembered wondering if the same fate would one day befall him, remembered scoffing at the idea. Yet he had behaved the same way at sight of the valley.

Now, staring into the comforting fire, Nate grinned and slapped his leg, amused by his foolish behavior. It was all right for kids to be afraid of the dark and other imaginary demons; they didn't know any better. But he was a grown man. He'd slain grizzlies, wolverines, and Apaches. He had nothing to fear but fear itself.

Later that night, snug under his blankets, his head propped on his hands, his gaze on the multitude of sparkling stars, Nate laid his plans for the next day. In the distance a coyote yipped, closer by an owl voiced its unique question. Gradually he drifted into dreamland and was on the verge of deep slumber when he heard something which made him sit bolt upright and grab for his Hawken.

From the west, from farther up the valley, wafted a menacing, guttural snarl totally unlike those of the wolves. It was deeper, louder, more ferocious, resembling muted thunder more than anything else, an elemental sound that inspired elemental dread.

Nate listened breathlessly. When the snarl died, he laid back down and tried telling himself the incident was of no consequence. So what if the panther was still in the valley? So what if it was on the prowl? He reminded himself that panthers seldom attacked people. To be on the safe side, though, he added fuel to the fire until the blaze was twice the size it had been. Then he reclined on his side, facing the woods, and cupped a palm around a pistol.

Sleep was a long time claiming him.

A pink glow tinged the eastern sky when Nate woke up and heated the coffee left over from the evening before. The strong brew and jerky sufficed for breakfast. His saddle went on the stallion, his parfleches and packs on one of the pack horses, and off he rode, savoring the tangy nip in the air. On all sides birds serenaded the rising sun.

Morning was one of Nate's favorite times. It gave him a wholesome sense of renewal, of starting each day with a clean slate. He looked forward to the work he had to do, and to raising his first beaver. In a few days he would have some pelts ready to sell. In six weeks he would have bales of them.

First things first. Nate watered the horses, then rode westward, noting the locations of lodges and spots where trees had recently been felled. Midway up the valley he established his permanent camp in a sheltered clearing bordered by thickets on two sides, dense spruce on the third, and the stream on the fourth.

Taking a half-dozen traps, Nate retraced his route

and placed them at suitable points. Most went close
to lodges, others near runs made by the beaver when
leaving or entering the water. He had to wade out into
the stream, then position the set traps deep enough under
the surface to drown the animals when caught. Each
trap was baited with castorum, a yellow substance taken
from their glands. The scent drew beavers like flowers
drew bees.

Done with the first batch, Nate went back to camp and
spent the next two hours erecting a sturdy lean-to, angled
so it blocked the prevailing northwesterly winds. Some
trappers liked to build their shelters of hides, but Nate
considered the practice a horrible waste of prime fur.

The frame for stretching pelts was Nate's subsequent
chore. He used firm, trimmed limbs and lashed them
together with whangs from his buckskins. A graining
block had to be set up. And when that was done, Nate
piled a store of wood.

Plenty of daylight remained, so Nate took his sack of
Newhouses and went westward along the stream placing
trap after trap. Newhouse was the name of the man
who manufactured the traps, and many now called his
product by his name. In additions Newhouse published a
manual known as *THE TRAPPERS GUIDE*, a somewhat
misleading book that had lured countless gullible souls to
the mountains in search of fortune. Newhouse claimed
trapping was a 'gentlemanly' occupation, and proved
it by illustrating his guide with drawings of so-called
trappers in refined city clothes doing things like skinning
beaver and shooting game.

Still, the man made a fine steel trap. He'd wisely
designed the jaws to be smooth, not jagged, so the
fur wouldn't be damaged. A disk at the bottom was
the trigger that caused the leaf springs to fly up and

lock the jaws in place. It all happened so fast, there
was no time for an animal to pull its foot from harm's
way once the disk was stepped on.

Nate had to be careful. Quite a few trappers had lost
thumbs or fingers after accidentally snaring their own
hands in the snapping jaws. A moment's distraction was
all it took. He'd learned to concentrate on the trap and
nothing but the trap when setting the trigger and lowering
the device into the water.

Sixteen traps Nate was able to put out that afternoon.
The sun crowned the mountains when he tied his sack
to his saddle and trotted back to camp. Along the way,
he double-checked to be sure he had blazed trees near
each of the traps so he could find them again.

That night Nate ate rabbit stew spiced with wild onions
and herbs. He treated himself to sugar in his coffee to
celebrate the laying of his line. His dreams that night
were of piles and piles of glossy peltries.

The next day was a repeat of the first. Nate succeeded
in placing nearly half of his traps by sunset, and that
evening, when making his rounds, he found the first
snared beaver, a husky male with a lustrous coat.
The animal had tried to bite its leg off to escape
but fortunately failed.

By the end of the fourth day all the traps had been
set out and Nate had his hands full tending to the hides
of those caught. It always happened that more beaver
were caught right after a trap line was laid out than
later on. Once the beaver population started to dwindle,
the survivors exercised more caution, steering clear of
anything that smelled of man or metal. A trapper had to
use more ingenuity in order to keep on catching them.

Nate had no such problem for the time being. Day
after day went by, each rewarding him with five or six

more beaver. His routine was always the same. Up at dawn to eat a hurried breakfast, a check of all the traps to retrieve any animals caught overnight, each of which had to be lugged to camp, then the late morning and early afternoon hours were spent working on pelts. Late afternoon was devoted to another patrol of the stream. Finally came supper, and more curing and scraping until he was too tired to stay awake another minute.

In this way four weeks elapsed. Nate lost all track of time, he was so immersed in his work. He trapped the main stream out and started on several branches where younger beaver had been driven by population pressure to establish their own lodges. Not once did Nate see another human being. Animals were his sole companions in the remote valley, deer and elk and countless smaller creatures.

Nate loved every minute. He often thought of his former job as an aspiring accountant in New York City, and he marveled that he had once seriously considered spending the rest of his life chained to a desk. He remembered the small work area he'd been given, and being huddled over ledgers late into the night to get caught up for a client. He remembered the reek of the lamps, the sore eyes, the cramps in his back. How could he have been so stupid?

All Nate had to do was pause and gaze at the majestic splendor all around him to see his former folly for what it had truly been. Give him the invigorating mountain air, spiced with the earthy scent of pine! Give him the deep blue sky, the rich brown earth and deep green forests! Give him the freedom to live as he damn well pleased instead of having to bow to every whim of a fickle employer! This was the life! The only life!

Early on, Nate forgot about the panther, forgot about

his premonition, forgot about his feelings of unease. Trapping took all his time from sunrise to midnight. There weren't any idle moments to spend in worthless musing. Gradually his collection of peltries grew and grew, and after a month he was the proud owner of one hundred and five hides.

Everything went extremely well until the day Nate approached his camp with a forty-pound beaver slung over a shoulder and heard his horses nickering. By their tone Nate realized they were upset. Grasping his Hawken tighter, he jogged the rest of the way and came to the edge of the clearing in time to glimpse a tawny form vanishing into the thicket on the other side. So fleeting was the glimpse that Nate couldn't be sure if he'd seen a panther, a bobcat, or something else entirely.

The black stallion was nervously prancing back and forth. Dropping the beaver, Nate ran over and calmed the troubled horse before it could break loose from its tether. He scoured the underbrush but saw no sign of their visitor. Not satisfied, he tiptoed into the thicket and crouched low to the ground where he would be more likely to spot movement. The still plants mocked him. Whatever had been there was apparently gone.

Nate searched in vain for tracks, thanks to the hard soil and the thick grass. He made a circuit of the camp to see if the animal had left prints elsewhere and was disappointed to find none.

Vaguely troubled, Nate resumed working. The horses hadn't been harmed and none of his belongings had been disturbed, so he shouldn't be worried. Yet he couldn't shake a persistent, nagging, trifling sense of impending trouble.

Butcher knife in hand, Nate set the beaver on its back and slit down the back of each hind leg. Cutting slowly, he opened a straight slit from the chin to the tail. Then, using his fingers, he peeled the beaver's hide down over its head as he might peel a stocking from his foot. While peeling he had to cut ligaments and muscles holding the hide in place, remembering to always hold the edge of the knife slanted toward the body and not toward the hide to avoid nicking the valuable fur.

While the hide was still pliable, Nate attached it to the stretching frame he had made. A rough stone sufficed as a scraper, and with it he removed shreds of muscles and fat that had clung to the inside of the pelt. He also trimmed off a few ragged edges. Overall, though, the hide was as fine as any he'd ever collected.

That evening Nate half expected the horses to get the scent of something and act up again, or to hear the throaty cry of the giant panther. Neither occurred. Bad nerves again, he figured, and turned in when the fire was so low it was almost out.

What woke Nate up, he couldn't say. One second he was sound asleep, the next he was lying there in near total darkness listening to his horses stomp and nicker. Instantly he pushed erect, rifle tucked to his shoulder. The snap of a twig to the west showed him which way to turn, and as he did he saw something at the edge of the spruce trees. He took a hasty bead, wishing he could see the thing clearly, when it suddenly disappeared. Puzzled, he bent at the waist and dashed forward.

Nate reached the thicket and halted. He glanced right, he glanced left. There was no sign of the creature. The horses were even more agitated now, the stallion trying to rear, one of the pack horses tugging furiously at its rope.

"Damn," Nate muttered. He had no choice but to dash to the horses and try yet again to quiet them down. The stallion did so immediately but the pack horse was in a panic, forcing Nate to seize the tether and hold fast to stop the animal from trying to break free.

In the thicket to the east arose a faint rustling.

Nate twisted, whipping the Hawken up with one hand. He realized the nocturnal prowler had circled completely around his camp. Was it the huge panther? Or something else? The pack horse continued to strain against him and he was of half a mind to pound the rifle stock onto its thick skull to teach it a lesson, but he had never been one to brutalize animals and wasn't about to start.

The rustling ceased. An eerie stillness gripped the gloomy forest. All Nate could hear was the sighing of the wind in the trees and the soft purling of the stream. Giving the rope a last pull to show the pack horse who was boss, he darted to his blankets and hastily crammed his pistols, knife, and tomahawk under his belt. Then, donning his hat, he sped into the thicket to the east, making no attempt to move stealthily in the hope he would flush the beast.

A flitting hint of a flashing inky shadow was the only clue Nate had to the creature's location. He promptly veered toward it, but whatever the animal was, it easily outdistanced him, racing off with a speed even the black stallion would be hard pressed to match. Into the adjacent woods it ran, and there, oddly, it paused in the open and seemed to look back.

Nate sprinted in pursuit. As yet he had not had a clear view of the thing. The general shape, though, and its fluid, incredibly swift movements were consistent with those of a panther. He was within twenty feet of the creature and raising the Hawken when once again the animal fled.

In the act of slowing since he had no chance at all of

catching it, Nate was mildly surprised when the cat—if such it was—stopped once more and looked back. The inexplicable behavior confused him. Was the panther taunting him or merely curious? Whichever, he couldn't afford to let a panther skulk about his camp at will and perhaps eventually bring down one of his horses when temptation proved too much to resist. So he pressed on, his thumb resting on the Hawken's hammer.

The big cat let him approach within twenty-five feet, then wheeled and flowed like quicksilver further into the trees. Yet it only ran another thirty feet or so when it halted again.

Nate was thoroughly confounded. He'd never heard tell of any panther behaving as this one was doing. The only explanation he could think of was that the cat had seldom if ever seen a human being and wasn't sure whether he was a threat or not. In a way he regretted having to dispatch it. He slowed, thinking the cat would be less likely to run off, and lowered the Hawken to his side.

The panther waited until Nate was less than twenty feet away, then spun and glided into undergrowth to the south. Nate hurried to the vegetation and sank to one knee, seeking a target. Darkness and bushes were all he saw. Frustrated, he moved a few yards to the left to vary the angle. Somewhere in there the cat was hiding. He was sure of it.

But Nate was wrong.

A minute had gone by when frightened whinnies brought Nate to his feet in dismay. His gut balled into a knot as he perceived that the panther had circled once again, this time back to the clearing, back to the horses. Nate flew toward the camp, his moccasins slapping the earth in regular cadence. The whinnies grew more strident, loudest among them the deep cries of the stallion. But where the pack horses, all mares, were neighing out of fear, the stallion was in a fury. Nate prayed the black wouldn't tear loose and fight the cat. The stallion was one of the best horses he had ever owned and he didn't care for anything to happen to it.

Suddenly the whinnies of the stallion took a new, harsher tenor, and mingled with the stallion's snorts and bellows were the low growls of an angry cat.

Nate's worst fear had come to pass. He could distinguish the stallion through the thicket, rearing and kicking in wild abandon, the firelight highlighting the rippling muscles under its satiny coat. Clutching the rifle in both hands, he plunged into the thicket and barreled his way through to the clearing, there to behold a sight few men had ever witnessed.

The black stallion was engaged in mortal combat with a panther of such immense proportions it appeared more like a monster from prior ages than a mountain lion. Long of body, unnaturally thick through the middle, and powerfully endowed with bulging sinews, the cat was easily evading the stallion's flailing hoofs. It leaped from side to side with effortless ease, its ears flattened against its round head, its lips curled to reveal its wicked teeth. At any second it might see an opening and pounce.

"No!" Nate roared, closing. Here was the clear shot he needed and he was going to take it, but as he brought the Hawken to bear the panther streaked out of the clearing to the west, a molten blur impossible to hit.

Nate cursed and stopped. He wasn't going to make the same mistake twice and follow the cat into the forest. Simmering with baffled wrath, he glanced at the stallion, which was standing still, its sides heaving, its eyes fixed on the spot where the panther had entered the spruce trees.

"Well now," Nate declared bitterly, "this changes everything, big fellow. I'm not about to leave this valley until I'm done trapping, so I guess that means we're in for a heap of trouble." He shook the rifle at the trees and repeated softly, "A heap of trouble."

Chapter Four

Old Satan.

As the story related time and again over the years went, some of the very first trappers ever to set foot in the Rocky Mountains ran into a bestial fiend that qualified as Evil Incarnate. Four hardy men from Pennsylvania had gone into unexplored territory despite warnings from friendly Shoshones to stay away from the region for fear of encountering the legendary Devil Beast. The whites had understandably scoffed at the silly notion of a panther renowned for ferocity unmatched by any living creature, a panther that had lived more scores of years than any man could remember, that had been shot with arrows time and again and pierced by lances and knives and yet lived on unharmed.

Into the unknown the quartet went, and they paid dearly for neglecting to take the Shoshones seriously. One of the men was pounced on while he slept and dragged off into the brush. When the body was found by his companions the next day, it was scattered in small pieces as if the panther had ripped it to shreds in wanton feline glee.

The remaining three had packed up and headed out of the country, but the panther wasn't about to let them go. It shadowed them for days, often showing itself beyond rifle range and keeping them awake at night with its unearthly screams. Their horses were driven off, never to be seen again.

A second trapper lost his life when he heeded Nature's call and forgot to keep one eye behind him. This man had his head shorn from his body and his entrails clawed out.

Days later the two weary survivors took their only good shot at their tormentor. Both were experienced woodsmen. Both were excellent shots. Yet, somehow, both missed, because the panther simply stared at them for a few moments after the thunder of the gunshots receded in the distance and then calmly walked off as if taking a stroll in a city park.

Miles from the Shoshone village one of the trappers, worn out from lack of food and sleep, stopped to rest on a log while his companion hastened ahead for help. When the rescue party arrived, the only article of the trapper's on the log was his rifle. A smear of blood led the last trapper and the warriors into a glade where the torso of the hapless dead man was found. His arms and legs, however, were missing.

Thus started the undying saga of Old Satan. The sole survivor told other trappers, and they in turn passed on the story, and so on and so on until every trapper became familiar with it. Trappers loved to talk, to swap tall tales around their campfires, and no tale was more popular than that of the monster panther. Somewhere along the line the cat received a fitting name. Now and then others would claim to have seen it but no one believed them. Monstrous panthers simply didn't exist.

Now Nate knew better.

The story came to mind the next morning as Nate was saddling the stallion to go make his rounds of the traps. He had decided to take his horses with him every time he left camp. It was either that or risk losing one and he needed them all to pack out his plews. Sliding a loop over the neck of the lead pack animal, he rode into the rising sun, staying close to the water's edge so he could see if the traps had done their job.

Less than a hundred feet from the clearing Nate came on a gravel bar rimmed with mud bearing the same enormous tracks he'd seen previously. The panther had squatted to lap the cold water, then leaped from the end of the gravel bar to the far bank, a jump of eighteen feet.

Nate resumed his morning routine. Four beavers had to be transported back to camp and skinned. That evening he made his second sweep, and this time he made a shocking discovery.

A wide tributary of the main stream contained two lodges. Nate had already trapped the nearest. The second was in a ravine gouged into the side of a neighboring mountain where the ravine widened and the runoff from on high formed a serene pool. A narrow strip of solid footing between the sheer face of the ravine and the water had permitted Nate to get close enough to the lodge to plant his traps.

Now, as Nate dismounted at the mouth of the pool and hiked along its perimeter toward the lodge, he noticed a strange crimson tint to the water flowing sluggishly by. He stared at the red stain until its meaning hit him like a ton of falling boulders. Then he broke into a run.

49

Two of the traps had contained beaver. One trap had been dragged, stake and all, clear out of the pool. The other was at the bottom, lying on its side. In the jaws of both dangled the shorn legs of the beavers.

Nate clenched his fists in rage and scanned the ravine from one end to the other. The panther was long gone but its handiwork was impossible to miss; the pair of beaver had been ripped apart, their organs, limbs, and hides forming a gory mess at the base of the wall. From the evidence, Nate doubted any of the meat had been eaten. The panther had done it for the sheer hell of it.

A cat that would enter water? Nate recalled hearing of panthers seen fording rivers, but he was under the impression they only got wet if there was no alternative. This one was different. It had deliberately gone in after the beavers, as if it had made the connection between Nate and the traps and knew that killing the catch would anger him.

That was a crazy idea! Nate told himself. Animals couldn't think, at least not the same way people did. An animal acted out of instinct and reflex. Complex plotting was beyond them. Everyone knew that. But how else could he explain the deaths of the beavers?

Nate gathered the traps and opened the jaws of each so the imprisoned legs fell out. Slinging the Newhouses by their chains over his shoulder, he walked to the horses and secured the traps to one of the pack horses. Not without some difficulty, because the horse's sensitive nostrils picked up a whiff of blood and it shied.

The ride to the camp was spent in somber thought. Nate hadn't trapped all of the tributaries yet. Making a rough guess, he pegged the total number of beaver still to be caught at forty. Enough for a new rifle for his son, or a lot of foofaraw for his wife and daughter. He wasn't inclined to pass that many pelts up.

Which left Nate with the pressing problem of how to deal with Old Satan, as he had taken to calling the beast. Tracking it down would take too much time, make him late for his reunion with Shakespeare. He didn't have poison or he'd bait a dead beaver and let the cat's own bloodthirsty nature do it in. Snares and other kinds of traps would probably be useless against such a wily creature. So what was left?

One thing was for sure. Nate couldn't tolerate having the beaver butchered. Yet he also couldn't be everywhere at once. While he was checking downstream, the panther might be upstream wreaking havoc, or just the opposite. Somehow he had to draw the cat within range of his Hawken.

Easier thought than done. How, Nate wondered, was he to lure in an animal as naturally wary as a mountain lion? What would interest it? A low nicker behind him gave him the answer, and he shifted in the saddle to regard the three pack horses. The scheme was fraught with risk, but if he did it right, it just might work.

Nate plotted the rest of the ride. He ate beaver meat for supper, then walked close to the stream where the soil was softest and began scooping dirt with a broken limb. Sweat was trickling down his back by the time he had a suitable depression excavated. With an eye on the setting sun, he accumulated brush from the thicket and piled it next to the depression.

Picking the pack horse was easy. Nate chose the one that had given him the hardest time since leaving home. Gripping its lead rope, he escorted the mare to the stream bank and fastened the rope to a log too heavy for the mare to drag off. He took measured paces from the log to the depression, counted fifteen, and nodded in satisfaction. Ideal range.

The stallion and the other two mares were tied within spitting distance of the blaze. They disliked being so close, but it was either that or leave them in the dark at the mercy of the panther.

Nate sat and sipped black, strong coffee for the next hour. He might need to stay awake all night and the brew would help. All was quiet during that time, except for the horse by the stream which kept whinnying. It was upset at being separated from the others and didn't like being left in the dark.

Presently Nate threw enough limbs on the fire to last for hours and went to the depression. Lying on his side so he was facing the decoy, he then covered himself with the brush until he was completely concealed. From a distance the blind should fool Old Satan.

Now all Nate could do was wait. He set the rifle in front of him, shifted onto his stomach, and rested his chin on his forearms. A mild breeze fanned the tops of the trees, and off to the right a cricket chirped.

Would Satan come? That was the burning question. Nate hoped he wouldn't wind up staying awake all night and then not get a shot at the cat. Losing sleep was a sacrifice he could ill afford, not with all the work yet to be done before he could leave the valley, but going without would be well worth it if he bagged the panther.

The minutes dragged by, becoming a full hour. The mare continued to whinny every so often. On occasion the stallion answered her. Several times she threw her weight against the rope, which held fast.

Nate did his best to stay fully awake and alert, but despite his best intentions his mind strayed. Fatigue and the deceptive quiet lulled him into a drowsy state. Memories washed over him, memories long forgotten. . . . or avoided.

Another time, another place.

In a newly painted frame house in a well-to-do section of New York City, a boy of twelve was on his bed, his head propped on his pillow, reading a book. Into his room stalked a square-jawed man with eyes the hue of flint.

"Here you are. I should have known you'd be wasting your time, as always."

The boy lowered the book and dutifully sat up. "I'm not wasting my time, Father. I'm reading."

"Reading what, as if I can't guess?" the father responded. He took the book from the boy and examined the cover, his mouth scrunched up as if he had just tasted a bitter lemon. "*Prometheus Unbound* by Percy Bysshe Shelley. Why do you read this drivel?"

"Poetry is good for the soul, father."

"Where did you ever get such a silly idea? From your mother? The woman should stick to her knitting and cooking and stop trying to turn you into a hopeless romantic." The father flipped a page and started reading. "My soul is an enchanted boat, which, like a sleeping swan, doth float upon the silver waves of—" He glanced up, shook his head in disgust, then tossed the offending volume to the floor. "Enough. I won't have you reading such trash."

"But, Father—"

"But nothing." The man gripped the boy's arm and pulled him off the bed. "Listen to me, and listen closely. I have a job for you to do and I want it done right."

"What sort of job?" the youngster asked. "I already did my chores."

"Don't give me sass, son," the father warned. "Come with me and I'll show you."

They walked without speaking down the hall, down the stairs, and along another hall to the kitchen. In the corner near the stove the father halted and pointed. "There."

The boy looked but only saw the white wall and the polished baseboard. "There what?"

"At the bottom, by the stove. Don't you see it?"

There was a small hole in the baseboard, no bigger than the boy's thumb. "That?"

"Kill it."

"Sir?"

"I want you to kill it."

"Kill what?" the boy asked, although he knew full well.

"The mouse, dunderhead. What else?" Scowling, the father motioned at a nearby table. "Your mother saw one this morning when she was setting the silverware out. About gave her a heart attack." A thin smile transformed his scowl. "You know how women are. Afraid of their own shadows."

The boy barely heard. "You want *me* to do it?"

"Why not you?" the father rejoined sternly. "Your brothers have other jobs to do. And you certainly don't expect me to devote precious time to so simple a task? A girl could do this."

"I've never killed a mouse before."

"It's easy. Set some cheese out and when the dirty little rodent shows itself, bash its brains in."

"I've never killed *anything* before."

The father sighed. "So? It's about time you did then,

54

isn't it? You're too squeamish for your own good. Why, when I was your age, I regularly chopped the heads off chickens and often helped my father, slaughter hogs. Sometimes I waded in blood and gore up to my ankles, but it was great fun."

The boy bit his lower lip.

"Do you know what your problem is? I've been too damn easy on you, spared you from life's realities. And those ridiculous poetry books don't help matters any. Life isn't all sugar and spice, son. You must learn to take the sour with the sweet." The father strode to the wood box and selected a stout length of firewood. "Here."

"You want me to use that?"

"You can kick the mouse to death for all I care," the father said, shoving the bludgeon into his son's hands. "But this will work nicely. Just remember to smash it in the head. I don't want its guts spread all over the floor. Your mother won't like that one bit."

The boy stared at the club and gulped. "I'll do my best, father."

"Of course. I knew I could rely on you."

The mare whinnied for the hundredth time, only this time there was a new note, a high-pitched quality that snapped Nate out of his reverie and returned him to the present. He automatically lifted his head and accidentally rustled the brush covering him. Freezing, he gazed at the mare and saw her staring out across the stream.

Was Satan coming? Had the cat taken the bait? Nate probed the night, his finger on the trigger of his rifle. He must be ready to fire at an instant's notice in order to protect the mare. She moved and stared to the northwest. Nate did the same yet was unable to spot the mountain lion.

Vibrant with expectancy, Nate slowly raised the Hawken to his shoulder. It suddenly occurred to him that he had a clear shot in front of his hiding place but the brush obstructed his view to either side. Should Satan charge from those directions he would have virtually no time to react. You idiot! he reflected. Why didn't you think of that sooner?

Behind Nate the stallion and two other mares added their nickers to those of the decoy. The horses were making so much noise Nate wouldn't be able to hear the panther cross the stream. Annoyed, he twisted to shush them, or started to, when his startled eyes fell on Old Satan. The monster wasn't more than ten feet off to the west, crouched belly to the ground, its long snakelike tail twitching madly as it glanced from the unsuspecting decoy to the horses by the dwindling fire and back again.

Nate was flabbergasted. He'd had no inkling the panther was so close. Evidently the mare was gazing at something else, or the panther had moved upstream and crossed without the mare seeing it. In order to shoot he would have to rise to his knees and swing around, giving the panther all the forewarning needed to bound off unscathed. Should he try anyway? Indecisive, he held himself rigid, waiting to see if the cat would move closer.

Satan appeared equally indecisive, continuing to divide his attention between the decoy and the other horses. At length the panther concentrated solely on the lone mare and crept toward her, claws extended.

Nate held his breath. Once the cat came near enough, it would be all over. As quick as panthers were, they couldn't evade a shot at point-blank rage. He counted down the feet and girded himself to spring from hiding. Eight feet. Six feet.

At the very moment Nate was about to leap up, Satan halted and looked directly at the brush. Directly at *him*. Nate could practically feel the panther's infernal eyes boring into his, and he couldn't repress a slight shudder at a mental picture of the cat leaping on him before he could stand and rending him limb from limb. He'd be pinned down, helpless to resist.

Nate had no idea whether the panther knew he was there or whether it was merely suspicious. Had the beast heard him? He hadn't moved since spying it. Had his scent given him away? Not likely, since the wind was blowing toward him. What, then?

Satan abruptly uttered a low growl that carried to Nate's ears alone; as yet, the decoy was unaware of the predator's presence. Muscles working like coiled steel springs, the cat inched its right leg forward, then its left. But instead of creeping toward the decoy, it came straight toward the depression!

Nate was in a dire predicament. So long as the element of surprise had been in his favor, he had an edge. His advantage gone, there was only one option. He must jump up and shoot. Unfortunately, doing so would hasten the cat's attack. And he held no illusions about which one of them was the fastest.

The stallion voiced a challenge that prompted the panther to stop and glare. Nate heard his horse stomp its forefeet, saw Satan hiss and turn a few degrees toward the fire. That was all the opening he needed. Surging from concealment, he trained the Hawken on the cat's ribs, cocked the hammer, and tapped the trigger. Swift as he was, he couldn't compare to the panther.

As the brush burst upward, Satan whirled and flashed toward the spruce trees, clearing twenty feet at a leap. In the middle of the cat's second leap, Nate fired, his slug missing by a hair and thudding into the dirt under the panther's hindquarters. Satan's speed didn't allow for a second shot.

The undergrowth closed on the lion as Nate snatched at his powder horn and rapidly reloaded. Although his twin pistols were heavy-caliber, he'd rather have the sheer stopping power of the Hawken at his disposal. Precious seconds were lost as he fed powder, ball, and blanket wad down the barrel. Then, although he stood no chance of overtaking Satan, he raced into the trees, slanting toward the stream as the cat had done. Maybe, just maybe, he'd get at least one more shot.

Nate broke from cover near the water and squatted. Disappointment racked him on discovering the lion had effected its escape. He smacked his leg in anger, then stiffened as the night was torn by a ferocious snarl— *coming from the camp!* Satan had used the same ruse as last time, circling around while he chased shadows!

Witnesses would have been dazzled by Nate's fleetness of foot. Panicked whinnies mingled with raspy growls spurred him to his peak, and he weaved among the pines with abandon born of desperation. The horses were being set upon, the stallion and the mares by the fire, and from the sound of things they were in grave peril.

A single tree blocked the clearing when a strident neigh foretold a stricken horse. Nate's blood turned chill. He gained the camp and saw the panther clinging to the haunches of one of the mares, its wicked claws gouging deep furrows in her buttocks, thighs, and flanks. He took a stride to obtain a better angle and the mountain lion, which hadn't been looking in his direction but seemed somehow to sense his presence, sprang to the ground and fairly skimmed the grass as it fled.

"Not this time!" Nate shouted, swinging the rifle to compensate. He stroked the trigger, felt the stock smack into his shoulder. The panther jerked to one side, nearly fell, recovered, and gained the brush with a prodigious leap.

Nate yanked out a flintlock and ran to the thicket. He longed to see the cat convulsing in the bushes, but he should have known better. Satan was gone. There wasn't so much as a broken branch to show which way the lion had headed.

Turning, Nate dashed to the hurt mare. The fire had died to flickering fingers of flame so he added several pieces of dry wood. In the flare of light the deep cuts resembled a welter of scarlet ribbons. Blood flowed down the mare's rear legs and formed a spreading pool under her tail. Wincing in sympathy for the agony the horse was enduring, Nate set down his rifle and collected handfuls of grass which he used in an attempt to stanch the flow. Throughout, the mare stood as docile as a lamb, head bowed, saliva drooling from her chin.

The grass slowed the bleeding but didn't stop it, compelling Nate to resort to a crude remedy he'd once seen a Shoshone warrior employ. The Shoshone had been on a buffalo surround during which his favorite war horse had been gored in the stomach by an enraged bull. In a bid to save the prized mount from certain death, the warrior applied regular mud packs to the holes. Nate had secretly doubted the treatment would be of any benefit, yet to his amazement the horse recovered.

There was plenty of mud along the stream. Nate made eight trips, carrying as much as he could hold without getting it all over himself. The mare fidgeted when he applied a thick, dank layer, as he might the frosting on a cake, into the furrows the panther had torn from her flesh. When he was done, Nate stroked the mare's neck and stared over her shoulders at the benighted woodland. "I'll get you yet, you bastard," he declared grimly. "Wait and see."

As if in defiant answer, from the vicinity of a mountain half a mile to the south wafted the shrill shriek of Old Satan.

Chapter Five

"I'll get you. Just wait and see."

The boy squatted next to the mouse hole and hefted the club taken from the wood box. He had to use two hands to swing it with any force. Leaning back against the wall, he stared at the piece of cheese lying a yard away. Sooner or later the mouse would come out after the morsel and the boy would do as his father wanted and bash the creature's brains in. The very thought made the boy's stomach churn but he fought the sensation. He had to do as his father told him. He had to prove he wasn't an idler and worthless dreamer as his father believed.

The boy wanted his father to be proud of him. If he killed the mouse, maybe his father would stop being so critical. Of late they spent all their time arguing, a situation that got worse the older the boy became. He didn't understand why. When he had been younger, he'd gotten along wonderfully with both his parents. Now he was always being criticized, always being labelled as lazy and worthless. Yet he was the same person he had always been, and he never griped about doing his fair share of the chores. So why was his father forever carping about every little thing he did?

Troubled, the boy looked up as a shadow fell across the floor. He beamed in delight at the woman who entered the kitchen and said softly, "You won't have to worry about this mouse much longer, Mother."

She paused, blinked at seeing him, and frowned at the hole. "So your father picked you, did he?"

An edge to her tone prompted the boy to ask, "Is something wrong?"

The mother's face clouded and she gripped her dress so tight her knuckles turned white. "No, son. Everything is just fine. You be sure and do as your father tells you."

"He said the mouse gave you a bad scare."

"Did he indeed?" She averted her gaze. "Well, if your father said it, it must be true."

"I can't believe a little mouse would bother you. You're too"—the boy paused, seeking the right word, and chose—"mature."

He was greatly startled when his mother unexpectedly turned, came quickly over, and gave him a hug that threatened to bust his ribs. When she stepped back, she spun around before he could see her features.

"Are you all right?"

"I'm fine, son," she said, her voice rather husky.

"You sure?"

"Of course. Now stay quiet so the mouse will come out." Off she went, her head bowed.

The boy was puzzled by her strange behavior. There had been a time when his mother had been full of life and laughter and being around her had made him all warm inside. Now she upset him terribly because she was always so moody. Yet she had no reason to be. Grown-ups were impossible to figure out.

The boy wagged the bludgeon, concentrated on the hole, and waited.

The next morning dawned grey and somber with a promise of moisture in the rarified air. Nate was no sooner out of the blankets than he checked on the mare. She was dozing and only cracked an eye when he gently touched her. Her hind quarters were terribly swollen but thankfully the bleeding had stopped. Nate replaced the dry mud with a new layer. Then, and only then, did he warm his stomach with four cups of steaming coffee. Usually his morning brew perked him up. Not today. Circumstances forced him to make a decision he would rather not have to make.

The mare was too weak to go anywhere. Nate either left her in camp while he made his rounds of the traps, which would leave her at the mercy of Satan should the panther show up, or he stayed in camp until the mare was strong enough to tag along. That would take days, though. And during that time the mountain lion would wreak vengeance on any beaver caught in the traps, destroying their pelts.

Nate quaffed the last of his fourth cup, then set the cup on a flat rock beside the fire. No matter what he decided, he stood to lose. Which did he value more? The mare or the hides? The horse had been loyal and had never given him cause to complain, but by the same token he couldn't very well stand by and do nothing while the hellish cat made mincemeat of the beaver. He was damned if he did, damned if he didn't.

The sky gradually brightened although the sun was

unable to put in an appearance thanks to the growing cloud cover. Nate made no move to mount up. Twice he examined the mare. At length he voiced a string of oaths and prepared to leave. He hesitated with a foot in a stirrup, glanced at the fire, and had a brainstorm.

It took twenty minutes to gather enough wood for four more fires, arranged in a ring around the suffering horse. To each he added enough fuel to last an hour, minimum. "This is the best I can do," he told the mare. "Cats are afraid of fire. Maybe this will keep Satan at bay until I get back."

Then Nate climbed onto the stallion and rode off with the two other pack animals in tow. He intended to hurry, but along a northern tributary he found five beaver and up another he found three, the most caught at any one time since his arrival. Each had to be retrieved, the traps reset and placed elsewhere. Several hours elapsed. By his reckoning the time was close to noon when he caught sight of the camp. And something else.

A large, ungainly black bird was gliding down toward the clearing, pinions spread wide to soar on the currents, its reddish head cocked to one side.

Nate took one look and prodded the stallion into a gallop. As he clattered past the thicket he discovered five more buzzards either perched on the mare or next to her. Several had strips of bloody flesh hanging from their breaks. Some hissed on seeing Nate appear. As he bore down on them they hopped into the air and flapped frantically, fleeing every which way.

Nate paid them no heed. He vaulted from the saddle and dashed to the mare. Feeling for a heartbeat wasn't necessary. She had been dead for some time, her throat slashed wide open, her jugular severed. A pool of blood was soaking into the soil. Other claw marks were on her neck and head. Portions of her side had been torn out in bite-sized chunks.

"Satan!" Nate stated harshly, his fists clenched. A survey of the clearing turned up three partial prints, enough to tell the story.

The mare had most probably been asleep, the fires long out, when the panther sprang out of the spruce trees and in a few mighty bounds pounced on her neck. Two or three swipes of its razor claws had been enough to rip her throat apart. Then the cat had slashed and bit its prey numerous times in savage glee.

Her death bothered Nate. He tried telling himself it shouldn't, that such incidents were commonplace in the Rockies. Violence and dying were an integral part of Nature. Each and every day countless animals fell victim to hungry meat eaters. Nate knew he should be accustomed to the endless cycle of killing by now, but this was different. The mare had been a companion of sorts, not just another wild beast.

And, too, Nate was incensed at Satan. The wily lion had outmaneuvered him—again. Was it out there right this minute, observing his every move? He searched the vegetation without success.

A pressing problem presented itself. The mare was too big to bury. Nor could the carcass be left there to rot, not if Nate intended to call the clearing home until it was time to rejoin Shakespeare. Finding a new spot to camp, moving all the supplies and pelts, and erecting another lean-to would cost him another day or two. Since he wasn't too fond of the idea of staying in that valley a minute longer than necessary, he had to think of a means of moving the mare.

Nate selected the thickest limb he could carry, wedged an end under the mare, and tried flipping her body over.

The limb snapped like kindling. Relying on a lever proved a waste of energy.

Undaunted, Nate walked to his packs and found the long coil of rope he invariably brought along. Getting the rope around the mare's body took considerable effort and ingenuity and left blood smeared on his leggings and moccasins, prompting a trip to the stream to wash up. Then he mounted the stallion and tried hauling the mare off, but although the obedient black strained and tugged and heaved, the weight was too much for any one horse to move.

"I'm not licked yet," Nate declared, swinging down. Drawing his butcher knife, he sliced the rope in half, giving him two. One end of the severed length was tied to the mare, the other end around the neck of one of the remaining pack animals. Grasping the stallion's reins and the pack animal's lead, Nate guided them toward the thicket to the south. When the ropes lost all slack and both horses stopped, he gave a pull and urged them on with shouts of encouragement. Gradually, inch by laboriously gained inch, the mare's body was moved.

The job took nearly two hours. Nate was afraid the ropes would break so whenever they seemed on the verge of splitting he rested the stallion and pack horse a few minutes. In this manner he was able to drag the mare a distance of forty yards.

Untying the ropes, Nate rode back and rekindled the fire. He spent the afternoon skinning beaver and working on their hides. With the red sun hovering above the stark western peaks, he made his customary circuit of the traps and was mildly disappointed to end up empty-handed.

"Maybe I should leave early," Nate said to the stallion. "Maybe there aren't as many beaver left as I thought." He'd developed the habit of talking to the big black as if it was his best friend, and the stallion accommodated by pricking its ears whenever he spoke. "I've got enough as it is, anyway. Why be greedy?"

No buzzards swooped over the clearing this time, but there was something far worse. Nate rounded a spruce tree and drew rein in consternation, his face flushing beet red. "What the hell!" he roared. "I'll nail that panther's hide to my cabin wall!"

Old Satan had paid the camp a visit in Nate's absence. The mountain lion had scattered parfleches and packs all over, tearing many open. Worse, a small bale of plews, representing two full weeks of work, was missing.

Nate was fit to be tied. He stormed about the clearing hunting for tracks. Finding none, he insured the Hawken was loaded and hiked in ever widening circles around the camp, determined to find the missing bale before darkness set in. Time worked against him. So did his own common sense when he realized he had left the horses unattended. Reluctantly, he gave up after only a few minutes.

A magnificent full moon adorned the heavens but Nate wasn't in any frame of mind to appreciate the celestial spectacle. He sipped coffee and mulled what he should do next. Obviously the panther had it in for him. Perhaps Satan regarded the valley as its exclusive domain. Whatever the reason, the cat had to be the most spiteful beast alive, and it was as plain as the nose on Nate's face that it would continue to torment him until he departed.

Running went against Nate's grain, yet what else could he do? The loss of another horse or bale would be disastrous. Better to cut his losses while he could. Later on maybe he would return with a few Shoshone friends and settle accounts.

Nate slept fitfully that night. Up before daylight, he hid the rest of his bales in the spruce trees, using the ropes to hoist them high onto sturdy branches. Convinced the plews were safe, he secreted his packs in the depression he had dug near the stream, then covered them with brush.

"That ought to do it," Nate announced. Forgoing coffee, he climbed on the stallion and started collecting the Newhouses. At midday he brought those he had gathered to the clearing and immediately rode out after more. By late in the day he had reclaimed two-thirds of the traps. He could have collected another half-dozen or so, but he still wanted to scour the area around his camp for the missing bale.

Tethering the pack animals in the very center of the clearing where they would be able to see the panther if it came at them and whinny in alarm, Nate, acting on a hunch, rode the stallion into the spruce trees. The bale weighed upwards of fifty pounds and would be hard to drag off, even for Old Satan. The thickets were too dense for the cat to make much headway, and Nate couldn't see the lion lugging the bale across the stream. Making the spruce trees the best bet.

The guess turned out to be accurate. Beyond the spruce trees lay a meadow. Nate gazed out over it and saw brown spots among the high grass. Applying his heels, he galloped to the nearest one, his anger surging at the sight of a pelt that had been torn into ragged sections. It was the same with the next hide, and the next. Satan had used teeth and claws to rend the plews asunder.

Not once in Nate's entire life had he heard of a panther doing such a thing. He made a sweep of the entire meadow and discovered only three hides intact. These he took with him.

Mountain Cat

The prospect of another night in the valley was mildly unnerving. Nate was actually anxious to leave, but he had the remainder of the traps to bring in. Provided that luck smiled on him, he'd be ready to go by noon of the next day at the very latest.

As an added precaution, Nate tore out bushes by the roots and piled them in a waist-high circle in the clearing. The barrier didn't offer much protection, but the panther would be unable to get at the horses and him without leaping over it. And if he had to, he could set the barrier alight to drive the cat off.

Nate ate glumly, wolfing beaver meat without relish. Afterward he sat up sipping coffee until well past midnight. To his surprise, Satan didn't appear, nor did the valley echo to the lion's throaty snarls. Propped against his saddle, he fell asleep with a pistol in each hand.

A whinny awakened Nate hours later. By the positions of the stars and constellations he knew the time was about four in the morning. All three horses were excited by something south of the barrier. Rising and stepping to the stallion, he gripped its mane and quietly straddled its broad back. From his vantage point he commanded a sweeping view of the clearing.

Satan was so close to the barrier Nate could have hit the cat with a stone. In the pale moonlight its coat had a whitish sheen. The lion appeared baffled by the wall of brush and was silently pacing back and forth.

Nate extended both flintlocks slowly so as not to draw attention to himself. He aimed carefully at the panther's head and curled his thumbs around the hammers. They would click when cocked, which couldn't be helped. The worst that might happen was the monster would run off. If not, the smoothbore .55-caliber pistols would end Satan's career then and there.

Grinning in anticipation, Nate jerked the hammers back. They did indeed click, loudly, too, and the panther reacted accordingly before Nate could fire. However, not in the fashion Nate expected. Instead of racing off, the mountain lion whirled, took a single leap, and cleared the top of the brush barrier with feet to spare, springing straight at Nate.

In the blink of an eye Nate compensated, training both pistols on the hurtling cat, but as he did the black stallion reared and he had to clutch at the stallion's mane to keep from being thrown off. In the act of rearing, the stallion pulled free of its tether.

Satan alighted in front of the stallion and raked the horse with its claws, then evaded a flurry of pounding hoofs. Nate raised one arm to fire. Again he was thwarted when the stallion abruptly leaped and sailed over the brush. Nate tried to stop the horse before it reached the thicket but the stallion ignored the pressure of his legs and arms.

"Whoa!" Nate shouted frantically. "Whoa, big fellow!" He jammed the flintlocks under his belt to free his hands so he could grab at the rope dangling from the stallion's neck. Bending forward, he snatched it and straightened just as the black burst from the thicket and entered the forest.

Nate looked up, saw a low tree limb sweeping at his face, and ducked. The limb struck his beaver hat sending it flying. He glanced back, wanting to note the exact spot so he could come back later, but the dark shadows made the area a murky soup.

"Stop, damn it!" Nate thundered, hauling on the rope with all his strength. The stallion, fired with fear, sped onward into the night.

Nate tried not to think of what might be happening

to his mares. Repeatedly he tried to halt the stallion. When it wouldn't obey, he tensed, preparing to leap off and run to the clearing to prevent the mountain lion from slaughtering the pack horses, if it hadn't already done so.

Bracing both hands on the stallion's back, Nate shoved upward. Too late he glimpsed another limb rushing toward him. He threw up his arms to protect himself. The limb smashed him in the temple. Excrutiating pain racked him from head to toe and he was catapulted end over end. Dimly he was aware of crashing down, of the drum of the stallion's hoofs rapidly receding.

Then all went black.

Somewhere else. Long ago.

The boy felt a hand on his shoulder and his eyes snapped wide with fright. He stared into the hard features of his father and inwardly struggled to calm himself.

"Is this how you do a job I ask you to do? You fall asleep?"

"I'm sorry, Father. It's been hours and the mouse hasn't shown itself."

"Oh?" The father pivoted, pointed at the cheese. It had been gnawed clean through and half of it was missing. "See those little teeth marks? What do you think the mouse was doing while you were being your usual lazy self?"

"I didn't hear it!" the boy blurted.

"That's your excuse? The mouse should have been polite enough to make more noise so you could wake up and kill it?"

"I didn't say—" the boy began, and recoiled when he was cuffed on the ear.

"What have I told you about sassing me, son?" the

father demanded in a strained tone. "Haven't I told you again and again never to talk back to your mother or me?"

"Yes."

"Yes, what?"

"Yes, sir."

A protracted sigh issued from the father and he slowly stood. "What am I going to do with you? I try and try to teach you how to be behave. I do my best to show you what it takes to be successful in this vicious world of ours. But you won't pay me any mind." He sadly shook his head. "I've never known anyone so lazy in all my days."

An angry retort reached the boy's lips but went no further. His ear still stung terribly.

"I know what you're thinking," the father declared. "It's just a tiny mouse. Why am I making such an issue of it?" He nudged the cheese with a toe. "There must be some way of impressing the point I'm trying to make."

"I won't fall asleep again. I promise," the boy said.

"You'd better not or I'll tan your backside," the father warned. "You're not too old for a switching." Turning, he took a few paces, then drew up short and snapped his fingers. "Of course! I saw him just a few minutes ago on my way home! Drop that piece of wood and come with me."

"Where are we going?"

"Don't ask questions," the father barked. Grabbing the boy by the shirt, he hurried to the front door. The sidewalk was packed with people, while in the street a steady stream of creaking carriages and rattling wagons flowed to and fro.

The boy was hustled two blocks to an intersection

with a main avenue. Here there were many more people, many more carriages. His father stopped in the midst of the bedlam and grinned. The boy looked all around in confusion, afraid to ask a question for fear of being ridiculed.

"See him, son?"

"Who, father?"

"One Leg, of course. Over by that wall."

The beggar had a name but no one knew it so everyone in the neighborhood called him One Leg. He was ancient, with wrinkles in his wrinkles, his clothes little more than grimy rags. Every day of the week except the Lord's day he could be found on this particular corner, battered tin cup on the ground in front of him to receive whatever alms were offered.

"Do you understand now?" the father asked.

No, the boy didn't. So he hesitated, uncertain of the right answer, and his father went on excitedly.

"This is what comes of being lazy, son. This is why I try to instill in you a dedication to hard work and discipline. I don't want you to end your days like One Leg." The father's voice dripped contempt. "He doesn't have to make a living this way. There are jobs he could do if he really wanted to. But all he does is sit on his backside, depending on the kindness of strangers for his livelihood. Do you want to be like him?"

"No," the boy said. In his heart he was deeply sorry for anyone who had to suffer so much.

"Good. I'm delighted you finally see the light. Now let's go home so you can kill that mouse. And if you start to doze off again, you just think of One Leg. That should set you straight."

"Yes, sir," the boy agreed, although truth to tell he was at a loss to see how his father could compare the beggar's pathetic plight to killing a lowly rodent. After all, One Leg hadn't asked to lose a limb.

"One day you'll thank me for this lesson," the father said proudly.

"I'm sure I will."

Chapter Six

Warm sunshine tingling Nate King's face returned him to the land of the living. He sat up with a start and immediately regretted doing so when a tremendous bolt of anguish shot through him. Groaning, he placed a hand on his temple and felt his palm grow sticky with half-dried blood. He flinched as he probed gently with his fingertips, tracing the outline of a ragged gash.

Propping a hand under him, Nate pushed to his feet, swayed at an onslaught of dizziness, and would have fallen had he not reached out and leaned against a tree. By the height of the sun he guessed he'd been unconscious for four or five hours. He scanned the woods for the stallion but saw only chipmunks.

"Damn," Nate muttered. For all he knew, the black was halfway to Shoshone country. He would have to rely on one of the mares. At the thought he stiffened. Then he shuffled toward the camp, drawing both pistols when the thicket came in sight. He feared the worst, and his fears were realized.

Part of the brush barrier had been destroyed, barreled aside by a terrified pack animal. Drops of blood showed the mare had been hurt, and also showed she had fled eastward. The second horse hadn't been so lucky.

Satan had brought the animal down by severing the tendons on her rear legs. Once the mare had been hamstrung, the panther had finished her off at his leisure, clawing great chunks from her body, slicing her neck to ribbons, and taking bites from various spots. The horse had died awash in a thick bath of her blood, and what remained was coated with crimson.

Not content with slaying the pack animal, Satan had turned his wrath on Nate's belongings. The saddle bore a dozen claw cuts. The blankets had been frayed. A parfleche had been reduced to scrap leather. Not a single item was worth being salvaged.

Where was the Hawken? Nate wondered in dismay. He needed the rifle if he was to have any hope of escaping the valley alive. A search of the bloody area inside the barrier was fruitless. He expanded his search to the clearing with the same result. Pulse quickening, he hunted among the spruce trees. Persistence kept him at it for half an hour, at which point thirst took him to the stream. He was kneeling to dip his hands in the crystal clear water when he saw his rifle lying nearby. Grinning, he dashed over and scooped it up. Other than teeth marks on the stock, the rifle was undamaged.

Renewed confidence invigorated Nate. He drank heartily, then washed his wound, gritting his teeth against the torment. Going to the depression, he removed some of the brush and withdrew a parfleche containing jerky and pemmican. This went over his left shoulder.

He rummaged in a pack for an old blanket he kept on hand as a spare. From this he cut a wide strip, dabbed the strip in the stream, and wrapped it once about his head, securing it with a knot at the back.

Nate was almost ready. The rest of the bales were safe in the trees. The rest of his provisions were hidden in the depression. The traps he placed deep in a thicket where the rain couldn't get at them. Then Nate hiked eastward, staying close to the stream where the going was easy. He chewed on jerky and kept alert for sign of Old Satan. All he wanted was one good shot, one chance to pay the monster back for the pain and all he had lost. Remaining in the valley would be foolish. Nate planned to head south and find McNair. The two of them would come back for his things, get in and out in a single day in order to avoid the panther. It was the best he could do under the circumstances. He should be thankful that he had enough pelts left to bring in a tidy sum at the rendezvous.

Nate recalled how his heart had leaped into his throat when the panther leaped at him the night before, and he marveled yet once more at the cat's actions. Such relentless conduct was so extraordinary he doubted anyone would believe him when he told the tale. If he told the story. It embarrassed him to think he had been beaten by a wild beast. He'd long believed that with a little hard work and discipline a person could surmount any problem, could overcome any hardship. Yet here he'd been put to the test and found wanting.

Hours later Nate came abreast of the hill he had descended to enter the valley. Scaling it on foot was an arduous labor. He often had to pause to rest. On reaching the crest he turned and gazed down on Satan's shaded valley, and in an act of sheer spite he cupped a hand to his mouth and voiced a series of Shoshone war whoops. They echoed off the mountains, rolling out across the valley in both directions. Wherever Satan was, he was bound to hear them.

Chuckling, Nate squared his shoulders and resumed trekking southward. Despite the nightmare, he was in fine spirits. He had food, he had ammunition. He had his rifle, pistols, knife, and tomahawk. He could live off the land almost as well as any Indian. In short, he was supremely confident he would reach his friend within a few days and his ordeal would be over.

The wildlife afforded ample entertainment. Whether it was squirrels scampering in the trees or ravens winging overhead or deer spooked from cover, there was always something happening. Once Nate spied moving brown spots on steep cliffs to the west. Bighorns, they were, bounding along the cliff face with unmatched ease, as unaffected by the dizzying heights below as if they were on solid ground.

Later, Nate spotted a small herd of shaggy mountain buffalo. He stopped, lifted the Hawken, then changed his mind. It had been ages since he ate a juicy steak, and merely looking at the grazing brutes made his mouth water, his stomach rumble. But he couldn't eat a whole buffalo at one sitting and he didn't have the means of packing the excess out. So rather than waste so much meat, he continued walking.

The sun arced westward, lengthening the shadows. Nate nibbled on jerky and looked for a spot to camp for the night. His head was torturing him. He'd turn in early, enjoy a decent sleep, and be full of vigor and vim come daylight.

A hare provided Nate's supper. Lacking a pot to cook stew, he chopped the meat into square bits, then skewered them on a sharpened stick and held them over the fire until they were done. He ate with relish, wiping his greasy fingers on his leggings. For a bed he spread pine needles and grass to form a mat an inch thick.

That night Nate slept better than he had in days. Leftover hare was his breakfast. As the sun peeked above the horizon, he adjusted his possibles bag and ammunition pouch, shouldered the spare parfleche, and headed out.

Nate whistled as he walked, his rifle balanced across his left shoulder. The more distance he put between himself and the valley, the happier he felt. His previous worries seemed downright silly, and he convinced himself that he had let his imagination get the better of him by exaggerating Satan's prowess. Toward the end there he had regarded the panther as if it had been a demon instead of just another oversized cat. True, it had an incredibly savage temperament. But Satan was a run-of-the-mill panther, nothing more.

Noon found Nate at a creek. Upon slaking his thirst he removed his bandage and washed the wound. It was healing nicely and gave no indication of being infected. He stripped off his buckskins and sat in a small pool splashing cool water on his chest and back. Refreshed, he followed the creek for over a mile, until it angled eastward and he had to journey on to the south.

Nate had hoped he would reach Shakespeare's valley before the second day was up, but since he was making a beeline for the valley instead of taking the easiest route as he had on the stallion, the exceptionally rugged terrain slowed him down. Deadfalls, ravines, and cliffs all had to be skirted or negotiated with extreme caution. Consequently he was several miles from his destination when twilight claimed the mountains.

Nate's sleep was even more restful than it had been the first night. He had chosen a sheltered spot close to the bottom of a towering cliff, as he had once before. At dawn he was up, eager to go on. Taking a piece of pemmican from the parfleche, he bit down and started walking, absently gazing at the cliff above. A patch of brown against the background of solid rock arrested his attention and he stared at it to see if it would move, certain it was another bighorn. Seconds later the creature rose off its haunches and walked a few yards, and when it did, Nate's mouth went slack and the pemmican fell to the grass.

The animal wasn't a bighorn at all.

It was Satan.

Long ago. Far away.

The boy was growing drowsy again. To keep from falling asleep and arousing his father's anger, he stared out the kitchen window at the big oak tree in the back yard. A robin sat on a branch chirping its little heart out. The boy smiled, envying the bird its lust for life. And its freedom. The robin could go where it wanted, when it wanted. It never had anyone telling it what to do or how to live its life. How the boy wished he might have the same sort of freedom!

Motion registered at the corner of the boy's eye and he swung his head around. Although he should have expected to see what he saw, he was nonetheless stunned to behold a mouse nibbling on the cheese. A tiny, harmless rodent with big, appealing eyes, its whiskers twitching as its mouth worked in a hungry frenzy.

The boy was mesmerized. He gawked in fascination, completely forgetting about the club in his hands. Never had he seen mice close up before. He hadn't realized how very teeny they were, how delicate they appeared. The thought of crushing this one to a pulp caused his tummy to flutter.

A distant sound made the mouse suddenly stop eating and raise its head high to sniff the air. When assured there was no threat, it bit into the cheese with renewed enthusiasm.

Reluctantly the boy firmed his grip on the club. He had a job to do, whether he liked doing it or not. As his parents had pointed out, where there was one mouse, there were always more, and if left to breed uncontrolled they could infest a house from cellar to attic. Worse, they sometimes carried diseases. So the rodent had to be exterminated for the good of his family.

But the boy hesitated, unable to bring himself to perform the deed. The mouse was so fragile looking, so innocent. How could he kill it?

Over a minute went by and the dainty creature polished off most of the cheese. The boy had to do something soon or it would scurry into the hole. Girding himself, he raised the wood over his head, but he did so slowly, not with the speed required to strike in time to stop the mouse from escaping. The rodent predictably whirled and scurried into its sanctuary. Rather than being upset, the boy grinned.

"What do you think you are doing?"

Shocked, the boy looked up to find his father framed in the doorway. "I tried to kill the mouse," he blurted even though he knew better.

"If there's one thing I can't stand, it's a liar," the father said gruffly, advancing and cuffing the boy on the head so hard the boy was knocked onto his backside. "I just stood there and saw you deliberately let that mouse get away. Why? What in the world were you thinking of?"

David Thompson

The boy rubbed his ear and clenched his teeth.

"Two days now you've been at this and you haven't killed a single mouse," the father criticized. "When I was your age, I would have had six or seven squashed by now. What excuse do you have?"

"None," the boy confessed.

"No, you don't. And frankly, I'm tired of this nonsense." The father went to the cupboard and obtained another small piece of cheese. "Listen to me, young man," he declared. "You're going to do as I want whether you like it or not. I won't have a shirker in my family. When there's work to be done, we do it."

"Yes, sir."

The father deposited the cheese at the same place on the floor. "I want you to know that if it was up to me, I'd use poison. But your mother is afraid her darling dog would get hold of some. So we have to do this the hard way." He glanced at the mouse hole. "You might be wondering why I don't go out and buy one of the traps available. Why should I waste the money when you can do the job just as well or better?"

"You have always taught us to be thrifty, Father."

"Take my advice. The sooner you get this done, the sooner you can go waste your time reading." The father walked to the door, then looked over his shoulder. "Sometimes we have to do things we don't like doing, son. We have to take the bad with the good, as it were."

"I know."

"Do you? I wonder." The father frowned. "If you learn nothing else from this experience, learn this. The bad things in our life just don't up and vanish because we want them to go away. We have to face problems head on and overcome them or they'll keep coming back to haunt us later."

* * *

Nate King gaped at the monster cat in disbelief. A wave of apprehension washed over him and there was a sinking sensation in his gut. It couldn't be! And yet there the panther sat, gazing down at him from its lofty roost! The damn beast had trailed him all the way from the valley, had no doubt been shadowing him all along. Why? What did it have in mind?

The answer was obvious. Satan had no intention of allowing him to get away. The panther was stalking him, biding its time until it could take him unawares. The hunter had become the hunted.

But the very notion was preposterous! Nate reflected. Panthers didn't track down people as they would other game. Quite the contrary. Panthers went out of their way to avoid human beings. Or most did, anyway, because there was no denying the testimony of his own eyes.

Nate raised the Hawken, realized he would be wasting the lead ball, and jerked the rifle down again. What should he do? Go up after the cat? No. Attempting to climb the cliff would be certain suicide.

Cradling the rifle in the crook of an elbow, Nate marched southward. Perhaps he was becoming over-wrought for no reason. The panther hadn't attacked him since he left the valley, had it? And before nightfall he would be back with Shakespeare, wouldn't he? If the cat showed itself then, the two of them would ride it down, and whoever shot it would have a glorious trophy to mount on the wall of his cabin.

At the edge of the pines Nate glanced up. The mountain lion was gone. He raised a hand to shield his eyes from the bright sunlight reflected off the cliff face and scanned the rim to where it sloped down into the forest a quarter of a mile ahead. There was a chance he could ambush the panther if he could get there before the cat did.

Nate ran for all he was worth. Satan had outsmarted himself by taking to the high ground. There was just the one way down, since not even a mountain lion could descend a sheer rock wall. Nate would soon have the predator right in his sights!

Only someone with iron sinews and superbly conditioned to the high altitude could have reached the side of the cliff in so short a time. Crouching behind a boulder, Nate scoured the slope. Satan was bound to appear at any moment. He cocked the Hawken, rested the barrel on top of the boulder, and smirked. I'm ready for you, you hoodoo killer! he thought. Come and be rubbed out!

By all rights the panther should have appeared. Minutes dragged by and it didn't. Perplexed, Nate climbed on top of the boulder to see if he could spot the tawny shape somewhere above. Either Satan was hiding or the cat had gone the other way.

On a spur of the moment decision, Nate ran up the slope to the rim. He couldn't let this golden opportunity pass. The panther wouldn't be expecting him to go after it, so he'd have an edge. Stealthily working his way along the narrow shelf that crowned the cliff, he held his finger lightly on the trigger.

To say Nate was upset when he had gone over fifty yards and not found his quarry was an understatement. He stopped, ascended a jumbled pile of boulders to the uppermost slab, and surveyed the shelf before him. It was as if the ground had opened up and swallowed the panther whole.

Just then, in the forest at the bottom of the south slope, a mountain lion coughed.

Nate swung around and glowered in exasperation.

Somehow, Satan had gotten to the woods before he got to the slope. All the time he had been looking for the cat at the top of the cliff, the cat had been resting in the shade of the evergreens. It was enough to make him want to hit something, so he did, slapping the slab and stinging his palm.

Retracing his steps, Nate was presently among the pines again. He figured Satan was ahead of him, and he searched diligently for tracks. The cat was too clever for him. All he located was a partial print that might or might not be that of a panther.

As Nate straightened he noticed the wildlife had fallen totally silent as it had that day he'd been en route to the dark valley, leading him to speculate on whether Satan had been stalking him far longer than he supposed. It was a disturbing feeling to find oneself the prey of one of the most fierce carnivores inhabiting the Rockies. Now he knew how a deer or an elk felt under similar circumstances.

Except there was an important difference. Unlike a deer or an elk, Nate could easily slay the big cat if he could only get a shot at it. To this end he vigilantly advanced. The eerie stillness rasped on his nerves, and he was almost grateful when a squirrel commenced raising a racket off to the right. Then it occurred to him that the cause of the squirrel's outrage might be the mountain lion.

Changing direction, Nate went from cover to cover until he spied the chattering denizen of the upper terraces high on the limb of a fir tree. The squirrel was staring at undergrowth a score of yards from the trunk. Flattening, Nate studied the wall of vegetation. He was certain Satan was in there, and equally certain there must a method of luring the cat out.

A rock suggested a means. Nate picked it up, hefted it a few times, then hurled the rock as far as he could to the left. It hit in a tree and clattered off a number of branches before thudding to earth.

A patch of underbrush moved.

Nate sighted on the spot and held the Hawken steady. As soon as the panther showed its hairy face, he'd core its brain with a lead ball. He waited, and waited. The squirrel kept on chattering. The breeze increased, swaying the branches overhead. And the panther failed to materialize.

Again Nate tried to entice the lion into the open by tossing a rock, this time close to the underbrush where Satan was concealed. Not so much as a twig stirred. Puzzled, Nate crawled forward, setting his elbows and knees down gently to muffle the noise.

Every mountain man knew that it was easier to see a moving object when low to the ground. An erect man might miss spying a moving buck in a thicket because the color of the buck's hide blended so well into the background. The same man, if crouched or lying down, would be more apt to detect the difference because the angle reduced the effect of the background.

So Nate remained flat on his stomach, and when he came to the undergrowth he snaked into its depths rather than stand and walk. A pungent odor stopped him. He didn't have to look hard for the source, a pile of raccoon droppings by his elbow, droppings so fresh they were runny.

Was that what the squirrel had seen? Nate mused. A raccoon? Avoiding the pile, he wound farther into the recesses of the brushwood. Suddenly, a flurry of activity erupted thirty feet distant. There was some sort of struggle going on. Nate lurched into a run, stooping to pass under scrub trees. He saw a tawny form and another, smaller shape, swirling around one another.

Nate was almost upon them when the tawny creature sped to the northwest. The outline of the panther was unmistakable and he couldn't resist dropping to one knee, aiming, and firing. Whether his shot was on the mark or not was impossible to tell. Apparently not, since Satan faded into the greenery without slowing the slightest bit.

Reloading on the run, Nate came to where the commotion had been and found a large male raccoon lying on its side, its lifeblood gushing from a ruptured throat, its intestines spilling from a ruptured belly. The panther had attacked it but not bothered to carry it off to eat. Wanton slaughter was all the beast seemed to live for.

The raccoon looked up at Nate and hissed. Its forepaws, uncannily like human hands, twitched and flexed.

"I'll get him yet, for both of us," Nate said softly. The coon's small, dark, appealing eyes reminded him of something but he couldn't quite pin down the memory.

Shortly the animal broke into violent convulsions. Gasping loudly, the raccoon breathed its last and went limp.

Nate finished tapping the ball and wad down on top of the powder and slid the ramrod into its housing. He trailed the mountain lion a few dozen yards, seeking spoor, and wasn't overly disgruntled when he didn't find any.

The panther was as devious as it was bloodthirsty. Satan never made mistakes, never left enough sign for anyone to follow. Experience or an inherent disposition had transformed the mountain lion into a living engine of destruction with an instinct for self-preservation that bordered on the supernatural.

A wry grin curled Nate's mouth. He'd done it again, ascribed human traits to an animal. He must keep reminding himself that the panther was just that and nothing more. It could be killed just like any other panther. All he'd need was a bit of luck.

No. That wasn't quite right.

All he'd need was a *lot* of luck.

Chapter Seven

A deathly hush gripped the verdant woodland as Nate King hastened southward. It had been over an hour since he found the raccoon and not once had he so much as glimpsed the panther, but he knew the cat was close by, knew it was stalking him. Intuition, instinct, logical deduction, all were in harmony on that one point. Satan intended to slay him, and it was only a matter of time before the mountain lion tried.

Nate's senses strained to their limits. Often he paused to listen. His eyes constantly roved over the terrain, noting possible spots where the panther might jump him, spots to be avoided unless there was no choice, and in that case they were to be approached with the Hawken leveled and cocked.

Uneasiness rested heavily on Nate's broad shoulders. He was edgy and knew it. While not the sort to harbor irrational fears, he couldn't suppress a feeling that the worst was yet to come, that he might finally have met his match. Luck, more than skill, had seen him through numerous clashes with hostiles and beasts, and his luck in this instance seemed to have forsaken him. Already he'd lost all his horses and had to abandon his traps and other fixings. He was afoot, low on food. When he eventually became fatigued, he didn't dare lie down and sleep because he might not wake up again.

There was one bright note in the gloomy outlook. Nate would be safe once he reunited with Shakespeare McNair. He held that comforting thought uppermost in mind as he walked. It bolstered his confidence, allowed him to discount the early setbacks as minor occurrences. Then he came to the gorge.

As gorges went, this one was small. Narrow at the top, only two hundred feet from top to bottom, it nonetheless posed a formidable obstacle. Nate glanced right and left and was disheartened to see he would have to walk over half a mile in either direction to go around. Any delay at this point was costly since it meant he wouldn't rejoin McNair until well after dark.

There might be a means of gaining the far rim sooner. Nate turned westward, looking for a way down. He was beginning to regret taking the straightest course to save time. Just the opposite had happened. He would have been much better off going the easy way, as he had on horseback.

No means of reaching the bottom presented itself, but Nate was sure he spied a game trail in the midst of the heavy brush below, which meant there had to be a way. If so, it eluded him. He chafed with impatience and resigned himself to going all the way around.

Presently, Nate skirted an immense boulder balanced on the edge and stopped in delight on beholding recent deer prints leading over the rim. Sinking to one knee, he studied the side of the gorge. Long ago a section of wall had buckled, and now a steep slope consisting of crumpled rock and earth formed a treacherous incline dotted with many small boulders. The deer tracks wound to the bottom and disappeared in a thicket.

Nate started to ease over the edge, then hesitated. If he was wrong, if there was no way up the other side, he'd waste hours. Did he care to run the risk of another night alone? He glanced back, checked the forest for sign of the panther, and when assured it was safe to proceed, he carefully lowered himself onto the slope. Immediately a lot of dirt and small rocks cascaded out from under him. The footing was treacherous, maybe too treacherous, and he considered whether to climb back up and go on around just to be safe.

The sudden sound of onrushing feet alerted Nate to his peril heartbeats before Satan struck. Nate was in the act of spinning to confront the cat when his left foot slipped out from under him and he toppled backward.

The misstep saved Nate's life. He felt a puff of air fan his hair as the lion's paw just missed his head before the panther's body slammed into him. The impact bowled him over and he tumbled down the slope. Frantically, he tried to dig in his heels. He clutched at boulders but couldn't arrest his momentum. To the contrary, he fell faster, gaining speed the farther he went.

Nate involuntarily cried out when his left side smashed into a boulder. A bone distinctly cracked and the subsequent pain was enough to make his head whirl. The Hawken went flying. Nate hit another boulder, and another. Severely stunned, so disoriented he couldn't tell which way was up and which way was down, he continued tumbling end over end for an eternity.

A gut-wrenching impact ended Nate's descent. Dimly,

he was aware of loose earth and dust raining down upon him. Flat on his stomach, he tried to lift his head but couldn't. He was weak, his vision blurred. He also felt nauseous. Bile rose in his throat and he swallowed it. Gritting his teeth, he was about to try and sit up when he heard something coming down the slope toward him.

Satan!

Nate was in no shape to fight. He sucked in air and held it, then lay as limp as a wet rag, feigning death. His sole hope for salvation rested in convincing the mountain lion that he was dead. It might leave him alone if it wasn't hungry, although in light of its extremely bloodthirsty nature, that wasn't a certainty.

Light footfalls came close to Nate's head. Raspy breathing pinpointed the panther's exact position. Nate felt soft pressure on his shoulder and listened to loud sniffs. Warm breath touched his neck, his jaw, his cheek. The cat's face was inches from his own, so near its whiskers scraped his skin.

Stark panic welled up within Nate. It took every iota of self-control he had to keep from leaping up and striking out in blind terror. A paw nudged him once, twice, three times, and the third time claws bit into his flesh, not deep, but deep enough to cause him to bite his lower lip to choke off a yell.

Nate's lungs were at their limit. He had to take a breath, and once he did the mountain lion would be on him so fast he'd be unable to offer much resistance. The soft crunch of calloused pads worked their way toward his feet and he relaxed a smidgen, thinking Satan was going to leave. Suddenly tremendous anguish lanced his left ankle. Satan had bitten him! He almost screamed, but instead bit his lower lip and suppressed a shudder. Warm blood trickled down over his foot.

Satan gave another loud sniff, swatted the bloody moccasin once, and loped off.

Relief flooded Nate's being. His lungs were close to bursting but he held his breath a bit longer, afraid the panther would hear. Only when he was on the verge of blacking out did he swiftly cup a hand over his mouth to muffle the noise, then exhaled. His body shook as he gratefully gulped in fresh air while cautiously raising his head for a look around.

The mountain lion was gone, but whether up to the top of the gorge or somewhere in the brush along the bottom, Nate had no idea.

Nate saw an isolated pile of earth and stones nearby and dragged himself into its shadow. Propping his back against it, he took stock. His head hurt again, abominably, but there were no new wounds. His chest hurt, too, possibly from a fractured or broken rib. And there was his foot, which bothered him the least but was bleeding quite badly. Miraculously, neither the pistols, the butcher knife, nor his tomahawk had fallen loose during his headlong plummet, and the powder horn, ammo pouch, and parfleche were intact. The only item he'd lost was the rifle, the one he needed the most.

Nate peeled off his left moccasin and examined the puncture marks. The cat had nipped his flesh, no more, so the damage wasn't severe. Drawing his knife, he cut a wide strip off the bottom of his left legging and wrapped it tightly around his ankle. Several whangs tied into a long string sufficed to secure the bandage in place. He gingerly pulled the moccasin back on, drew a flintlock, and slowly rose.

There was still no sign of Satan so Nate shuffled to the slope and began climbing. He wasn't about to leave without the Hawken.

A rifle was an essential part of a trapper's gear, the single most indispensable item he owned. It enabled him to hold his own against fierce beasts and bloodthirsty hostiles. It made possible slaying game at distances no pistol could ever reach. Overall, a rifle made staying alive easier, and frequently was the deciding factor in whether a trapper lived or died.

Nate King intended to live. The only problem was that boulders covered the slope like warts on a toad, scores of them, and the incline itself was uneven, dotted with ruts and bigger depressions. The Hawken could be anywhere. He might miss seeing it even if he was right on top of it.

Climbing slowly, Nate peeked behind every boulder, in every crack. Thanks to the immense boulder at the top, the one he had been near when the panther attacked, he had a fair idea of the path he had taken to the bottom. Allowing for a five yard margin one way or the other, he could reasonably confine his search to a belt a dozen yards wide.

The climb became increasingly difficult the higher Nate ascended. He had to grab hold of boulders to keep his footing, and often he slipped despite the extra purchase. The loose earth slid out from under him no matter how lightly he set his feet down.

Sixty feet from the bottom the inevitable took place. Nate was easing around a boulder for a better look into a wide hole when the dirt underfoot swept out from under him and he fell backward. Arms flailing, he attempted to regain his balance. Gravity thwarted him, and he grimaced as he slammed onto his back and shot toward the bottom. Nothing he did stopped his slide. By twisting and turning he was able to avoid most of the boulders below him, but not all. At length he rolled to a stop in a choking cloud of dust, battered but not gravely injured.

Coughing and wheezing, Nate pushed to his feet and glared at the incline. It would be the height of folly to try again. Yet he refused to leave without the Hawken. If he could regain the rim, he might be able to spot it. But the only way to do that was to find a way up the other side and then to circle around.

Nate moved eastward, into the brush bordering the base of the south wall. The deer tracks led in the same direction. Too bad, he mused, that he didn't have tapered hoofs like they did; then he'd be able to scale the slope with ease.

A glimmer of blue was visible ahead. Nate ducked under a limb, passed a thornbush, and emerged in a clearing dominated by a picturesque spring. He squatted, tested the water by dipping a finger in and touching it to his lips, then drank his full. The spring explained why the deer visited the gorge regularly. They could eat, drink, and lie low, safe from predators.

Not now, though. Nate twisted and scanned the vegetation. Was Satan out there, watching him? Or had the panther gone elsewhere in the belief he was dead?

Pistol in hand, Nate entered the growth beyond the pool. The tracks brought him to a thin strip of bare earth adjoining the base of the wall. He was encouraged by the fact most of the tracks led in the same direction, which implied another way out of the gorge. In his eagerness to find it, he exerted himself more than he should have, and abruptly he was racked by intense spasms in his chest. Groaning, he doubled over, staggered to a low protruding finger of rock, and sat down.

The rib must be worse than he thought, Nate realized. It had been aching terribly since his second fall, but this was the worst yet. If he had any common sense he'd rest for a while to let the discomfort subside. But he was running short of time. Night loomed several hours off.

Nate picked up a thick twig, jammed it between his clenched teeth, and strode on. Whenever his ribs flared, he bit down hard. In this way he covered hundreds of yards and came to the path leading up to the south rim.

Actually, it wasn't so much a path as a series of skeletal switchbacks extending from the bottom to the very top, switchbacks wide enough for deer with their slender hoofs but hardly wide enough for a grown man's feet. Nate looked and would have swore if not for the twig in his mouth. The prospect of scaling them in his condition was daunting, but it was either that or attempt to climb the steep slope again.

Nate squinted at the sun, well on its western arc, then moved up the first grade to the sharp bend. Here the path was no more than six inches wide. He had to step sideways to get to the next grade. Treading with consummate care, he climbed to the second bend. Once more he moved sideways. And so on and so on it went until he was halfway to the top and half out of breath with his chest in acute torment. Halting, Nate leaned against the wall and stared at the switchbacks below. It was strange, but from that high up they reminded him of a series of steps, cellar steps, specifically, steps he hadn't thought of in many a year.

Long ago. Many miles away.

The boy sat at the bottom of the cellar steps, the club in his left hand, his bored expression fixed on a mouse hole in the wall beside his father's workbench. He heard footsteps above him but didn't turn around.

Mountain Cat

"Well, look at this, Sherm. He's still at it."

"The mice must be smarter than he is, Lou. That's all I can figure."

There were scornful snickers and a hand fell on the boy's shoulder.

"What the dickens is the matter with you, little guy?" Lou asked. "Over a week you've been at this and you haven't killed one lousy mouse."

"Keep it up and you'll spend the rest of your life down here," Sherm declared. "Father is so mad at you we can't even mention your name when he's around."

Hiding the ache in his heart, the boy shifted and gazed at his two brothers. "I haven't seen one yet."

"Don't lie to us, brat," Sherm said, giving the boy a slap on the back of the head. "We were all at the dinner table when father told us about the one you could have smashed but didn't." Smirking, Sherm leaned down. "Why didn't you? Were you afraid it would tear you apart?"

"Go away, Sherm."

"Don't tell me what to do."

Lou gave Sherm a shove. "Quit picking on him. Can he help it if he doesn't like killing things?"

"Yes, he can," Sherm snapped. "Think of how the other kids will act if word of this gets around. We'll never hear the end of their teasing."

"I'm the one they would tease," the boy noted.

"Wrong, milksop. We'd be picked on too because we're your brothers. Everyone will say it runs in the family, that the King boys must be girls." Sherm slapped the boy again. "And all thanks to you, you jackass."

"Father doesn't like us to swear," the boy said.

"Father isn't home right now," Sherm countered. He gestured angrily at the mouse hole. "What are you waiting for? Crush one of the damn things and he'll let you off the hook."

"I can't kill one if I don't see one."

Sherm bristled and would have jumped on the boy if not for Lou, who intervened by grabbing Sherm's wrists and holding fast. "I won't let you beat him up again. He's doing the best he can."

"Damn you both to hell!" Sherm said, yanking loose and moving to the next higher step. "You're always taking his side, Lou, even when you know he's wrong. He'd be better off if he didn't have you around to protect him. Maybe then he'd learn about life."

"Listen to you," Lou said. "Those are Father's words, not yours."

"They're true. He spends all his time with his nose buried in books. What's he going to amount to when he grows up?"

The boy stood and faced his brothers. "I don't know what I'm going to do," he told Sherm. "Sometimes I think I'd like to be a writer. Other times I think I'd like to work with figures since I'm good at arithmetic. And there are times, when I'm off hunting with Uncle Zeke, that I think I might like to live in the woods like an old hermit and have just the animals for company."

"You're touched in the head, you know that?" Sherm responded. "Zeke is a lot of fun, but he's missing a few marbles somewhere. And Father and him don't get along so well."

"I like him," the boy insisted.

Sherm started up the steps. "Do as you want, idiot. I've had my say." Stopping, he glared down. "But I'm warning you, Nate. If we get teased over this mouse business, I'm going to lick you proper."

"You can try," Nate said.

The door slammed behind Sherm. Lou sat down and crossed his arms over his knees. "Why make it worse by talking back to him the way you do? You know how he gets?"

"I should let him bully me all the time?"

"No. No, I guess not." Lou focused on the cause of the argument. "The whole family's upset, and all because of some stupid mice. Makes you wonder."

"I really will kill one," Nate mentioned.

"When?"

"When I have the chance."

Lou made a clucking sound. "Little brother, I come down here quite a lot to be alone, to think. I couldn't begin to count the mice I've seen when it's all quiet, especially at night. So tell me. And be honest. How many have you seen, just today?"

"Four."

"And you didn't club one?"

"I couldn't bring myself to do it." Nate held the club out as if about to cast it from him. "I know how easy it would be to bash in their skulls. I know they're just mice, and we can't have then overrunning the house. But they're living things, just like us."

"Wrong, little brother," Lou interrupted. "They're animals. We're not. They don't think like we do, don't feel like we do. They don't have souls like we do. You start making them equal with us and you might as well go live like a hermit because you won't be any better than they are."

"Are we better? Really and truly?"

"Dumb question. You like poetry. Know any mice that have written poems? Or painted beautiful art? Or sculpted statues?"

"But does that make us better?"

Lou cocked his head and regarded Nate quizzically. "Maybe Sherm and Father are right. Maybe you do read too much. How else would you come up with some of these crazy notions of yours?" Rising, he climbed to the door and paused with his hand on the latch. "You'd better get your thoughts straightened out. You say you like Uncle Zeke. Then remember what he told us about puny thinkers, as he calls them. There's a right way to think and a wrong way to think, and it seems to me you're in the wrong. Why, if everyone felt the way you do, we'd all be eating nothing but vegetables and fruit and we'd never have milk to drink or be able to go horseback riding. Gophers would ruin all the yards, cats and dogs would be living wild in the streets, and there'd be so many mice they'd be in your bath water." He opened the door. "You're smart enough to see the truth. You're just afraid to admit it."

Nate watched the door close quietly. As usual, Lou saw right through him and had hit on the heart of the problem. He took a seat on the bottom step, placed the club across his legs, and rested his chin in his hands. One mouse. All he had to kill was one mouse.

He stared at the hole and waited.

The switchback became harder to negotiate the higher Nate King climbed. Sometimes he had to leap over gaps, and at other times he had to cling to the gorge wall with his fingernails to keep from falling over the edge. His chest hurt worse as time went on, much worse, the pain so excruciating that he halted every few minutes to rest.

At long last the rim reared just twenty feet above Nate's head. Arm pressed tight against his ribs, he was making good headway when he came to where a four foot ridge of earth had buckled. There was no way to go around. He had to jump, so he moved to the very edge, crouched, and tensed his legs.

Movement in the gorge below drew Nate's attention to the spring. Barely controlled rage boiled within him as he watched Satan approach the pool and drink. There was the cause of all his troubles, and if only he had the Hawken he could have picked the panther off. He saw the cat sit and yawn, saw it idly gaze around and then look up. Right at him. Their eyes locked, and although the distance was too great for Nate to clearly see the mountain lion's features, he swore Satan's features lit with bestial glee.

Then Satan headed for the switchbacks.

Rather than be worried, Nate laughed. "That's it!" he declared. "Come on up here! By the time you reach the top, I'll be waiting for you with both pistols cocked. Come on!"

Thinking of how joyous it would be to plant two balls in the cat's brain, Nate leaped across the gap. Or tried to. Distracted by grand thoughts of rubbing his nemesis out, he failed to concentrate as he should have, and as a result he came down inches short of the other side. Mere inches, but it might as well have been miles. Quickly he thrust out both arms and caught at the lip. For a few seconds he held on, his legs flailing as he desperately tried to find purchase for them. His right moccasin found tenuous footing, and he was in the act of bracing for an upward lunge when burning agony seared his chest and made his head spin. Of a sudden he went weak.

Nate felt his fingers slipping and tried to gouge them into the soil. He kicked wildly but was unable to find solid footing. Panic tore at the core of his being. "No!" he cried, and helplessly plummeted over the side.

Chapter Eight

Blood rained out of a stormy sky, big, moist drops that splattered onto Nate King's face and beard and plastered his hair to his head. Blindly he struck at the dark downpour, striving to block the drops. Some got into his nose, some into his mouth. He sputtered, swallowed, gagged. High above him the storm clouds shifted, changing shape, transforming from simple clouds into a gigantic feline that snarled and hissed and clawed at him while a torrent of spittle, red spittle, showered from its mouth. "No!" Nate shouted, swallowing more damp liquid. "Stop it! Stop it!"

Suddenly Nate realized that he was sitting up and swinging wildly at thin air. Thunder rumbled overhead and raindrops were hitting his face. He blinked in confusion at the darkness enveloping him and wondered where he was until he remembered Satan and the pain in his chest and falling, falling, falling.

Nate groped the ground, looked down, then up. The

outline of the rim was faintly visible. He discovered he was still high on the gorge wall, on a switchback about fifty feet from the top. Had it not broken his fall, he would have been smashed to a pulp when he hit bottom.

Nate peered at the inky floor of the gorge and the lower switchbacks, puzzled by Satan's absence. The panther had been coming after him when he slipped. Why hadn't it finished him off? More importantly, where was it now?

A vivid bolt of lightning briefly lit up the heavens, attended by a tremendous clap of thunder. Nate was buffeted by winds so strong he had to hold on tight to keep from being plucked from his perch. The storm was intensifying. He had to reach the rim before the lightning or the wind accomplished what the fall had failed to do.

Rising to his knees, Nate winced as his chest again throbbed with torment. He tried to stand, but the instant he put his full weight on his left foot the leg was jarred by pain and he nearly buckled. Sitting once more, he gingerly felt his ankle and foot. Both were hugely swollen, whether as a result of the fall or due to the bite he had no idea.

Another jagged spear of lightning reminded Nate of his precarious position. Being so high up, he was a prime target. He had to find shelter swiftly.

Since he couldn't stand, Nate crawled up the grade, negotiated the switchback, and went on. His gravest worry was blundering onto one of the gaps and falling again. To prevent that from happening, he tested the ground ahead before advancing. This held him to a snail's pace but he would rather be safe than pay the ultimate price for being rash.

Gradually, painstakingly, Nate worked his way ever higher. The rain fell in buckets, drenching him to the skin. The lightning flashed continuously, the thunder boomed. Worst of all, the wind tore at him, trying to rip him loose and fling him to earth. His lips grim with determination, Nate kept on going.

The first gap Nate encountered was a small one, one he recalled from earlier, and was handily crossed. The next, being wider, took some doing. Nate had to inch both knees to the edge, guess where the upper incline was situated, and lunge at the same time he did a frog hop, throwing both arms straight out. He landed on firm ground and gave silent thanks.

At length Nate came to the gap where his mishap had occurred. He knew it was the one even though he couldn't see it clearly. Edging to the brink, he waited for another streak of lightning to illuminate the wall. In the garish glare, the gap seemed more like a chasm, an insurmountable gulf only a madman would try to hurdle. But hurdle it he must.

This time Nate focused on the patch of earth he must alight on and nothing else. Bunching his legs, he took a few deep breaths to compose his nerves, and when the next streak of lightning brightened the sky, he pushed off on his good leg, throwing himself across the open space as if shot from a cannon. Rain battered him, the wind lashed him, and then he was smacking down on his hands and knees and clinging fast to the slick, dank soil. He squatted there a while so his pulse would stop racing, then he crawled upward.

Many minutes elapsed. At last Nate attained the summit. He collapsed, exhausted, and shivered as the cold rain chilled him to the bone. Rousing himself, he limped into nearby undergrowth, into the densest bushes he could find, and curled up underneath them. Here the rain hardly touched him, the wind left him alone. He could relax for the first time since being attacked. Closing his eyes, he folded his arms across his chest and tried to rub warmth into his body. His rib was on fire, his left foot pulsing. Surprisingly, neither stopped him from promptly falling asleep.

Singing birds brought Nate around. He sat up, amazed to see the sky was clear, the day hours old. His chest didn't bother him as much but his foot was worse. One look was enough to show him why. Grinding his teeth so he wouldn't cry out, he pried his moccasin off and examined the discolored flesh. There was no doubt. The foot was infected.

Nate bowed his head, mentally resisting the tide of despair threatening to engulf him. A fractured rib, an infected foot, no rifle, low on food, and in dire need of water. What else could go wrong? Even though he had slept a long time, he felt extremely tired, and he wearily pressed a palm to his forehead. His brow burned with fever, hotter than it had ever been.

"Now I know," Nate muttered. He squeezed his foot into the moccasin, rose, and hobbled from the brush. Forest stretched southward into the distance. A short search turned up a broken limb the proper length, and using this as a crutch, Nate went on.

Reaching Shakespeare was more critical than ever. The mountain man had lived among Indians so long and learned so much from medicine men he knew more about healing than most doctors. Shakespeare would know how to treat the infection and tend the rib. All would be well.

Nate reassured himself with that thought repeatedly. But his condition steadily deteriorated. Presently he broke out in a sweat. His body would be hot one minute, cold the next. At times he wanted to throw off his buckskins, at others his teeth chattered.

A peculiar feeling seized hold of Nate, a lethargy so overwhelming he seemed to be moving in slow motion. It took forever for him to take a single step. His arms were so sluggish they were leaden.

Nate was familiar with the symptoms of tainted blood. He'd known a trapper who had succumbed after getting a foot caught in a trap. And there had been a Shoshone warrior, wounded by a Cheyenne arrow, who had died from the ailment. Certain herbs were supposed to be an effective treatment but he didn't know which ones they were.

Nate's sense of time was all askew. He plodded on because he refused to quit, relying on the crutch more and more. His leg was now swollen midway to the knee. In addition, his rib acted up again. And the whole time the fever raged.

Habit caused Nate to stop at noon and sit on a log. He closed his eyes, then jerked them wide when he began to drift off. He couldn't sleep yet. There would be plenty of time for that luxury once he found Shakespeare, which, if his strength held out, should be before nightfall.

While not hungry, Nate forced himself to eat to maintain his energy. The jerky tasted tangier than usual, making his mouth water. He stuffed a piece in his cheek, shoved up off the log. The top of his crutch had rubbed the skin under his arm practically raw, but it couldn't be helped. It was either go on or die.

Nate traveled southward for the longest time. His existence became a mechanical routine of forcing his good leg to take a step, then employing the crutch. Nothing else mattered. He had to reach Shakespeare and the only way to accomplish that was to keep on going even if his brow was hotter than a burning ember. His chest felt as if something was boring through his flesh from the inside out, and his left leg was in such pain he couldn't bear to put his foot down.

On and on and on Nate went. He was terribly thirsty but couldn't remember exactly where the streams were located. His mind was sluggish, almost numb. Conscious thought took so much effort he didn't bother thinking. He just plodded along, minute after minute, hour after hour.

At length Nate looked up and saw he was in a field of high grass. Bordering it to the south was a ribbon of a creek. The sight of cool, refreshing water sent a shiver down his spine. He cried out, a formless cry of hope and relief. From an internal reservoir he tapped the last of his waning strength and hurried forward.

A yard from the creek Nate let go of the crutch and threw himself flat on the ground. His lips touched the water and he drank as might a person who had been lost in a desert for a week. His thirst was unquenchable. He gulped and gulped until his belly bulged and he couldn't swallow another drop. Then he rolled onto his side and splashed water onto his fiery forehead and face.

It felt so indescribably wonderful to simply lie there and rest. Nate sank both arms into the creek up to the elbows, luxuriating in the chill sensation. He wanted to drink more but was afraid he'd be sick. Absently gazing skyward to learn how many hours of daylight were left, he was confounded to see the sun wasn't where it should be.

Nate had been heading south for ages. Or so he'd believed. The sun, therefore, should be to his right, to the west. Instead, the blazing orb hung in the heavens to his left. If the direction he thought was west was actually east, that meant he had either been walking in circles or had become completely switched around and been hiking northward for most of the afternoon.

"It can't be!" Nate declared as the full magnitude of his mistake hit home. He'd counted on finding McNair before nightfall. Now he didn't have the slightest idea which way to go. Was he still due north of Shakespeare's valley, or was he to the west or east of it? There were no landmarks nearby he recognized, no way to get his bearings.

I'm as good as dead! Nate reflected, and had to bite his lower lip as a flood of despondency rose within him. He closed his eyes and shook his head, fighting the feeling of hopelessness. He couldn't give up! He didn't want to die, not this way, not there, where no one would ever find him, not all alone, left there to rot and have his bones be bleached by the sun like that warrior whose remains he had found in the meadow. He'd never hold his beloved wife in his arms again or see his son and daughter. He couldn't, he wouldn't, let his end be so meaningless.

Nate sat up. He wasn't going to give up the ghost meekly. Since he could no longer count on being treated by his mentor, he had to quit being sorry for himself and treat his wounds the best he knew how. Shifting, he rested both feet by the creek. He tried pulling the moccasin off his left foot but the foot was now so horribly swollen he couldn't get the top of the moccasin down over his ankle.

The blade of the butcher knife gleamed in the sunlight when Nate pulled it from its beaded sheath. He removed the parfleche and stuck the strap between his teeth, then carefully worked the tip of the knife under the top of the moccasin. In order to cut the moccasin off, he had to twist the knife so the sharp edge was against the leather. Doing so produced waves of torment. Nate bit down on the strap, resisted the agony, and sliced away.

Winona had made the moccasins. The love she bore him, and the pride she had taken in her craftsmanship, were reflected in her work. The soles were exceptionally thick, the tops barely less so and quite supple. The moccasins had been made to hold up under the toughest of wear in the roughest of weather. Cutting through the leather was a chore for one as weak as Nate had become, but he persisted.

Perspiration dotted Nate's brow and made his buckskin shirt cling to his damp torso. He stopped cutting every so often to splash more water on his face. The moccasin loosened somewhat the lower he went, and after fifteen minutes was loose enough for him to remove, but only with great difficulty.

Nate's foot was ghastly. Discolored, two times its normal size, with a festering sore as large as his fist, it made his stomach churn to look at it. He lowered the foot into the creek and mustered a grin at the temporary soothing the water produced. Lying back, he closed his eyes. Before he knew it, he dozed off.

The caw of a raven woke Nate up. He sat, saw with a shock that twilight had descended. His foot had stopped hurting so he lifted it from the creek and examined the sore, which appeared to contain a pint of pus. He glanced at the knife lying beside him, then at the sore. His hand closed on the knife hilt.

Nate placed the parfleche strap in his mouth again, poised the blade over the sore. He hesitated, dreading what he had to do. Then, biting down hard, he jabbed the knife in. Two things happened simultaneously; the sore exploded in a sickening spray of yellowish-green pus and pain exploded in his head. He sagged onto his back, vainly trying to keep his wits about him. A dark veil enfolded his mind.

When next Nate opened his eyes it was night. The moon had risen and stars dominated the firmament. Wind from the northwest shook the trees and grass and fanned his hair as he bent forward to inspect his foot. The sore had drained of pus and was now deflated, thin shreds of skin hanging down. Some of the swelling had lessened and the pangs weren't as intense as they had been when he moved.

Nate soaked the slit moccasin in the water, then pulled it back on. He cut off more whangs and looped them around the top of the moccasin to hold it in place. Tucking the crutch under his arm, he stood. Since blundering through the woods in the dark tempted fate, he looked for a spot to curl up until morning. A small pine, its lower limbs eighteen inches above the ground, offered a haven. He crawled under, set both pistols in front of him so they were in easy reach, and rested a cheek on a forearm.

Nate's stomach rumbled with hunger but he made no move to open the parfleche. The little jerky and pemmican he had left might have to last him a long time. He would ration it and hope for a clear shot at game.

Having slept so much in the past twenty-four hours, Nate doubted he was tired enough to fall asleep very soon. He didn't take into account the ravaging effects of the rampant fever and the severe toll the hours of walking had taken on his weakened constitution. In no time at all he was snoring.

And dreaming. Adrift in a Stygian limbo, he felt something pulling at his leg, and when he looked down he beheld a tiny mouse nipping at his toes. The mouse grew in size, changing shape as it did. Suddenly the mouse was gone, replaced by a snarling monster, by Old Satan himself. Satan reared back on two legs to claw at Nate's face. Overcome by fright, Nate swatted at the panther's paws. His fingers were ripped off, leaving bloody stumps, and he was disemboweled. He opened his mouth to scream but no sound came out. Cringing in terror, he tried to flee and pitched into a black well. The mountain lion jumped down after him, coming closer, and closer.

The snap of a twig woke Nate up. Dawn wasn't far off. He saw a black-tailed doe at the creek, drinking. It was a perfect shot if he didn't scare it off. Moving slowly, he picked up a pistol and cocked the hammer. At the click the doe snapped its head on high, its ears swiveling, its nose twitching.

Nate fired but couldn't see if he'd hit the deer or not because the cloud of acrid gunsmoke hid it from sight. He blinked, coughed, snaked to one side, and was appalled to see the doe was gone. How could he have missed? The answer was that he couldn't, not at that short range, as he learned when he crawled out from under the tree and saw the twitching doe expiring in a growing crimson pool.

Forgetting the crutch, Nate limped over, drew his knife, and began carving before the doe stopped convulsing. He sliced off a patch of hide, lanced the blade deep into the flesh, and cut out a sizeable chunk. Ordinarily he would have taken the time to make a fire and to roast the meat until it was well done. Ordinarily, though, he wasn't this famished, this in need of nourishment.

Blood dripped from the chunk but Nate didn't care. He closed his eyes and bolted the meat cold, chomping as might a starving wolf. Gore and blood trickled down over his chin onto his throat and he wiped himself clean with the back of a sleeve. Seldom had a meal tasted so delicious.

Upon finishing that first piece, Nate carved out a second, bigger portion. Working as rapidly as he could, he got a fire going, transfixed the piece, and held it so close to the flames the outer surface was singed. His appetite had barely been whetted; he couldn't wait to dig into more. Mouth watering, he fidgeted and fussed over the meat until it was done. Then, unfazed by the hot fat that seared his palms, he gripped the portion in both hands and chomped down.

New vitality radiated outward from Nate's belly. Every morsel swallowed added that much more strength to his limbs. He felt like a new man when he was done, in spite of his chest and his leg. Moving to the creek, he leaned down to slake his thirst and had his good mood wrecked by a track imprinted in the mud to his left. It wasn't one of his tracks, nor one of the doe's.

It was Satan's distinctive paw print, so big no other panther in the Rockies could have made it.

Nate was jolted to realize the mountain lion had passed within a dozen yards of his hiding place sometime during the night. Thankfully the wind must have been blowing the other way or Satan would have detected his scent. He saw another track a few feet past the creek near where the cat had gone into the forest.

A new thought intruded itself. How far had Satan gone? Was the panther close enough to have heard the shot? Forgetting about a drink, Nate swiftly reloaded the spent pistol and crawled back under the pine. Maybe he could make the situation work in his favor. By lying low, he might be able to get a shot at the mountain lion if it came to investigate.

The waiting was harrowing in itself. Nate turned at every slight sound, jumped at the rustling of underbrush. The breeze now wafted into the forest, carrying his scent and that of the doe. Either or both should bring Satan on the run.

The better part of an hour went by and there was no sign of the cat. Nate concluded it was safe to ease into the open and was on the verge of sliding out when a chattering squirrel deep in the woods abruptly fell silent.

Nate flattened, went as rigid as a board, both cocked pistols in front of him. Satan was finally coming. He knew it in his marrow, knew he had to end their conflict while he was still invigorated from the meal and could still think clearly.

A fluid, tawny specter materialized in shadows fifteen yards away. Satan prowled in a half-circle, testing the wind, enticed by the intoxicating odor of fresh blood. Any other panther would have rushed into the open to tear at the doe, but not Satan. The panther had spent a lifetime cultivating caution and honing its feline instincts to an extraordinary degree. Satan's sensitive nostrils registered the hated man scent underlying the blood scent of the doe, and Satan knew that the two-legged creature he desired to kill was nearby.

Nate watched the cat pacing back and forth and had to curtail an impulse to fire. Satan needed to be closer for the pistols to be effective. He toyed with the notion of attempting to sneak up on the cat and wisely didn't. Let Satan come to him.

The panther paused, its blazing eyes raking the trees, the creek, the field. It snarled, not so much out of anger

as to see what would happen. Oftentimes its snarl caused
prey to bolt from cover, but not this time. The two-legged
creatures never did as other animals would do. They were
different, a challenge to hunt, to kill. Which appealed to
his predatory nature.

The panther unexpectedly vanished and Nate scowled.
Satan never did as Nate expected, never did the predict-
able. He intently scrutinized the vegetation. Nothing. He
scanned low tree limbs since sometimes cats took to
the trees. Nothing. He studied every bush close to the
creek. Nothing. Then, anger getting the better of him, he
glanced to his left and cursed under his breath. Or would
have, had he not seen Satan on his side of the creek, eight
feet off in the thick grass, staring right at him!

Their eyes locked, held. Neither moved. Nate wasn't
sure he could get off two shots before the panther reached
him and it would take both balls to bring the cat down.
He lightly fingered the triggers, waiting for Satan to
make the first move. When it came, it was so fast
Nate was almost taken unawares even though he was
ready for it.

One instant Satan was crouched in the grass, the next
instant Satan was ducking under the low limbs to get at
Nate and Nate was squeezing the trigger on his right
flintlock. The pistol boomed, the cat recoiled, then leaped
in again, paws flashing, claws extended. Nate raised the
other pistol to put a ball in the lion's brain but the lion's
paw was quicker. The pistol sailed out of Nate's grasp.

Scrambling backward, Nate threw the spent flintlock at
Satan's head. He grasped his tomahawk, yanking it out as
he rolled out from under the tree and rose. In the excitement of fighting for his life he forgot about his left leg,
and when he stood, his leg gave way, causing him to stag-
ger to one side, toward the creek, just as Satan charged.

Nate drew back the tomahawk, stroked it forward. The edge bit into Satan's skull but the angle was all wrong and it didn't slice in deep enough to stop the mountain lion. Satan slammed into Nate and they both crashed down, landing in the water, Nate on his back with the cat on top.

Nate King looked up into the contorted mask of ferocity incarnate and knew his end had come.

Chapter Nine

Certain moments in every man's life are so remarkably vivid, so profoundly intense, they are never, ever forgotten. Some are tranquil moments, such as the first time he is intimate with a woman or the birth of his first child.

Some are perilous moments, such as a knife fight, or being shot at, or set upon by savage beasts. These are events that call forth a man's courage, that test his manhood as few others can. In those moments of extreme danger when his life hangs in the balance, he is more totally alive than at any other time. Every one of his senses is at peak performance. His whole mental concentration and personal focus are on the danger at hand, and nothing else. He thinks deeply, feels deeply, lives deeply. If he survives, he reflects on them often, marveling at his deliverance, at the courage he didn't know he had before he was put to the test.

Nate King looked up into the snarling features of the creature about to slay him and was overcome, not by abject fear, but by a calming courage. The panther was too heavy for him to throw off, especially as weakened and in anguish as he was. His arm holding the tomahawk was pinned under the cat's paw and he couldn't lift it. Kicking at the lion would only enrage it further and result in his innards being ripped out by its rear legs.

Nate saw Satan's wicked teeth lowering toward his jugular. He looked the panther in the eye and girded himself to die as a man should die, bravely and without complaint. There would be no screaming, no pleading, no whining.

No one was there to witness Nate's death. He had nothing to prove except to himself. The ultimate trial loomed and he accepted it as inevitable.

But at that very instant, the instant the panther's teeth were about to close on Nate's soft flesh, Satan suddenly straightened and glanced around. A shriek of pure rage was torn from the cat's lips and its tail whipped wildly. Then, in a single bound, it cleared Nate and the creek and landed at the edge of the undergrowth, into which it vanished.

Nate was too flabbergasted to move. He didn't realize he wasn't breathing until his lungs ached and he had to gulp in air. Dimly, he heard drumming, as of many hoofs. He tried lifting his head for a look but he was too weak to do so. The hoofbeats grew louder and louder, and Nate managed to twist his neck in time to see the best friend he had in all the world vault from the white mare and race toward him.

"Dear Lord! No!" Shakespeare cried, dropping to his knees in the water to prop an arm under Nate's shoulders. "How bad is it, son?" he asked. "Where did that panther get you?"

Nate was speechless with amazement. He was going

to live after all! His time had not yet come! A happiness so acute it brought tears to his eyes gushed up within him and he placed a hand on his mentor's arm.

Shakespeare, misconstruing, inquired anxiously, "Where does it hurt the worst? I don't see any blood."

"I'll live," Nate croaked huskily.

"That critter didn't get its claws into you?" Shakespeare asked in surprise. "You don't know how glad that makes this old coon. When I spotted you tussling with that thing, I figured you were a goner." He glanced at Nate's head, at Nate's left leg. "Seems to me you're battered up some, though."

"You don't know the half of it," Nate assured him.

The mountain man cracked a grin. "Well, now that you've had your yearly bath, what say we get you dried off?" Grunting, he got his other arm under Nate and stood.

"I can walk," Nate protested.

"Hush. I need the exercise." Shakespeare carried Nate from the creek and deposited him near the doe. "How thoughtful," he quipped. "You knew I was coming and wanted to have a meal ready."

Nate propped himself on his elbows. "How?" he asked.

"How did I find you? You can thank him," Shakespeare answered, pointing.

Twisting, Nate was shocked to see his black stallion standing with McNair's pack animals.

"He showed up in my camp all sweaty, about ready to keel over," Shakespeare explained. "Must have galloped the whole way from your camp to mine. I saddled up pronto, threw my peltries and fixings on the pack horses, and went to find you. Been looking every since."

The emotion in the older man's voice brought a lump to

Nate's throat. He swallowed, coughed, and commented, "You timed it just right."

"Not on purpose," Shakespeare admitted. "I found your camp easy enough, and I have to admit it worried me some seeing that dead horse and all that blood everywhere. I yelled and yelled and fired my gun but you never showed so I decided to track you down." His expression turned grimly serious. "It wasn't so hard at first. Then I came to that gorge where you took a tumble, and rather than go down in it, I rode all the way around, hoping I'd find where you came out. Sure enough, I did, but your tracks showed there was something wrong. You were walking unsteadily, and in a circle, no less. And now and then I came on the painter's prints." Shakespeare glanced at those by the creek. "Never set eyes on tracks so big in all my life."

"Satan would have finished me if not for you," Nate said softly.

McNair's eyebrow arched. "Satan? You've named it after that old legend?"

"It's fitting," Nate said. His rib acted up again and he had to lie back down. "I'll tell you the whole story as soon as I feel up to it."

"What's the matter?"

Nate explained about his rib. Shakespeare retrieved an old blanket which he cut into wide strips and wrapped tightly around Nate's chest. Shakespeare also bandaged Nate's head and applied an herbal paste to the punctured sore.

"I can't leave you alone for two minutes," the mountain man complained as he carefully bound the foot. "How in tarnation did you ever wind up tangling with that cat?"

While Shakespeare roasted venison and boiled coffee, Nate related his ordeal, concluding with, "I'm lucky to be alive, but I suppose I should count my blessings. I still have some hides left, and the stallion." He stared into the fire. "I only wish I hadn't lost my Hawken."

"That reminds me," Shakespeare said. Hustling to the far side of one of his pack horses, he was busy for a few moments. He returned proudly bearing a familiar rifle.

"You found it?" Nate blurted, half rising in his excitement.

"That I did, son," Shakespeare said, handing the Hawken over. "Spotted it from the top of that gorge. Had a hell of a time climbing down, I don't mind saying. Without my rope I never could have gotten to it."

Nate fondly clasped the rifle in his lap and stroked it as he might his wife's hair. "Thought I'd never see you again!"

"We can get attached to those things, can't we?" McNair chuckled, squatting beside the bubbling pot. "Here. How about if we warm your insides a mite?"

The coffee was perfectly delicious. Nate savored the first cup, sipping the potent brew and rolling it on his tongue. In a short time the venison was done and he ate with cheerful relish. The meat he had eaten earlier had only whetted his appetite. He was famished, as he demonstrated by gorging on half a haunch. When his stomach was full to bursting, he wiped his greasy hands on his leggings and settled back wearing a smile of supreme contentment. "Life doesn't get much better than this," he mentioned.

Shakespeare nodded. "We'll let you rest up tonight. Tomorrow is soon enough to go after your plews." He bobbed his head at his pack horses. "From what you've told me, I figure we should be able to pack them all onto my animals."

"If we can't, I'll tie the rest on the stallion," Nate suggested without thinking.

"And then what?" Shakespeare snickered. "Walk all the way back to your cabin with your leg in the shape it's in? You'll have to have it amputated if you try a featherbrained stunt like that."

"I won't leave any of my hides behind," Nate insisted.

"Quit fretting. You won't have to. We can always rig a travois if there are too many."

Nate hadn't thought of that. Indians used travoises all the time to transport their lodges, personal possessions, even their small children. The contrivances were ingenuously simple. First a pair of long poles were tied crosswise behind a horse's head. Next, behind the animal's rump, a pair of crosspieces were lashed a couple of yards apart. A latticework of thin but sturdy branches and buffalo tendon was constructed, forming an ideal platform on which to carry anything under the sun. "Good idea," he said.

"I like to have one at least once a month. Keeps me on my toes."

Somewhere in the forest a twig snapped. At the sound Nate sat up as if hurled from the ground by the grass itself. He cocked and pointed his rifle at the trees. Eyes narrowed, he raked the woods, his finger nervously rubbing the trigger.

"A bit jittery, aren't you?" Shakespeare commented.

"It could be the panther."

"It could be a chipmunk."

Slowly Nate lowered the Hawken and with marked reluctance let down the hammer. "We can't be too cautious where Satan is concerned."

"This panther really has you spooked, doesn't it?"

"If you'd been through what I've been through, it

would have you spooked too."

"I suppose," Shakespeare said, pressing his tin cup to his lips. Over the rim he studied his young companion closely. "I knew a free trapper once who let himself get spooked by a glutton," he remarked as he put the cup down.

"Oh?" Nate responded absently. A glutton, as he well knew, was a common nickname for the wolverine.

"Yep. He had himself a nice little dugout in Flathead country and had done real well raising beaver that year. One day he came home and found that something had broken in and made a mess of his fixings. The tracks told him it had been a wolverine. He was mad enough to spit nails, but he didn't think much else of it at the time because it's not out of the ordinary for a curious critter to make itself at home in a lodge or cabin or whatever." Shakespeare paused. "Then one day he came home again and found the same thing had happened."

"What did he do?"

"What you or I would have done. He set traps around his dugout and baited them with fresh meat. Damned if the glutton didn't swipe the bait without being caught." Shakespeare poured more coffee for both of them. "That wolverine grew fond of the trapper's place and came around every chance it got. Scared off some of his horses, ate every scrap of food it could find, and had the annoying habit of biting holes in his buckskins and blankets."

"Didn't he get a shot at it?" Nate wondered, now interested in the outcome.

"He tried. Mercy, how he tried. He became outright obsessed with rubbing that glutton out. Stopped trapping entirely. Hardly ever hunted. All he could think about was that furry varmint and how to go about killing it."

"Did he, finally?"

"No one ever knew. Came a time when a bunch of us stopped at his dugout to see him and he wasn't home. From the evidence, we guessed he hadn't been there in ages." Shakespeare took a swallow. "But we found plenty of wolverine sign."

Nate supported himself on an elbow. "You never tell one of these yarns unless you're trying to get a point across. Are you saying that I'm acting the same way toward Satan as your friend did toward the glutton?"

"Let's just say my yarn, as you call it, could be taken as a warning."

"You wasted your breath. I'm not about to go crazy on you over an ornery panther."

"I hope not."

Nate laughed and forgot about the matter until later that night when Shakespeare was snoring on the other side of the fire and sleep eluded him. He gazed thoughtfully at the star-dotted canopy overhead. No matter how hard he tried, and he was trying, he couldn't put the mountain lion from his mind. Over and over again he relived that last attack, relived being knocked onto his back in the creek and staring up into the cat's bestial features as its fangs dropped to his neck.

Why couldn't he shake the memory? Nate mused. It wasn't as if he hadn't been attacked by wild animals before. Bears, wolves, snakes, name it and he had found himself on the receiving end of their wrath. So why did Satan bother him so? The idea of the panther going unpunished after all that had happened agitated him terribly.

It was foolish.

Wasn't it?

* * *

Many years before. New York City.

The boy named Nate was crouched on top of his father's work bench, the club clutched in his right hand. He stared at the mouse that had emerged from the hole moments ago and a tingle of excitement rippled through him. Here was his chance! All he had to do was jump and swing.

Nose twitching, the mouse warily approached the cheese. It took a nibble, then another, and began eating in earnest, convinced it was safe.

Nate balanced on his heels, tensed to leap. Then he mentally pictured the end result of his club crashing down on the rodent's head, and he hesitated. The creature was so small, so very innocent. How could he take its life? Why didn't his father just plug up the holes so no mice could enter the house? That would be better than pounding this one to a pulp.

A second mouse appeared, poking its head out and looking right and left. Seeing its fellow eating the cheese, it dashed out to join in the feast.

Nate remembered his father's words: "Where there's one mouse, there are always more. If we don't prevent it, they'll overrun the house in no time. Your mother will find them in the pantry, in the flour, in the bread. Mouse droppings will be everywhere." Here was living proof his father had been right, yet still Nate couldn't bring himself to jump.

What's wrong with me? Nate quizzed himself. Was he so weak-willed he couldn't do what had to be done? Was he a puny thinker, as his Uncle Zeke described some people who didn't see things the way they were? He thought of Percy Bysshe Shelley and his other poetry books and was staggered by a mature insight; poetry, grand, glorious poetry, those golden words he loved so much, had no bearing at all on the day to day things that people did. Poetry didn't put food on the table, or keep a person clothed, or teach someone how to deal with vermin.

As if to prove that point, one of the rodents below paused in its chewing long enough to excrete waste.

Nate's mouth curled in heartfelt disgust. For the first time in his young life he looked at another creature and felt an urge to kill. Legs uncoiling, he sprang, swinging as he dropped. It was ridiculously easy. The first mouse had no inkling of danger and died with cheese bulging its cheeks. The second mouse froze, petrified with terror, giving Nate an opportunity to dispatch it with a single blow. He stood looking down at them, then hefted his club and smiled.

It took only a minute to reach the front room where his father sat reading a newspaper. His father glaced at him, saw the mice dangling by their tails from his hand, and frowned. "You should have known better than to bring them up here. What if your mother saw them?"

"I knew she's off shopping. And I wanted you to see."

"You did the job you were supposed to do. What do you want? A pat on the back?"

"I killed two of them."

The father folded his paper and regarded the boy a moment. "What did you kill, son?"

"Sir?" Nate responded uncertainly.

"What did you kill?"

The answer was so obvious that Nate was at a loss to understand why the question was even asked. "Two mice, Father."

"Look at them."

Nate did as directed, noticing how the brains of one trickled from its split skull. To his surprise he didn't feel queasy.

"What do you see?"

Confused, Nate studied them intently. What was he supposed to see? "Two dead mice."

"Nothing else?"

"No. Just two dead animals."

"Then what was all the fuss about? Why did it take you so long to do a simple chore?"

"I told you, Father. I've never killed before."

"How do you feel now that you have?"

"I'm glad I did as you wanted."

"You don't regret killing them?"

"No. It had to be done, just as you said."

His father smiled, a rare genuinely warm smile, and beckoned Nate closer. He draped a hand on Nate's shoulder and gave a gentle squeeze. "Remember this lesson, son. There's an old saying that life isn't a bowl of cherries, and nothing could be truer. We have to work hard to get what we want in this world. We have to overcome difficulties every step of the way." He nodded at the mice. "Often there will be things we don't want to do, don't like doing at all, but they have to be done whether we like doing them or not. The measure of a man is that he accepts his responsibilities and performs them without complaint. Do you understand?"

"I think so."

"Excellent. Now take those mice out back in the alley and leave them there for the cats."

"Sir?"

"You've seen how many cats and dogs run loose in this city, haven't you?"

"Of course. There must be hundreds."

"Thousands," his father corrected him. "All because people won't take responsibility for their pets. They let them breed like rabbits, and when they have too many, hey just throw those they don't want out on the street where the animals have to fend for themselves." He lowered his hand to his lap. "It was different when I was young. Back then if people had too many cats or dogs they just took them and drowned them in a bucket or bashed their brains in. We didn't have the problem New York City has now with strays."

"So you want me to leave these mice for the cats to eat?" Nate said, amazed by this rare display of kindness.

"I want you to stack those old crates we have out in the alley and hide behind them. When a cat comes to eat the mice, you club it to death. Kill as many cats as you can before the mice are all gone."

"Sir?"

"Are you hard of hearing?"

Nate stared at the mice, at his club. "Oh. I'm to use the mice as bait like I used the cheese."

"You're learning." His father picked up the newspaper and went to unfold it.

"Can I ask you something?"

"Yes."

"Why do you want the cats killed?"

"There always has to be a reason with you, doesn't there?" His father tapped the paper. "Very well. Of late some cats have taken to standing on the fence late at night and caterwauling so loudly the racket wakes your mother. Then she has a hard time falling asleep again. Perhaps if we kill a few of the cats that call the alley their home, the caterwauling will stop."

Nate remembered their first talk about the mice. "So you want me to do this for Mother's sake, just like you wanted me to kill the mice for her sake?"

"You find that odd?"

"I just figured I was doing it for you."

David Thompson

"Would that make a difference?"

"No, sir."

"I'm glad to hear it. As for your mother, one day you'll have a wife of your own and then you'll understand why everything I do is for her benefit."

Nate was stunned. Clearly his father bore his mother tremendous affection. He had never given much thought to how much his parents loved one another. Based on all the arguments they had, he'd assumed they barely tolerated each other.

"A husband owes it to his wife to provide things like a decent home and fine clothes," his father was saying. "And to do all the little things he can to make her life easier. Of course, don't go overboard."

"Sir?"

"Like everything in life, women have their proper place. Take this business about granting them the right to vote. Whoever heard of such nonsense? Their minds are too shallow to grasp the complexities of politics. Can you imagine your mother casting an intelligent vote for mayor or president?"

"Yes," Nate said.

His father stared at him, then sighed. "Just when I was beginning to think there was some hope for you." He made a shooing motion with his hand. "Off with you, son. Do as I told you. And don't bother bringing the dead cats in to show me. Just pile them in the back yard and I'll count them later. I don't know if I can trust you to give an accurate tally."

"Whatever you say, sir," Nate responded, turning away quickly so his father wouldn't see the feelings his face betrayed. The mice in one hand, the club in the other, he ran from the house as if the fires of Hell were lapping at his heels.

Chapter Ten

"Watch out below," Shakespeare McNair shouted, and clamped his hands on the rope to stop the bale's descent. He waited until Nate moved aside, then continued lowering the hides to the ground. Once they were down, Shakespeare let the rope slip over the top of the stout spruce limb that had supported the bale's weight. He watched it fall, grasped the limb, and cautiously descended.

"This is the last of them," Nate said.

"Thank goodness," Shakespeare said, running a palm across his perspiring forehead. "If you ask me, I think you got yourself hurt just so I'd have to do all the heavy work."

"How did you guess?" Nate responded with a smirk.

"What's left?"

"We already have my fixings, so that leaves the traps."

"Where'd you hide them? On top of some mountain, I suppose?"

"In a thicket nearby. I'll show you."

Shakespeare picked up the heavy bale and threw it over his left shoulder with an ease belying his advanced years. "We'll have to go slow on our way back. My pack horses are going to tire easily toting as much as we have."

"We could leave some of my belongings here," Nate proposed.

"Be sensible. If you leave your traps, you run the risk of them rusting out on you unless you cache them good and proper, which is more bother than it's worth where traps are concerned. You can't afford to lose your packs and parfleches so we have to take them. And we sure as blazes can't leave your hides."

Nate didn't disagree because he knew his friend was right. Still, he felt uncomfortable putting Shakespeare to so much trouble. He held the Hawken in both hands and hopefully surveyed the valley.

"Still looking for that painter?" Shakespeare commented, chortling. "You just can't let it rest."

"You wouldn't either if it had happened to you."

The mountain man squinted at the younger man. "Don't get your britches in an uproar. I didn't mean to imply you haven't been through the wringer. But we haven't seen hide nor hair of Satan since that tussle you had at the creek. He's long gone and not likely to bother us again."

"You're wrong."

"How so?"

Nate didn't take his eyes off the forest. "Satan is in this valley somewhere. It's his home, his sanctuary. He's out there right this second spying on us, just waiting for his chance to sneak in close and do us harm. I know he is. I can feel him in my bones."

"If you ask me, son, you're getting a bit carried away with this whole affair," Shakespeare cautioned. "You've been making this Satan of yours out to be some kind of demon, and he's not. He's no different than any other painter."

"You don't know him like I do. You haven't seen him up close. He's not a demon, but he is the biggest panther that ever lived, and the smartest, too."

"Crafty, maybe, but not smart in the same way people are smart. There's no denying that animals can be clever sometimes, especially those that have to prey on others to get a bite to eat. But you're still ten times smarter than this Satan."

Nate didn't reply. He knew his friend was wrong, but how did he go about convincing a man who had dwelled in the Rockies more years than Nate and his wife combined had lived that this mountain lion was unique, a rare specimen endowed with unmatched cunning and viciousness? Engrossed in his thoughts, Nate emerged from the last rank of spruce trees and saw all the horses gazing intently eastward. He did the same and drew up in midstride.

Satan stood by the stream less than a hundred yards off, head held low, tail swishing slowly. Evidently he had been working his way toward the clearing.

Dashing to the left for a better shot, Nate rammed the Hawken to his shoulder and tried to take a bead. Satan foiled him by bounding across the stream and into saplings lining the bank. "Damn!" Nate fumed. Spinning, he ran to the black stallion and vaulted into the saddle. A jerk of the reins and the stallion erupted in a gallop, speeding along the stream toward the spot where the panther had disappeared.

"Nate! Wait!" Shakespeare called.

The shout was wasted. Nate was only interested in one thing. Disregarding a lancing pain in his chest, he forded the stream and raced to the edge of the slender saplings to where he rose in the stirrups to try and spot the panther. Again he was foiled. It had only taken him twenty seconds or so to get there, but Satan was nowhere in evidence.

Nate circled the saplings, hoping against hope the cat was hiding in the stand. A complete circuit turned up nothing, not even tracks. Chagrined by Satan's escape, he rode slowly back to the clearing and dismounted.

"I could have told you that you were wasting your time," Shakespeare said, and received a glare that would have withered a plant.

"You could have helped. You could have gone to the other side of the stand to cut him off."

"Wouldn't have done any good," Shakespeare said, refusing to be ruffled. "I spotted the painter running off through that thicket north of the saplings as you were riding up to them."

"Why didn't you say something?"

Shakespeare shrugged. "I figured it wouldn't have done any good. As touchy as you've been acting today, you'd have ignored me."

"I have not become—" Nate began, and caught himself. He wouldn't insult McNair by lying to him. Especially not when his friend was telling the truth. He had indeed been irritable, ever since they entered the valley, and it didn't take a genius to figure out why.

"Let it go, son," Shakespeare said kindly.

"I don't know if I can," Nate said, limping toward the thicket. He'd forgotten all about his foot in the excitement and now he felt as if someone was repeatedly stabbing it with a dagger made of living fire. Grimacing, he checked the position of the sun, saw there were only two hours of daylight left. "We'd better hurry if you want to put this valley behind us by nightfall."

"Point to the traps and I'll fetch them."

"I'm not helpless," Nate grumbled. Ducking low, he worked his way to the Newhouses. Three trips were needed to bring them all out. As he assisted in tying them onto the pack animals, he looked at his mentor. "I've been thinking."

"A dangerous habit," Shakespeare said, and quoted his namesake. "Heaven make thee free of it."

"You haven't heard me out."

"I don't need to."

"Are you clairvoyant now? Do you know my thoughts before I speak them?"

"I know you, young sir."

"You think you do."

Shakespeare became somber. "Methinks I am a prophet new inspired, and thus expiring do foretell of him. His rash fierce blaze of riot cannot last, for violent fires soon burn out themselves."

"Are you talking about me or the damn panther?"

"Perhaps both. Perhaps neither."

Nate finished tying a sack and turned. "I hate it when you talk in riddles."

Soon they were ready to depart. Nate assumed the lead, a pack horse trailing his stallion. The Hawken rested across his thighs, handy for immediate use. He scoured the adjacent slopes, the woodland, the open spaces. Deep down he knew without a shadow of a doubt that Satan was observing their every move, and all he asked for was a single good shot.

They were in an unspoken race with the sun but they couldn't ride as fast as they would have liked, not with the pack horses so overburdened. And, too, Nate deliberately went a shade slower than he might otherwise have done in order to increase his chances of spying the mountain lion. As it was, despite this, they would have reached the crest of the ridge bordering the valley to the south if not for an unexpected occurrence.

Nate was seeking a shorter route to the ridge when he saw a large brown animal move in pines to the southwest, across the stream. Automatically he brought the Hawken to bear in case it was a grizzly. Seconds elapsed, and the animal stepped into the open and lowered its muzzle to graze on grass. "My other mare!" he blurted, drawing rein.

Shakespeare came alongside. "She's lucky the painter was busy dogging you or she'd be a goner by now."

"We need her," Nate declared, transferring his lead rope to McNair. He moved to a pack animal and removed another rope from a pack. "Take care of the rest. This shouldn't take long."

"You never know. She's been running wild for a few days. Sometimes being free gets into their blood."

"The stallion can catch anything," Nate boasted. However, in order not to wear the black out in a long chase, he bent low over the saddle and took advantage of all the cover available until he reached the stream. Here he had no choice. Galloping into the open, he crossed the stream in a spray of water and gained the opposite bank. It was then that the mare bolted, mane and tail flying as she fled eastward.

Nate applied his heels and pursued. He had to catch her for her own good. As Shakespeare had noted, now that Satan was roaming the valley again, it was only a matter of time before the panther found her.

The mare, however, evinced no desire to be caught. She stuck to flat, open country, to the high grass, leaving a path of flattened stems in her wake.

As usual, the black stallion responded superbly to the challenge. The horse loved to run, loved to put its strength and endurance to the test. Head low, muscles rippling, the black gradually narrowed the gap.

Nate was holding the Hawken in his left hand. He now transferred it to his right, the same hand holding the reins, to free his left for slipping the rope over the mare's neck. Ahead, the mare glanced back, saw they were gaining, and went a smidgen faster. Nate did likewise, constantly scanning the ground for animal burrows or other holes or ruts that might pose a danger to the stallion. He could ill afford to lose the black to a busted leg.

The mare displayed surprising stamina. A full mile had fallen behind them when she finally began to show fatigue and slowed slightly. This was the moment Nate had been waiting for, and he let the stallion have its head. The mare swerved as they swooped toward her, swerved again when Nate came near enough to swing the loop at her.

"Hold still!" Nate bellowed, leaning far to the side. He almost got the rope over her but she angled away, abruptly wheeled, and galloped westward.

"Contrary cuss," Nate muttered, hauling on the reins so the stallion would turn. Again he overtook her, again she cut to one side. He remembered the time his family had visited Santa Fe, remembered seeing *vaqueros* at work on a nearby ranch, and wished he knew how to use a rope, or *reata*, with the same skill they did. He'd have the mare caught in no time.

Although winded, the mare had enough spunk to keep

dodging and weaving. Nate reached the limits of his patience and stopped. So did the mare, twenty yards off, her head drooping as she breathed noisily.

Nate was about to try a ploy that might bring success. Most horses, when goaded into motion, started out briskly enough, then picked up speed as they went. Some, like the black stallion, had a knack for vaulting into a full gallop the instant they were urged to do so. He gave the stallion a few pats, adjusted the rope so the loop was by his leg, then jammed his heels in and hollered, "Heeeyaaah!"

The stallion streaked like an arrow at the mare. She snorted, tried to flee, but this time she was much too slow. Nate flashed next to her, his arm flicked out. The noose sailed over the mare's head, tightened on her neck, and Nate had her. He yipped like a Shoshoni, exuberant.

Once she was caught, the mare's resistance evaporated. She followed docilely as Nate headed back. He noticed deep slash marks on her hindquarters made by Satan that night in the clearing. They were healing nicely, and in a couple of weeks she would be as good as new.

By now the sun had dipped close to the horizon. Nate knew they would be unable to leave the valley before darkness set in but he wasn't upset. Rather, he looked forward to spending one more night in Satan's domain since there was every likelihood Satan would make an appearance.

As Nate rode, he pondered memories long neglected.

Years before. A cluttered alley in New York City.

The stacked crates formed a wall on three sides, while behind Nate was the fence. He had left a gap so he could dash out and brain any cats that strayed by, and for half an hour he had crouched in readiness, doing his best to avoid looking at the pair of dead mice.

His young mind had been whirring with new thoughts since his conversation with his father, thoughts he dared never voice in front of his father for fear of receiving a dreaded visit to the woodshed.

Minutes ago Nate had made a decision. To him, it was no different from the dozens of decisions he had to make each and every day, no different than deciding which clothes to wear or which book to read next. Had he been a little older, he might have realized this wasn't the case. No, this decision was exceptional, one of the most important any person could make. He didn't know it at the time, but it would have a profound impact on his life later on, when he was older, on the verge of manhood.

Presently Nate spied a pair of cats prancing down the alley toward him. He grasped the club, dipped lower, only an eyeball peeking out. One of the cats was yellow, the other brown. Both were lean, much leaner than house cats normally were.

It was the yellow cat that caught sight of the mice first. Pausing, it sniffed the air, looked all around, then ran to the rodents and took one into its mouth. Its companion dashed to the second mouse, bit down.

Neither feline saw Nate. Neither suspected he was there. Nate rose slowly, raised the club on high. He looked at the yellow cat, then the brown one. His shoulders bunched and he swung, driving the club down onto the crates, smashing so hard he cracked the wood.

The crash startled the cats, caused them to leap away, to fly for their lives with their prizes clutched in their jaws. Neither so much as glanced back.

Smiling, Nate stepped through the gap and stared at

smears of blood in the dirt where the mice had been lying. He went into the back yard, tossed the club down, and marched into the house, straight to the room where his father still sat reading the newspaper. His father looked up.

"You killed one already?"

"Not exactly, sir."

"Then why are you inside?"

"I made a mistake."

The paper was forgotten. "What kind of mistake?"

"I lost the bait."

"The mice? How, pray tell?"

"Some cats took them."

"You didn't use your club?"

"I swung," Nate said. "But you know how fast cats are. I'm sorry, sir. They got away."

His father's displeasure was transparent. "I suppose I shouldn't be surprised. I'm disappointed, though. I expected better of you."

"Do you want me to kill more mice and try again?"

"What would be the use? No, I'll have your brother Sherman attend to the cats. He knows how to follow instructions to the letter."

Nate had to secretly pinch his leg to keep from cracking a grin.

"Tell me the truth, son," his father said.

"Sir?" Nate responded, feeling a rush of fear. Did his father suspect?

"You weren't paying attention to the job you had to do, were you? You were daydreaming and let those cats sneak right up to the mice. Am I right?"

"No, Father. I would never do that."

"Be honest with me, son. I won't punish you for telling the truth."

"I saw them coming. Two of them. I swung the club just like I said."

"And missed." Somehow his father contrived to make the two words a harsh rebuke. "When will you learn, Nathaniel? How soon before you start acting your age? There's a right way and a wrong way to do everything in life, and you have to learn how to do things the way they should be done."

"I'm trying to do what is right. Believe me, Father. There's nothing I want more."

"I'm very pleased to hear you say so. Perhaps there's some hope for you yet."

"Thank you. I sure hope there is."

His father stood and stretched. "Well, what's done is done. Run along and find something useful to do. Don't bury yourself in those ridiculous poetry books your mother is so fond of."

"Never again."

"What?"

"I'm tired of them."

"Since when?"

"Since today. I think I'll read that book you've been wanting me to read, *Robinson Crusoe*."

"An excellent choice," his father declared, placing a firm hand on Nate's shoulder. "I'm quite delighted. To you this might seem insignificant, but you've taken a big step toward manhood today."

"By giving up poetry?"

"There's a fine line between being a boy and being a man. You cross that line when you're willing to relinquish the silly ideas and things of your childhood and devote yourself to mature pursuits."

"And when we learn the difference between right and wrong," Nate reminded him.

"That too, son. That too."

*   *   *

Nate King sipped his coffee and stared across the blazing fire at his mentor. Since sundown he had been wrestling with his decision and how best to convince McNair. He cleared his throat and began by remarking, "Do you think that it's hard sometimes for a person to tell right from wrong?"

"Here it comes," Shakespeare said, leaning back against his saddle.

"Here what comes?" Nate asked in feigned innocence.

"You've got it into your head that you have to rub out Satan and you're about to give me your reasons."

Nate was impressed. "You really are clairvoyant."

"Balderdash. You're as obvious as a pimple on a baby's bottom. But go ahead anyway, if it will make you feel better."

"You don't agree it has to be done?"

"I haven't heard your reasons yet."

"There's only one that counts," Nate said. "Satan is a man-eater. I'm sure of it. If we don't put him under, one day another trapper will wander into this valley and his death will be on our heads."

"Ahhh." Shakespeare stared into his cup and swirled the coffee. "Whether 'tis nobler in the mind to suffer the slings and arrows of outrageous fortune, or to take arms against a sea of troubles, and by opposing end them."

"I say we take arms."

"And our pack horses? What do they do while we're off chasing your fiend?"

"One of us will have to stay with them at all times."

"Which one?"

"I'm the one Satan nearly killed."

"Figured as much," Shakespeare said, and fluttered his lips in vexation. "I do beseech you, by all the battles vherein we have fought, by the blood we have shed together, by the vows we have made to endure friends, hat you directly set me against this hellish cat."

"I'm the one," Nate insisted.

"But your foot? Your head? Your rib?"

"He's hurt too. I think I put a ball into him, and I know I landed a solid blow with the tomahawk. We'll be fairly matched."

"Fair?" The mountain man snorted. "A fool in good clothes, and something like thee. 'Tis a spirit: sometime it appears like a lord; sometime like a lawyer; sometime like a philosopher."

"I've lost your trail."

"A painter knows nothing of fairness. To Satan life is survival, and he'll do whatever it takes to survive. He knows the valley, you don't. His senses are ten times sharper than yours. He can move like a ghost, you can't."

"Is this your way of boosting my confidence?" Nate joked.

"It's my way of saying you're loco."

Nate set his cup on a flat rock and gave his friend a searching look. "When I was a kid I learned that a person has to do what he or she thinks is right no matter what the consequences might be. We can't live with ourselves otherwise." He paused. "We all have to answer for our actions in the end."

There was a long silence. Eventually Shakespeare McNair poked a stick into the flames and remarked, "We see it through, then, no matter what."

"No matter what."

Chapter Eleven

The Rocky Mountains teemed with life. Daytime or nighttime, various birds, mammals, and reptiles were always abroad. During the evening and morning hours the wild creatures were most noticeable since it was then that most ventured forth to forage for food and water.

One hour in every twenty-four was different, however. During that time the Rockies were unusually quiet, enjoying an atmosphere of well deserved serenity. It was the hour before dawn, when most of the nocturnal prowlers were retiring to their dens or burrows and the animals normally abroad during the day had not yet risen.

During this peaceful interval, the forest seemed to snatch a few precious moments of rest. Often the trees themselves stood straight and still, for even the wind died down during this time. Rarely did so much as a single bird chirp, or an insect buzz. Creation slumbered at the feet of its Creator.

Any noise, however slight, was like a gunshot in a library and instantly caught the attention of anyone or anything within earshot.

So it was that Nate King's eyes flicked open when his ears registered a sound his brain couldn't identify. He slowly sat up, prodding his sluggish mind to life, and gazed at the horses. When danger threatened, their keen hearing provided the first warning. But they were dozing, as they always were at this time of the morning. McNair dozed too, although he was supposed to be keeping watch.

Shaking his head at his edginess, Nate reclined on his side and tucked his hands under his chin. He hadn't slept all that well out of concern Satan would pay them a visit. That the panther hadn't shown puzzled him. Satan knew they were there, and Satan didn't tolerate intruders in the valley. The cat should have put in an appearance.

Nate considered waking McNair and teasing his friend about falling asleep, but didn't. Sunrise wasn't far off, as indicated by the pale shade of pink suffusing the eastern sky. Let Shakespeare get a few minutes of rest. They both needed to be at their best once the hunt began.

From upstream came a low sound, the same that had awakened Nate, and he lifted his head to listen. It was a swishing sort of noise, like the flurry of small wings. He mentally pictured a flock of sparrows taking wing, then realized the significance and rose to his feet, Hawken in hand.

None of the horses were agitated and Shakespeare slumbered on. Nate wondered if he was being unduly nervous again. He didn't want to raise a fuss and be made the fool when his fears proved groundless. Perhaps he should investigate first.

Nate padded to the stream and paralleled the bank.

The morning air was crisp and cold, chilling his lungs when he breathed. Dew clung to the grass, moistening his moccasins with every step he took. It was light enough for him to see several fish a few yards away, and to spot a lone bull elk in a clearing high on a neighboring mountain. He smiled, relishing the simple fact of being alive.

McNair's herbal remedies had worked marvels. Nate's leg was stiff, his foot a trifle sore. He still limped, but only a little. His rib ached dully, his head hardly hurt at all. Compared to his condition two days ago, he felt like a new man.

Nate covered a hundred yards without incident. The woods were as quiet as a tomb. Other than the bubbling of the stream, the world lay hushed, girded for the swirl of activity the dawn would bring. He halted, convinced he was wasting his time, and turned to go back.

The faint chittering of an early-rising chipmunk attracted Nate to a bald hillock to the northwest. He raked the hill, saw no reason for the chipmunk's agitation, and was twisting to continue walking when he beheld Satan and gasped. The panther was crouched on top of the hill, staring at him, its tawny coat blending into the background so well it was nearly invisible.

Nate brought up the rifle, then realized the range was too great for an accurate shot. "Stay there, you bastard," he said to himself. "I'm coming for you."

Shakespeare leaped erect when Nate flew into camp. The mountain man watched as Nate grabbed his saddle, and remarked, "Going somewhere?"

"I just saw the painter," Nate said, using the same word his friend and many of the old-timers did to refer to the big cats.

"You think you can catch it?"

"I'll try my best." Nate threw his epishimore on the stallion and smoothed it out. "With any luck I'll be back by noon, dragging that devil behind me."

"It might be wise to wait until there's more light."

"Satan will be gone by then."

"Maybe we could shoot a buck and hang it out as bait to lure him in close. Panthers love venison."

Pausing, Nate said, "We've been all through this. Quit worrying. I'm perfectly able to take care of myself."

"It seems to me that any man walking around with a busted rib, a bashed head, and a lot of teeth marks in his foot is playing fast and loose with the truth when he claims he's the careful sort."

"I have no time for this," Nate said. Every moment spent talking to McNair was another moment Satan had to get away. He placed the saddle on the epishimore and adjusted the cinch.

Shakespeare wore an unhappy expression. "I'd go with you if I could. You know that."

"I swear. Sometimes you're worse than a mother hen. Quit feeling guilty. One of us has to stay with the pack animals, as we decided." Nate mustered a smirk. "Just don't fall asleep again when you should be keeping watch."

"I still think I'm the one who should do the chasing. You're in no shape for a long, hard ride."

"We'll find out soon enough, won't we?" Lifting a foot to a stirrup, Nate swung up and gripped the reins. "Try not to get too bored. I'll return as soon as I can."

"Don't rush on my account," Shakespeare advised. "Shoot sharps the word."

"Don't I know it." Nate touched a finger to his brow, wheeled the stallion, and was set to gallop off when McNair said his name.

"Aren't you forgetting something?" Shakespeare held up a parfleche. "If you don't eat, you'll be too weak to hold your own against that varmint."

"Thanks," Nate said. He sheepishly took the bag and secured it to the saddle. They exchanged meaningful looks, then he was off like a shot, riding low over the stallion as the splendid mount sped along the south bank to the approximate spot where Nate had spied the panther. Much to his amazement, Satan hadn't moved.

The stallion took the stream on the fly. Nate couldn't understand why Satan didn't run off, why the big cat just sat there as Nate rode steadily nearer. He lashed the stallion with the reins, wishing it could go faster.

The ground leading up to the hillock was rocky, sprinkled with large boulders. Often Nate lost sight of Satan for a few seconds as he skirted them. A mere forty yards separated Nate from his quarry when, on going around yet another boulder, he saw Satan glide into pines on the north slope.

Nate angled to intercept the cat. He reached the base of the hill and plunged into the trees, alert for movement in front of him. When he saw it, it wasn't in front, it was to the right. Satan was in full flight, clearing twenty-foot stretches with prodigious leaps.

"Not this time!" Nate said somberly. He pursued, wending among the pines with reckless abandon, resolved to end Satan's life even if he had to chase the panther to the ends of the earth. The mountain lion glanced around, saw him, and ran faster, its fluid body a copper blur as it flowed over the rugged terrain with an ease few creatures could match.

The stallion knew what was required of it. On scores of occasions Nate had ridden down buffalo, elk and other game, and once the stallion knew which animal was being chased, it took to the challenge of the race with a passion almost human in its intensity.

Down the hillock. Across a grassy meadow. Up the slope of a mountain. Satan held to a straight course as if he had a definite destination in mind. Two hundred yards up the mountain, the cat bore to the east.

Soon Nate discovered why. The woodland gave way to a tract of land where a geologic upheaval ages ago had caused massive buckling. There were many steep gullies, treacherous washes, narrow ravines.

Nate suspected that Satan had chosen the area on purpose, knowing the stallion would be hard-pressed to keep up. Every gully, every wash, every ravine slowed the horse down, while Satan took each obstacle in stride, leaping from rim to rim where possible, skirting them with lightning speed where it wasn't.

No one would ever guess, judging from Satan's performance, that the cat had been shot at close range and struck with a tomahawk. Nate figured the shot had done no more than graze the beast, and the tomahawk must have only broken the skin.

For over fifteen minutes the mountain lion put a lie to the widespread belief among free trappers that panthers lacked stamina and would collapse after running short distances at top speed. Satan showed no sign of tiring and didn't stop until clear of the buckled landscape. Then he halted on a clear slope and looked back, tail switching like a whip.

Nate had lost considerable ground despite the stallion's valiant performance. He wanted to scream in baffled fury when Satan made for another expanse of forest. Once he lost sight of the panther, he might as well give up since tracking the lion to its den would be next to impossible. Either he caught up quickly or he would have to try again another time.

The stallion seemed to sense Nate's frustration and redoubled its efforts. Coming to the lip of a ravine, it vaulted high into the air, front legs tucked tight, completing an arc that brought it safely down on the opposite lip. Earth crumbled out from under its rear hoofs and for a couple of harrowing seconds Nate thought they would go over the side. But the black dug in its front hoofs, threw its weight forward, and galloped onward.

Presently Nate came to the forest and entered at the same spot as the panther. As he had dreaded, Satan was nowhere to be seen, nor were there any prints. The ground was too hard. He went a dozen yards, then worked in a half-circle, seeking tracks anyway, refusing to give up.

At length, thirty yards from the clearing, Nate came on a partial paw print in a patch of bare earth. It wasn't much, but it was enough to show Satan's direction of travel so Nate went the same way. Apparently the cat was heading higher, toward the lofty heights panthers invariably called home, perhaps toward its den.

Gradually the clustered pines gave way to scattered stands of firs interspersed with shimmering aspens. Above them grew dwarf pines, sprouting among a sea of boulders.

Nate drew rein at a boulder field and surveyed the steep slopes above. There had been no more prints to guide him. He was relying on intuition and logic. Somewhere up there Satan was holed up. He was sure of it. Locating the den was crucial.

A glint of white off to the right aroused Nate's curiosity. On riding over, he spied bones, reminding him of the dead Indian. The last thing he expected to find was more human remains, yet that was exactly what he had discovered. Dismounting, he knelt to examine them.

Another warrior had gone on to the realm of the Great Medicine Spirit. These bones were much older than the previous set. Nate estimated the Indian had died a year or so ago. The cause of death was easy to ascertain; there were teeth marks on the arm and leg bones and the skull had been partially crushed by immense iron jaws.

"Satan," Nate whispered to himself. He picked up the skull, turning it in his hands. What had the man been doing there? Hunting elk? Bighorn sheep? Or had he been after Satan and the panther had turned the tables on him?

Reverently, Nate set the skull down in the same exact spot and stepped back. "Rest in peace," he said softly. "I aim to rub out the hellion that did this to you."

Nate forked the saddle. Four or five hundred feet higher reared craggy cliffs, their seamed rocky surfaces glinting dully in the bright sunlight. He rode toward them, the Hawken resting on his thighs.

At this elevation the wind howled almost constantly, shrieking over the rim of the cliffs and sweeping down across the slopes below. Nate and the stallion were buffeted severely. In order to stop his eyes from watering, Nate tucked his chin to his chest and peered upward through slitted eyelids.

The cliffs formed a formidable wall extending over half a mile. Nate could readily imagine the number of secluded nooks, crevices, and caves there must be. Locating Satan seemed a hopeless chore, akin to finding the proverbial needle in a haystack. Yet he had it to do.

Nate tilted his head back to scour the stony ramparts as he drew nearer. Fifty feet from them he turned and

bore westward, his eyes now glued to the dusty groun
A single track was all he needed to give him some id
of Satan's whereabouts, but he traveled a quarter of
mile and didn't see one.

The sun hung in the western sky when Nate came
where the cliffs tapered off. He slid down so the stallio
could rest and sat with his back against a stunted tree
facing the ramparts. The whole day was nearly gone an
he had failed to find Satan. He might as well return t
camp and resume hunting in the morning.

Nate had vowed to stay in the valley as long a
it took to bring the panther to bay. The discovery o
the dead warrior had fueled his resolve. But was he
being realistic? How long would it take to hunt Sata
down? Another day? Two? A week? A month? He'
seen how easily the cat could elude him. Unless the
animal walked right up to him and begged to be shot o
he was extraordinarily lucky, he might end up wasting
lot of time and energy and have nothing to show for it

Nate knew that Shakespeare didn't agree with his plar
and was only staying because of their deep friendship.
Such devotion was rare, which made him appreciate
McNair's feelings all the more and caused him to question whether he had the right to endanger his friend's
life to satisfy his personal sense of justice.

What to do? Nate asked himself. He mounted and
headed down the mountain, casting frequent glances at
the cliffs in the vain hope of spying Satan.

The glow of a beckoning fire served as a beacon and
brought Nate right to the camp as twilight blanketed the
countryside in a gray mantle. Shakespeare was whittling
and looked up but made no comment. Wearily, Nate
stripped off his saddle and took a seat.

"I don't need to ask how it went."

"Give me another day," Nate said.

"That's all? I thought we were sticking until we have the painter's pelt."

"I wanted to, but I had a chance to do some thinking today. And it wouldn't be fair to you."

"There you go again."

"What?"

"Using that favorite word of yours." Shakespeare stroked his keen knife into the piece of broken tree limb he held, carving off a chip. "Don't worry about what's fair for me. If you want to kill this cat, we kill it. Simple as that." He stared at the younger trapper. "This above all, to thine own self be true. And it must follow, as the night the day, thou canst not then be false to any man."

"It's hard, sometimes, being true to our convictions," Nate commented.

"Health to you, valiant sir."

"Why do you say that?"

"Mine honor keeps the weather of my fate. Life every man holds dear, but the dear man holds honor far more precious-dear than life."

"Are you saying that about me or about yourself?" Nate asked.

McNair chuckled and quoted more of the Bard of Avon. "Here's Agamemnon, an honest fellow enough and one that loves quails, but he has not so much brain as ear wax."

To divert his friend from the subject at hand, Nate nodded at the limb being whittled. "What is that you're making? It looks to me like a stake of some kind?"

"I rest my case," Shakespeare said softly. Then, in a normal tone, he answered, "Very perceptive, Horatio. It's a stake of the only kind." Shifting, he revealed a pile of five additional stakes lying behind him.

"What are they for?"

"Your feline friend," Shakespeare said. "I've lived i
these mountains a long time, so long I know them a
well as city folks in the States know their puny bac
yards. I know all the animals that live in these moun
tains, including painters. So I wasn't too surprised whe
you showed up empty-handed." He resumed shaping th
stake. "Grizzlies have reputations for being the fierces
beasts in the Rockies, and wolverines are known for thei
cunning and savagery, but in this old coon's humbl
opinion neither can hold a candle to a riled panther."

"How will a bunch of stakes help us kill Satan?"

"Think, son," Shakespeare said. "You're tired, that'
plain to see, but use that noodle of yours." He hefte
the stake he was working on. "Once, years ago, a glut
ton snuck into a Flathead village and made off with
little baby. The father decided he was going to kill tha
wolverine come Hell or high water. He tried everything
Tracking, hunting from horseback, setting out bait an
hiding nearby, but none of his ideas worked. One day h
dug himself a pit, lined the bottom with a lot of stakes
and covered the pit with thin branches, grass, and leaves
He made the covering strong enough to hold the weigh
of a fawn he killed, which he gutted and laid out as pretty
as you please for the wolverine to find. Then he went on
back to his lodge."

"Did the glutton fall for it?"

Shakespeare laughed. "I'll never poke fun at your wit
again." He nodded. "Yep. The very next day he went
back and found that wolverine turned into the hairiest
pincushion you ever did see."

"So you're fixing to do the same with Satan?"

"I have to do something useful," Shakespeare said.

"While you're off gallivanting around tomorrow, I'll begin on the pit. If you haven't rubbed Satan out in a day or two, maybe we should try the Flathead's way."

"I'm game," Nate said.

McNair chortled merrily. "Twice in one minute. You're on a roll, Nathaniel. You truly are."

Smiling, Nate idly gazed into the fire at the blazing wood, and suddenly vivid, painful memories of another time and another place blanked everything else from his mind.

The shed smelled of dank earth and freshly chopped wood. Propped in one corner was a large axe. To one side, piled chest high, was the wood the family used in their fireplace.

Nate stood facing the rear wall, leaning forward with his arms bracing his weight. He heard his father moving behind him and tensed for the first blow.

"I warned you, didn't I? I told you that you're never too old for me to give you a licking?"

"Yes."

"Yes, what?"

"Yes, sir."

"The next time I tell you to do something, maybe you'll see fit to do it. I won't tolerate being disobeyed, not by you or any of your brothers."

"The doves wasn't hurting anyone, Father. I saw no reason to kill them."

"I explained all that to you when you first objected," the elder King said with exaggerated patience. "Those doves were sitting in that tree every morning and evening, getting their droppings all over the flower bed. Disgusting birds! We shooed them off time and again but they kept coming back. All you had to do was hide

around the corner with that bow Zeke gave you and pu
an arrow into one or both of them. Was that too muc
to ask?"

"I won't kill an innocent dove, not for you, not fo
anyone."

"Do you know what this reminds me of? That tim
two years ago when you gave me so much trouble ove
killing a few filthy mice and some pesky cats. Do yo
remember?"

"I've never forgotten it."

"Then I'd think you should have learned an importan
lesson. Sherman took care of those cats for me, just lik
he took care of the doves when you wouldn't. What goo
did being so stubborn get you? The doves still died."

"I'll only kill when *I* think it's right, Father. And
don't care whether it's a mouse or a bird or a deer."

"Where did I go wrong with you?"

Nate made no reply. There were swishing sounds to
his rear as his father swung the strap to warm up.

"I regret having to discipline you, son. I truly do. Bu
you leave me no other choice."

Still Nate did not answer.

"I will not abide being treated with disrespect," his
father snapped. "Respect is the most important part of
any relationship."

"I thought it was love," Nate finally spoke.

The next moment the strap bit into him. He arched
his back and ground his teeth together, refusing to give
his father the satisfaction of seeing him cry. Not this
time! Not ever again! Wincing with each blow, he mentally counted them off: "One, two, three, four, five, six,
seven. . . ."

And on and on it went.

Chapter Twelve

In the rosy blush of blazing dawn the sheer cliffs changed from their typical dull brown hue to a bright flesh-colored tint, seeming to come alive, to glisten with vitality.

Nate King sat astride the black stallion, his gaze roving over the high ramparts as he diligently sought a clue to Satan's whereabouts. The panther had not shown itself during the night, much to his disappointment. He'd stayed up late just in case the cat did, and now he felt the lingering effects of having gone without a decent night's sleep.

Stifling a yawn, Nate rode eastward. Yesterday he had checked the west end of the cliffs; today he would scout in the opposite direction. A piece of jerky served as breakfast. He had been in too much of a hurry to partake of the fine flapjacks Shakespeare had been preparing when he left.

Nate regretted being so impetuous. His stomach growled without letup and he craved a hot cup of coffee. Well, he reflected, what's done was done and he might as well buckle down to the matter at hand.

An animal appeared high above, then another, and another, all moving with fearless precision along the cliff face, bounding from outcropping to ledge to shelf. At times they were balanced on knobs of rock no bigger than a man's fist. Yet they were as sure-footed in their element as a mule would be on terra firma.

"Bighorns," Nate said to himself. One day soon he was going to honor a promise and take his son Zach bighorn hunting. The elusive creatures were prized for their taste, which most mountain men compared favorably to that of mutton. Many claimed bighorn meat was tastier and juicier. A few trappers made it a point early each spring, when the bighorns inhabited lower elevations because of deep snow on the crags, to bring one of the animals down and hold a grand feast. Nate had been to one of the raucous affairs, and it was there he'd first savored a bighorn steak. He couldn't wait to enjoy another.

But today the presence of the bighorns above was bothersome since it meant Satan wasn't in the area. Nate trotted on along the base of the cliffs, alternating his attention between the heights and the ground.

Midmorning found Nate at a place where a dozen or so boulders had fallen from on high. He ground-hitched the stallion, carried his parfleche to a rock slab on which he took a seat, and pulled the last piece of pemmican out. A few more hours and he would have traveled the entire length of the cliffs. If he didn't spot Satan by then, he was inclined to call off the search and give McNair's pit a try. It couldn't hurt.

Nate chewed and thought and didn't realize several minutes had gone by until the strident screech of a bird of prey drew his interest to a bald eagle soaring on the uplifting air currents. He watched the eagle sail in a small circle, then swoop at the crest. Again and again it did the same thing.

Intrigued, Nate hopped off the slab and stepped backward until he had a clear view of the top. The eagle would dive at the rim, flap its wings a few times, then swerve aside, regain altitude, and repeat the behavior. Either it was trying to snare a small animal, or it was trying to drive something off. But what could be up that high, Nate mused, other than a bighorn or a marmot?

Inspiration jarred Nate to his core. Wheeling, he sprinted to the stallion and mounted. A hard ride brought him to where the cliffs came to an end. Swinging around the rock wall, he saw a gradual slope leading up toward the summit.

The eagle was gone but Nate wasn't taking anything for granted. He grasped the Hawken in his left hand, the stock supported by his thigh. As usual the ground was too packed to bear prints although he did come on a smudged print that resembled a cat's.

It was well past noon when Nate found large black and white feathers scattered over a small area near the rim. Close by was a short tree in which the second eagle had probably been perched when set upon. A trail of feathers led upward.

Nate cocked the rifle and warily advanced. So far as he knew, panthers rarely attacked eagles. The bald variety, and the golden kind too, was formidable when provoked. Satan had to be very hungry to risk having his eyes gouged out.

The feathers were spaced at irregular intervals. Presently they led Nate to what appeared to be a wide cleft. Sliding off the stallion, he squatted near the edge and peered downward. The ghastly sight below made him recoil in astonishment.

At one time the ground had cracked and split wide forming a thirty foot trough extending northward from the cliff rim. Littering the bottom of this trough were jumbled bones piled three feet high. Buffalo bones, deer bones, bighorn bones, they were all there. So were those of marmots, badgers, ferrets, beavers, raccoons, opossums, and assorted smaller animals. In the midst of the tangled mass lay the skull of a small horse.

Nate blinked, then leaned over the edge. He had never seen so many skeletons collected in one spot. They were a morbid record of Satan's kills over the past decade, or longer. Easing onto the grade below, he stepped carefully to the pile and picked up the leg bone of a buffalo calf. As he did, he noticed a human skull among the assortment.

Quickly Nate pried the skull loose to study it. The victim had been a child, judging by the size, most likely a boy. It was very old, proving Satan had been a confirmed man-killer years ago.

A sudden scratching, as of claws on rock, reminded Nate of the peril in which he had put himself. He quietly set the boy's skull down and turned toward the mouth of the trough. Was it his imagination or did a shadow flit across the opening?

Hawken leveled, Nate crept to the crest of the cliff. Here the trough angled lower into a funnel shaped hole in the stone surface large enough to permit a steam engine to pass through. From lower down on the mountain the opening would have been impossible to spot.

Sliding on his backside, Nate worked his way toward the hole. He felt confident, alert. His left foot hurt just a bit and his rib ached dully, otherwise he felt fine. Near the hole the rock surface flattened, enabling him to squat and peek into a dimly lit cave.

He'd done it! Nate had found Satan's den! Now that he had, there was the question of how to flush Satan out so he could end the monster's vicious reign of terror. An eight or nine foot drop would take him to the dusty floor, which wasn't much of a drop at all, but landing would aggravate his left leg and might throw him off balance, giving the panther the opening it needed to pounce on him before he could snap off a shot.

Then, too, there was no way back out that Nate could see. Once down there, he'd starve to death if Satan didn't get him first, and he didn't care to end his days on such an ignoble note after having gone to so much trouble. Unfortunately, he hadn't thought to bring a rope along. Nate straightened, hefted the Hawken, and debated whether to tell Shakespeare of his discovery so they could work out a plan together.

A bloodcurdling snarl erupted directly above. Spinning, Nate glanced up and beheld his worst nightmare come true.

Satan was poised on the rim of the trough, the dead eagle hanging limply from his mighty jaws, dry blood plastering his chin. The panther's eyes were alight with primal fury. His sanctuary had been violated by the frail creature he had tried to kill several times without success, and the entrance to his haven was blocked. His inherent bloodlust swelled, dominating his being, and he took a stride nearer.

Nate was in dire straits. He couldn't retreat very far with the cliff rim at his back. Nor could he go more than a few feet to the right or the left. His sole avenue of escape was up the funnel to the trough, and Satan had him cut off. He fingered the hammer of his rifle, hesitant to shoot for fear of provoking the panther into charging since even if he killed it, the beast's momentum might knock him back over the edge or into the hole.

What else could he do, though? Nate realized, and jammed the stock to his shoulder. As he did, Satan dropped the eagle, snarled, and sprang. Then everything happened so fast, Nate had no time to react. The Hawken boomed, a cloud of gunsmoke bloomed, preventing Nate from seeing the onrushing cat, and the next heartbeat he was sent flying by a heavy impact on his shoulder. Frantically he flailed his arms, seeking a purchase, but there was none.

The shock of smashing down on his back whooshed the air from Nate's lungs. Above him he saw the cave opening, saw Satan's head appear and heard the mountain lion vent its rage with a rumbling growl.

Nate scrambled to his feet and backed away. Somehow he had kept his hold on the rifle. Holding it in his left hand, he drew a pistol, aimed it at the feline's feral visage, and cocked the piece. Satan promptly vanished.

Halting, Nate wedged the flintlock under his belt again and hurriedly commenced reloading the Hawken. He glanced at his surroundings and learned the cave was much bigger than he had thought, so big, in fact, it qualified as a cavern.

From outside came more growling. Nate's fingers flew. When the rifle was ready, he slid the ramrod into its housing and leaned against the rock wall to catch his breath.

The temporary respite gave Nate the opportunity to study the cavern closely. Enough sunshine poured through the gaping entrance to bathe the interior in light for a score of yards in all directions. Beyond the radius of the sunlight, to the east, reared bulky shadows, boulders, Nate guessed.

The floor was level where Nate stood and in the middle, where he had fallen, but on the east side it seemed to angle downward. The walls were smooth, as was the ceiling. There were no stalagmites or stalactites.

Nate focused on the opening. Sooner or later Satan would see fit to jump down after him. His wisest recourse, then, was to wait there and put a ball in the panther's brain when it did. Accordingly, he inched nearer to the center of the chamber.

The growling above had ceased.

Butterflies fluttered in Nate's stomach and he tried to calm his nerves by sheer force of will. He licked his dry lips, then stared at the east end of the cavern. Those bulky shapes were clearer now, and he saw that they were broken chunks of rock of varying sizes, some taller than he was, evidently all that was left of a toppled wall.

Where was Satan? Nate wondered. Why wasn't the panther coming in to get him? He walked directly under the rim and craned his neck for a glimpse of the lion or its shadow but saw neither.

After five minutes elapsed and there was no activity above, Nate moved to the other side of the hole, cautiously keeping out of sight. The new angle proved no better. Puzzled, he cast about on the floor and found a suitable rock which he then threw upward. It clattered noisily but failed to spark a response.

Nate didn't know what to make of this development. He didn't believe Satan would simply wander off, not when he occupied the panther's lair. Was it biding its time, waiting up there for him? Or—and here a new idea hit him—was there another way into the cavern, a way only Satan knew?

Venturing into the murky realm fringing the entrance, where the floor angled gradually downward, Nate came on piles of earth and heaps of stones, additional residue from the crumbled wall. There were more huge boulders than he had imagined, and he threaded his way among them with supreme care.

The cavern turned out to be enormous. Beyond the boulders the floor became level again. No sunlight filtered through, but Nate's eyes had adjusted sufficiently to the dark to enable him to distinguish inky outlines. He walked forward taking small steps, testing his footing before applying his whole weight. Caves often contained nasty surprises such as crevices and pits, and he didn't want to blunder into one.

Nate had gone over fifty feet by his reckoning when a soft puff of air struck his cheek. He halted, elated. A breeze meant there was another opening somewhere near, perhaps a means of reaching the outer world. Turning this way and that he tried to pinpoint which direction the breeze came from.

Satisfied the answer was off to the right, Nate worked toward a wall. It appeared solid enough, and there were no telltale points of light. Had he erred? No, because another whisper of air caressed his face, a little stronger this time.

Stopping, Nate ran his hand over the rough surface, feeling for a crack or a concealed passage. He moved to the left and squatted to check lower down. Immediately a blast of wind hit him head-on.

What was this? Nate asked himself excitedly. Groping over a wide area, he discovered a ragged hole the size of a melon. Through this the breeze wafted.

Nate kept searching in the hope there was another opening, one big enough for him to crawl through. But there wasn't, and in his frustration he clenched his fist and swore under his breath.

Hugging the wall, Nate sought another way out. He refused to give up, refused to give Satan the satisfaction of prevailing. A troubling thought occurred to him a few yards farther on: What if Satan was smart enough to know that he would eventually succumb to hunger and thirst? What if the panther had no intention of coming in after him until assured he was good and dead?

That couldn't be the case, Nate reflected. There wasn't a mountain lion alive that smart, that clever. He kept looking, searching every nook and cranny, making a complete circuit without finding the yearned after escape route.

Suppressing an impulse to panic, Nate returned to the entrance. The sunshine sparkled as it fell through the hole, lending the setting an enchanted aspect like in a child's fairy tale. But there was nothing enchanting about the certain fate awaiting Nate unless he found a way out of the trap in which he had unwittingly put himself.

A turtle-shaped boulder offered a tempting seat. Nate loosened the pistols for instant use and studied the rim nine feet up. How the dickens was he going to reach that high to pull himself out? He couldn't very well sprout wings or build a ladder. And he couldn't jump with his leg in the shape it was in.

The turtle-shaped boulder gave Nate a brainstorm when he slapped it in annoyance, stinging his palm. He looked down at it, frowned, then drew back as if it had slapped him in the face in return. Of course! he mused. Why hadn't he thought of it sooner?

Hurriedly Nate moved about, seeking boulders light enough to lift and flat enough to be stacked one on top of the other. Right away he located two and lugged them under the rim, wincing as his hurt rib protested the exertion. One more brought the height to just over two feet.

Nate gauged the distance to the edge of the entrance and nodded. Climbing onto the top boulder, he perched like a hawk about to take flight. The top of the hole was less than a foot above his head. All he had to do was jump and seize hold. Only one thing stopped him, uncertainty over Satan's whereabouts. Nate would be totally helpless for the few seconds he hung there before climbing up, and in that span Satan could take his head off with a single swipe.

Nate jumped down and went in search of another flat boulder. He had to look longer this time, but he found one and added it to his stack. Now when he stood on the top he could straighten high enough to see over the lip. Still, he paused, straining his ears to catch any sounds. A growl, heavy breathing, the pad of paws, anything.

The deep silence was unnerving. Nate slowly rose on his toes and risked peeking out. To his amazement, Satan was nowhere to be seen, not in the area of the funnel nor in the part of the trough visible from the entrance. Inexplicably, the panther had gone away.

Nate didn't waste another moment. Resting the Hawken on the lip in front of him, he placed both palms flat, coiled his shoulders, and shoved upward. Once on firm footing, he grabbed the rifle and dashed up the incline into the trough and from there out onto open ground. Still, Satan didn't show.

To say Nate was happy was the understatement of the century. He had stared death in the face, as it were, yet again, and lived to tell the tale. Maybe Shakespeare was right. Maybe he did have more luck than most two men combined.

Grinning at his deliverance, Nate turned to mount the black stallion and did a double take on finding the horse gone. A few partial prints told the story. Satan had tried to bring the stallion down, but the powerful black had fought back and fled with the mountain lion in earnest pursuit.

So now Nate knew why Satan hadn't been waiting outside the cavern. He began running, pacing himself so he wouldn't become fatigued too quickly, anxiously seeking sign of his horse and the cat. Thankfully he was going downhill.

Nate covered hundreds of yards before a sharp pang in his side compelled him to rest briefly. Striding to the crown of the cliff, he gazed in reverent awe out over the magnificent expanse of verdant countryside unfurled below the heights. On his way up he had been so intent on spotting tracks, he hadn't paid all that much attention to the tremendous view.

Nate swore he could see almost to the broad Mississippi. Majestic mountains mingled with rolling emerald hills to the north and the south, forming undulating waves that grew smaller with distance. A sea of verdant forest covered most of the landscape, except for brown breakers where stark peaks and cliffs such as the one he was on reared skyward. Far, far to the east, at the very horizon, lay a stretch of grassy flatland like a green shoreline, perhaps the prairie itself.

Movement below shattered Nate's contemplation of Nature's awesome grandeur. He spied the black stallion making for woods flanking the heights. Satan still gave chase but was hopelessly outdistanced.

Nate continued jogging. His foot began aching terribly, and not to be outdone, his rib did the same. Regardless, he forged on, oblivious to everything except the need to save the stallion. Often he had to slow to allow his foot and chest to stop throbbing.

The afternoon waxed, waned.

On the brink of exhaustion, Nate halted close to the bottom of the cliffs, within an eighth of a mile of the forest into which the stallion had gone. Dripping with sweat, he sat on a rock and collected his strength for the next spurt. He looked up, saw the long shadow of an isolated tree spearing at him, and realized how very late it had become. Shifting, he was troubled to note the sun had partially dipped from sight. Twilight was minutes off.

From the frying pan into the fire, as the old saying went. Nate rose and hastened toward the trees. At least there he could find shelter, find a spot to hide until daylight, hopefully somewhere that offered some protection from the panther.

Nate knew that Satan would be on his heels eventually. Once the mountain lion gave up its pursuit of the stallion, it would venture back and pick up his scent. He had to be in a defensible position before it caught up.

The shadows of the foremost phalanx of pines formed a dark band on the paler grass. They blanketed Nate as he came to the forest and entered their gloomy dominion. An eerie quiet gripped the woods, a bad omen.

Nate found the stallion's tracks readily enough and trailed them. It was doubtful he could overtake the horse before nightfall closed in, but he would try. He didn't care to spend the night in the woods if he could help it.

To the west the sun sank steadily, painting the sky brilliant streaks of red, orange, and pink. The northwesterly wind increased, as always. To the south an elk trumpeted, a rare sound at that time of year.

Nate crept anxiously along, his grip on the Hawken

as steely as the gleam in his eyes. More than ever he burned with a desire to put an end to Satan, to give the panther a small measure of its due for those who had fallen prey to its insatiable butchery. Satan was a deviate specimen, a freak of Nature, a lion that lived for the pure joy of slaughter rather than to merely fill its belly when hungry.

Suddenly Nate stopped, his eyes widening.

Coming toward him was the feline terror.

Chapter Thirteen

Nate King was filled with fleeting shock on seeing the scourge of the Rockies not fifty feet off. Satan had spied him the same moment he had spied the panther and, voicing a guttural snarl, the mountain lion bore down on him at incredible speed. Nate cocked the rifle and snapped off a shot, in his haste neglecting to aim properly. At the blast Satan swerved into the undergrowth and was swallowed by the gloom.

Whirling, Nate ran, fleeing in uncontrolled fear. He went only a few yards when shame brought him up short. Turning, he whipped out a pistol, then stepped to the side to a fir tree. Low branches provided firm purchase, and in seconds he had climbed twenty feet and was squatting in the fork of a pair of thick limbs.

Nate glimpsed a tawny coat to the east and took precise aim, but Satan wasn't staying in one place. The panther blended into a thicket. Although Nate scoured the vegetation intently, he saw no trace of the big cat.

Now what should he do? Nate quizzed himself. The lion had him treed, effectively trapped again, just like in the cavern. Only this time his stallion wasn't close at hand to lure the panther elsewhere. And this time Satan could spring at him from any direction, at any time. His being in the tree made little difference to a predator capable of scaling the vertical trunk and reaching him in two swift leaps.

Nate set the flintlock at his feet and rapidly reloaded the rifle, stopping only once when a twig cracked behind him. He spun to see if Satan was sneaking up on him. Breath bated, he scanned the plant growth, saw a chipmunk scampering from cover to cover. Thus reassured, he finished ramming the ball and patch into the barrel.

All that remained of the setting sun was a crimson crown. A spreading pall of darkness obscured the landscape, and the shadows were now themselves in deeper shadow. Soon the moon would rise.

Replacing the pistol under his belt, Nate sat, his legs curled under him. If he was Satan, he'd wait until night had the forest firmly in its inky grip before attacking, but panthers were known for being unpredictable. Satan might not want to wait that long.

Nate peered upward, marking the positions of limbs. With a bit of luck he'd be able to climb another twenty feet. After that the branches were spaced too far apart.

The only problem with going higher was that the limbs higher up were thinner, less able to bear Nate's weight. And nowhere was there as wide a fork as the one supporting him. Better, he reasoned, to stay right where he was and bide his time until the panther made a move.

Nate rubbed his eyes and fought a yawn. He'd been up since well before dawn and had not partaken of food or water since the night before. Since his parfleche was on the stallion, he'd have to do without a while longer.

The heavens dimmed to black; the canopy of blue gave way to an indigo canopy sprinkled with sparkling pinpoints. In the east blossomed the gleaming moon, bathing the Rockies in its iridescent light. A coyote greeted its advent with a wavering howl and was answered by another elsewhere.

Holding the Hawken on his knees, Nate leaned forward, bending low over one of the branches in order to make it harder for the panther to distinguish him from the tree. A flutter of wings to the west heralded the flight of a large owl, and Nate watched as the aerial artist looped upward and was silhouetted against the radiant lunar surface.

Typical night sounds reached Nate's ears: the lonesome wails of wolves, the snort of a black-tailed buck as it fled on smelling Satan's scent, the grunt of a roving grizzly to the southwest. Noticeably lacking was any sound made by Satan, which did not bode well for Nate. His skin pricked as if from a rash, and he had the sensation of being spied on by unseen eyes. But try as he might, he couldn't locate the panther.

Nate had to change position after an hour due to a cramp in his left leg. He tried to do so noiselessly but his left legging scraped the branch loud enough to be heard yards away.

There was plenty of time for Nate to think, about Shakespeare, about Winona, about Zach, and his daughter, Evelyn, and how each time he braved the wilderness he gambled his life that he would ever see them again. The wilderness was a harsh taskmaster. Those who survived the lessons it taught were those who never let their guard down for a moment.

Was it worth it? Nate speculated. Was it worth being a free trapper when he stood to lose everyone and everything he truly loved every time he went up against a bestial nightmare like Satan or tangled with a war party of hostile Indians? Was the pure, precious freedom he enjoyed living in the wilderness worth the price he might have to pay for it?

There could only be one answer: Yes! A million times, yes! Freedom was worth any price. Not the watered-down kind of freedom found back in the States where politicians conspired to dictate how people should live, but true freedom, that personal state where men and women could live as they damn well pleased without being accountable to anyone other than their Maker.

Such thoughts, and many others, occupied Nate for some time. Two more hours went by, then a third. The moon climbed steadily. Nate yawned frequently and fought off an urge to sleep.

About midnight Nate found himself dozing fitfully off and on. His leaden eyes would close, his chin would sag, then he would realize what he was doing, jerk his head up, and try to stay awake until the next time.

Nate probed the nearby vegetation over and over but did not see the panther. By about three in the morning he began to suspect that Satan had left and there was no need for him to remain vigilant. Fatigue eclipsed his caution, and despite his intentions, he slipped into a deep slumber.

Nate would never know what awakened him. One moment he was asleep, the next his eyes were open and it was much lighter than he remembered it being and he was staring at one of the limbs forming the fork in which he sat and there on the limb, crouched low, ears drawn back, was Satan.

The instant Nate saw the panther, Satan sprang. Nate clutched the Hawken and tried to bring it to bear but his sleep-dulled reflexes were much too sluggish. Satan slammed into the rifle, batting it loose with a single sweep of an iron paw, and landed on the limb inches from the fork, close enough to disembowel Nate with the next stroke.

Only Nate wasn't there any longer. He threw himself backward and deliberately let himself fall, taking the chance he wouldn't break his neck hitting a branch on the way down. A jolting impact lanced his hip with agony, then he was falling again. He hit the ground hard, rolled, and rose to one knee.

Satan was already in midair, snarling fiercely, claws extended.

Nate took a hasty bead. His finger was constricting on the trigger when the mountain lion plowed into him with the force of a battering ram, sending him tumbling. He felt his shirt rip, felt blood drawn. But the new wound was far from fatal, and when Nate stopped tumbling he pushed to his feet and grabbed at his pistols. His arms twin blurs, he drew and aimed and cocked and fired, just as Satan reached him. The twin balls bowled the cat rearward but it was up in a flash and pressing its attack.

A paw nearly took Nate's leg off at the knee. He retreated, throwing the pistols at Satan's head, making the panther duck and giving him the opportunity to grasp both his butcher knife and his tomahawk. Then Satan closed in.

Now the fight was joined in earnest. There was no time for Nate to think, no time for him to plot a means of beating the monster, no time for anything other than simply staying alive, for preserving his life as best he was able.

Satan came in low, trying to bring Nate down by tearing into his legs. Nate countered with a wicked slash of the tomahawk that drove Satan to one side. The panther spun, angled in again, and was again driven back by a flick of the butcher knife. Baffled, the lion stood still a few moments, growling and hissing.

Nate lunged, aiming a tomahawk blow at the panther's skull. In doing so he noticed a recent gash where he had struck the cat by the stream days ago. Evidently Satan remembered too, because the mountain lion wanted no part of the tomahawk. Whenever Nate swung it, the panther darted aside, giving the weapon a wide berth.

Satan started circling, walking swiftly, steely body hugging the ground, tail snaking back and forth. Every so often Satan would swipe a paw as if probing for weakness. Nate had to keep turning in order to keep facing the feline fury. When the panther swung, so did he, holding Satan at bay.

The stalemate lasted minutes. Nate's blood raced, his temples pounded. He didn't need to be told what would happen if he made a single small mistake. Satan would be on him before he could blink, tearing his flesh from his body. No matter what, he must not blunder!

But he did.

It happened in this fashion: Nate was turning, always turning, inadvertently bearing to the left as he did, his gaze locked on the panther to the exclusion of everything else, and so it was that he failed to see a short sapling growing right under his nose until, as he pivoted yet one more time on his heel, his foot bumped into the obstacle and he tripped, tripped *forward*, toward the panther.

Satan recoiled, but not quite quickly enough to evade Nate's knife which by sheer chance speared into Satan's left eye. Nate came down on all fours, saw Satan tense, and barely got the tomahawk up before the mountain lion leaped. The edge of the tomahawk bit into Satan's face but hardly slowed the enraged beast. Nate was bowled over, the cat on top, his tomahawk arm under the panther's chin as he desperately tried to stop Satan's razor teeth from finding his throat. Claws tore his shirt, his leggings. In desperation Nate plunged his long knife into Satan's side, over and over and over.

Without warning Satan jumped off, whirled, and came at Nate again. Nate attempted to rise, to meet the rush standing, but his speed compared to that of the savage feline was as that of a tortoise to a hare. He thrust the knife, burying the blade to the hilt, as the panther bowled him over. By a quirk of fate he wound up flush against Satan's side so he looped an arm around the lion's thick neck and held tight while simultaneously stabbing again and again and again.

Satan became a whirlwind, spinning and flipping and clawing in a frenzied bid to shake the tormentor off. Nate clung on for dear life, stabbing, stabbing, always stabbing. He nearly lost his grip when they rolled into a tree or a boulder. Fangs sank into his shoulder, causing him to cry out. The next moment, there in front of him, was Satan's other eye, and as the lion drew back, he rammed the blade into it.

No one could have held onto the panther after that. Satan erupted into a berserk rage, twisting and jumping and rolling as if demented. Nate lost his grip on both the knife and the lion and flew through the air, smacking against a pine. Sitting up, he was startled to discover he had lost the tomahawk. He pushed upright, empty-handed, defenseless, and backed against the tree, prepared to sell his life dearly even though he was feeling weak and faint.

Abruptly, Satan emitted a high-pitched shriek and vaulted straight up into the air, clawing at the emptiness in a last act of ferocious defiance. Then Satan crashed down, convulsed, and was still.

Nate gaped at his bestial foe, unable to believe his own eyes. He took a halting step, searching for the Hawken and the pistols, when suddenly a wave of vertigo brought him low, buckling his legs and pitching him onto his face. The last sight he saw was a patch of grass sweeping toward him.

The pungent scent of wood smoke brought Nate around. He sniffed, opened his eyes, and went to sit up, stopping when he found a blanket covered him to his chin and realized he was propped on a saddle. His own saddle.

"Glad you could join the world of the living."

Nate stared across the fire at his mentor. "You?" he croaked. "How?"

"How else? I was a mite worried when you didn't show for supper so I came looking for you. Had to track by torchlight, which is as hard as the dickens to do unless you know what you're doing. I was up on the cliffs when I heard shots." Shakespeare poured coffee into a tin cup and brought it over. "I found you this morning about dawn."

The afternoon sun told Nate how long he had been unconscious. "Thanks for coming after me."

I'm just glad I found you when I did. You lost a lot of blood, son. You're damned lucky to be alive."

"Where did you find the stallion?"

"I didn't. It came wandering into camp about the middle of the morning." Shakespeare handed over the cup. "Careful. That's hot."

Nodding absently, Nate took a slow sip. "It's over," he said softly.

"Sure is. I skinned the painter for you." Shakespeare grinned. "'Course, the pelt won't amount to much with all the holes you put in it." He gently touched Nate's brow. "There's no fever. Do you feel all right?"

Nate King felt the warmth in his belly from the delicious coffee, felt the wind in his hair and the pleasant sunshine on his face, and he smiled in heartfelt contentment. "Never better, my friend. Never better."

WILDERNESS DOUBLE EDITION

SAVE $$$!

Savage Rendezvous by David Thompson. In 1828, the Rocky Mountains are an immense, unsettled region through which few white men dare travel. Only courageous mountain men like Nathaniel King are willing to risk the unknown dangers for the freedom the wilderness offers. But while attending a rendezvous of trappers and fur traders, King's freedom is threatened when he is accused of murdering several men for their money. With the help of his friend Shakespeare McNair, Nate has to prove his innocence. For he has not cast off the fetters of society to spend the rest of his life behind bars.

And in the same action-packed volume...

Blood Fury by David Thompson. On a hunting trip, young Nathaniel King stumbles onto a disgraced Crow Indian. Attempting to regain his honor, Sitting Bear places himself and his family in great peril, for a war party of hostile Utes threatens to kill them all. When the savages wound Sitting Bear and kidnap his wife and daughter, Nathaniel has to rescue them or watch them perish. But despite his skill in tricking unfriendly Indians, King may have met an enemy he cannot outsmart.

_4208-8 $4.99 US/$5.99 CAN

Dorchester Publishing Co., Inc.
P.O. Box 6640
Wayne, PA 19087-8640

Please add $1.75 for shipping and handling for the first book and $.50 for each book thereafter. NY, NYC, and PA residents, please add appropriate sales tax. No cash, stamps, or C.O.D.s. All orders shipped within 6 weeks via postal service book rate. Canadian orders require $2.00 extra postage and must be paid in U.S. dollars through a U.S. banking facility.

Name_____
Address_____
City_____State_____Zip_____
I have enclosed $_____ in payment for the checked book(s).
Payment <u>must</u> accompany all orders. ❑ Please send a free catalog.

WILDERNESS

BLOOD FEUD

←——————————————→

David Thompson

The brutal wilderness of the Rocky Mountains can be deadly to those unaccustomed to its dangers. So when a clan of travelers from the hill country back East arrive at Nate King's part of the mountain, Nate is more than willing to lend a hand and show them some hospitality. He has no way of knowing that this clan is used to fighting—and killing— for what they want. And they want Nate's land for their own!

___4477-3 $3.99 US/$4.99 CAN

WILDERNESS

#25
FRONTIER MAYHEM

<————————————————————————>

David Thompson

The unforgiving wilderness of the Rocky Mountains forces a boy to grow up fast, so Nate King taught his son, Zach, how to survive the constant hazards and hardships—and he taught him well. With an Indian war party on the prowl and a marauding grizzly on the loose, young Zach is about to face the test of his life, with no room for failure. But there is one danger Nate hasn't prepared Zach for—a beautiful girl with blue eyes.

___4433-1 $3.99 US/$4.99 CAN

WILDERNESS

#24

Mountain Madness

⟵————————————⟶

David Thompson

When Nate King comes upon a pair of green would-be trappers from New York, he is only too glad to risk his life to save them from a Piegan war party. It is only after he takes them into his own cabin that he realizes they will repay his kindness...with betrayal. When the backshooters reveal their true colors, Nate knows he is in for a brutal battle—with the lives of his family hanging in the balance.

_ _4399-8 $3.99 US/$4.99 CAN

Dorchester Publishing Co., Inc.
P.O. Box 6640
Wayne, PA 19087-8640

Please add $1.75 for shipping and handling for the first book and $.50 for each book thereafter. NY, NYC, and PA residents, please add appropriate sales tax. No cash, stamps, or C.O.D.s. All orders shipped within 6 weeks via postal service book rate. Canadian orders require $2.00 extra postage and must be paid in U.S. dollars through a U.S. banking facility.

Name_____
Address_____
City_____State_____Zip_____
I have enclosed $_____ in payment for the checked book(s).
Payment <u>must</u> accompany all orders. ❑ Please send a free catalog.
CHECK OUT OUR WEBSITE! www.dorchesterpub.com